TO CATCH A TIGER

TIGER SHIFTERS 7

KAT SIMONS

T&D PUBLISHING

TO CATCH A TIGER

Published 2016 by T&D Publishing
Cover art design © 2016 and 2019 The Killion Group
Interior book design © 2019 T&D Publishing
ISBN-13: 978-1-944600-18-1 (Trade Paperback Edition)

This is a work of fiction. All of the characters, places, organizations, and
events portrayed are either products of the author's imagination or are used
fictitiously. Any resemblance to actual persons, living or dead, business
establishments, events, or locales is entirely coincidental.

First printing: April 2019
For information, contact T&D Publishing www.TandDPublishing.com

Dr. Ryan Yin stared at the prone forms of the two tiger shifter females, so stunned he couldn't speak.

The small, rectangular room Gregory had led him to was only just wide enough to leave a walking space between the two single beds, each bed holding one woman. The one on the left, a dark-haired, dark-eyed woman, wore black dress slacks and a cream-colored button up shirt that made her look like she'd just come from work, except her clothes were wrinkled and dirty. The blond-haired woman on the bed to the right wore brightly patterned yoga pants and a light blue tank top. Neither had shoes on, and their hair was mussed and tangled against the pillows.

The room's plain white walls, the white sheets on the beds, and the lack of any other furniture served as a starkly simple background to the horrific sight of the two captives. Their eyes were wide and they were conscious, but neither moved as he and Gregory stood staring at them, not so much as a muscle twitch or change of expression.

The stench of their fear and anger was so thick in the air, Ryan could almost see it. The flavors of their terror, like spoiled fruit, coated his tongue and made him want to gag.

Over the last three weeks…actually it must be closer to four weeks now, three tiger shifter females had gone missing.

This was not where Ryan expected to find them.

"Make sure they don't die, doctor," Gregory said.

He stood just behind Ryan, at his shoulder. His proximity made the fine hairs on the back of Ryan's neck stand up.

"What…?" Ryan had to swallow and start again. "What are they doing here? What have you given them?"

"Just look after them. Make sure they keep breathing. And everything will be fine."

Ryan dragged his gaze from the women to stare at Gregory. The tall, young male, with his dark hair and eyes, might have been a handsome shifter if it weren't for the stench of crazy surrounding him.

A little less than a year ago, Gregory had started gathering young male tiger shifters to him, making promises about mates and new laws. The rhetoric appealed to many males, and Gregory had raised a small army in that period of time. Most of them even ignored the fact that Gregory had very little acquaintance with sanity. He said what they wanted to hear, so they followed him. Even when he started talking rebellion.

Until now, though, Gregory had carefully remained

within the rules of tiger shifter society. Ryan had been sent into the group to watch for any breach of the law, any excuse to take Gregory down. Yet for all Gregory's talk, he hadn't done anything outright that could get him or his group arrested and locked up.

But this…kidnapping tiger shifter females…this broke so many laws, it guaranteed a death sentence. For Gregory's entire group.

Ryan took a calming breath. Then he said in as level a tone as he could manage, "What have you given them?"

He forced down all the anger and horror clogging his throat. The women needed him alive. If he pissed Gregory off, he ran a good risk of getting himself killed before he could do anything to help them. And if the crazy bastard had taken all three of the missing females, then there was still one more out there somewhere. She'd need Ryan's help, too.

Gregory tilted his head to one side and stared for a long moment. The stench of his crazy washed over Ryan, an almost chemical smell mixed with a sickly sweet scent like rotting leaves on a forest floor, but Ryan had gotten used to that smell in the last nine months and ignored it. How the other young tigers could, he didn't know. The smell had become more pronounced since Ryan had first met Gregory. It was like a dark miasma of fog around the male now, not just an underlying strangeness in his scent signature.

"The drug is new," Gregory finally said. "There's no name for it."

"Where did you get it?"

"You'll find this ironic, doctor. I got it from that human serial killer who tried to murder your sister all those years ago."

Ryan blinked very slowly, sure he'd misheard. The serial killer—Bradley Williams—had tortured and murder a tiger shifter female eleven years ago. He'd used a drug on her to keep her contained, immobile but able to feel. The woman, Su-jin Lee-Bennett, had been Ryan's sister's best friend, and in her need for revenge, his sister had come close to getting killed, too.

Hiding his emotions was significantly harder as he asked, "Why?"

"Why did I deal with a tiger killer?" Gregory asked.

"That. And why have you used that drug on our own?"

"Williams was a pawn. Convenient. He's improved his drug, you know. Less is required to keep them from moving."

"Williams killed one of our people. A female. How could you have anything to do with him?"

"He was the only one with the drug. I couldn't get access to the lab where that bitch elder Elizaveta keeps the old version."

"Again, I will ask, why have you drugged and kidnapped tiger shifter females?"

"Do you really have to ask?" Gregory tisked and shook his head. "Doctor, doctor, doctor. What do you think we've been aiming for all this time?"

"Mates. Voluntary mates. Not…" He gestured to the two women. "Not kidnapping and rape."

"They'll be willing. Eventually. Just make sure they don't die."

Gregory walked out of the small room without looking back.

One of the two males standing guard beyond the door closed it after Gregory, and a lock clicked loudly into place.

Ryan felt ill. His stomach rolled in violent waves and for a heartbeat, he thought he might actually throw up. He'd made it all the way through medical school and a tough residency without once losing his lunch. Or control of his tiger nature for that matter. But this…

He knelt by the woman on the bed to his left. Her eyes were open and she tracked his movements with her gaze, but she didn't so much as twitch a muscle otherwise. She was conscious, but obviously couldn't move. Since the drug was an improved version from the one used by the serial killer, it likely worked just as it had on Su-jin—which meant that even though this woman was immobile, she could probably feel everything done to her.

"Sonofabitch," he murmured, too quietly for the tiger guards outside the door to hear. They were loyal to Gregory in every way. If they knew what Ryan was thinking in that moment, even a little bit, they'd drag him out of here and execute him.

"I'm a medical doctor," he said to the woman, holding his hands up so she could see them. "I need to examine you. Please try to relax. I will be as quick as possible."

He took her pulse, checked her pupils, did a cursory exam of her limbs and body, making sure his touch was clinical and impersonal. His skin crawled from the vulnerability of the two women, and his tiger's anger was turning his vision red. His rage spiked when he moved to the second woman. Her eyes were closed now, and her pulse was thready. She was barely breathing.

"Fuck." He hurried to the closed door and pounded on the steel-covered oak.

One of the guards opened the door and stared at him without comment. Ryan knew the man, but not well. His name was Harlon…something. He'd joined Gregory's group about three months ago. He was a huge male, strong and fierce in a fight. Gregory had not only taken Harlon into his fold, he'd given him a place of "honor" as one of his closest guards.

"I need my medical gear," Ryan said, using every ounce of arrogant cockiness expected of a surgeon.

When they'd dragged him from his home in Boston, blindfolded, ears blocked, and a disgusting smelling rag over his nose to keep him from being able to track where they took him, they'd been smart enough to bring his large medical kit. It was the one thing in all this he was grateful for. He had emergency oxygen and, if necessary, a portable defibrillator. Those would help him keep the women alive. He hoped. He had to keep the unconscious woman breathing and her heart going long enough for the fucking drug to wear off.

The door closed in his face, but it wasn't soundproofed so he heard Harlon order the other male—another relatively new member of the group whose name Ryan couldn't remember—to get the medical kit. At least that was something.

Ryan returned to the woman who was in the most trouble. He knelt by her bed, held her wrist in one hand to monitor the fluttering of her pulse, and kept an eye on her breathing, preparing to start CPR if necessary.

"What the fuck were they thinking?" he muttered.

The first woman he'd examined twitched, her fingers moving against the mattress. That small movement made his heart thump harder. The drug was wearing off, thank god.

At least he hoped her twitch was a good sign. He had no idea how long the women had been with Gregory, or how much of the drug they'd been given. If these were the same tigresses who'd been taken over the last three or four weeks…

Damn it, how were they even still alive?

In a barely audible whisper, he said, "Keep fighting it. You're almost free. Of the drug at least."

He glanced at the locked door. They were seriously outnumbered at the moment. Even if she fully recovered, he didn't have much hope of getting the women away from here yet.

Especially since he had no idea where *here* was.

The young males who'd *escorted* him here had ensured his shifter senses were blocked. They'd driven for what felt like days, based on his hunger and need to sleep and pee. Then they'd shoved him into some sort of aircraft and flown for what had seemed like several hours. From the muted sound he felt through his body more than heard, he was pretty sure they'd been in a helicopter, but he couldn't be sure of that.

Between the days of driving and the flight, he could literally be anywhere in North or Central America right now. Maybe even South America. He thought they hadn't crossed any major oceans, but even that was mostly a guess. They'd done too good a job screwing with his tiger senses, and they'd left him disoriented for so long he was still recovering from it. The inside of the building didn't give him any clues either because they hadn't removed any of the blocks until he was just outside the door to the small room where the women were being held.

Gregory had never fully trusted him, but he had accepted Ryan as one of his disciples. The fact that he'd gone to so much trouble to ensure Ryan didn't know where they were couldn't be a good sign.

He couldn't worry about that now. First he had to make sure both women survived the drug. He had to find out where the third was. Then he'd have to find a way to get them all out of here. Before anything worse happened.

By the time the guard entered with Ryan's equipment, the first female was flexing her fist. She stilled the minute the door opened, and Ryan had to hide his smile. Smart. The guard set the heavy box next to Ryan where he knelt on the ground between the two beds, then left again without a word, locking the door behind him.

The first female went back to flexing her fist. Her arm twitched a few times and one foot jerked.

"Keep fighting," Ryan said under his breath as he opened the large, plastic orange box that held his emergency gear.

He snapped on a pair of gloves, then pulled out the

oxygen canister, inspecting it for possible damage before assembling and testing the valves and oxygen stream through the face mask, and then he placed the mask over the unconscious woman's mouth and nose, ensuring an appropriate flow rate. He got the pulse oximeter out, checked to make sure the woman didn't have nail polish on her finger or anything else that might inhibit the readings, then gently inserted her first finger into the small clip-like device to monitor the percentage of oxygen saturation in her blood. Tiger hemoglobin levels were different than humans and his pulse oximeter was designed for humans, but it at least gave him an idea of how much oxygen was moving through her veins. Next, he took out his stethoscope and listened to her heartbeat. Slow, but as he counted, he was relieved to discover it was steady.

He turned back to the first woman. Her jaw was tight now, her head tilted back just a little.

He moved so he would be in her line of sight and said, "I'm going to check your heartbeat."

He held up the stethoscope so she could see it. To his surprise, she gave a slight head nod.

When he was sure her heart wasn't going to explode, he settled back on his haunches and breathed. "You'll be okay soon." *I hope.* "Try to stay calm as you come out of the drug. I don't know what kind of after-effects it'll have."

As far as Ryan knew, Williams had only ever used the drug on victims he killed so he hadn't particularly cared about residual after-effects.

Ryan glanced at the door. Then next to the woman's ear

he said, "The longer we keep the guards from realizing you're recovered, the better."

She blinked and he took the gesture as a sign that she understood.

Damn Gregory for using something like this on their own people. What the hell had the crazy bastard been thinking? Female tiger shifters were so rare now, every single one was important. Killing one, even accidentally, wasn't just a horrific crime against the woman, it was a crime against their entire species.

The notable absence of the third missing female settled a sense of doom in Ryan's chest. He hoped she was still alive somewhere, but since she wasn't in this room and Gregory hadn't mentioned her, Ryan feared the worst.

He continued to monitor the unconscious woman while the other slowly broke free of the drug. He glanced at her regularly to ensure she was doing okay, but he didn't want to crowd her as she regained control of her body.

He didn't know her, but that wasn't unusual. She looked old enough to have started her Mate Runs. Males weren't allowed any contact with unmated females outside the Run that might give them an advantage during the Run. And Ryan didn't run. Unless he'd inadvertently seen her at the elders' compound in West Virginia, or she was a good friend of his sister's, he'd have no reason to recognize her.

She was quite pretty—dark hair and eyes, sharply angled features, her skin smooth with a light flush of pink in her cheeks. Her scent was a surprisingly spicy mix, like allspice and cinnamon, combined with the earthy essence of her as an individual. He could smell the drug throughout her scent signature, the bitter bite of it making his throat tight. And under that disturbing element, he realized she also had just a faint hint of…

"Ah hell," he muttered. "You're nearing your estrous cycle, aren't you?"

She nodded.

Ryan closed his eyes. This was a disaster. A female in estrous around all these desperate males… Gregory's tigers weren't likely to keep things civilized. Ryan's earlier fears punched him again. He had a sister. And a niece. He might not approve of the Mate Run—the only way for a male to earn a female tiger shifter mate under tiger law—but the thought of rape was abhorrent to him.

He leaned a little closer to the still-unconscious woman and pulled in a deep breath, studying her scent. He blamed the residual effects of the rag they'd used to block his sense of smell for not noticing this right away. Just as he was afraid, under her scent signature and the bitter tang of the drug was the faintest, faintest hint of her estrous approaching.

Leaning back he tried not to curse aloud, but in his head he was running through every hard word he knew—in two different languages.

To the recovering woman, he murmured, "You're both going to come into estrous soon. Probably why Gregory picked you. I'll do what I can to protect you. But we are very outnumbered here. Gregory has at least forty loyal tiger males with him now. I'm not sure if they're all here— wherever here is—but even half that number is too many for the three of us to fight. Even if he lets you two recover completely."

Even as he said that out loud, his stomach heaved again.

"I'll try to keep him from giving you any more of the drug. At least I can do that much. But I'll need your help." He spoke at the almost subsonic levels shifters could manage in close confines. He didn't want this part of their conversation overhead by the guards just outside the door.

She rolled her head to look at him and though no real sound came out, she mouthed the word, "How?"

"No matter how strong you feel once the drug wears off, I need you to pretend you're weak and groggy from it. For as long as you can. I'll have to convince Gregory it's too dangerous to use again. And hope he believes me. You being slow to recover might help. Plus, if things get really bad, you'll have the element of surprise on your side."

She nodded, slowly but distinctly, and her dark eyes narrowed to dangerous slits as she focused on the wall behind him. He could only guess what she was thinking, but whatever it was, from the look in her eyes, he could tell that Gregory had picked the wrong woman to kidnap.

Ryan smiled faintly as he returned his attention to the second woman. Her heartbeat and breathing were steady now, but she was still out cold. That worried him. From what he knew of the drug, it wasn't supposed to render a victim unconscious. That was the point, to keep them immobile but awake and aware.

"They knocked her out first," came a faint, rusty sounding voice.

He turned to see the first woman rolled fully onto her side, staring at her unconscious friend.

Without looking at him, she said, "She fought. Check her head. They hit her really hard."

Ryan nodded and did, gently moving his gloved fingers over her scalp, under her hair. There was a very small lump behind her ear on the left. He bit back another curse.

"How long have you been here?" he asked, reaching for a penlight from his kit. He eased open the woman's eyes, checking her pupils and blowing out a relieved breath when they were reactive and even. But worry still tightened his gut.

Shifters healed really fast. For that lump to still be there, either the women were just taken a few hours ago, the drug had slowed down her ability to heal normally, or they'd hit her hard enough to fracture her skull. None of those options were good.

Even worse was the fact that these probably weren't the same women the community already knew had disappeared. There was no way the unconscious woman would have survived weeks of a head injury that had done enough damage to still have the bump present.

"Not sure," the first woman breathed. "Got me with the drug. Used me to distract her. Was a…Wednesday? I think when they took me. Hard to remember."

"The drug has played with your senses. Have you been injected more than once?"

"Yes. Can't remember how many times."

"Fucking sonofabitch."

He wasn't sure how long ago they'd picked him up. A

few days at least. If they'd taken the women first, before coming for him, or even at the same time as he'd been taken, then the two had been captives—and given that fucking drug repeatedly—for days now. As long as a week?

And they were likely the fourth and fifth females to disappear. Which meant the three original tigresses were still missing, women he couldn't even be sure Gregory held.

His anger raged through him. His tiger, usually a pretty calm part of his nature, was literally clawing to get out and rip the other males to pieces. He breathed slowly, controlling his animal side so his human side could better look after his patients.

"Has she been unconscious most of the time since you were taken?" Ryan asked. She'd had her eyes open when he'd first come in but had passed out only minutes afterward. If she'd been mostly unconscious for days…

Gregory was lucky she wasn't dead.

"Yes," the woman said. "Not sure how much time passed between them taking me and taking her, though."

That news meant the conscious woman could still be one of the original missing three. Ryan wasn't sure if that made him feel better or not, because it meant the conscious woman had been held and drugged for much longer than a few days.

"But she's been out for a while," the woman continued. "Even when she's opened her eyes, she hasn't really…been there. They kept injecting us with that drug every time we showed any signs of movement. Was too scared to hide it at first."

She murmured the last so quietly, Ryan almost missed it. "You've done good. You're still alive. You just have to stay that way."

"I'll die before allowing rape," she hissed.

"I'd rather those weren't your only choices," he said dryly, but inside he wasn't sure how to stop it.

Drugged, she wouldn't be able to prevent the males from raping her. Even at full strength, she was in the middle of a group of very desperate tigers who had no ethical issues with rape. At least that was the impression they'd given Ryan over the last nine months. And if they *did* allow her to be free of the drug, she'd fight—he could see it in her eyes—and she'd die.

Both women would die unless he could find a way to get help. Soon.

He was running through options, his hand on the unconscious woman's wrist as he absently kept track of her pulse, when he felt the other woman's stare. He met her gaze.

"You'll help us?" she asked.

"I'm going to try. I just don't know how yet."

She rolled onto her back and stared up at the ceiling. "I don't want to die," she murmured.

He didn't know what to say to that, so he just took her hand and squeezed briefly. He pulled away immediately after, afraid she'd take the physical gesture the wrong way if he maintained contact too long. Given her situation, Ryan couldn't abide causing her any more distress than she was already under.

He kept thinking of Sarah and her daughter, and of them being in a situation like this. He almost couldn't breathe around the shot of terror the thought of that invoked.

"What's your name?" he asked quietly, as much to distract himself as her.

"Lakshmi. Lakshmi Das."

She wasn't one of the original three missing females. She and the still unconscious woman were the fourth and fifth victims, then. Ryan closed his eyes to rein in his anger.

"I'm Ryan Yin," he said, because he owed her that much. "It's a pleasure to meet you."

She snorted, and the faint sound eased some of his tension.

He recognized her name, of course. The males knew all the females, by name if not by sight, because there were so few of them to know—only 148 in total in the US, both mated, unmated, and children. Lakshmi wasn't from the East Coast, so even if he did take part in Mate Runs, he'd never have encountered her. If not for this disaster. Males were only allowed to participate in Mate Runs near their home territories. A female could open her Run to more males from different parts of the country, or even different countries, if she didn't find any of the local males to her liking. That happened rarely, though. Most females had a large number of males to choose from and didn't often need to bring males from other regions in before they found a mate.

The restrictions placed on males, the entire Mate Run, was designed to protect the females while still ensuring each one mated with a tiger shifter male. The species was on the brink of extinction and the females were drilled from birth that it was their responsibility to have children. The only way tigers could breed was with other tigers.

At least, that was the thinking until recently. The discovery of hybrids between tigers and humans had opened up alternate possibilities. Whether that was good news or bad for the species depended entirely on which tiger was asked.

Since Ryan never intended to take a tiger mate, he had no real opinion on the matter. But the possibilities had fed the hunger of the young males Gregory led. They wanted an end to the Mate Run, they wanted a new way of getting a mate and reproducing, and they weren't particularly concerned with how the females felt about any of this.

Ryan shook off the line of thought. The reproductive politics of his people weren't his concern right now. Right now, he had to find a way to keep these two women alive and safe long enough to get them out of here.

"Do you have any idea where we are?" he asked, without much hope.

Lakshmi shook her head. "They kept us in the back of a van on the way here. Strong smell of blood in it. Couldn't track direction or anything."

He sighed. "Similar means of getting here. With the addition of a…helicopter I think. An aircraft of some kind anyway."

He was about to say more when a faint movement from the unconscious woman distracted him. He turned his full attention to her, hoping to ease her out of the drug as quietly as Lakshmi had recovered.

CHAPTER TWO

Lakshmi watched the male's back as he focused on Erin.

He looked normal enough, dressed in blue jeans and a white t-shirts that emphasized the thick muscles in his broad shoulders and torso. His black hair was cut short but a little loose like he was due a haircut, and his eyes were a rich brown color that reminded her of dark tea.

Nothing about him screamed threat. He was obviously a predator, just like any other tiger shifter, but he didn't raise her hackles the way the other males did.

Dr. Ryan Yin.

She wasn't sure who he was, outside of the fact that he was a tiger shifter, but that wasn't unusual. There were a lot of tiger shifter males. She did know he hadn't been part of her Mate Runs, so his territory wasn't near hers in Southern California. Which meant they'd have had no opportunity to meet before this.

This was a pretty sucky way to meet.

Her heartbeat lurched with a combination of fear and anger that was almost crippling. Until the appearance of Dr. Yin, she'd been so terrified she'd worried she'd kill herself with her own damned fear before she could regain enough strength to fight her way out of this.

She wasn't used to feeling helpless. In fact, most of the time, Lakshmi felt powerful and strong—not just because she was a tiger shapeshifter. Her tiger was extremely strong, true. But she'd always felt powerful in her own right, in her femininity and intelligence. It helped that she had a strong, beautiful mother who'd passed that confidence on to her daughter.

Her mother owned five business, raised four children, and taught classes in economics at University of California San Diego. She was a woman Lakshmi was proud to call Mom.

Being at the mercy of males was not something Lakshmi had ever expected to experience. She wasn't the least bit afraid of human males, despite what had happened to Su-Jin Lee-Bennett all those years ago at the hands of a human killer. She was a much stronger female than Su-jin, and it never occurred to her that she'd fall victim to a human.

She'd been right about that. She wasn't at the mercy of a human killer now. She was at the mercy of males of her own species.

That shouldn't have happened either. That was the promise the elders gave all the females in exchange for participating in Mate Runs and attempting to have children.

There was a lot of pressure on females to procreate because the species was on the edge of extinction. And the number of females was dangerously low compared to males. Two hundred years ago, that had resulted in chaos for her people—rapes, death matches, bloodshed and violence that had nearly destroyed them. The institution of the Mate Run had saved her people. It gave the males the illusion of competition and the females freedom to choose from any number of mates. It succeeded in putting an end to the extreme violence.

The only reason—literally the only reason—Lakshmi tolerated the Mate Run was because it was supposed to protect her from…well from the very situation she found herself in right now.

Her heartbeat thumped hard again, more anger than fear this time. So much anger she was sure the doctor was drowning in the smell of it. She didn't care. She wanted them all to know how angry she was—especially because it helped her to overcome the terror.

Having control of her body again helped, too. A little. She was still locked in this room, surrounded by who-knew-how-many tiger males, in the middle of who-knew-where. But if she could control her body, she would escape. Or die trying.

She was less worried about death than rape. That probably said something about her, but she was too tired to think about what.

She considered the doctor's back again. His scent did as much to ease her fear as being out from under the effects of the drug did. Something about it was comforting. Strong and solid. A hint of earthiness, but also—strangely—blood. Yet the blood didn't raise her predatory instincts, or call to her animal in a dangerous way. It was odd. The very faint metallic tang mixed with all the other flavors of his scent to create a kind of warm, comforting sensation, like a hug. Maybe it was because he was a doctor. He did seem to have a decent bedside manner—given the circumstances.

Her father had encouraged her to go into medicine, but she didn't have the temperament. She wasn't sure she'd be able to calm her tiger's hunger around the blood.

"She's coming to," Dr. Yin said quietly, without looking at Lakshmi. He removed the oxygen mask carefully, and then paused, seeming to listen to Erin breathe.

"Her name is Erin. Erin Blum," Lakshmi told him.

Lakshmi didn't know Erin very well, but they did know each other. Their territories were across the country from each other—Erin had her territory in Texas. But they both took self-defense classes from Alexis Tarasova, a former Tracker and basically a legend among the female tigers. Since Su-jin's murder, all the females took self-defense classes from Alexis, learning how to fight by more than just tiger instinct. Those lessons had made Lakshmi feel even more powerful and strong.

Too strong for this. She wasn't supposed to be here. She wasn't supposed to be vulnerable.

Those thoughts spiked her fear so she pushed them down. Anger was better. Anger would help her hold it together long enough to escape.

"Erin." Dr. Yin leaned a little closer to her. "Erin, my name is Dr. Ryan Yin. I'm here to help you. You've been given a drug that makes it impossible to move, but it should be wearing off now. You also took quite a blow to the head. You might experience a headache or blurred vision. When you can, please tell me if you have these or any other symptoms. I'll do what I can to help."

Lakshmi stared at him. He was being very gentle with both of them. Ensuring he explained everything he was doing. That helped. If a strange male doctor had come into this room and started examining her without that effort, she would have felt violated. Instead, he was reassuring and comforting—those characteristics in his scent as well as his voice.

Erin groaned and rolled to her side. "Head hurts," she muttered. "Not as bad anymore."

Lakshmi let out a quiet breath at the signs of Erin's recovery.

"You could feel the pain even under the drug?" Dr. Yin asked.

"Yes. Could feel everything."

That had been the worst part for Lakshmi. She could feel everything—their touches, gropes, the way they carried her around and deposited her here like a sack of grain. She couldn't fight, she could barely breathe, but she could feel each sensation. It was horrible.

And, she realized suddenly, that type of drug reaction was…familiar.

She hadn't gone through this personally before, but she was finally putting it together. A similar thing had been done to Su-jin by the human killer. Almost eleven years ago.

Something Dr. Yin and the leader, Gregory, had said came back to her then. Gregory had made a comment about getting the drug from a serial killer, hadn't he? She'd been so scared and angry and desperate, she'd barely heard anything they'd said to each other. She'd been trying too hard to move, to force her body into action. But now that she could think, she had a vague memory of Gregory saying something like that.

"Is this the drug that was used on Su-jin Lee-Bennett?" she asked Dr. Yin's back.

He faced her, his expression bleak and angry. "An improved version, apparently. Williams hasn't stopped working on it over the years." He snarled and his hands flexed into tight fists. "The elders should have let my sister kill him."

He muttered the last, but not so quietly that she didn't hear it—or realize what it meant. "Your sister…Su-jin's best friend Sarah Chu?"

He nodded but didn't look at her.

Sarah Chu and Su-jin's brother, Joseph Bennett, had tried to kill Williams all those years ago. They'd been stopped, and Sarah had gone on to marry and have children. As far as Lakshmi knew, Su-jin's brother was still going in and out of confinement because he continued to hunt Williams. Tiger shifters weren't allowed to kill humans. Doing so was punishable by death. It was because they were so close to extinction, they couldn't afford to attract the attention of human authorities. They certainly couldn't afford to have human forensic teams uncovering evidence of tiger shifters. Not when they were so outnumbered by humans and humans were a notoriously fearful race that would no doubt declare war on her people.

Lakshmi understood all this, but she'd secretly hoped Su-jin's brother would kill Williams and be done with it. She wasn't afraid of the human or his drug, but she wanted him dead for what he'd done to one of theirs.

All of this had happened when Lakshmi was a teenager, but she remembered it well, and remembered the effect it had on the community, the effect it still had.

Did the elders know that human bastard had continued to develop his drug?

"Why would Gregory deal with a serial killer, someone who'd murdered a tigress?" she asked aloud, without expecting an answer.

Gregory was nuts. It was all over his scent. He probably didn't see the conflict in dealing with a female killer or kidnapping females to force matings. It was well known he and his young males were against the Mate Run. There were rumors of rebellion. But she'd just assumed the elders had the situation under control. They couldn't have possibly expected this…

Could they?

"Do the elders know about…?" She wasn't sure how to finish. She didn't actually expect Dr. Yin to have answers, despite the fact that his sister worked for a facility run by the only female elder—and arguably one of the most powerful of the remaining eight.

"Gregory wanting rebellion and being crazy?" Dr. Yin said dryly. "Yes. This drug? I don't know. That Gregory is using it to kidnap female tigers? I sure as hell hope they know now. Do they know you're missing? Probably, since other females have gone missing in the last three weeks or so as well."

"I thought that was…"

Dr. Yin looked at her. "What?"

She pressed her lips together before answering. "I thought the females who went missing were just…trying to get away from the attention and pressure. I didn't think they were truly missing, like the rumors said."

"They're really missing," he said, his voice very soft. "The Trackers are looking for them as we speak. And I'm sure they're looking for you, too. With luck, help is on the way."

She swallowed. What if they didn't know Gregory was responsible yet? How long would it be before someone found them?

Everyone paid attention to the females—where they were, what they did, where their territories were, when they were in their territories, even when they cycled and which Mate Run territory they used. She'd spent her entire life knowing everyone else in the community knew about her and what she was doing.

At times, she'd found it annoying. In that moment, she was extremely grateful for it. Even if her parents didn't realize she was missing—though she was sure they did; Lakshmi talked with her mother on the phone every day—someone would notice a female was out of touch and *not* hunkered down in her territory for privacy.

Two females, she reminded herself. More even, since

those she'd heard about before being taken were apparently really missing.

She heard sounds at the door before she could say more and instantly rolled onto her back, forcing herself to lie as still as possible.

She couldn't tell if Erin did the same thing, but she heard Dr. Yin murmur something to her and hoped he was coaching her to do as he'd suggested Lakshmi do. They'd been speaking in barely audible tones, because of the guards outside the door, but as the door swung open, she still had a moment of terrifying dread that they knew she was revived and would give her another shot of that awful drug.

That fear kept her frozen, even more than her own efforts might have.

Dr. Yin stood and faced the man who walked in—a young male who'd been with Gregory when Lakshmi was taken.

"How are they, doc?"

"As well as can be expected. You shouldn't be using this drug on them. They're too damned valuable and we don't know what it will do."

Dr. Yin's voice was full of irritation and annoyance, but she didn't hear the anger she'd sensed from him earlier. In fact, now that she thought about it, she couldn't smell his anger anymore either. She couldn't smell discomfort or fear or any of the complex mix of emotions she'd picked up when the door was closed. All she got was a tang of annoyance over his ordinary scent.

What the hell?

"They've been training with Alexis," the young male said. "Did you know that? If not for the drug, they might have accidentally been killed when we picked them up. They'd have tried to fight before recognizing the opportunity we're giving them."

She wanted to snarl and attack. She wanted to rip and tear the arrogant bastards to shreds. But she held still, keeping all her anger in a tight grip. She could smell the stench of it, the heat of a fire burning under her skin, and she was sure the males could, too. She didn't care. She wanted them to know she was pissed.

"Kidnapping females isn't the answer, Richard," Dr. Yin said. "You know it's not."

"Gregory thinks it is. Are you going to argue with him?"

Silence followed. She couldn't see Dr. Yin's face, and for some reason, she still couldn't read his scent, so she couldn't judge his reaction to the question.

"Keep an eye on them," Richard said. "Once they're stable, you have more work to do. And we'll have two more here by tomorrow for you to doctor."

Dr. Yin's back stiffened. "More? Damn it, Richard, that's going to bring the entire community down on our heads. What the hell is Gregory doing?"

"Taking what's rightfully ours." With that, Richard left the room.

The door lock clicked into place behind him.

"Are you a prisoner, too?" she whispered. Dr. Yin didn't know where they were and they kept locking him in here. But he knew the other males by name. He seemed to have an idea what was going on. She narrowed her eyes at him when he turned to face her.

"Not like you are," he said. "But Gregory has never completely trusted me."

"Why are they leaving you in here with us, then? Aren't they worried about what you might…do?"

"No. I'm the doctor." He snarled, then shook his head and said, "If they hear anything they object to, they'll pull me out."

He didn't clarify, but she had a stomach-churning impression that the males wouldn't care if the doctor took advantage of her and Erin's weakness. She rolled onto her side again, bile rising and the need to throw up strong. She choked it back but only barely. Throwing up would make her feel even weaker and more helpless than she already did. She couldn't abide any more weakness.

Dr. Yin settled on the floor again, between the two beds, and met her gaze. "You're safe with me," he said.

His voice was so quiet she felt more like she was reading his lips than hearing anything.

"I would never have done anything like this to a female. I wasn't in on Gregory's plans and had no idea he meant to do something so…desperate. I have a sister. Her best friend was killed while under the control of this drug. I will do whatever I can to help you both. And any other tigresses brought here. I promise."

She held his gaze, studying his expression, his scent— now full of earnestness and that anger that had vanished when Richard entered the room—looking for lies and seeing none. She nodded her understanding, hoping against hope she was reading him right.

"Do you think you could eat yet?" he asked after a few quiet moments.

"I thought you didn't want them to know we were recovering from the drug's control?"

"They'll know you're free from the drug soon, even if I don't tell them. You need to keep up your strength." He took off his disposable gloves and tossed them into his open medical kit.

"I'm too nauseous to eat right now," she muttered but looked at Erin.

Erin shook her head and put a hand over her mouth.

That gesture had Dr. Yin coming up on his knees and moving closer. "Are you going to be ill? How is your head?" He opened Erin's eyes and examined her pupils. "Blurry vision?"

Erin grunted a no, but she still held herself very still. "Just sick feeling," she said.

"Sonofabitch bastards," he muttered very quietly.

The violence in his tone was almost enough to make Lakshmi smile.

"You likely have a concussion," he said to Erin. "You should have healed from it by now, but the drug has slowed things down. I need you to stay awake and with me for a little bit so I can make sure your body is going to fix itself. Can you do that, Erin?"

"Try," she whispered.

For the first time since regaining control of her body, Lakshmi sat up. Erin didn't sound good. And a concussion could be very serious. Especially in a tiger shifter since it was so hard to give them a concussion. Shifter bodies healed quickly. This wasn't good.

"What can I do to help?" she asked.

Dr. Yin motioned to the large, orange plastic box with his medical equipment in it. "If you're well enough to stand, could you please hand me one of the instant ice packs in there."

She dropped to her knees by the box near the foot of her bed and hunted for the ice packs. Behind her, she heard the doctor murmuring quietly to Erin, asking her about her symptoms. Lakshmi turned back with one of the packs as he told Erin he couldn't give her any medicine for her headache.

"Until I'm sure the other drug is out of your system," he said, "we'll have to use other methods. I'm sorry about that."

Erin started to shake her head but Dr. Yin stilled her. "Just rest. Don't move much." He took the ice pack Lakshmi held out to him and crushed the middle to activate it.

Lakshmi was swamped again by a sense of helplessness. She knew a lot of things about running a business and entrepreneurship, about accounting and economics. But she'd never learned anything about first aid. It just had never been an issue—her family was made up of shifters, they healed quickly, and she had human employees that were trained in first aid for humans. It wasn't a skill she'd ever considered necessary to her life.

She'd put it on her list of things to learn once she got out of here. If she got out of here.

Would Dr. Yin teach her first aid?

She stared at the side of his face as he gently held the ice pack over the bump on Erin's head. She really hoped he was as kind and honorable as he seemed. She didn't trust him…couldn't trust him because he knew Gregory and his males too well. But there was something about him.

If he was the man he seemed to be, she could like him. If not…she was a fool.

CHAPTER THREE

Ryan woke from dozing on the floor and immediately checked Erin who'd gone to sleep once he was sure she was healing. She was breathing soundly and seemed to be comfortable. He turned to check on Lakshmi, to find her sitting up in bed, leaning against the cool, white wall, watching him.

"Are you okay?" he asked. "Do you need something?"

Her full mouth quirked at one corner. "A bathroom would be nice."

He hadn't even thought… "Of course. Sorry." Very quietly, he said, "Try to…appear disoriented still, a little weak."

She jerked her chin up in a nod of understanding.

Rolling to his feet, he moved to the door, knocking to get the guards' attention.

"I need to take one of the women to the bathroom," he said, infusing his voice with the authority he'd earned as a surgeon, a tone that worked well on most of the young tigers when Gregory wasn't around. "Then they'll both need food."

Ryan had always been that much older than the rest, and not really one of them even though he was accepted into the group. He was here because Gregory needed his medical skills. And because Ryan was very, very good at pretending to believe the same things the rest of these males did about the Mate Run and how males should be allowed to claim mates.

It helped that he actually was opposed to the Mate Run and considered it antiquated and mildly barbaric.

The guard, a new male Ryan had never even met before, nodded at the requests. "I'll show you the way," he said.

Ryan figured they wouldn't just let him walk around the…building or whatever this place was by himself with one of the females. He didn't like leaving Erin alone, but he didn't want to send Lakshmi off on her own either.

He motioned her out of the room. She stood and wobbled a little, making a show of straightening her shoulders and firming her stance before moving away from the bed. Ryan met her gaze and hoped she saw his slow blink as the encouragement it was meant to be. To aid the show, he held out his arm so she could use his support to "steady" herself. She glanced at him a moment, her eyes narrowed, then slid her hand around his elbow in a tight hold. The contact calmed a restlessness in his tiger that Ryan hadn't even been aware of, and something inside him seemed to settle. The reaction was odd and a little disorienting, like nothing he'd experienced before, and all from a simple touch.

He attributed it to the stress of their situation, blinking it away to focus on the moment.

He waited just outside the door until the remaining guard, a male named Sanjay who was loyal to Gregory but not prone to rash actions, locked the door. So long as Sanjay remained on this side of that room, Erin should be safe. Ryan followed their escort, keeping Lakshmi close to his side. She leaned against him just a little and stumbled once, grunting as she did.

Their guard glanced back. "What's wrong?"

She snarled at him in answer.

"She's been subjected to that drug for days," Ryan said. "She's weak."

Lakshmi's grip tightened hard and fast on his arm, proving she was anything but weak in that moment, and Ryan almost snorted in amusement.

He hid his near slip in a scowl directed at the guard. "Bathroom," he ordered, and the guard started moving again.

Ryan studied their location as best he could, but the walk to a bathroom didn't give him much insight. The walls were plaster, white, and unadorned—just like the room the women were being kept in. The temperature inside was mild, he assumed controlled by a central air system from the vents near the ceiling. It was a little cooler than a human might have found comfortable but perfect for a tiger shifter with their fast metabolisms. There were no windows in the hallway and all the doors they passed were closed.

Everything looked the same as everything else. All the doors were the same steel reinforced heavy oak, with a similar ball knob and a reinforced frame that would make the doors impossible to break down, even for a tiger shifter. Ryan couldn't tell one room from another. In fact, it was difficult to even discern the sizes of the various rooms they passed. Without windows to show the time of day, Ryan wasn't sure if it was day or night, but the hall's recessed ceiling lights were soft and muted.

The entire corridor conspired to confuse his senses and made orienting himself to his surroundings impossible. For a shifter, that was more than a little disconcerting.

Their guard opened one of the many doors, seemingly at random, revealing a small half-bath. No shower, but a pedestal sink and a toilet, all spotlessly clean and white. Not surprisingly, there wasn't a window either.

Lakshmi met his gaze as she released her hold on his arm. The strange settling sensation filled him again, but the loss of physical contact brought back his tiger's restlessness. Before he could analyze the conflicting sensations, she turned to glare up at the guard and stalk into the bathroom. She leaned against the doorframe on the way in, as if dizzy, then slammed the door behind her. The lock clicked loudly into place.

Ryan and the guard leaned against the opposite wall and waited.

"This is a bad idea," Ryan muttered, without looking at the other male.

"Taking her to the toilet?"

Ryan rolled his eyes. "No, you idiot. Kidnapping females. This is only going to bring the elders down on us. We might as well have declared war against them outright."

The guard didn't comment, but Ryan sensed his unease and caught just a faint hint of nervousness in his scent, a tang of musky suppressed fear.

That gave Ryan hope. If the other males were as worried about this latest move of Gregory's as he was, he might be able to find a few allies among them, to help him get the women out of here safely.

The bathroom door opened before he could say more to the guard or even get his name, but Ryan memorized his scent signature. Lakshmi emerged from the small room and turned back toward her "room" without looking at him or the guard. They followed her in silence.

She made a show of wobbling a little, and when Ryan moved forward to offer support, she waved him away. He knew why—any female tiger would resent feeling and showing weakness in this situation and she was playing the part perfectly. But for some reason, his tiger objected to being brushed off when Lakshmi appeared to need his help.

He was relieved to see Sanjay still at the women's door, looking as if he hadn't moved from his post. With both women's estrous approaching, Ryan couldn't trust any of the males to remain civil, even if they might under ordinary circumstances. Just one more reminder that he didn't have much time to get the women to safety. Before the guards locked them back in, he reminded them to bring food. He was a little surprised they didn't make him leave the room now that Lakshmi at least seemed to be recovering, even though she'd shown them signs of being weak. Maybe they could tell Erin still needed his supervision.

When the door locked shut, he turned to Lakshmi. "You need to eat when the food arrives. Even if you aren't hungry. You need your strength." He glanced at Erin, still asleep. Out of habit, he went to check her pulse and breathing. "She'll need to eat as well, if she can once she wakes up."

"I'll try to eat."

Lakshmi didn't sound very convincing, but at least she'd make the effort.

"You need food, too," she said quietly.

"Don't worry about me. I'll eat when I'm sure you two are okay."

"We won't be okay until we're away from this place and safely back with our families."

He couldn't argue with that truth, even in an attempt to offer comfort.

"When was the last time you ate?" she asked.

He rubbed a hand over his face and up through his hair. "I don't remember." He settled on the floor, putting his back against the wall at the head of the two single beds.

"If you're going to help us," she said in the almost inaudible tone they'd been using, "you need your strength, too."

"I'm fine. I can go weeks without eating properly."

"Your tiger is that strong?"

He smiled a little. "My residency was that demanding.

It trained me to survive on sporadic sleep and random eating habits."

"How long ago was that?"

"Doesn't matter. The habits are ingrained now." He shrugged. "But I finished my surgical residency three years ago."

"Do you like being a surgeon?"

"I do. I wouldn't have gone into it if I didn't enjoy it." He winced a little. "Okay, I probably would have gone into medicine whether I liked it or not, for a few years anyway. My parents... They *encouraged* medical school."

She chuckled quietly and the sound went a long way toward easing the worst of his tension.

"My father wanted me to go to medical school, too," she said.

"I'm assuming you didn't?"

"No. Not my calling." She met his gaze for a few moments. "How do you deal with all the blood?"

He shrugged. "Same way any other shifter does who goes into medicine, I suppose. My tiger and I have an understanding. When I'm at work, blood means I need to help, not eat. Probably made my residency easier, actually. I had to talk myself out of being hungry so often, I just stopped being hungry at the hospital."

"Do you hunt anymore?"

"Sometimes. The occasional deer. Mostly, I eat like a human."

"Was that hard, giving up that part of your nature?"

"Not as hard as it might be for some. This *was* my

calling—even without my parents' urgings. I was meant to be a doctor."

"My dad would like you. So would my mother."

That made him smile fully. "So what do you do?"

"I own a couple of businesses, one sundry store and a coffee shop, and I manage the business end of my father's restaurant. He supplies my coffee shop with our food and pastries, and I make sure his business runs smoothly."

She sighed, a half-smile, half-frown playing around her mouth, an expression he read as worried.

"I'm also in the middle of opening a new clothing retail store," she said. "It's at a delicate point. Being away..." Her expression turned to a full scowl as she nibbled her bottom lip.

"What kind of clothing?" he asked.

"Adult, women's clothing mostly with a small section for men. Casual, everyday wear. At least at the moment. I'd like to expand eventually to include items for the whole family, and maybe a section for formal wear... Or maybe that will be a second shop. I have to see how this store works out."

"So you're rich?"

She dropped her chin, giving him an assessing look. "Are you?"

"I do okay. Despite my medical school bills."

"Me, too," she countered with a smug little smile.

The easy conversation helped Ryan forget the tightness in his stomach and the anxiety clawing at him. She seemed to be recovering well, which was a relief all on its own. But the casual, normal discussion had a similar effect on his tiger as the physical contact had earlier, lulling him into a kind of contentment, just sitting quietly with her and chatting.

All the anger and worry came roaring back when he heard the door lock click. He had his feelings, and his scent, under control by the time the thick door swung open.

Yet another new male brought in a tray loaded with food. He was around Ryan's height, with light blond hair, tanned skin and blue eyes. Ryan had only met this tiger once. He recognized his scent signature but it took him a few moments to remember the man's name—Justin? No, Jason. Jason was so young, Ryan was surprised he was even thinking about mating enough to join Gregory. The man couldn't have been more than twenty—very young for a long-lived tiger shifter male.

Jason stared for a long moment at Lakshmi, who stared back, her anger strong in her scent. The young male looked away, glancing at Erin who was still asleep, then he met Ryan's gaze.

"If you need anything more, I'll get it for you. Just let me know. Gregory has put me in charge of making sure the females are fed."

"Are there drugs in that food?" Ryan would smell most things, but there were a few drugs tiger shifters were vulnerable to that were difficult for even them to smell.

"No," Jason said, holding Ryan's gaze.

Ryan analyzed his scent: worry, anxiety, excitement… but no lies. Jason was taking his job of feeding the women very seriously. Ryan let his shoulders relax and nodded for the kid to leave the tray he was carrying on the floor.

"You need any food," Jason said, "just let me know, doc. Gregory will see you in an hour."

He started to come a little farther into the room, but when Lakshmi growled, he stopped and put the tray down where he was, backing out of the room without taking his eyes off her. As soon as he was clear of the door, the guards locked it again.

Ryan snorted a half-laugh under his breath as he rose to get the tray.

But Jason's flash of fear worried him. If the males believed Lakshmi or Erin were capable of attacking at random, they wouldn't hesitate to drug the women again.

Frankly, he was surprised they'd allowed Lakshmi to remain undrugged this long. The room they were in was designed to hold a tiger prisoner. But Lakshmi wasn't making any attempt to hide how angry she was, and they had to know she was gearing up to fight, even if they thought her still weak from the drug.

That worried him, too. He had a feeling they'd all have to fight to get out of here, but the odds weren't in their favor. Too many enemies, too few allies.

And now Gregory wanted to see him.

The tiger was so unbalanced, with an ever growing cult-leader complex, there was no telling how he'd react or what he'd do at any given moment.

Ryan could hide his feelings from tiger senses, showing other tigers only what he wanted them to see. It was a rare trait, one that helped in his job and was the reason he was part of this group. But it was also the reason Gregory didn't fully trust him. Despite not being able to sense or smell deception on Ryan, the crazy bastard knew Ryan was hiding things from him. Ryan played a very delicate balancing act with Gregory.

This situation was going to change that balance, one way or the other.

"Are you afraid of Gregory?" Lakshmi asked.

He set the tray next to her on the bed and lifted the lids, sniffing at the contents to double check for drugs. Nothing he could smell.

"No," Ryan lied.

"Why not?"

"I have no reason to be." More lies. He tasted some of the nearly raw steak on one plate, decided it was safe and handed the plate to Lakshmi. "If you can stomach it, eat all that."

She didn't even bother with utensils, just picked the steak up and started munching on it, ripping pieces off and chewing quietly as she considered him.

"I'm not sure I believe you. About Gregory. But I can't smell a lie."

She was talking in the nearly inaudible tone again, but he still glanced at the door.

"Why do you think I'm lying if you can't smell it?" he asked without meeting her gaze. He tried some of the potatoes and vegetables on the tray, small bits to check for drugs before approving those plates for Lakshmi to eat from.

"Not sure," she said. "But your scent changes, depending on who's in the room. I've never met a tiger who did that. Even the elders and their assistants don't change their scents. They just don't reveal anything. Yours seems to…adjust to the situation. I didn't think that was possible."

He shrugged. "Maybe your senses are off because of the drugs." He motioned to the potatoes. "If your stomach is queasy at all, those will help."

"The steak is good. I have a healthy appetite under most circumstances."

He smiled a little. Then sighed when she didn't drop the subject of his scent.

"I can tell what every other tiger who enters this room is feeling," she said. "That last male, he was both anxious and excited. And when he mentioned Gregory there was just the faintest flash of fear mixed with awe."

Ryan didn't comment, pretending to focus on the rest of the food and the two flasks of liquid—both water.

"You're one of them, aren't you?" she asked.

"Meaning?"

"You know these males. You're one of Gregory's group."

He handed her a flask. "Water will help flush the drug out faster. But sip if you're feeling any nausea."

"You are, aren't you, Dr. Yin?"

"I'm their doctor. Yes."

"Why?"

"Why what?"

"Why are you with them? You don't seem…like the rest."

"Drink," he ordered and turned to check on Erin.

"You're not going to answer my questions?"

"I'm not sure what to tell you."

"Do you believe in the Mate Run?"

"No."

"Do you want rebellion against the elders?"

He looked away from Erin and met Lakshmi's gaze. So quietly it wasn't even really a sound, he said, "No."

"Then why are you here?"

"To make sure no one dies." And he turned back to Erin.

That was as much truth as he could give Lakshmi.

CHAPTER FOUR

L akshmi devoured her steak, surprised by her own hunger given how horrible food had sounded even just a few minutes ago. She watched Dr. Yin the entire time she ate, confused and more than a little annoyed by the fact that he confused her.

He didn't make sense. He seemed to be as angry about what Gregory was doing as she was, and yet he was part of Gregory's group. Willingly. Before now anyway. He could disguise his scent. She was sure of it, even if he wouldn't admit it. And not just to hide what his scent told other shifters—the elders could ensure their scent didn't reveal their thoughts—Dr. Yin seemed to transform his scent at will, giving off whatever impression he wanted.

If she was right about what he could do, it meant he could hide what he was thinking from everyone—Gregory included. Maybe even the elders. A handy trick.

But it also meant she definitely couldn't trust him. Not

that she did, but she kept thinking of him as…help. An ally. Now she had to wonder if he was a plant, put in here by Gregory to do more than just keep them alive.

The problem was, she wanted to trust him. She liked him, on a basic, instinctive level guided mostly by her tiger's sense of things. Her tiger was typically a good judge of character and situations. Her tiger thought the doctor was a friend.

Her tiger also thought the doctor was incredibly handsome.

That was annoying. She was too pissed and too scared. She shouldn't be thinking about his looks. Worse, if she allowed herself to be distracted by his looks, she might miss some vital sign of the danger he posed to her.

But she couldn't stop remembering that strange rightness she'd felt when she'd taken his arm on the way to the bathroom. How it felt so natural, even though he was a stranger. Given her situation, physical contact with any of the males should make her skin crawl. Yet the heat of Dr. Yin's skin against her palm had warmed her somewhere deep inside. It was so odd. She couldn't understand why her tiger would feel possessive of the doctor when she should be leery and on guard.

Her reactions to Dr. Yin made no sense, and that worried her as much as being kidnapped.

She was still contemplating the puzzle of him when the door opened again. Just before it swung inward, she caught a flash of worry in his scent and then it was gone. One of the earlier guards, the one who'd carried her in here originally, came in and motioned Dr. Yin to his feet.

The doctor glanced at her. "When Erin wakes up, encourage her to eat. If anything changes with her condition or yours, please send the guards to get me."

She nodded, but narrowed her eyes at his back as he left. A completely irrational part of her had a moment of panic as the door closed, the sense that her only help was leaving and she was alone now, at the mercy of any number of dangerous males. She had to bite the inside of her cheek to keep from calling after him as her heartbeat sped.

Concentrating on breathing, she talked herself down from the panic. She didn't know Dr. Yin well enough to feel so dependent on him. In fact, that might be the very reason Gregory had allowed him to stay so long—Gregory wanted her and Erin to trust the doctor, maybe even rely on him. A form of control.

She couldn't allow that to happen. Which meant, whether he was a friend or not, she needed to rely only on herself. She ate one of the baked potatoes—skin and all— drank an entire flask of water, and then checked on Erin.

Lakshmi simply couldn't trust any male right now. She and Erin were on their own; they'd have to find a way out of this. They'd have to regain their strength, and they'd have to fight.

Still…

That part of her that had panicked kept watching the door, waiting for the doctor to return. Hoping no one else walked into this room before he got back.

And because that watching, waiting part of her annoyed her and made her feel weak, she made a concerted effort to ignore it.

She needed a plan. One that didn't rely on the good doctor. As Erin started to rouse, Lakshmi focused on getting her to eat even as she ran through their options.

A way out. They needed a way out.

* * *

R yan held his composure by a bare thread as he was led through non-descript white hallways with more closed doors. There was no real scent to follow, no trails. And there seemed to be a constant, low-level hum of white noise that prevented him from tracking anything using his acute hearing. Wherever they were, the place was big. Wondering why Gregory needed a complex this large nipped at Ryan's heels, pestering him with more worrisome possibilities than he wanted to imagine.

His control was stretched even more as, with each twist and turn through the endless sameness, his tiger kept pushing him to return to Lakshmi. A low level of panic tightened his muscles the farther he got from her, making it hard to concentrate on the confrontation to come. The perfectly logical argument that he could be more helpful to Lakshmi by convincing Gregory to stop using the drug did nothing to shut his tiger up.

After seemingly miles of walking, he was finally marched into what he could only consider a throne room, and it took every ounce of self-control he had not to roll his eyes or reveal his disgust in his scent.

The high-ceilinged, rectangular room had walls lined with light wood and cream-colored silk wallpaper. The natural wood floor was polished to a painful shine, and a long red and gold rug ran from the door to a low dais at the far end of the space. Three huge crystal chandeliers lined the flat ceiling, providing the only light in the windowless room. At intervals along the wall, white and gold marble pedestals dripped with green, vining plants, adding a pleasant fresh scent to the lemon polish smell of the room.

This was the first area he'd been in that was anything but white and actually had a smell to it. Which might have been a relief to his senses but for the crazy tiger sitting in a throne on the dais at the far end of the huge room.

The wide, high-backed chair was also wood, though darker than the other woods in the room, and the thick armrests and ornamented back were decorated with gold filigree. Two males in their tiger forms flanked the throne, sitting on the dais with their tails wrapped around their front paws. The pose was deceptively placid and stylized, so that the males almost looked like statues instead of living animals.

In the throne, Gregory sat with his head tilted down but his glittering gaze fixed on Ryan.

Under different circumstances, Ryan suspected the room was supposed to be a large, formal dining room or maybe even a ballroom. The fact that Gregory was using it as an audience hall shouldn't have really surprised him.

Ryan gave Gregory a slight nod of greeting, his only show of deference. The man didn't need any encouragement in his king delusion. From the way the two tigers flanked him and sat like guards, Ryan figured Gregory was getting enough encouragement as it was.

"How are the females?" Gregory asked.

"Recovering. No thanks to that drug. You can't give them any more. It's already slowed down Erin's healing and the head wound she got is causing her serious problems." He didn't mention it was Gregory's fault she had that head wound. "We just can't trust that bastard human and anything he's created. As a doctor, I have to insist you don't use the drug anymore."

"Lakshmi and Erin won't be given another dose unless it becomes absolutely necessary." Gregory finally raised his head to look more directly at Ryan. "Now that Erin is recovering, I'll need you to see to the other women."

Ryan's chest tightened. "What others?"

"The first two we brought here… Well, the drug killed one. We've been more careful since, but it seems to have adversely affected the surviving female. I'll need you to do what you can for her. The other two females are arriving soon. Their travel wasn't as complicated as we anticipated."

Six. Gregory had kidnapped *six* females.

So far.

Ryan's tiger roared in his head and his knees actually shook from the surge of adrenaline and disgust.

Gregory's nose twitched, and Ryan knew he hadn't been able to disguise his reaction, so he didn't try. He'd made it clear he didn't like these kidnappings already. It made things more believable when at least some of what he showed Gregory was absolute truth.

"You don't approve, doc," Gregory said.

"Of course not. This is too much. You killed a valuable

female already! You can't risk any more. You have to stop. Let the women go. Then maybe, just maybe the elders won't send an army down on your head."

Gregory smiled. "Let them. We're prepared."

Ryan wasn't sure he'd ever heard anything quite so terrifying. He shook his head and pretended ordinary irritation. "Where's the other prisoner?"

Gregory raised a brow at Ryan's tone but motioned to the guard standing at Ryan's right shoulder—Pat, a tiger who'd been with Gregory practically since the beginning. "Take the doctor to her. Bring his medical equipment. He'll need it."

"What about Lakshmi and Erin?" Ryan asked.

"They're recovering. They aren't your concern anymore."

"Erin still needs attention. Her head wound isn't healed."

"Then you'll be brought back to her once you've seen to Megan."

Megan… That had to be Megan Yankova. She was one of the original females reported missing more than three weeks earlier. Gregory really was responsible for all the disappearances then. Fuck.

But…three women had been missing before Gregory's young males had come for Ryan. Gregory said he'd brought two females here. One died, the other was Megan… What had happened to the third?

Dread dropped heavily onto his shoulders as he considered where Gregory had gotten the drug. The sonofabitch wouldn't have given a human serial killer one of their few females in exchange for that drug, would he?

The idea, the implication was too much for Ryan to take and still maintain his sanity. He had to concentrate on keeping the women here alive and finding a way to help them escape. Thinking about Gregory's dealings with the serial killer would only distract him.

Breathing slowly to calm his pulse, Ryan asked, "And when…*if* Erin and Megan recover? What then?"

"They'll be moved to more permanent accommodation."

"Just Erin and Megan or all of the women?" A thread of panic tightened in his gut. Lakshmi was recovered enough to fight. She might just risk it if they separated her from Erin. If she fought, she'd be killed.

It was one of the most serious crimes a male tiger could commit—killing one of the few, valuable females left to their population. Gregory had already killed one. He might even have handed another over to a human murderer. He obviously didn't care about the law or the lives of the women. Which meant any of them could be killed. They weren't protected by their gender or value to the community.

"Leave Lakshmi with Erin," Ryan said, trying to prevent disaster. "It helps keep Erin settled and calm, which is what she needs to recover fully. Any more stress will ruin all my good work."

He infused all the arrogant authority he possessed into his voice. He'd intimidated many a resident and fellow doctor with that tone.

From his scent, Ryan could tell that Gregory wasn't intimidated and still suspicious, but he gave a slight nod.

"I'll defer to your expertise, doctor," Gregory said. "For now."

Ryan bit his tongue to keep from saying anything that might antagonize Gregory. With a curt flick of his hand, Ryan motioned the guard Pat to take him to the woman he hadn't seen yet.

He ran through every curse he knew as he made his way there.

* * *

Ryan had barely made it through the basement room's steel door when the stench hit him hard. Piss and blood, and worse. Despite years of training, working around human waste and body fluids, the overwhelming smell still made him gag.

He spotted the cage as his eyes adjusted to the dim light. Then he saw the ragged form of a naked female in her human form.

She snarled at them when they entered, hissing and chuffing as she might if she were in her tiger form. She started to shift, russet fur running down her arms, her face distorting into the wider, longer features of her tiger. Then abruptly her body snapped back to human form.

Ryan frowned. His species didn't do half shifts, and typically once they started to go tiger, they went all the way. They could go back and forth, but not halfway and back.

Normally.

"What's happened to her? Has she been able to fully shift since you brought her here?" He spun on Pat, glaring as anger roared through his blood.

"Only those almost shifts," Pat said. "It's like she's gone tiger, but her body can't make the change with her mind." He swallowed hard and didn't look directly at the female as he spoke.

Ryan snarled and went to the cage. "And after this, and a dead female, you still fucking used the drug? On more females?"

He was so enraged, so absolutely disgusted, his tiger was clawing to get out and do damage to the assholes responsible for this. He felt the change just under his skin, and only years of control kept him from going tiger.

The cage holding Megan had shifter-proof bars, but even if it hadn't, Ryan wasn't sure she'd have been able to break out. She was certainly angry enough, but in her current state, he wasn't sure she'd have the strength. As he neared, she swung to face him and snarled, baring teeth that were too long and sharp to be in a human's mouth.

"Jesus," he muttered. His heart hurt for her.

He steadied his breathing, with no little effort, and pushed his anger out of his mind so he could concentrate on helping her. Then he adjusted his scent to give off the calming, tranquil, safe signals he used so often in his role as a doctor. Even humans, whose sense of smell was decidedly weaker than a tiger shifter's, reacted to that subtle scent, relaxing in his presence so he could better do his job.

Faced with a half-crazed shifter female, made that way

by other tigers, it took more willpower than usual to force down his darker emotions and let the calming essence fill his scent. She needed this from him, though, so he didn't rush his examination. He sat down outside the cage and let his scent fill the space around them, let his patience give her the reassurance she needed to believe he was safe and meant her no harm.

He remained that way on the hard concrete floor for a long time, waiting her out as she paced the confined space, snarling and chuffing, keeping her distance, occasionally charging the bars and lashing out at him with fingers part human and part claw. The sight of her faltering attempts to shift broke his heart. But he continued to keep his anger at Gregory and the others out of his scent so he could reassure her.

"What's your name?" he asked quietly, when she finally stopped pacing and stared at him.

He needed to give her the power of giving him her name—even though he already knew who she was. He needed to give her some sense of control. He also wanted her to hold on to her human side for long enough to discuss her symptoms with him, and using her human name would help with that.

Her lips lifted in a little snarl, almost like the reaction was involuntary. She grunted a few times, cleared her throat and forced out, "Megan."

Her voice cracked, sounding broken and not entirely human.

"My name is Ryan Yin, Megan. I'm a doctor. I'm here to help you, but I won't touch you until you're ready for me to. I understand you've had a very bad reaction to the drug they gave you. I don't dare give you anything to counteract it. I'm not even sure there is anything that can counteract it. But with time and patience, it will leave your system and you'll be back to normal."

"Can't shift. Tigers fighting to get out and can't."

"I noticed. Can you calm her at all? The less she struggles, the faster you'll heal."

He was working entirely on instinct. He didn't actually know if that was true or not. But any kind of internal fight between Megan and her tiger was bound to wear her body out, and the weaker she was, the longer it would take for the drug to finish metabolizing.

Over his shoulder, he asked Pat, "How long has she been like this?"

"Two weeks."

Ryan closed his eyes. "When was the last time she was given the drug?"

"Yesterday."

He growled. He couldn't help it. They were *still* subjecting her to the fucking stuff? Were they insane? Well, he knew Gregory was, but this…

When Megan moved around, her eyes going larger and her lip twitching in another snarl, he realized he'd let some of his inner anger slip into his scent. He dialed it back. She would probably be more reassured by his anger after she recovered.

If she recovered.

He waited for her to settle again before attempting to speak with her. She stalked around the cage like a tiger in a zoo, but as he watched, her circuit slowed and her muscles relaxed enough so the stalking looked less stiff and harsh. Eventually, she was pacing in an almost human manner.

Finally, she stopped and faced him again.

"My tiger wants to kill," she said.

He could hear the damage done to her throat. "Get her some water," he ordered Pat.

When the man hesitated, Ryan turned and narrowed his eyes. "Get her some water," he said again slowly, pronouncing each word distinctly. "Now."

The guard glanced at Megan then looked away, a shudder jerking across his big shoulders before he left the huge concrete room.

Ryan faced Megan once the door closed behind Pat.

"I can't begin to tell you how sorry I am that this has happened to you," he said, using the same almost inaudible tone he'd used with Lakshmi upstairs, so any nearby shifters wouldn't overhear him. "The elders do know females have gone missing and they're looking for you. Help should be here soon. In the meantime, I will do whatever I can to keep you and the others safe."

"Others?"

He sighed. "There are two more women upstairs. And two on their way."

"I was taken after another… She died."

Tears made his eyes burn. He forced them down. "Yes. I just learned that."

"Will I die?"

"Not if I can help it."

"I wanted to die. I wanted to let go and give over to the tiger completely."

"You don't have to."

"I can't trust you."

"I know. It's okay. I am a doctor, and I will try to make sure you recover and are healthy. But I won't push you."

She jerked her head in a nod.

"After the guard returns, may I examine you?"

"He's here, my tiger is too angry. She'll attack you."

Her voice sounded more and more human the longer the guard was away, too. Obviously, Ryan's scent helped calm her tiger, but having the other man around would make it impossible for him to do his job.

"I'll send him away after he's brought water." He glanced around the large open room and spotted his medical kit near the door. He rose.

"Wait!" Megan banged against the bars, reaching toward him.

"I'm not going anywhere." He pointed to the large, orange, hard plastic case with medical symbols on it. "Those are my supplies. I'll need them for the examination when…and if you're ready."

"What about the other women?"

Ryan had been trying not to worry about Lakshmi and Erin, especially since Megan so obviously needed his help. But the mention of them made his stomach tighten.

"They're both recovering," he said, "and I've insisted they aren't given any more of the drug."

He ruthlessly forced the stench of worry and anxiety out of his scent. That would only set Megan's tiger off again. But the emotions churned in his belly. Without him around to act as a buffer, he couldn't be sure what Gregory or the others might do to the two women upstairs. He was torn between the need to return to them and make sure they were safe and his need to help Megan.

"Once you're feeling better," he said over his shoulder as he retrieved his kit, "I'll see if I can arrange to have you all put into the same rooms."

"He won't. He's afraid of us."

"Gregory?" He didn't really need to ask, but he wanted to keep her talking. The longer she talked, the more human she sounded and the less twitching and half-shifting she did.

She nodded. "He knows we can fight now. The first female he took—Anna—she almost killed one of his men in a fight before they could even use the drug. It's why he gave her too much. Why he killed her. He's afraid. He won't allow us to join together. We'd be too strong."

"There are only three of you now." He snarled. "Five by tomorrow. And me," he added very quietly. "Six to…about forty is still not good odds. No matter your training and skills."

"I'd rather fight and take my chances."

His lips twitched, an almost smile. "Lakshmi said the same thing."

"Who are the two upstairs now?"

"Lakshmi Das and Erin Blum."

"Do the elders know they're missing?"

"Hopefully. When you and Anna went missing, the elders knew pretty quickly."

"You're Sarah Chu's brother, right? Her husband is a Tracker. Is that how you know all this?"

He didn't miss a beat when saying, "Yes. The community knows there are females missing. The Trackers are hunting for you now."

"The elders will send the Trackers here. They'll attack this place."

"As soon as they find it."

Her green eyes flickered. "You don't know where we are either?"

"No," he admitted. "They blocked my senses to get me here."

"Are you a prisoner, too?"

The exact question Lakshmi had asked. "Not exactly. Not like you. But I won't be let free either."

"So you can't tell the others where we are." She nodded as if this settled something for her.

"They will find us. There's no place on the planet Gregory could take five females where the Trackers wouldn't find you. You just have to survive long enough for help to arrive."

"Survival isn't my biggest worry."

There was a deadness to her tone, a hollowness that made his every nerve jump to alert. He opened his mouth to ask what she meant and realized he might not want to know yet. Because if she told him she'd already been raped, given the shape she was in, he knew his tiger wouldn't be able to take that without killing someone. And if he attacked any of the other males now, he'd be killed. That wouldn't help Megan or Lakshmi or Erin.

He pulled in a deep breath and let it out slowly, calming the disgust and anger that threatened to choke him.

Megan narrowed her eyes. "Your scent is…interesting."

Before she could say more, the guard returned, saving Ryan from having to make excuses or explain without explaining.

He was having a much harder time than usual controlling his scent. Lakshmi was already suspicious, though he hadn't confirmed anything. If he wasn't careful, everyone would realize how well he could manipulate his scent.

Ryan met Pat near the door, not allowing him any farther into the room, and took the cold bottle of water from him.

"You need to leave now," Ryan ordered, "so I can examine her." Even as he spoke, he watched Megan start pacing again. "She's too agitated with you around. I won't be able to help her unless we're left alone."

"Gregory said to keep an eye on you."

"Then stand outside the door." Ryan gestured to the huge, gray cement basement, with its obvious lack of windows or anything else but the cage in the center of the room. "I'm not going anywhere."

The guard hesitated, glancing between Ryan and the cage. "I need to stay."

"If you stay, she'll probably die. Gregory doesn't want her dead."

Pat's scent flared with worry and something very subtle…a light tang of disgust, like the flavor of fish just starting to rot. Maybe he didn't want any more females to die either. Ryan could hope.

"I'll be outside the door," Pat finally said. He tossed Ryan a key. "For the cage. Though, you're taking your life in your hands if you open the door, doc. I'd examine her from out here."

Megan growled, low in her throat, her tiger rising to the surface.

Ryan ignored the threatening sound and motioned the other man out. "I'll take my chances. Don't come back in until I knock on the door. If she kills me, find another doctor that can help the women."

Pat snorted an almost laugh and sauntered out, pretending at a confidence his scent clearly said he didn't feel.

Ryan shook his head at the retreating man. When the door was locked, he turned back to the cage.

"Will you kill me if I let you out?" he asked Megan matter-of-factly, without showing any sign of worry. "If you do, it could take weeks for them to get another doctor here."

She was still pacing, but she let out a half-chuckle, a strange sound, as much tiger as human.

He waited outside the cage door until she was calm again. When he was sure she was in control of herself, he turned the lock and went in, leaving the door wide so she didn't feel trapped with him.

She glanced at it, then back at him. "I could kill you. Ambush the guard. Then make a run for it."

"You could. Might be a good plan. I'd rather not die yet, though. I have two more patients due in soon."

He spoke without meeting her gaze as he did a visual

assessment of her body, ensuring his movements, expression, and scent all remained clinical and detached. She didn't show signs of broken, badly-healed body parts. Her pale skin was covered in a layer of dirt mixed with some old blood, and her dark brown hair was knotted and caked with grime. But beyond the dirt, he didn't see any current bleeding or obvious damage.

"May I examine you now?" he asked when he was confident her tiger had relaxed fully.

She nodded.

He set about his examination carefully and with a great deal of reassuring talk to explain everything he was doing or intended to do. Megan's health took up most of his thoughts as he concentrated on what the drug had done to her.

But in the back of his mind, he felt the clock ticking, and he couldn't stop worrying about Lakshmi.

CHAPTER FIVE

Lakshmi came to her feet, almost instinctively, when a small phalanx of five males marched into the narrow room. Erin, despite having just complained of feeling woozy, swung up to a sitting position on the bed and focused on the threat. Lakshmi moved to stand in front of the other woman, positioning herself so she could protect Erin if necessary but wouldn't be in Erin's way if she was able to attack.

The male standing at the center of the five took one step farther into the room and motioned at Erin. "Stand. You're being moved."

"Why?" Lakshmi said. In the back of her mind, she wondered where Dr. Yin was and when he'd return.

Or if he'd return.

"We have more permanent accommodations for you," the group's spokesman said.

He was a tall, broad shifter, with blond hair, blue eyes,

and a lean look about him that put her on edge. He didn't smile or leer, but his gaze was a little too focused on her. His scent was a mix of determination, excitement, and a faint wisp of lust.

She stared him down and her tiger wanted to snarl, to force him to look away, but she wasn't sure if that would make things worse.

"Erin is still too unsteady," she said. "Dr. Yin didn't want her moved yet. I need to stay with her to make sure she stays awake."

"If she can't walk on her own, one of my men will carry her."

Erin shuddered and shook her head, though Lakshmi could tell the gesture cost her. When she started to stand, Lakshmi jumped to her side to steady her.

"I'd rather crawl than have one of them touch me," Erin said to Lakshmi but plenty loud enough for everyone in the room to hear.

One of the five guards growled. Another snorted a laugh. The spokesman's expression never changed, his gaze still uncomfortably intent on Lakshmi.

She was used to men staring at her, particularly other tiger shifters. She was rare among her kind and that made her valuable in ways that had nothing to do with her as a person. She ignored those stares. It meant nothing to her, because it wasn't about her. But even being used to that kind of attention didn't help her feel any more comfortable under the scrutiny of these five males.

She gripped Erin around the waist with one arm to hold

her upright and patted her shoulder with the other hand, a gesture meant to comfort them both.

"You're moving us against doctor's orders," Lakshmi said. "That could come back to haunt you."

The spokesman blinked but didn't answer. A couple of the guards moved from foot to foot, the discomfort in their scents like a bite of pepper. She wasn't sure what caused the discomfort specifically, but it gave her information to store. They were worried about her and Erin's health. At least there was that. It gave her time to plan an escape.

The fact that they weren't giving them any more of that awful drug wasn't lost on her either.

At a signal from the spokesman, the other four shifters surrounded her and Erin. The males crowded close, impossible not to in the narrow room, but didn't touch them.

"If you try to run," the spokesman said, "you'll be drugged again."

She nodded in understanding. She needed to remain in control of her body and if that meant cooperating while she studied her surroundings and her guards, she'd do it.

A tremor ran through Erin at the mention of the drug. Lakshmi hugged her closer.

They were led through very nondescript corridors, all painted a blinding white and spotlessly clean. The wooden floor was even whitewashed. The effect made Lakshmi think of insane asylums for some reason, and it was all she could do not to bolt for the nearest door. She'd never wanted to see a splotch of color so much in her life.

The scent of the place didn't tell her much either. It was almost sterile, it was so bland. She could clearly scent the five males around her, as well as herself and Erin—and their approaching estrous. But beyond the smells of tiger shifters, she caught only the faintest bite of a bleach-based cleaner and just a hint of the paint used on the walls and floor. Her nose actually twitched at the lack of smells, the absence so obvious to her and her tiger.

"How did you scour away all scent?" she asked the spokesman, not really expecting an answer.

She wasn't disappointed. Only one of the males even glanced at her. His eyes sparkled with that look she dreaded, the lust she saw during her Mate Runs in the eyes of males she had no interest in. It only took a glance for her to know she'd never have allowed this particular male to catch her.

Except now she was at his mercy.

The injustice of it caught at her throat and cut off any more questions. Anger rose over her like a wave, mixing with her worry and fear. Her tiger wanted to roar her outrage before ripping her way out of this mess. And Lakshmi wasn't sure how much longer she'd deny her tiger that option because the fear of what could happen was swamping her logic.

For now, though, she forced her tiger side to quiet so she could attempt to think rationally. She had a feeling they were prepared for her to go tiger, which meant she had to do what they didn't expect if she had any hope at all.

She memorized the path they took through what appeared to be a huge complex, as they walked a set of narrow stairs up two levels and then wound through even more blank, white corridors. She realized the non-descript walls and lack of landmarks made this place something of a labyrinth. In fact, if she hadn't had a very keen sense of location, she might easily get lost in all these same-same corridors, without even scent to help her backtrack.

Her own scent might leave a trail for long enough that she could return to the original room. But whatever they were doing to make the air so bland would probably mask her scent trail before long.

It crossed her mind to consider how Dr. Yin might find them if he couldn't follow their scents. She forced down her scowl, not wanting the surrounding males to misinterpret the expression, but it irritated her to no end that part of her kept turning to Dr. Yin as an ally. She didn't know him and certainly didn't know enough about him to consider him a friend. He was part of this group. She had to start thinking of him as a potential threat.

She couldn't trust any male right now. Not even the kind, handsome Ryan Yin.

After a few more turns and twists designed to further confuse them, they finally stopped in front of a set of large white doors. The spokesman pushed them open and gestured her and Erin inside. Past the entrance was the first hint of personality she'd seen in the building.

A huge room spread out before her, with several very large beds set on low daises decorated with thick quilts in jewel-toned colors and piled high with pillows. The wood floor was polished to a shine—not white-washed here—and laid with thick, colorful Persian rugs. The walls were hung with swaths of sheer curtains in a rainbow of colors. And the overhead lighting was softened and recessed, giving the room the impression of sunlight even though there were no windows.

Decorations in metallic gold paint added a glint to the room, as if the designer of the space had tried to make it look opulent. The wall to her right had been painted to resemble an intricate blue and white tile mosaic. To her left was a small, rectangular green and pink tiled pool that resembled a large fountain or ancient bath, the water in it crystal clear and fresh smelling.

Next to the pool was a small door she assumed went to a bathroom. There were a few white columns at intervals around the area, set in pairs with decorative arches over them, giving the illusion of multiple spaces and doorways in the large room.

And though she couldn't actually see any signs of incense burners, the air was scented with a mix of frankincense and sandalwood.

As she and Erin were ushered inside, Lakshmi frowned. The place reminded her of something, but she couldn't quite place it. It only hit her after the males left and the door locked behind them.

The room reminded her of a Hollywood version of a Turkish harem.

* * *

Ryan didn't even try to hide his anger as he was brought before Gregory this time. Gregory wouldn't believe him—and would know for sure something was strange about him—if he didn't show Gregory how mad he was at what he'd just seen.

"You have to stop using this drug, Gregory," he said without waiting for Gregory to speak. "I mean it. No more. On any females. Ever. I have no idea if Megan will ever recover fully. She might be permanently damaged, thanks to that crap you've been giving her."

"How is she at the moment?" Gregory didn't show any emotion at Ryan's outburst, but his dark eyes glittered.

Ryan straightened his shoulders. Showing his anger was one thing. Showing any fear at all was out of the question right now.

"She's doing a little better," he said, "because she's calmer. You have to keep the other males out of that room. They agitate her too much and make matters worse. Her body can't heal if she's not calm."

"Is she sufficiently recovered to be moved?"

"Only if you want the faces ripped off any male who tries to get near her. Or you want her dead." Ryan narrowed his eyes when Gregory didn't immediately respond. "You can't drug her again to move her. You'll kill her."

Gregory stared without answering.

"Damn it, Gregory. You *have* to stop using this drug. Do you understand me? If you don't, you will kill more of these women. It's bad enough you've killed one female already."

Something flickered in Gregory's eyes. Nothing else in his expression or scent changed. But the little flicker, the very slight tightening of his eyes, made Ryan's stomach roll as he remembered there was a third female whose fate was still a mystery to him.

"It has only been one female, right?" Ryan said, his jaw tight with his rage.

"Let me know when Megan is ready to move. You can accompany her to her knew accommodation, if it makes you feel better."

"Gregory…" There was warning in Ryan's tone.

This time Gregory's gaze narrowed and the bite of displeasure filled his scent, like burning trash.

"Watch your tone, doctor. You're not indispensable."

Ryan held his tongue, but only barely and because he'd been practicing for so many months now. He let his gaze slide away from Gregory's and made a show of contrition.

Gregory leaned back in his throne, his expression relaxing into a slight smile.

Ryan searched for a way to get more information from him without pissing him off, but before he could think of anything, the door behind him opened. He looked over his shoulder as one of the many guards walked in and bowed his head at Gregory, like he really was a king.

"The female, Lakshmi, is asking for the doctor. She says Erin needs his help."

Ryan frowned. "What's wrong? Is she conscious? Headache?" He was already moving toward the door, forgetting Gregory—a bad move.

"Doctor, I haven't given you leave yet."

Ryan closed his eyes and resisted a snarl. He turned to face Gregory. "Erin has a serious head injury. May I see to her now?"

"Of course, doctor. That's why you're here. When you're finished, Jason will take you to get some food. You've been busy since arriving, and I've been told you haven't eaten yet."

His tone was so calm and magnanimous as he made a show of being a "good" leader. It made Ryan want to growl and spit. Instead, he nodded thanks and motioned the male who'd brought Lakshmi's message to lead the way.

He stopped at the door and looked back at Gregory. "I'll need my medical supplies again."

"They'll be delivered." Gregory motioned toward one of the tigers flanking his throne. The animal stood and left through a side door.

"And Megan needs water to wash in and fresh clothes. The more human she feels, the better. But she needs to be left alone while she bathes."

Gregory's eyes narrowed just slightly but his tone was light. "It will be done."

Ryan left with his stomach still tight from worry. He felt Gregory's gaze on his back until they'd turned a corner in the complex.

* * *

Lakshmi had only just sent word that they needed Dr. Yin when the door to their luxurious prison opened again. One of the males who'd brought them here stepped inside—the one whose lust had disgusted her. He was taller than her by a few inches, with short dark hair and eyes, and an average build. In most circumstances, he was the kind of man she never looked at twice. He wasn't ugly, but he wasn't particularly handsome. Ordinary. Forgettable. And that look in his eyes brought back her earlier thought that he was the type of male she'd never let catch her during a Run.

"You're to come with me," he said.

Panic at being separated from Erin started her heart thumping hard. "I need to stay with her. She's gotten worse. I've sent for the doctor." She didn't move from the bed where Erin was lying.

Out of sight of the male, Erin gripped her wrist tight, whether out of warning or to keep her near, Lakshmi couldn't tell. But no doubt Erin scented the same sick lust Lakshmi did on the young male.

He came two more steps into the room, his gaze locked on Lakshmi. "Gregory's orders. He wants to talk to you." He nodded to Erin. "The doctor will be here to check on her soon."

Something in his scent was wrong… It didn't match his expression or his words. There was too much excitement and anticipation.

Every nerve in Lakshmi's body went on alert. She glanced at the open door. She could sense the two guards outside still, but neither interfered or questions that she was to be taken from the room.

The thought of going anywhere with this particular male repelled her. And yet, if she refused, they might drug her again. Still, her instincts were screaming that she should not allow them to separate her from Erin.

He'd said Dr. Yin was on the way. She held onto that

hope. If she could stall long enough, he'd arrive and she'd have an excuse not to go anywhere.

Unless they hadn't really sent for him…

"Come on," the man said, nodding to the door. "If you don't move, I'm to drug you and carry you."

"But Erin…" Panic swept through her, leaving a metallic taste in her mouth and making her dizzy. She couldn't be drugged again. She wouldn't survive it. She couldn't allow it. But every part of her rebelled at leaving the room with this man.

"Now," he said.

"Don't," Erin whispered.

Lakshmi wasn't sure she had a choice. She had to stay in control of her body. Swallowing hard against the taste of her own fear, she rose. Erin clung tighter to her wrist for a moment more but Lakshmi glanced down at her and shook her head.

"Dr. Yin will be here to check on you soon," she said. "Tell him Gregory sent for me."

Erin tightened her lips into a line and glanced at the male, conveying all her worry and fear in that single look. Finally, though, she released her hold. "Be careful."

"You too."

Lakshmi followed the male, reluctance making her limbs feel heavy. She risked a glance at the two guards outside the door. Neither met her gaze or made any sign that something was amiss. Maybe Gregory really had sent for her, and she was misinterpreting her escort's scent.

Though, facing Gregory all on its own was terrifying.

She didn't want to be in the same room with the crazy bastard, not by herself.

What if that was why the male leading her was so excited? What if Gregory was bringing her someplace to be raped?

She almost balked, almost ran back to the harem room, though it wasn't any safer than any other part of this building. The instinct to bolt was so strong, she trembled with it.

Concentrate, Lakshmi. Look for exits.

Panic was making it hard to breathe, nonetheless think. She had to calm down, she had to focus. Study her surroundings, look for a way out. They were giving her a chance to gather information. She had to take it. She wasn't drugged. Yet. She could fight if she had to. Spots danced in her vision, but she blinked hard to clear them away and then dug deep for her anger. Anger would override the panic. Anger would keep her alert.

Anger didn't bury the panic in time.

Her escort swung around so abruptly, she had no time to react. Before she knew what was happening, he'd slammed her against the corridor wall, his body pinning hers. And to her horror, he held a syringe in one hand, the point set against her cheek.

He smiled, grinding his hips into hers. She wanted to throw up when she felt his erection.

"Now, pretty," he said against the cheek opposite the syringe, "you're going to do exactly what I tell you to do. No fighting. No struggle. Or I'm going to shoot you full of this stuff and do what I want anyway."

"Why…? Why here?" Terror raced adrenaline through

her body but she couldn't think. The needle of the syringe dinted her skin, not piercing yet, but the threat was enough to send her into full-blown, deer-in-the-headlights frozen panic. She panted, trying to pull in oxygen.

"You smell so good," he said, burying his nose against her neck.

She bit back a whimper. She had to do something. She'd trained for this. She knew how to defend herself. Oh god, but the syringe…the drug…

"You don't remember me, do you?" he said, pulling back to stare at her.

"Should I?"

"Your first Run. You let some other asshole catch you."

"That's how it works." *Do something, Lakshmi. Fight!* But the needle was too close. A wrong move would push it under her skin.

"You didn't give me a chance. Now you'll give me exactly what I want."

She didn't answer. She stretched her head to one side, trying to move away from the syringe, instinct more than strategic thought. Her heart pounded so hard if felt like it was going to burst from her chest. When her assailant grabbed her breast, she let out a sound somewhere between a whimper and a growl.

Her tiger rose then, bringing her animal instincts and anger, swamping her logical but panicked human thoughts. A roar built in her throat even as the male started to lick and bite her neck, pulling at her clothes with his free hand.

He'd made a mistake not binding her hands. Her tiger pulled on her self-defense training, the moves turned into muscle memory by years of practice. Free from the panic, she struck, her hand darting out to grab the wrist of the hand holding the syringe and twisting it backward, breaking his wrist and sending the syringe flying out of his grip in a single move. He screamed, but Lakshmi was already bringing her other hand to his dick, taking it in a tight grip and twisting hard enough to bring him up off the ground. She pushed him back a step, two, until the wall wasn't in her way, then she shifted her body weight and flipped the male onto his back.

Her roar of outrage and anger echoed in the hall.

She moved to stomp on the male's neck, but he grabbed her foot and twisted hard and fast before she could react, breaking her ankle. The pain so sudden and surprising, she couldn't breathe enough to scream. With only the leverage of her calf, he tossed her backward. The move was clumsy and awkward but was enough to drop her onto her ass. Through the haze of pain in her ankle, she scrambled to find the syringe. She had to get it before he did.

He rose up over her, his violent anger a stench that made her gag. He kicked at her side, hard. She was already rolling away, but his foot still made contact with her waist, enough to feel like a gut punch, robbing her breath yet again.

Her ankle was already healing but not fast enough for her to put weight on it, so she rolled to her knees. There was no time to shift to her tiger form. That took long minutes and while she was mid-shift he could easily kill her —or inject her with the drug. The only good thing was that he couldn't shift either.

He wasn't a trained fighter, that was obvious when he charged her again, not bothering to protect himself from her next attack. Despite being on her knees, she used his own momentum against him, and ducked under him, bracing her hands against his stomach to toss him almost without effort into a nearby wall. As he collapsed to the ground, she scanned the corridor, hunting for the syringe again.

Damn it, where was it.

From somewhere farther away, she heard the sound of running feet. No! Not more of them. She couldn't let them overwhelm her.

Frantic, she finally spotted the syringe and scrambled toward it. But her assailant caught her by her injured ankle and jerked her backward, away from her goal. She screamed this time, a combination of pain, frustration, anger and fear, and kicked back with her good leg, slamming her bare foot into his jaw, hard enough that she heard the bone crack. He didn't loosen his hold on her leg, though, and kept dragging her close, his fingernails scoring her skin under her pant leg. She kicked again, aiming for the same place but missing and hitting him in the neck, a glancing blow that didn't slow him at all.

She yelled again, kicking without even bothering to aim beyond trying to get close to his face. She pulled at the ground, dragging herself farther away from him, and reached toward the syringe. Too far.

The sound of others approaching got louder. Time was running out. She flung herself away from her assailant with a violent stream of kicks and thrusts, pulling out of his grip for a split-second before he caught her again.

And then the corridor was full of noise and shouting. The grip on her leg released abruptly, making her launch awkwardly forward. In her panic, she scrambled toward the syringe, but someone picked it up before she reached it. She almost cried as fear rose up to choke her again. She shuffled around to put her back to the wall, trapped, desperate and wild.

She jumped when hands touched her cheeks and lashed out with a quick body punch. The new threat caught her wrist mid-motion. She struggled, kicking and slapping, too desperate now to remember her training. It took almost a full second before a familiar, calming scent penetrated the panic and slowed her thrashing. She focused on the man holding her, realized it was Dr. Yin, and all the fight and fear drained away in a flash of relief so strong her body felt like jelly.

"Lakshmi," Dr. Yin said, his voice quiet, "it's me. It's Ryan. I've got you. Are you injured?"

"Ankle's broken," she said through gritted teeth as shock took hold and she started to tremble. "He was going to drug me. I couldn't… I couldn't…"

"Shh. It's okay now. He'll be taken care of."

Without taking his hands from her, he glanced over his shoulder. "Get him out of here."

Lakshmi realized there were two other males besides the doctor in the corridor. One leaned down and lifted her assailant off the floor, ignoring his protests and grunts of pain.

"Take him to Gregory. I'll look after her," Ryan said.

"She's ours to fuck," her assailant said through his

teeth. "Gregory said so. Why are you stopping me? This is why she's here, you fucker. Give her back to me. She's mine."

Ryan ignored him as he was dragged away. He caressed Lakshmi's cheeks until she looked away from her departing assailant and met his gaze.

"I need to look at your ankle," he said in his quiet, calm voice. "Is that okay?"

She nodded. Then another kind of panic rose through her shock. "Erin! She's alone."

"We'll go back to her now. My medical equipment will be there, and I'll be able to look after you both. Can you walk?"

She tried to stand, bracing against the wall behind her to balance, but between her shaking limbs and her half-healed ankle, her knees buckled and she nearly hit the floor again. Ryan caught her before she fell and scooped her up into his arms, strong and reassuring.

She didn't argue, she didn't have the strength. The fact that she leaned into Ryan instead of being revolted by his touch wasn't lost on her.

She was just too drained to worry about it.

CHAPTER SIX

It took almost all Ryan's self-control—what little he had left—to keep his scent full of the calm she needed and not the rage he felt. His tiger roared in his head, clawing at his will, demanding to get out and exact revenge. The only thing that kept his tiger under even a semblance of control was the fact that Lakshmi was injured and needed him.

When he heard her roar, panic at what was happening sent him into motion without thought, racing through the corridors to reach her. He'd barely noticed when a second guard joined him and his original escort, all of them running toward the shouts and thumps of the fight. Every cell in his body was focused on getting to her, saving her from whatever had put that much rage in her voice.

Her scream had almost stopped his heart.

It never occurred to him to wonder how he *knew* it was Lakshmi in trouble. He just did. And he had to save her.

He took in the sight of a male he didn't know scrambling at her leg as she desperately tried to get away, then he'd leapt over them both to jerk the male away from her. He'd tossed the man carelessly against a wall, even though his tiger wanted him to break the male's neck, because the sight of Lakshmi frantic, her back to the wall, her dark eyes wide and wild had caught Ryan's compassion and overwhelmed his tiger's fight instincts. In that moment, he needed to comfort and see to her wellbeing. The bastard who'd attacked her would wait.

Now that she was safely in Ryan's arms, though, his tiger was raging for revenge again, the emotion far more powerful than Ryan would have expected given Lakshmi was a virtual stranger and Ryan hadn't even known the male. He was appalled by the man's attack on Lakshmi, sick with the thought of what could have happened, and obviously angry. None of that surprised him. He'd been angry at the situation from the beginning. The thought of rape made him ill. Harm coming to any of the women was enough to make his blood boil. The actions of the strange male only brought home how dangerous their situation was, putting into sharp relief all the many reasons he had to get the women away from here.

But somehow his emotions seemed a lot more…violent than he could explain. Because the male had attacked *Lakshmi.*

Shaking that off, he turned his concentration to ensuring she remained calm and comforted. He could sort through the mess of his emotions later.

He'd expected to be led back to the original room

where the women had been held, but instead, his escort brought him to a new set of double doors flanked by two males he hadn't seen before this. He knew them both—Jim and Mathew—but this was the first time he'd encountered them since arriving.

"How many of you are here?" he asked his escort, hugging Lakshmi a little closer when she flinched.

"Some are still out hunting," his escort said. "Everyone will be here soon."

Ryan snarled. This was so bad on so many levels it made his head spin. He made a sharp head gesture for the guards on the double doors to open up so he could take Lakshmi inside.

Mathew opened the doors, his glance moving between Lakshmi and Ryan. "Your medical supplies were just dropped off," he said.

Ryan noticed neither Jim nor Mathew asked what had happened to Lakshmi. That lack of concern only emphasized what her attacker had claimed—the women were here for the men to do with as they saw fit. Ryan's gut tightened into a ball of disgust. The horrible truth finally sank in—he wasn't likely to get help from any of them.

He went through the door trying to keep his anger and an overwhelming sense of hopelessness at bay. He'd just have to save the women without help. He shouldn't have expected anything else.

He was inside the room and hunting for his medical kit before the room's décor hit him. When it did, he froze and stared. The door behind him closed, but he barely noticed.

There were huge swaths of bright material everywhere

—drapes covering windowless walls, pillows, silky sheets on a scattering of mattresses. Gold leafing glittered from the ceiling and off decorative pillars. The wood floor was covered with plush rugs and tassel-covered pillows. The whole thing was bright, gaudy, and reminded him of…

"A harem," Lakshmi said, her quiet voice breaking into his shocked awe.

He glanced down at her, his arms unconsciously tightening around her, as if he could protect her from the weird room. "Harem?" he asked.

"He made the room up to look like a fucking harem," she snarled. "Or like a fake Hollywood version of one, at least."

Ryan felt his mouth drop open. He snapped it shut with a groan. "Great."

He glanced around, looking for a place he could set Lakshmi down to look at her ankle, and noticed Erin, half-sitting half-lying on a mattress set on a low marble dais. The bed was covered in more colorful silk material, gauzy veils, and piled high with pillows in different shapes. The sight of Erin reminded Ryan of his original reason for coming back to the women. He carried Lakshmi to the bed and set her down gently next to Erin who'd dropped back against the pillows.

"Is she okay?" Erin asked.

"Broken ankle," he said quietly.

"It's healing," Lakshmi said, her teeth gritted. "Not too bad."

"Anything worse?" Erin whispered.

"No," Lakshmi said, reaching out to take her hand. "Could have been. He had a syringe."

Erin closed her eyes and her shoulders shook with a shudder.

As Ryan gently lifted Lakshmi's ankle and examined it, he said, "Erin, how are you? Dizziness, nausea?"

Erin remained passively on the pillows, gripping Lakshmi's hand, but her dark eyes when Ryan glanced at her were clear and alert.

"I'm fine, doctor," she said in an almost inaudible murmur. "Lakshmi was worried about you, so I'm pretending. Thought it would be a good excuse to get you back." She glanced at Lakshmi. "Seems it was a very good idea."

Lakshmi let out a sigh, then hissed when Ryan hit a sore area on the side of her foot.

"You were worried about *me*?" He glanced up at Lakshmi, his eyebrows raised.

She made a face and rolled her eyes, a surprising pink blush coloring her cheeks. "They moved us while you were gone. And you were away for a while."

He nodded and turned his attention back to her ankle, suppressing a completely inappropriate smile. "Your bones seem to be healing well," he said instead. "Doesn't look like I'll have to re-break anything."

"Thankfully," she said. "That hurt like hell. I've never broken a bone before. It's nothing like when our bones rearrange themselves during a shift, is it?"

"No, it's not," he said. "Not for our species anyway. Keep the ankle still for a minute. Let me see if I have a brace. The less movement, the better until the bones have completely knitted back together."

He glanced around and spotted his medical kit by the door. Unfortunately, he didn't have a brace that would keep her ankle immobile so he pulled out a role of bandages, draped his stethoscope around his neck, and, at the last minute, picked up his penlight. If Erin was going to all the trouble of pretending to be more ill than she was, he wanted to help her with that illusion.

He returned to the bed, studying the room and its awful décor as he went. "This place is really gaudy," he said as he wrapped Lakshmi's ankle with the bandages, pulling them tight enough to form a semi-stiff brace.

"It's disgusting," Lakshmi said, her lip curling in a snarl.

He moved from Lakshmi to Erin's side and examined her scalp, focusing on the area around her head wound. To his relief, the bump was gone. "Do they have cameras in here?" he asked.

"I've found three so far," Lakshmi said.

He checked Erin's eyes, running through the exam he'd typically do, putting on a show for the cameras but pleased to see Erin seemed mostly recovered from her injury and the drug.

"How long have they had you here?" he asked.

"Hard to tell," Lakshmi said, "but it's felt like a while. They moved us not long after you left. How long have you been gone?"

"Few hours. Maybe four." He was basing that solely on his level of hunger.

"They have trunks with clothes in them," Lakshmi said. "Disgusting stuff."

"Disgusting how?" He was almost afraid to ask.

"Harem crap. Like *I Dream of Genie* stuff. If that crazy fucker thinks I'm going to play harem girl, he's even more delusional than I thought."

Ryan pressed his lips together so he wouldn't smile. This wasn't an amusing situation, but Lakshmi sounded a lot better now, stronger and less shocky. His relief at that was a heady thing.

An instant later, though, he frowned. "They have cameras in here."

Most tigers didn't really think too much about nudity. They had to strip to shift and often did that around other tigers. They weren't known for their modesty. But something about the fact that the males here had set up cameras to spy on the women and expected them to change clothing while being monitored felt…perverse.

"There's a bathroom without cameras," Lakshmi said. "But even then, I wouldn't put on genie pants. Terrible style. Not sure why he thought those would be flattering."

This time he couldn't hold back his snort of amusement. Fashion probably wasn't topmost in Gregory's imagination when he'd had those clothes put in here, but the fact that Lakshmi sounded more offended by poor fashion choices than the spying made the queasiness in Ryan's gut ease a little. Her voice wasn't shaking anymore, and the fine tremors that had shivered over her skin while he carried her seemed to have eased. Ryan noticed his tiger had calmed as well. The driving need to kill the male who'd harmed her was not as strong, so he could concentrate on the situation at hand.

Without being too obvious about it, he glanced at the room again. "Where are the cameras?"

"Two are behind us," Lakshmi said, "at the top of the pillars, one pointed toward this bed, the other pointed toward another of the beds."

"The one facing this bed," he said, "can they see our mouths when we're like this?"

"Hard to say, but from the angle I'd say no. The third is above the door, part of the ceiling decorations. I'd guess that one can see most of the main parts of the room."

He nodded imperceptibly. "So we're going to have a hard time making plans in here."

"Do you know where we are yet?"

"No. The other female, Megan, is in the basement. I haven't even seen a window yet."

"How is she? Megan… Megan Yankova?"

"Yes. And she's not good. When I think she can control herself, I'll have her moved here. It'll be easier to escape if we don't have to go all over the complex, breaking you all out of different rooms."

"Have you noticed the smell here?" Lakshmi asked, shifting a little on the bed so she was closer to Erin.

"Lack of it?" he asked. "Yes. I think it's smaller than they want us to believe."

"Like they're walking us in circles through the same corridors?"

"Exactly. And the white noise in the halls…"

"Damned irritating," she said. "Is Megan still drugged?

Is that what you mean by her not being able to control herself?"

He winced, not really wanting to tell her this, especially after what had just happened to her. But it was important all the women knew and understood what the drug could do. Especially since Gregory wasn't the only male who could get his hands on the drug and potentially use it.

"They gave her too much," he said quietly, "and it's had a strange effect on her. Her tiger keeps trying to get out and can't."

"She can't shift?" Lakshmi's voice filled with horror.

"She makes partial shifts and then snaps back to her human form."

Lakshmi shuddered, and Erin closed her eyes tight.

"That's horrifying," Lakshmi said. "Will she be okay?"

"I hope so. If they stop drugging her. I've been pretty insistent with Gregory that he has to stop using the drug, but…"

"But he's psychotic so we can't know what he'll do, and my attacker was going to use the drug despite what you've said, which means any of them could ignore your medical orders," Lakshmi finished for him, a combination of anger and fear in her scent, trembling in her tone. "How soon can you get her here? Maybe Erin and I can help her recover."

Her compassion for another woman, after what had just happened to her, the strength it showed to push past her own trauma and want to help Megan, awed Ryan. He wouldn't have been surprised if she'd burst into tears or curled up into a ball next to Erin, or even started tearing the room apart in a rage after her attack.

Instead, she was looking for ways to help her fellow prisoner. Her resilience humbled him, and without thinking about it, he set a gentle hand on her calf, just above her injured ankle. He wasn't entirely sure what he meant to convey with the touch, and realized the instant he did it that she might be uncomfortable with his hand on her when he wasn't examining her injury. He hated that he might cause her anymore pain than she'd already experienced.

But as he lifted his hand away, she caught his fingers, wrapping them in a tight hold. He met her gaze. Her scent was overwhelmed with too many different emotions for him to parse it all out at that moment, but he was relieved that none of those emotions seemed to be anger or disgust with him. He let out a long breath and made an effort to focus on the situation again. But he didn't let go of Lakshmi's hand, and she didn't release her hold on him either.

"At the least, Megan will be more comfortable with other women," he said. His lip lifted in an unconscious snarl when he murmured, "They have her in a cage now."

Lakshmi actually growled at that, the sound of her tiger clear and very close to the surface. For reasons he couldn't explain, that sound made him happy.

"Get her here as soon as you can," she said. "We'll protect her."

"Yes," Erin said without moving her lips. "I'll pretend to be more seriously injured for a bit longer so you have to keep checking on me. Will that help things?"

"It will," he said. "But you'll need to be careful. They'll

catch on if you push the head injury excuse too long. You are feeling better, right? No more headaches, blurry vision, dizziness?"

"I'm good, doc," she said. "Except for a little nausea."

He frowned. "Not sure if that's the head wound or the drug." Glancing at Lakshmi, he asked, "Any nausea?"

"Not now. Well, not from the drug. The situation makes me sick to my stomach. What just happened makes me want to throw up. But otherwise…"

He tightened his hold on her hand. "Gregory has decided I should be fed after this examination. I'm going to use the opportunity to scout the complex more. See if I can find a window and figure out where we are. The other two prisoners should be here soon. When I can, I'll arrange to have all of you put into the same room."

He didn't want to leave, even to eat. Not after what had happened to Lakshmi. He knew he needed to confront Gregory. He should find out what, if anything, would happen to the male who'd attacked her, or if he'd continue to be a threat. And Ryan was afraid this wouldn't be the only incident—not with both women so close to estrous.

Ryan had to find a way out of the complex.

But the thought of not being here to protect Lakshmi felt like he was trying to wrench away from one of his own body parts.

A knock on the door proceeded one of the guards.

"Sorry to interrupt, doc," Mathew said.

His tone was so polite and normal Ryan blinked at him. "What is it?"

"Time to leave. Gregory's orders."

"Erin is still dizzy and Lakshmi's ankle might need more medical attention." His tone and scent were ruthlessly neutral, but his tiger was right underneath the surface, hissing and chuffing.

Mathew's gaze dropped to Ryan and Lakshmi's entwined hands. "Time to leave, doc."

Ryan bit back a snarl, squeezed Lakshmi's fingers, and released his hold. She didn't at first loosen hers, holding him in place a heartbeat longer before finally letting go.

"The women have been traumatized," Ryan said as patiently as possible, treading a careful line, but pointedly not leaving his position beside the bed. "They still need medical attention. And neither of them can afford another…incident." He let a very slight growl into his voice on the last word.

Mathew didn't show any outward reaction to the quiet threat beyond a slow blink. "Gregory has sent orders. No males are allowed inside this room except him. And you, doc. But only for necessary medical reasons." Again, Mathew's gaze dropped to Ryan's hand, even though he was no longer touching Lakshmi.

"Lakshmi was taken from the room," Ryan reminded him.

"None of them are to leave this room either," Mathew said. "Except by Gregory's orders."

"That male said he was taking me under Gregory's orders," Lakshmi said, snarling.

"Only Gregory's trusted inner circle are allowed to move the women from now on," Mathew said, showing no reaction to Lakshmi's statement.

Ryan wasn't sure any of that made him feel better. Around a female in estrous, Gregory's inner circle weren't any more trustworthy than any of the other males. As Ryan continued to hesitate, Mathew took one more step into the room.

"You need to leave now, doc. Gregory won't tolerate any further disobedience."

"Further?" Ryan asked. What the hell did that mean?

"Go ahead," Lakshmi said quietly. "It won't do any of us any good if you get on Gregory's bad side."

Ryan had a feeling he was already on Gregory's bad side simply because he kept arguing against these kidnappings. But he didn't think he should comment with Mathew watching. He looked back at Lakshmi, then Erin, then Lakshmi again.

"Your ankle?" he asked Lakshmi.

"Better. Feels mostly healed."

He stood and held a hand out to her. "See if you can put weight on it."

When Mathew growled, Ryan glared at him. "I'm not leaving a patient before I know she's stable," he said.

Lakshmi took his hand and, with his help, stood. She kept most of her balance on her uninjured foot for a moment, then settled her bandaged foot firmly onto the floor. With her face turned away from Mathew, she gave Ryan a very small smile and winked. He took that to mean her ankle felt better.

But aloud, she said, "It's still a little sore, but I'll be okay." She shifted her weight to her uninjured foot, and held his gaze a moment before settling back onto the mattress.

He knew instantly she was doing the same thing Erin was, making a show of being weaker so she'd have an element of surprise on her side if she was attacked again.

But the male who'd come after her had had the drug… Surprise wouldn't help if she couldn't move.

"They're fine, doc," Mathew said. "No one will enter or leave while they're still healing."

"And the drug? You know what it's done to Megan?"

Mathew finally showed some sign of emotion. He flinched and looked away.

Ryan pressed his point. "*No one* can be allowed to administer that drug to any of them again," Ryan said firmly.

"Take that up with Gregory. For now, our orders are no one in, no one out. Except Gregory himself, or you for medical exams."

It would have to do. Ryan could tell Mathew wasn't going to let him stay any longer, not without a fight, because these were Gregory's orders. If Ryan pushed too hard, he might be banned from the room, too, and then he'd have a lot harder time helping the women.

"Fine," he said. He faced Lakshmi and Erin again, his back to Mathew. "Rest, and send for me immediately if you need assistance. Stay off that ankle until the bones have completely healed and there's no soreness left."

Lakshmi nodded, her gaze darting from him, to Mathew, then back again. "Thank you," she murmured. "For everything."

His tiger protested leaving her so strongly, for a moment Ryan wasn't sure he'd be able to go without someone physically pulling him away. But finally he convinced the instinctive part of his nature to listen to logic. He had to leave, so Gregory would let him come back.

"Anything," he said, "you need anything, send for me."

"We will," Lakshmi said.

He left, though it was one of the hardest things he'd ever done. He waited just outside the door, his gaze on Lakshmi until the door was firmly closed and locked. Then to Mathew, he said, "No on in, no one out."

"Those are the orders."

The male who'd brought Ryan from Gregory's throne room was still waiting in the corridor and he gestured for Ryan to follow.

Ryan risked one last glance at the double doors before allowing himself to be led away, worry a living, clawing thing in his gut.

His tiger kept insisting he'd left a part of himself behind in that gaudy harem room.

L akshmi couldn't rest after Ryan left. She sat against the bed, next to Erin, and stared at the door. Waiting. On guard. Trying very hard not to think.

She wouldn't have admitted it out loud, but she had no doubt Erin could smell her fear, that residual of terror still lurking beneath the surface. But it wasn't terror of nearly being raped that kept her staring at the door, even if that had been pretty fucking horrific. No, there was a deeper fear, one that shook her to her core.

When she'd felt the needle against her cheek, she'd panicked.

The idea of being incapacitated by the drug had over-whelmed all other thought, even the fear of being raped. It had overpowered the pain in her ankle, the shock of bone breaking, the years of self-defense training that had always filled her with confidence…everything had been subsumed under one dominant, panic-filled thought. *Don't let them give you that drug!*

Hearing about Megan, how she couldn't shift, only added an additional layer to that fear.

She knew if she couldn't control this particular terror, if she couldn't think when she saw a syringe, she wouldn't survive. She wouldn't be able to fight, plan, or escape. She wouldn't be able to help Erin or Megan, or any other female brought here. She'd become the one thing she'd never considered herself, in her entire life.

Helpless.

The very idea of it was intolerable. That they wouldn't even have to drug her, just threaten to drug her, and she'd be made helpless. She couldn't allow that. She couldn't.

She let her tiger swirl closer to the surface, grabbing hold of that part of her that was all instinct and strength, reaction without forethought. Her tiger didn't want to be caged by the drug either, but her tiger's response was rage and the need to strike out at the threat. Not fear. Not panic. Not helplessness. Her tiger only knew that if she saw another syringe, she was going to tear the limb off the male holding it.

Lakshmi smiled. Now, that was a much better idea. She took that feeling and wrapped it around herself, a shield as the minutes ticked slowly by.

CHAPTER SEVEN

Ryan sat in the small, featureless room with its single steel table and chairs, scarfing down the steak and venison stew Jason had brought him. The room was white and lacked any smells beyond the food in front of him, but at least with the door closed, he couldn't detect that barely audible white noise that screwed with his hearing.

That, the mostly rare steak, and the moment of privacy —the first he'd had since being taken from his home— were the only things he could be grateful for at that moment. There was a male hovering down the hall, waiting for him to finish eating, so Ryan couldn't explore the complex yet. And they hadn't passed any windows getting here. Worse, *here* was entirely too far away from Lakshmi. Gregory's orders or not, Ryan was terrified another male would go after her.

He glanced at the steel door, letting his senses stretch out to his guard. They hadn't bothered giving him a room of his own yet. Maybe they'd let him sleep outside the women's room? If he claimed he wanted to be close, in case of an emergency…

The food calmed his restlessness somewhat, but he still felt a pull back to Lakshmi. If it weren't for his high metabolism chewing through too many calories lately, he wasn't sure he'd have managed the food, not given how tight his stomach was with worry. But fortunately, the food stayed down. He was going to need the energy.

He was down to the last few bites of his meal when he felt a new male approaching the door. Mathew?

Ryan was on his feet as the door opened. "The women?" he asked before Mathew could speak.

"Are fine. Jim is still guarding them. With Sanjay."

That was something at least. Jim intimidated the hell out of Ryan. He was one of the best fighters in the group, and his blue eyes always looked so cold and intent, it was hard to face him. But he was extremely loyal to Gregory, which meant he'd never go against Gregory's order to stay out of the harem room. Sanjay was another member of Gregory's inner circle and would follow orders, too.

"If the women don't need me, why are you here?" he asked Mathew. "Is it Megan?"

"You have two new patients," Mathew said. "They just arrived."

Ryan put his hands on his hips and closed his eyes. He knew this was coming. Expecting it didn't make it any easier to bare. Two more women in this madhouse. Two more vulnerable and valuable females caught up in Gregory's sick games.

He shook off his anger and waved at Mathew. "Take me to them. My medical supplies?"

"Still in Erin and Lakshmi's room. I'll have the kit brought up if you need it."

He followed Mathew through the featureless corridors, trying unsuccessfully to get oriented. The place was maddening. He had no idea where he was at this stage, and it made him more than a little irritable that he couldn't find his way around on his own.

He was taken into the same holding room where Lakshmi and Erin had been before they were moved. For several long moments he stared at the two new captives without being able to process what he was seeing. When the reality finally sank in, his mouth dropped open in shock.

"You didn't," he breathed. "This can't be happening. Gregory can't be this suicidal." Spinning on the guard at his back, he growled, his tiger so angry Ryan could barely see around it.

"You idiots," he said through clenched teeth, his voice rising with each word, "kidnapped Isabella Tarasova-Romanov? Alexis Tarasova's daughter?" He roared the last word.

Alexis was a former Tracker and the only female Tracker in hundreds of years because most females hadn't been allowed to pursue the dangerous occupation since their numbers had dwindled so drastically. They were considered too valuable to risk on the job. Alexis hadn't let that stop her, and she'd been one of the most dangerous and deadly Trackers ever. She'd retired when she'd married, but now she trained Trackers—and those she trained were the best.

That by itself should have made Gregory stay as far away from her daughter as possible. But on top of Alexis' deadly skills, she just happened to be the adopted daughter of Elizaveta Chernikova.

"You kidnapped the granddaughter of an elder," Ryan said slowly and deliberately to Mathew. "You've ensured the others won't just attack this place and recover the females. You've guaranteed your death sentences."

Mathew didn't show any outward reaction to the news, but his scent filled with the acrid musky stench of his fear. The fact that he was finally reacting to any of this was a small comfort to Ryan, but it didn't help the situation.

"Gregory knows what he's doing," the young man said after a pause, ever loyal to his leader.

But Ryan heard the tremor in his voice.

"You better hope she hasn't been injured," Ryan said. "Your only hope of survival now is if she comes away from this unharmed. Christ, man, she's only seventeen years old! She's not even close to her first estrous yet."

"They're coming in early."

"What?"

"The younger females," Mathew said, finally meeting Ryan's gaze. "Gregory found out some of them are starting estrous early. Elizaveta has been trying to keep that knowledge from the community. Hiding females from us. Gregory says it's nature's way of helping the species, ensuring the females can breed earlier and longer. He says

Elizaveta is hiding the change to prevent more of us from having mates."

"Why the hell would she do that?"

"The elders only want their preferred males to get mates."

Ryan blinked. This was a new twist on the story Gregory had been feeding the young males. Gregory had poisoned them against the elders for months now with variations on the theme that the elders didn't want any of them to get mates. But this idea that the elders selected their favorite males as mates for the limited females was a new one.

"Don't be an idiot," Ryan said. "The females choose. They always have. If the elders actually had their preference, none of the females would marry or mate permanently."

He wasn't sure if that applied to all the elders—he was pretty sure Elizaveta encouraged permanent matings—but because of the low number of females, several of the other elders encouraged females to take many mates for "genetic diversification."

Ryan had always found that attitude distasteful. His opinion was actually counter to what Gregory preached, but it was still anti-elder, so Gregory didn't try to change Ryan's mind. Too often.

Ryan hung his head for a moment, as the full weight of the disaster swamped him. Alexis' daughter… Alexis was going to tear Gregory to pieces.

"They're probably on their way here now," Ryan muttered. "Okay, get out of here while I make sure the two women survive. Once I'm sure they're stable, we're moving them to the other room where Lakshmi and Erin are."

"Gregory might not want that yet."

"You know what? I don't give a fuck. We're moving them so all of the women are in the same place—a place where you bastards aren't allowed now, thanks to what happened to Lakshmi." He swallowed hard to choke down his rage. "If they're together, I can better ensure their health and survival. The only chance now…the *only* chance any of us have of coming out of this alive is if all five of these women survive. Unharmed."

Mathew's eye twitched, a tic Ryan couldn't quite interpret, then he stepped out of the room, giving Ryan space to examine his new patients.

As he had with Lakshmi and Erin, Ryan explained his every action to the drugged women. They were both conscious, he could see it in their eyes, and from their scents they were equal parts terrified and angry.

When he got to Isabella, it was all he could do to keep his overwhelming anger out of his scent. Tiger shifters aged differently than humans, and the females didn't become reproductively fertile until around twenty-five years old. At seventeen, Isabella wasn't just young, she was essentially still a child. The fact that Gregory had taken her with an eye toward mating was so beyond disgusting to Ryan he could hardly contemplate it.

Even if what Mathew said was true and the females were coming into estrous earlier than normal, it didn't justify…this.

He examined Isabella and ensured she was unharmed beyond being drugged. When he was confident they were both healthy, he banged on the door. Mathew entered immediately.

"You're going to carry one of them—very respectfully—back to the room where Lakshmi and Erin are," Ryan told him without preamble. "I'll carry Isabella. You will, at all times, be gentle. Do you understand me?"

"Gregory…"

"Enough with Gregory. Gregory has signed your death warrant with this. Mine, too. And since, thanks to that attack on Lakshmi, I can't have her brought here to help, you will do what I say. But I swear, if I even get a hint of something indecent in your scent, I will kick your ever-loving ass."

"You? You never fight."

He leaned in close, putting his face in the taller but younger man's face. "Doesn't mean I can't." He let every ounce of his anger and disgust into his scent, along with the seriousness of his threat.

Mathew blinked and took a step back, a telling gesture—and from his frown, he hadn't intended to reveal his unease. Ryan didn't care as long as he did what he was told.

"Doc, you're asking for trouble, you know?"

"Not your business."

The guard hesitated a moment longer, then gave Ryan a curt nod.

So the man wasn't entirely stupid.

He motioned Mathew to the side of the female he didn't know. She was tall, with spiky black hair and sharp blue eyes, dressed casually in jeans and a t-shirt. Her hand twitched when Mathew got closer and her eyes widened. Ryan knew letting the young male carry her was upsetting and he didn't want to, but there was nothing for it. He couldn't safely carry both women while they were still mostly immobile. And he couldn't send for Lakshmi to help. Not that he'd trust any of these assholes to bring Lakshmi here now. But having another woman to help would have been preferable to Mathew.

Ryan loomed over Mathew as he bent to lift the woman, ensuring the younger man acted respectfully and gently. Then he turned to pick up Isabella. She was wearing running shorts and a loose t-shirt. Like Lakshmi and Erin, neither woman had shoes on. He wasn't entirely sure why Gregory would have had their shoes removed. Tigers had tough soles that enabled them to run over forest floors even in bare feet. Depriving them of their shoes wouldn't prevent escape.

When Isabella's arm twitched, he let out a relieved breath. With luck, neither would suffer any side-effects.

Alexis…hell, Elizaveta was going to go ballistic when she found out about her granddaughter.

And he was going to have a lot of questions to answer —not the least of which was why he hadn't alerted them to the location as soon as he was here. Not that he'd had the time or opportunity. But given Isabella's presence, he wasn't sure Elizaveta would accept that answer.

Well, it was her damned fault he was here. And lucky for her, too, since he, at least, would try to protect all of the women.

He let Mathew take the lead back to the harem room because he still couldn't find the damned place on his own. But Ryan kept close enough to the other male to ensure he couldn't do or say anything lecherous or upsetting to the woman he carried.

As they stalked through the irritatingly similar corridors, Ryan found his thoughts turning to Lakshmi, wondering what she'd think if she ever learned the truth about why he was with the young males. Would she view him differently? Would she be glad to find out he wasn't *really* one of Gregory's tigers, or would she be pissed he'd lied to her about his reasons for being with the group?

He shouldn't care. When all this was over, she'd return to her life in California, to the Mate Run and her future mate or mates. He'd go back to Boston and continue his work. They wouldn't likely even see each other again. Her opinion of him shouldn't make any difference to his life.

He wasn't sure how to feel about the fact that it did.

But she wouldn't ever know the truth, so it didn't really matter. Beyond the elders, no one was supposed to ever know the truth. Even Ryan's own family, whom he was very close with, didn't know what he was doing. For his own protection, the elders said.

Protection. He almost snorted. If an army descended on this place while these women were here, none of the males would be given mercy. That included him.

Unless Elizaveta herself showed up to vouch for him.

He hadn't been lying to Mathew when he said Gregory had signed his death warrant, too. Everyone but the elders would consider him as guilty as the other young males, and given that Isabella had been taken, no one was likely to survive the impending attack.

Ryan's only hope was to get the women out of here before the elders' army found their location. He might even be able to avert the wholesale slaughter of the young males if he could reach help before the Trackers got here.

Maybe.

Isabella groaned quietly.

"Try to stay calm as you come out of the drug," Ryan murmured. "We're taking you to a more comfortable location with other females. You're not safe yet. But I'll do what I can to help."

When they reached the big double doors to the harem room, the two guards—Jim and Sanjay—frowned. Sanjay noticed the woman in Ryan's arms and his eyes widened briefly before he covered the reaction. But his scent gave away his surprise. Jim showed no reaction to Isabella, but he scowled at Ryan.

"They aren't supposed to be here yet," the large man said.

"Open the door, Jim. Or I will kick it open."

Jim's eyes narrowed, but Sanjay stepped into the tension. "Are they recovering?"

"They'll do that a lot better with Lakshmi and Erin. Open the door. Now."

Sanjay glanced at Jim, who was still glaring, but opened the door and stepped aside.

Lakshmi was already standing halfway between the bed and the door, semi-crouched in a fighting stance. Erin was on her feet too, a few feet behind and to the left of Lakshmi, closer to the bed, but still ready for danger.

Ryan waited just inside the doorway until Lakshmi recognized him. When she did, her stance relaxed and her expression softened. Until she noticed the girl in his arms.

Her eyes were huge when she met his gaze.

"I know," he said, with feeling. He nodded to Mathew who was standing just behind him. "Can you please take her. Mathew isn't coming inside."

Lakshmi, eyes still wide, hurried to take the other woman from Mathew. Ryan remained where he was, watching the exchange, ensuring Mathew remained careful. Ryan noticed Lakshmi went out of her way not to touch him as she gently cradled the other woman into her arms. Without another glance at the males outside the door, Lakshmi carried her charge to the bed she and Erin had been using.

"Close the door behind me," Ryan ordered. "They need some privacy to recover without side-effects." Sort of a lie, but he didn't care.

"You staying inside, doc," Jim said, threat and accusation in his tone.

"Until I'm sure they're out from under the drug. Yes. Since that's the reason you bastards brought me into all this. You want to argue the point, Jim, we'll discuss it when I'm done seeing to my patients."

He couldn't quite believe he was basically challenging Jim. Jim was one scary bastard. But Isabella's kidnapping was the very last straw for him—when he'd thought he had no straws left after Lakshmi's attack. In his current mood, Ryan had no doubt he'd be able to tear Jim apart.

He wasn't sure if Jim realized this, but Sanjay seemed to. He nudged Jim out of the way and closed the doors gently. The lock clicked into place.

Ryan carried Isabella to the bed, placing her down next to the other woman. Then he went to his medical kit, still just inside the door, and got the things he needed for a more thorough exam.

By the time he got back to the bed, Isabella was struggling to sit up. The other woman's arms and legs were moving sporadically, but she seemed to be regaining control a little slower than the girl.

He knelt beside her first. To Lakshmi, he asked, "Do you know her name?"

"Dr. Yin, meet Violet Kim. Violet this is Dr. Ryan Yin. Sarah Chu's brother."

He smiled a little at the formal introduction and dipped his head to Violet in greeting. Her head jerked in a kind of return acknowledgement.

The moment he heard the name, he knew who she was. As was typical among tiger shifters, her strong features and dark hair held a strong resemblance to her mother, but her blue eyes had come from her father, a man Ryan had actually met before at the elders' compound. Violet's territory was down south, near New Orleans, another woman he was unlikely to ever have known in person before this.

His smile dropped. This was a really shitty way to meet tigresses from other parts of the country.

· · ·

Lakshmi arranged the sheer drapings hanging from a canopy above the mattress as Ryan examined Violet, so that the bed was somewhat blocked from the various cameras. She'd uncovered another one while she waited on Ryan to return, and the idea of Gregory watching them, especially now with Isabella here, gave her the creeps.

Isabella managed to prop herself up against the pillows that made a sort of headboard on the bed. Her blue eyes were wide and a little wild as she looked around the gaudy room.

Lakshmi's heart broke. Isabella was just a girl. Not even close to her first estrous yet. She should have been safe from Gregory's sickness. Lakshmi squeezed her shoulder, trying to give what comfort and reassurance she could.

"Where are we? What's happened? What's going on?" Isabella's questions came out in a breathy rush, her voice hoarse from disuse.

"We aren't sure where we are." Lakshmi settled on the edge of the bed. She glanced at Ryan, before continuing. "You've heard of the problems with the young tigers…Gregory?"

Isabella nodded, then her already wide eyes widened more. "He's done this? How? Why?"

Lakshmi winced. "The why is…a little too disgusting to say aloud."

"Oh god," the girl breathed.

"It's okay." Lakshmi rushed to calm her. "They aren't allowed in this room, so you're safe in here." *For the moment, and only because one attacked me already.* But

Lakshmi wasn't about to say that out loud. Isabella looked so terrified, Lakshmi ached for her.

"That drug… I couldn't move, but I could feel everything." Isabella shuddered.

"I know. Dr. Yin is making sure they don't give us any more."

Lakshmi looked to him for confirmation and he nodded. She was still terrified of the drug, but she forced those thoughts away. Isabella needed Lakshmi to be confident, not afraid.

"We just have to stay alive until the others find us," Lakshmi said. "And they will. Your parents are going to tear the world apart to reach you."

Isabella smiled a little at that. Then she frowned. "If they find us."

"They will." Lakshmi put as much assurance in her scent as her words, feeling everything she wanted to convey. She needed to believe they'd be found soon or she'd go insane.

Ryan finished examining Violet, then gently went to Isabella. "May I check your heartbeat and blood pressure?"

She narrowed her eyes but nodded. As he had with all of them, he talked Isabella through the exam, keeping his voice soft, his touch clinical and gentle and his scent full of comfort.

Lakshmi watched him, only a little surprised she was finding it so hard to remain suspicious of him. She couldn't allow herself to trust him. She couldn't trust any male right now. But Ryan was…different in ways she didn't even fully understand herself. And her tiger kept leaning toward him, reassured by his presence.

That should probably bother her a lot more.

When he finished Isabella's examination, he stood back from the bed, wrapping his stethoscope into a compact circle. "I have to talk to Gregory," Ryan said. "I'll be back as soon as possible."

A moment of panic gripped Lakshmi, and she ruthlessly pushed it down. She was growing entirely too reliant on Ryan's presence to make her feel safe.

"Are you sure you should leave before Violet recovers?" she asked.

Violet was moving more, on the verge of having full control of her body. They didn't need Ryan to stay. In fact, Isabella and Violet might be more comfortable with him gone. But Lakshmi couldn't seem to resist asking.

He looked down at Violet as she rolled onto her side without help. A very faint smile lifted his lips before his serious expression returned.

"She's almost there," he said. "I'll be back to check on all of you as soon as I can. But Gregory and I need to have a few more words."

Lakshmi's stomach danced at the edge of menace and threat in his voice. His dark eyes were narrowed and his jaw set. He looked a lot more dangerous in that moment than he ever had before. To this point, he'd come across as comforting, safe.

He didn't look safe now.

And she liked the look on him. A lot. Which would

probably be embarrassing if she didn't have so many other things to worry about.

He met her gaze, catching her staring, but he didn't show any outward reaction. She still couldn't read his scent reliably—which was beyond irritating because in that moment she couldn't read his expression either.

He held her stare for a beat, maybe two before saying, "Stay safe. All of you."

She forced a smile. "We will. I'll look after everyone."

He returned her smile, quick and adorable, before becoming serious again. "Don't do anything to get hurt, if you can at all help it."

She nodded, not sure what else to say. She didn't like that she was relying on his help. But she was. And somehow, her instincts insisted that was okay.

Her tiger liked him. A little too much. But her tiger had always been a good judge of character. She'd stay cautious, but she was seriously leaning toward wanting to trust Ryan.

It wasn't lost on her that he'd become Ryan to her instead of Dr. Yin.

He hesitated a few moments longer, holding her gaze. Then he swept an assessing look over the other three women, nodded as if assured of their health, and left the room. She watched him go, not looking away from the door until the lock turned.

CHAPTER EIGHT

W hen Ryan was gone, Isabella said, "I like his sister a lot. What's he doing here? He doesn't seem like the type to fall in with Gregory's young males."

"I don't know," Lakshmi said, facing the girl and putting an arm around her shoulders in a small hug. "Do you know Dr. Yin?"

"Not really. Just what his sister says about him, and Sarah's husband Daniel seems to trust him. It's just weird."

"Have you noticed his scent?" Erin asked.

"You mean the way you can't read it well?" Isabella said. "I noticed while he was carrying me here."

"He seems to be able to change it, depending on who he's talking to," Lakshmi said.

"That shouldn't be possible, should it?" This from Violet, who was finally pushing herself up into a sitting position.

"Are you okay?" Lakshmi asked her, moving to help her lean against a huge pile of pillows.

"I'd be better if I hadn't been kidnapped," she said, snarling at the orange and purple silk cover on the bed.

That statement was answered by similar growls of agreement from the other women. Lakshmi could smell their worry, that they were all scared, but like her, they were controlling it with their anger. And an angry tigress was a thing to be feared.

Gregory was more than a crazy idiot. He was suicidal.

She faced Isabella again. Her presence only confirmed that assessment.

"Where were you when you were taken?" Lakshmi asked the girl. "Will your parents know already?"

Isabella frowned, her face scrunching up as she thought. "It's pretty blurry. I mean, I remember everything. Too much actually." She shivered and Violet patted her knee. "I was at my grandmother's house—my father's mother. Dad is still in an uproar over that breach in security a couple of months ago, when they brought the hybrid child to the elders' compound?"

Lakshmi nodded. She'd heard all about it, the details spreading through the tiger community like wildfire. An elder had died during that mess, which left the elders' council at an awkwardly even number of eight. Isabella's father, Victor Romanov, was the head of security systems for the US compound. Lakshmi wasn't at all surprised to hear he was still on the warpath to uncover the cause of the security breaches.

"So my younger brother and I have been visiting our

grandmother for the last few weeks. Mostly to stay out of the way and keep from being put to work."

She smiled and the expression made her look so young Lakshmi's heart squeezed tight.

"Was anyone around when you were drugged?" Lakshmi asked.

"No. They caught me on a run, in human form, in my grandmother's neighborhood."

"I was on my way home from running some errands before driving to my territory for a little break," Violet said.

"I'd just finished a yoga class at the studio in my neighborhood," Erin said. "They got me close to a van by using Lakshmi's presence in the back."

Lakshmi growled at that. "Bastards."

"I don't remember much about the attack," Erin said, her hand going to her head, where the bump had been.

"You fought like a champion," Lakshmi told her. "They hit you very hard before using the drug."

Erin's eyes narrowed as a distant look moved through her expression. While all of them had been well trained in self-defense, Erin was particularly skilled. Under different circumstances, had she merely been human or if female tigers weren't so rare, Lakshmi was sure Erin would have gone into some sort of military or police career.

For the first time, Lakshmi realized how difficult this must be for Erin in particular. Lakshmi was used to taking care of herself, too. Used to being strong and able to handle herself. She found her current vulnerability overwhelming. But Erin was a warrior, her confidence and skills going far beyond simple self-defense, and being this vulnerable must be intolerable for her.

"I was taken after a visit with my parents," Lakshmi said, "when I was on my way home. My next Mate Run is in a few days..." She frowned. "They caught us all during our normal routines. Everyday activities. Not during a Run."

"Too many other males around for that," Erin said.

"And Gregory hasn't run in a year," Isabella said. "According to my mother."

"I'm not sure any of the young males aligning with Gregory have run in a while," Violet said. "They aren't banned, right?"

"Not that I've heard," Lakshmi said. She thought about what her attacker had said, about being part of one of her earlier Runs... She met Erin's gaze, then chose her words carefully because she didn't want to scare Isabella more than she already was. "There was a male earlier... I didn't remember him but he claimed to have been part of one of my Runs, my first. I can't say if he's been part of them since."

She hadn't paid nearly enough attention to the looming threat of the young males. They all seemed to collect at the opposite end of the country, their little rebellion nothing to do with her or the males that were allowed to participate in her Runs. She'd been wrong about that, not even realizing males from her own Run had joined Gregory.

She couldn't recall which of her males had left the Run. There were usually about twenty involved. She'd sampled a few of them, but so far, she'd always been glad when her estrous ended without her being pregnant. She had had a lot of fun with a couple of them, for the three days they got to have almost non-stop sex. But she hadn't formed any kind of attachment to any of them. And the ones she hadn't allowed to catch her… Well, she hadn't noticed if they kept running or not. She only paid attention to the small handful she liked enough to let them catch her.

Not paying attention to what was happening with the males had been a mistake. Her own confidence in her power as a female tiger without any kind of caution seemed like a mistake now, too. One that had nearly gotten her raped, and left her in this terrible position.

She cursed silently and pushed down the sneaking edge of guilt. This wasn't her fault and she wouldn't blame herself. Any more than she would think to blame a seventeen-year-old girl for getting taken. In fact, if Isabella even thought to blame herself for this mess, Lakshmi would set her straight immediately. She couldn't do to herself what she would refuse to allow another woman to do.

No, the blame was firmly at Gregory and the other males' feet. And they were going to pay.

She glanced up at the four cameras she'd located. Without moving her mouth, and in that just barely audible tone, she said, "The room is monitored but we need to make a plan. There's another female—Megan Yankova. She's in bad shape, according to Dr. Yin. He said he would try to make sure she was brought here too, so we could all be together. Once she's here, we have to get out."

"Rescue?" Isabella asked quietly.

"We can't count on help finding us before someone

here gets…hurt." She swallowed hard, forcing down memories of her attack. "We have to take care of ourselves. We're outnumbered, but we have an ally in Dr. Yin. And we have our cunning and anger."

"What if they drug us again?" Violet asked.

It took a great deal of willpower not to shiver at the thought. Her deepest terror still lurked under her tiger's anger. She didn't want either Isabella or Violet to see that, though, so she wrapped herself up in her tiger's instincts and said, "Dr. Yin is trying to prevent that. We'll have to do what we can to prevent it, too. We may have to pretend at a docility we don't feel. Can you all do that?"

Erin narrowed her eyes, her snarl almost imperceptible. Lakshmi understood the reaction, but they needed the element of surprise that would come from pretending to be weaker than they were. Of all of them, Erin should see the advantage in that.

"Can you try?" Lakshmi asked her.

"Can you?" Erin returned.

Lakshmi rolled her eyes. "Fine. I'm not typically the docile type. But I'll make the effort if you will."

"Do they know about the self-defense training?" Violet asked.

"Word about that is finally starting to spread to the community," Isabella said.

The self-defense classes, mainly led by Alexis, had been going on for ten years now. But the females had decided the males didn't really need to know about it— again creating an element of surprise—and so the classes had remained mostly secret for all that time.

So much had happened in the community this year, though, Lakshmi wasn't surprised this particular secret had finally gotten out.

"If they hadn't known before, they would have figured it out when Erin attacked the males trying to take her," Lakshmi said. "She nearly killed them."

Erin's smile at that was feral and vicious.

"Mom says it's good if they know," Isabella said with a little smirk, "'cause the males will realize we can kick their asses now."

So long as they could move. Another flash of her attack, of the needle pressing against her skin, the heat of her attacker's breath on her face. She blinked hard against the memory but must have given something away because Erin reached out and grabbed her hand, squeezing tight. Lakshmi returned the pressure, acknowledging the comfort.

"Did any of you feel the males approaching?" Erin asked.

The slight change in subject gave Lakshmi a moment to recover from her lapse.

"I knew who kidnapped me because of the way they got me to the van to check on Lakshmi," Erin said. "But they didn't do that with the rest of you." She looked at Lakshmi. "You said the kidnapping part is blurry."

"I knew there were two males approaching me," Lakshmi said. "I thought it was weird, but figured they were just breaking the law about staying away from us in between Mate Runs. I could tell they were young. I assumed they were going to be joining my Run for the first time and were…trying to get in good with me ahead of time. Or something."

She frowned when she remembered the one female that hadn't been brought to this room yet. "There were three other missing females before I was caught, but I thought… with the attention…"

The other women nodded in understanding.

"That's what I thought, too," Violet said. "Despite the warnings coming from the powers that be to be careful, I thought a few females just got more clever about getting some privacy."

Erin said, "When the males approached me, claiming they'd found an unconscious female on the roadside and needed my help, it never crossed my mind it was a kidnapping attempt. Even knowing there were missing women. They were tiger males, our own kind… But it's been…four, five days since I was taken." She looked to Lakshmi with a frown.

Lakshmi shrugged. "That sounds about right, but honestly, my sense of time is really off. I think I was taken about three days before they went after you, but I'm not sure."

"How about the rest of you?" Erin asked. "Did you have any idea tiger males were responsible for the missing females?" She looked at Isabella. "Surely your parents are aware and warned you?"

"Actually, they did warn me to avoid all males except my brothers just the day before I was taken. My oldest brother was due to arrive within hours of my kidnapping, as added protection."

"If your parents knew the young males were a threat, why not bring you back to the elders' compound?" Lakshmi asked.

Isabella hesitated a moment, then said, "Because of the security slips that my dad is so mad about. When they heard about the kidnappings, they were afraid even the elders' compound wouldn't be safe."

"They were worried someone would help the young males there?" Lakshmi asked. "At the very heart of the elders' power in this country?" She could hardly believe that. "The young males are against the elders. There's talk that they want to overthrow the elders. I mean, this move to kidnap us is essentially a declaration of war on the elders and their power, isn't it?"

Erin frowned and looked around. "Gregory is crazy. We can't assume anything he does is consistent or makes sense."

"But we're not talking about Gregory here," Lakshmi said. "If Alexis and Victor didn't trust their daughter to the safety of the elders' compound, it means they're worried about traitors inside the compound. Traitors working against the elders."

"Or one of the elders is a traitor," Erin said.

They all fell silent at that, the air around them permeated with their worry, a miasma of musk and a scent like burnt citrus. Lakshmi and Erin exchanged a look. The elders were always in the middle of power plays and complex machinations too layered to dissect. But in the end, they always placed the good of the community above their own interests—even if they didn't agree with each other.

That was why there were generally nine elders, so a majority vote on issues was always possible. An elder working with the young males, maybe working to completely topple the entire tiger shifter governmental structure, would be bad news for everyone.

And it might mean help wasn't actually on the way. An elder could confuse any rescue operation, ensuring whatever force had been put together to recover them never found this complex. If an elder was actively helping Gregory…

They were in a lot more trouble than they thought.

Lakshmi shook off the fear clinging to her at the idea of an elder working against them. They had no actual information to confirm that, and they couldn't afford to lose hope over unfounded theories.

"We already knew we couldn't wait on help," she said. "It's coming. I'm sure it is." She gave Isabella a pointed look. "Even without the elders as a group, your family will be hunting for the people who took you with their own army of very angry tigers."

Isabella nodded. "No one could stop my parents from finding me. Not even the elders."

"Exactly. Our job now is to survive, stay safe, and try to escape at the earliest possible moment. With luck, we'll have the backup of an approaching army when we do get out of here. But no matter what, we're getting out of here. Soon."

"Better be soon," Violet said quietly. "You and Erin are

really close to estrous. Even the males who aren't as comfortable with this kidnapping thing will have trouble staying…civil soon."

Lakshmi swallowed hard. One had already disposed of civility with her. That was only going to get worse, despite Gregory's orders. Once her estrous came on fully, her own scent would work against her. Unconsciously, she reached down to rub her ankle. It was fully healed, no real soreness left, but a ghost of the pain lingered, a reminder of their precarious situation.

She was about to ask for escape plan ideas when a knock on the door had them all sitting up straighter, preparing for a fight.

The door didn't open, but the male beyond it knocked again. Lakshmi glanced at the other women, then went to the door, staying on her toes in case she had to move fast or fight. It wasn't Ryan outside, she could sense that much.

She hesitated near the door, standing to one side so it wouldn't hit her if it suddenly opened, trying to decide if she should answer the knock. The last time an unexpected male had come here… She forced down the jump of fear so she could think. Then a smell reached her through the thick wood and the pervasive background scent of frankincense and sandalwood—steak.

Her stomach growled loudly.

Hunger overrode her hesitance. She turned the door-knob, only a little surprised when it opened. The male who'd brought her food while she was recovering from the drug stood holding a large tray piled high with grilled steaks and potatoes. She frowned at him.

"Food," he said brightly.

She raised her brows at the obviousness of his statement.

He winced. "I mean, the doc said you needed to eat."

"Is it safe?"

"Of course. We don't want to hurt you."

She gave him a deadpan look. There was no way he hadn't heard what had happened to her already.

He shuffled his feet and dropped his gaze, holding the tray out to her.

She snatched it from his hands, careful not to touch him. "When will the other prisoner be brought here?"

He looked up but didn't quite meet her gaze. "I haven't been told yet. I understand the doc is discussing that with Gregory now."

She nodded, then stepped back a little and kicked the door closed with her foot.

She carried the heavy tray back to the bed and set it in the middle of the mattress. The smells were heavenly after so long without regular food. She'd been allowed to come out of the drug's effects just enough to suck down the protein drinks they fed her through a straw before her kidnappers had shot her with another dose of the awful drug. And the food Ryan had arranged for her earlier—how long ago now?—had already been churned up by her fast metabolism. Her attack and the fight had taken even more energy. Erin hadn't eaten anything yet, and Lakshmi had no idea when Isabella and Violet last ate.

By the way everyone fell on the food, she assumed they were all starved.

Silence descended as they devoured the steaks and piles of buttery potatoes, none of them bothering with the silverware provided. When her stomach finally felt full enough to slow down, she settled back on the mattress and looked at the others.

"So," she said in a quiet murmur, "anyone have ideas for our escape?"

CHAPTER NINE

Hours later, when the lights in the room had been dimmed from some outside source, giving the illusion that it was night, Lakshmi sat against a wall on a pile of pillows, listening to the other women's steady breathing as they slept.

She'd dozed a bit but had woken with a start for reasons she couldn't pinpoint and hadn't been able to fall back to sleep after. She'd kept searching the dark room, hunting in the shadows for danger. She was exhausted, so strung out she could barely think, but the adrenaline and terror of her situation made resting impossible.

So as not to disturb the others, she'd left the single bed they'd all remained congregated on and settled in a nook to the left of the door were the various cameras weren't directly pointed at her. She had no doubt their captors could still see her, but it gave her the illusion of privacy.

She stared at the room, the piles of silk pillows and gold

flecked pillars, the gauzy material draping walls and bed canopies. The sounds of water moving gently in the pool-fountain and the scent of frankincense and sandalwood might have been pleasant under different circumstances. Instead, it felt sinister and threatening.

But at least there was color and scent here. In the corridors the lack of sensory input, even smell, was so disorienting it left her feeling…blind.

Which she suspected was Gregory's aim.

She wanted to snarl at the thought of the tiger responsible for all this, but she was too tired.

They'd spent the hours before the lights had dimmed plotting potential escape plans. Most of those plans suffered from the fact that they had so little information about their situation.

They didn't know how big the building was. They had no idea where they were in the world, except that they were able to drive here because outside of Ryan, they'd all come to the complex in the back of vans. And with their sense of hearing and smell being disrupted outside this room, they hadn't been able to pick up any details that might help.

None of them had even been able to sense the number of tigers in the building—which they should have been able to do. She had a feeling the numbers kept changing, with males coming and going, and that was complicating things.

The best plan they'd managed—watch for an opportunity, then kill any male that got in their way as they made a break for it.

But a break to where? How? None of them even knew where a door to the outside was. Or what they'd encounter when they reached "outside." Or how far they'd have to run before they found help. Or even how many males would be in pursuit if they did manage to escape.

And Gregory still had the drug.

She bounced her head off the wall behind her, gently so as not to make any noise that might disturb the others. She felt so helpless. And she hated it to the depths of her soul.

Though she didn't want to admit it to herself, she'd spent the last few hours waiting for Ryan to return, too, and when he hadn't, she'd been a little too disappointed. She really had to stop waiting for him to show up, waiting for his help…watching for his return because he made her feel better. She tried to focus on the fact that she couldn't trust him, but even that wasn't enough to keep her from glancing at the door regularly, hoping to sense his approach.

Maybe it was because she was thinking about him, or maybe it was just coincidence, but she turned her senses to the door, searching out the guards that had been there, and realized someone new had arrived. She smiled, despite herself, and scooted over to the door.

She tried the knob but the door was locked, so she leaned against it, still sitting, and murmured, "Is that you, Dr. Yin?"

She knew it was. This close, she could smell him—his scent signature with its odd mix of earthiness and blood, though his emotions were still hard to pinpoint. She heard a slight bump, as if he'd leaned up against the door, too.

"You can call me Ryan, Lakshmi," he said.

His voice was quiet but loud enough for her to hear through the thick wood. She smiled, since she'd started thinking of him as Ryan already, and half closed her eyes so she could focus on his voice, and the scent and the feel of him.

"How did your meeting with Gregory go?" she asked.

"Bad. How are you? Your ankle?"

"It's all healed now."

"That's a relief. Full mobility?"

She huffed out a quiet half-laugh. Always the doctor. "Yes," she said. "Perfect working order."

"How are the others?"

"They fed us. A lot of steak. That helped."

"Good."

"Want to talk about the bad meeting?" She knew there were still two other guards in that corridor with him, a few yards away but near enough to hear everything he said, so she wasn't sure he could discuss much. She felt the need to ask anyway.

"He's changed his rhetoric. I'm not sure he even has a plan."

"What do you mean?"

He was silent a moment before answering. "Gregory has…accumulated the support of so many males by telling them he wants to ensure they all have mates who can give them children. He's blamed the Mate Run and the elders for the fact that they're without mates—"

"Conveniently leaving out the sheer lack of numbers of females," she put in with no little annoyance.

Ryan snorted. "That didn't really help his argument so he ignored it. Anyway, with the introduction of hybrids to the community, he's been telling us all that mates are readily available now. He claims there are hybrids all over the place and the elders are hiding them from us."

"How does he know that?"

"He doesn't. No one knows how many hybrids there are, or whether they're rare or common. My sister works on this issue. If anyone knows, Sarah would. And she doesn't. Not yet anyway. We do know the hybrids are likely capable of having children with shifters. Gregory has been using that fact, too."

"So why kidnap us? Why not go hunting up all these supposed hybrids?"

"It's just starting to get out now, but it turns out we can't sense hybrids, even the ones who can shift."

"Like the little girl brought to the elders a few months back?"

"Sarah told me the hybrids can sense us, but we can't sense them."

"Great advantage for the hybrids," Lakshmi commented.

"Definitely. It also means, we can't just go out and find them easily."

"The hybrids come from humans who can breed with tigers. Why not just fuck a lot of human women until they find one that can make a hybrid with them?"

"Since in all the years Elizaveta has been looking for humans who can mate with tigers, we've confirmed…what, one human male and one human female who can, the likelihood of randomly coming across one who can reproduce with a tiger is even worse that the likelihood of getting a tiger mate during a Mate Run."

She sighed. "So Gregory has turned his attention back to full tigers, then."

"Kind of. You're not here just to be mates."

He growled the word, a sentiment she echoed with her own sneer.

"You've been kidnapped," he said, "to…force the elders to negotiate."

"What?"

"He wants the elders to turn over the location of the hybrids."

"The elders don't know the location of any hybrids beyond…the adult female who can't shift and the little girl, right?"

"Right. But he's convinced that's a lie."

"Really convinced or just using it as an excuse?"

"With Gregory, it can be hard to tell. From his scent, he honestly believes the elders are hiding potential mates from us."

"His scent is full of crazy. How can you tell anything from it?"

He coughed, and Lakshmi thought he might be trying to suppress a laugh.

"Anyway," he said, "you're all here as hostages to be ransomed as much as captives to be…"

Though he trailed off, she knew what he had been about to say. "Breeders," she snarled. "We are more than just fucking uteruses."

"Unfortunately, our entire society has been so focused on survival, too many tigers view females as little more than breeders at this stage."

"Do you?"

"I have a sister."

"That doesn't answer my question."

Silence. Then, "No. I've never seen female tigers as simply breeders."

"You've taken part in Mate Runs?"

"No."

That surprised her, enough that she turned to frown at the door as if she could see him through it. "Why not?"

"My sister found a good mate, a good husband. They have children, and I get to be an uncle."

"You don't want children of your own?" For some reason, the fact that he didn't run, that he might not want kids disappointed her. She ignored the sensation.

"I have a very demanding career. I'm happy being an uncle."

"You're leaving something out."

She heard his sigh clearly. But several moments passed before he answered.

"I hate the Mate Run. It worked for my sister. She didn't mind it, actually." He fell silent for a beat before asking, "Do you?"

"Mind the Run? Not...really."

"You don't sound very certain about that."

"If it wasn't required of us, I wouldn't do it. Let's put it that way. But I haven't had any bad experiences or anything. In fact, I've enjoyed it for the most part."

"Then why wouldn't you do it if you had a choice?"

She wasn't sure, but his voice sounded strained when he asked, as if his jaw was clenched. Huh. She couldn't detect any change in his scent to indicate his mood, but he sounded…annoyed by the fact that she'd enjoyed her Runs. Interesting.

She smiled a little when she said, "I like the sex, don't get me wrong."

His almost silent growl made her grin widen. For some reason, Dr. Ryan Yin being jealous of her previous Run partners pleased her enormously.

"But it's not the best way to meet a potential husband," she finished.

"Not interested in changing mates for each child then?"

"No. I want what my parents have. A real partnership."

"They found each other through a Run."

He wasn't asking. He didn't have to. For the last two hundred years, the Mate Run was literally the only way tigers were allowed to permanently mate.

"And a lot of other couples have managed to fall in love and form long-term relationships through the Run," she said. "But…"

"But?"

"But it isn't working for me. It hasn't worked for a lot of females. Some don't care. They're the ones who want new mates for each child and aren't interested in a husband. The Run is great for them."

"None of your males have been…good enough."

She wanted to say something clever to wipe that smugness from his voice, but he was right, and she didn't feel like lying to him. "Let's just say I've never been upset by the fact that I haven't been pregnant at the end of an estrous cycle."

After another silence, he said, "How would you like to meet a mate?"

"I suppose the way other women get to meet mates."

"Going out on dates?"

"Being introduced to someone and getting to know him before letting our hormones get the best of us," she added.

"I thought you liked the sex."

She chuckled. "I do. A lot. But I'd like to know my partner a little better if I'm going to form a commitment to him."

"Because of your parents?"

"They clicked instantly," she said. "My mother once told me she knew the minute he entered the Run territory that he was the tiger for her. It only took them about four Runs before she was pregnant with my oldest brother. They've been married ever since."

"My sister met Daniel on her first Run. Actually I think they might have come across each other before she started her Runs… Anyway, it was the same thing for them as for your parents. She never let anyone else catch her. It took them a while to get pregnant, though."

"If that had happened to me," Lakshmi said quietly, "if I'd met *him* during a Run, I might feel differently about the whole thing. But I haven't. And I want what my parents have."

"So you keep running?"

"Well, I don't have much choice in that."

"And that's why I hate the Mate Run."

She frowned. "Because females have to participate? That's very…progressive of you."

He snorted at that label. "I don't want a female fucking me because she has to."

"We don't. We fuck you because we want to."

She grinned at the slight choking noise he made.

"I know you choose who gets to catch you. That's fair enough. But you are only participating in Runs because you have to. If not for that law, you wouldn't do it. You said so yourself."

"Not all females feel the way I do."

"Very few males seem to feel the way I do," he muttered. "The whole process just feels…forced. For all of us. Not like rape exactly, but…legally requiring females to reproduce seems barbaric."

"You're quite the feminist, Dr. Yin. Did you know that? Is your sister this progressive?"

He chuckled. "We've never talked about it much. It creeps me out to think about my big sister having sex. And discussing the details of her Mate Runs and sex is just… No."

She laughed. "So where do you come by this idea that we humble females should actually get a say in whether we have children or not?"

"I guess it came to the surface during my residency. I worked in the ER. I saw a lot of…bad things."

"Do I want to know?"

"Beyond the usual accidents and things, I saw rape victims, women bleeding to death because, for various insane reasons, they didn't have a legal abortion but tried to induce one themselves, women having babies they didn't want, children hurt or killed by parents who didn't want them… Just a lot of horrific stuff that…marked me."

Lakshmi shivered, trying hard not to imagine what he must have seen. His basic descriptions were bad enough. "I'm sorry you had to deal with all that."

"I'm not. I was able to help a lot of people. I help even more now as a general surgeon. And I'm good at it. But the work has affected my world view."

"Those were all human women, though."

"What does that matter? People should have a say in what they want and how they live. They shouldn't be legally *required* to reproduce."

"Even though we're almost extinct?"

"Even though."

"Is that why you joined Gregory? Because he advocates an end to the Mate Run?"

That would at least explain why he was here. Everything she'd learned about him so far… His being with the young males really didn't make any sense. Isabella had been right, he didn't seem the type. But maybe he hated the Mate Run enough to throw in his lot with the young males and their crazy leader.

He didn't answer her question, though. The silence stretched out for several minutes before she realized he wasn't going to.

She didn't want to end the conversation, so she hunted for something else to say. And decided they should get back to the immediate problem.

"Has Gregory sent a ransom to the elders for us?" she asked.

"Apparently. Right after his cohorts took Isabella. Crazy as he is, he knew that move would bring an army. He's playing a game."

"You said his rhetoric has changed? How? This all seems to play into what you've told me about him."

"He keeps changing his reasons, keeps claiming new and more convoluted things about the elders' efforts to prevent most males from mating. A few of his explanations contradict others and no one else seems to notice."

"You notice."

"I'm not looking for a mate," he reminded her.

Her chest tightened at that, and a punch of disappointment hit her again. She wasn't sure why and didn't want to think about it.

"I don't care about all the other stuff he preaches," Ryan continued. "So I suppose it's easier for me to notice the contradictions."

"How do the other males feel about this ransom thing?"

"Most support it. They want mates. They want children. And most of them won't ever have a chance at children if things continue as they've been."

Lakshmi had rarely considered the male point of view in the extinction issue. Oh, she knew the facts, knew there were too few females to the number of males. But she knew she'd have children one day. She wanted them and having them was never a question. She'd never considered how the males might feel about not being able to have children, or that so many of them just wouldn't.

"Do you think," she started quietly, "the hybrids will

help the species? Since they can probably have children with tigers?"

"I'm not sure we can avoid extinction," he said. "Even with the hybrids. It's still a matter of numbers because we've only found two of them so far. And our laws can't command hybrid women to breed with tiger males. We can't control them at all, even if the elders want to. Most of them will think of themselves as human. If they want human partners instead of shifter partners, there's nothing to stop them."

"So despite Sarah's work, you don't see any hope for us?"

Again a long silence. Then, "I think we're looking in the wrong direction. I think we need to find out why so few tiger females are born and survive. If we can't solve that underlying problem, we're dead as a species."

"I assumed our scientists were looking at that and just couldn't find an answer."

"But we can't just give up looking."

"If you...if you didn't need the Mate Run to find a mate, would you want a tiger mate? Would you want children? If things were different with our species?"

"I don't know."

His voice was so quiet, she only barely heard him through the door. She couldn't detect anything in his scent, but she was almost used to that now. She swallowed hard, nodding at no one, ignoring the fact that he couldn't see her. He would be able to read her scent, the disappointment like souring citrus she could smell clearly. It was on the tip of her tongue to ask him how he felt about her disappointment, because it seemed important to know if he cared, but a shuffling sound stopped her.

She rose to her feet, to be ready for anything, and listened as Ryan spoke to another male.

He was being called to help the woman they hadn't seen yet. He didn't even say goodbye through the door before he hurried off. She felt the loss of his scent almost physically. Even though she understood his rush, and maybe even his silence—it probably wouldn't go over well if the males thought he was currying favor with the captives —she couldn't seem to prevent her feelings from being hurt that he hadn't even wished her goodnight.

She was an idiot.

She sighed and returned to the bed where the other women slept, making an attempt to close her eyes. She should be more worried about Megan, still in a cage and not in control of her tiger, than she was about how Ryan felt about her.

Curling into a tight ball, her back comfortingly pressed against Erin, she forced her thoughts to quiet. She needed rest or she wouldn't be able to escape.

Dr. Ryan Yin was not part of that equation.

CHAPTER TEN

Ryan rushed into the basement area, slamming the door behind him so the male who'd brought him here wouldn't enter. Megan was pacing and growling, but at a glance, her body seemed to be sticking to its human form. She'd been brought fresh clothes and clean water to bathe in, so she looked and smelled better than she had when he'd first seen her. But her agitation overrode the improvements.

"I got here as quickly as I could. What's changed?" he asked her without preamble.

"I can't feel my tiger," she said. "I can't feel her at all."

"Can you shift?"

She shook her head, panic making her eyes wide and her smell ripe with musk and fear. "A day ago, I couldn't shift fully, but my tiger was there, fighting, trying to get out. Now I can't feel her. At all. I feel…cut in half."

"Okay, don't panic." He motioned her close to the bars,

so he could take her pulse and study her eyes. "Your tiger is still there. She's part of you. She can't just go away. It's your nature and that doesn't change."

"Then why the hell can't I feel her?"

He never liked to admit he didn't have the answers. It went against his medical training, to acknowledge he didn't know something before he'd had a chance to at least investigate. But he'd never even heard of this before.

Though tiger shifters often talked about their tiger as a separate entity, and often that aspect of themselves had its own ideas about what was what in the world, the human and tiger weren't actually separate. They were aspects of a whole being, not different beings inhabiting the same body. They couldn't *be* separated.

So Megan's tiger was still part of her. It wasn't gone. Her fundamental nature as a shifter hadn't been changed by the drug. That just wasn't possible.

Unfortunately, he didn't have any idea what *was* possible, or how this could happen.

After a cursory exam through the bars of her cage, he confirmed she hadn't gotten physically worse. From what he could tell, she should have been completely recovered from the side-effects of the drug.

Without a physical cause, his only answer was a mental block. But he hesitated to say that to her. In the tiger world, mental disorders were viewed…badly. Ryan had always been surprised Gregory wasn't ostracized for that reason, but somehow his rhetoric had saved him and made him a leader in a world that would normally have shunned him.

"Well?" Megan asked. "What's wrong?"

He couldn't bring himself to tell her he didn't know. Instead, he said, "You're fine. But you need out of this cage. I'll talk to Gregory now and have you moved immediately. When it happens, don't attack anyone or they will put you back in here. You need to be with the other women so your tiger is comfortable."

He wasn't certain, but he had a feeling that being inside a small cage like this had simply overwhelmed her tiger. At least, he hoped so. Getting her out of here and up with the others, where Lakshmi could look after her, was the only thing he could think of that might help.

"Try to stay calm," he said, pressing his hand to her shoulder very briefly. "I'll be back soon."

"Soon," she said and asked at the same time, her fear a tangible thing in the room.

He ordered the guard outside her door to take him to Gregory immediately. Somewhat to Ryan's surprise, he wasn't taken to Gregory's throne room this time.

He was led to a smaller room, on what he thought might be a different level, though it was hard to tell. The room had thick-cushioned, tan couches lining three of the four soft yellow walls, a low coffee table in the center, and heavy carpets covering the hard wood floors. There was a flat screen TV on one wall, turned off, and a small fridge in the corner. The room reminded Ryan a little of the living room at the cabin Gregory kept in the woods a few hours outside Baltimore—it was very clean and tastefully decorated, but it was much more casual and relaxed feeling than the cabin.

Gregory was stretched out on a couch, looking like a

man at home on a Sunday, his feet bare, wearing jeans and a t-shirt, flipping through a newspaper. He closed the paper and folded it over before Ryan could see where the paper was from, so it didn't give him any hints where they actually were in the world.

"What do you need, doctor?"

"I need Megan moved up to the room with the other women. Her tiger has gone quiet in that cage and it's causing her a lot of stress that could exacerbate her condition. She needs the security of having the other women around her."

Gregory pursed his lips and raised his brows, silently staring at the rug under Ryan's feet. "It will be done. Is there anything else?"

"Have the elders responded to the ransom demand yet?"

"Not yet. They will." He looked back down at the folded newspaper. "If that's all, I'll bid you goodnight."

Ryan opened his mouth to say more but decided against it. "Goodnight."

As he turned to leave, though, Gregory said, "I know you're unhappy with my strategy, doctor. You'll see soon that I'm right."

Ryan didn't answer. There was no point.

"Don't interfere in my plans, Yin." Now a slight growl filtered through Gregory's voice. "You don't know everything about what I'm doing."

"Maybe if you explained…"

"Goodnight."

Ryan suppressed his own growl and left. He didn't care what Gregory's plan was anymore—even if that was the entire reason he'd gotten mixed up with the young males to begin with. He had to find a way to get Lakshmi and the others out of here. Soon.

He'd accomplished the first part—ensuring all of the women were in one place. Tomorrow, he'd have to find a way to get outside and see where they were. He wasn't sure they had more than a day, maybe two before the elders' army descended on this place.

A day, maybe two to avert a war.

Sure. Easy.

* * *

Lakshmi woke with a start when the lock on their door turned. She launched off the mattress, landing in a crouch between the door and the bed, prepared to fight. She wasn't surprised when Erin landed next to her a moment later, also taking up a defensive position.

The door swung open but no one walked in immediately. Lakshmi sniffed the air and realized just beyond her view there was another female with three males.

No Ryan, though.

She stared into the black hole of the open door, contemplating whether they could make a run for it, until something in the darkness moved. A moment later a woman came into view.

"Megan." She hurried to her when she stumbled across the threshold, only realizing then that Megan had been shoved into the harem room.

Megan growled over her shoulder. When Lakshmi was

close enough to see, she was amused to realize the males were standing far back from the door in a defensive half-circle, staring at Megan like she was the crazy tiger in the building.

Lakshmi took her arm and guided her farther into the room. "How are you?"

Megan stared at her a few moments, her green eyes empty. Then she blinked and shook herself hard enough to dislodge Lakshmi's hand.

"Lakshmi?"

"It's me. Are you still under the drug? What can we do to help you?" She put her arms around the woman. Megan's eyes were haunted, her expression full of more pain than the confusion Lakshmi had seen when the other women were brought here.

"I can't feel my tiger," Megan whispered, her voice raw and harsh. "First, I couldn't shift. When I tried, it just… didn't go all the way. My tiger kept trying to get out and she couldn't. Then… I just couldn't feel her."

"Has Dr. Yin seen you? What did he say?"

"It's nothing physical. He arranged to have me brought here. I've been in a cage."

She choked as she said the last, and Lakshmi saw red, her anger spiked so hard and fast it almost dropped her to her knees.

Lakshmi hugged Megan closer and led her to the bed. Erin took up the other side, wrapping an arm around Megan's waist.

"You'll be okay," Erin said. "We'll look after you. I'm sure you'll be able to shift in no time."

"Absolutely," Lakshmi said. They eased Megan onto the bed next to the now-awake Isabella and Violet. "You just need some rest in a comfortable place, surrounded by other women."

"Can you shift?" Megan asked Lakshmi. "Is your tiger still there?"

Lakshmi felt whole, but she hadn't tried to shift since being drugged. She glanced at the others, all of them exchanging questioning looks.

With a determined nod, she rose from the bed and stripped, aware of the cameras but ignoring them. Knowing she could let her tiger out was more important than worrying about Gregory and his males watching her. A part of her, deep inside, thought, *Let them watch and see what they'll be denied.*

She took a few deep breaths, amazed she was even a little worried. She'd been shifting to her tiger form since the age of three. It was as natural as breathing, as instinctive as eating and sleeping. It was just something she did. All the time. The fact that there was even a little doubt shot a bolt of terror through her, sharp enough that she now understood Megan's haunted expression.

Afraid if she waited too long, she'd make matters worse, she closed her eyes...and let her tiger out.

The pull and twist of the shift washed through her, like the most delicious stretch, or the wonderful release from a good back crack. Her body rearranged itself, her tiger fur sprouted from her skin, her ears adjusted higher on her head, her nose and mouth reforming as a snout and whiskers sprouted, her teeth elongated, her body thickened and stretched, her tail unfurled.

By the time she dropped onto all fours and shook out her fur, she wondered why she hadn't done this sooner. She felt strong, powerful, free in this form.

And because she felt so good, she let loose a room-shaking roar, releasing hours, days of tension and fear in that long, echoing sound.

Isabella chuckled. Erin smiled and nodded. Violet glanced at Megan, frowning.

Lakshmi blinked as she adjusted to her new world view through her tiger eyes, then she studied Megan's face. The woman looked stricken, if possible even more haunted than before.

"And the rest of you?" Megan asked, turning to look at the other three women in turn.

Isabella was the first to strip out of her jogging shorts and shirt. She didn't hesitate the way Lakshmi had, just leapt off the bed and shifted. She shook out her russet, black striped fur and stood in her tiger form less than three minutes later—a fast shift and a sign that Isabella had definitely inherited her mother's strength.

Violet, somewhat more slowly, followed suit. Her tiger was a beautiful white Amur with thick black stripes and blue eyes the color of the ocean.

Erin was the last to try, and for several painful moments, she stood without shifting, staring at her own hands. Then, in the fastest change of any of them, Erin let her tiger spring forth, a thickly muscled Bengal with a beautiful white and russet ruff around her large head. In her tiger form, Erin's normally brown eyes turned gold, and they glowed in the dim lighting.

Violet loped around the room as if testing her muscles. Erin leaned forward on her front paws and stretched, the move sending her tail high. Isabella shifted back to her human form, crawled back onto the bed next to Megan, and took her hand.

Lakshmi saw Megan's fingers tremble before Isabella wrapped her hand around them.

"Do you want to try shifting?" Isabella asked.

Lakshmi jumped up onto the mattress and nudged the woman gently with her nose in wordless encouragement.

But Megan shook her head. "I'll try later. In the morning maybe. Or the day after. At least you all can shift. That's something."

"I'm sure you'll be able to shift, too," Isabella said, but she frowned at Lakshmi, concern obvious in her young eyes.

Megan nodded but the stricken look didn't leave her expression.

Lakshmi shifted back to her human form and slipped into her clothes before crawling onto the mattress next to Megan, opposite Isabella.

"Sleep," she encouraged, nudging Megan down onto the pillows. "We're here with you. You can rest. You'll feel better soon."

Still in tiger form, Violet and Erin joined them, forming a pile of feminine comfort as they all settled back into sleep.

Lakshmi held out as long as her tired body would let

her, making sure the others slept peacefully first, before finally letting exhaustion drag her under. Her last thoughts were to wonder if Ryan had any answers for Megan, and if they'd see him in the morning. She smiled a little just before drifting off, no longer quite so surprised that she was looking forward to seeing him.

* * *

Lakshmi opened her eyes a few hours later, or what felt like only a few hours, to see Gregory lounging on a pile of pillows a few feet away.

She was out of bed and crouching between him and the other women before she fully processed the sight of him. Erin, still in her tiger form, hissed from just beside Lakshmi a heartbeat later. Behind her, Lakshmi felt and sensed Violet crouching on the bed in front of Megan and Isabella.

Panic filled Lakshmi. How had he gotten in here without her noticing? How had she slept through the stench of his crazy? How long had he been there just watching them?

The questions and fears rolled through her in chaotic waves that left her speechless and unable to think clearly for precious moments. It didn't seem possible they'd have slept through him being in the room, through the intensity of his stare. Was she dreaming? Was this a nightmare?

Gregory smiled, just a little. His scent clogged her nose and coated her throat, the rank taste making her gag. She hunted the room with her senses open, but no other males were inside. Just Gregory. Staring. And smiling.

She snarled at him.

"Hello, Lakshmi," he said.

"What do you want? Why are you in here?" She didn't actually want answers to those questions. If he wanted what her previous attacker had wanted, Lakshmi was going to kill him. She barely had control of that impulse at the moment. She was too terrified. If Gregory got anywhere near her, she'd attack and tear him apart.

Close on that thought, she remembered the drug. He didn't seem to have a syringe anywhere in sight. He was dressed casually in jeans and a t-shirt, his feet bare. His hands were in plain sight on the pile of pillows cradling his big body. But that didn't mean he didn't have the drug on him or a syringe somewhere in the room.

She didn't dare take her eyes off Gregory, but she tried to search the room with her other senses—and realized Ryan was just outside the door. She turned her attention to his presence, the feel of him. Though it was hard to tell, he seemed to be pacing.

Her tiger relaxed just a little, knowing Ryan was so close. And with that, Lakshmi's panic eased, allowing her to think. She'd be bothered by that later, but she needed it so much now, she didn't care.

She straightened her shoulders and met Gregory's glittering gaze. "Well?" she asked. "Are you just going to stare or did you have something to say?"

"So strong," he murmured. "You were a good choice."

"Only if you want your ass kicked. I was a good choice for that."

He chuckled. "Please. Relax. Sit."

"No."

His slight smile fell away, his only sign of annoyance. "You'll get used to following my orders. After all, that's what females are for, isn't it? To follow their mate's orders."

"You're not my mate."

"I will be. You're all mine."

"No," she said again. Her answer echoed by a series of growls, hisses, and chuffs from the other women.

Gregory gestured to the bedroom. "Your surroundings belie your denial."

"Putting us in a harem room doesn't make us your concubines. No matter what your sick little brain seems to think."

"Not concubines. Wives."

She snarled. "Fuck you, Gregory."

"That is the point," he said, with a smirk. "And this is a good room for it, don't you think?"

Erin took a step closer to him, but Lakshmi set a hand on her shoulder, keeping her from attacking. Yet. Every ounce of Lakshmi's being wanted to kill Gregory and run. But once they did kill him, nothing would stop the rest of the males in the building from attacking. Not even Ryan pacing just beyond the door could stop that. She had to think logically, to plan and consider what she did next.

If Gregory had wanted to rape them, he could have drugged them in their sleep, or allowed other males in here to hold them down. He wanted something else from them in that moment. She just had to figure out what it was.

"You sure you should be risking this?" she asked. "Being in here alone with us? We could kill you."

"You won't. You've already figured out the repercussions of that."

"How do you know?"

"You're smart. I've been watching you."

"That's creepy, you know."

He laughed. "I've been very entertained."

"Gross," Isabella said from the bed.

Gregory flicked a glance at the girl, and Lakshmi panicked, moving to block his view of Isabella.

"Did you send that male here yesterday to rape me?" she asked him.

Isabella gasped, and Lakshmi immediately regretted her question. She'd have preferred Isabella never know about the attack. But she'd needed a way to distract Gregory from focusing on the girl and the question had just popped out. Now that she'd asked, though, she wanted an answer.

Gregory met her gaze. Under her hand, Lakshmi felt Erin's muscles bunch and flex, ready to attack.

"Karl was not following my orders," Gregory said, his tone serious.

"That was his name?"

"You didn't know? He'd been part of your Run at one stage, hadn't he?"

"So he claimed. I didn't remember him."

"Perhaps you should have paid more attention to him. Given him a chance."

"He just proved what a bad choice he would have been."

Gregory tipped his head to one side, a nod of acknowledgement. "At any rate, it doesn't matter anymore."

"Why?"

"He's dead."

Lakshmi blinked a few times, not sure she'd heard him right. "Dead?"

"Of course." Gregory remained relaxed against his pile of pillows, as if he were right at home, not casually discussing someone's death.

The sight gave Lakshmi a shiver of fear for reasons she didn't quite understand. "Why is he dead?" she asked. "When he was only attempting what you brought us here for."

"I brought you here to give *me* children," Gregory said, his stare intent.

"Just you? The others are under the impression we're here for all of you." Her stomach turned but she fought down the nausea. Gregory was willing to talk, and any information they got out of him was important.

"Oh my favorites will be allowed to fight for access to you. Only the strongest should be allowed to breed. And only at my discretion."

"So you killed my attacker because he…didn't get permission to rape me first?"

"No one takes what's mine without consequences." His dark eyes glittered as he said "mine."

"We're not yours," she said because she couldn't hold it in.

He glanced around the farce of a harem room, taking in

the beds in a lazy perusal, before meeting her gaze again, direct and unflinching. "I beg to differ."

"We are not now, nor will we ever be your wives. It'll be rape, not wifely acquiescence. And we'll fight."

He smiled. The look sent a bolt of terror through Lakshmi. When he pulled out a syringe and twirled it casually in one hand, her knees buckled. Only her hand on Erin kept her upright.

"You'll accept," he said, so confident and sure. "You'll welcome me."

"I'll rip you apart, limb from limb," she said, too scared to do anything but show her anger.

Her breathing came in short, fast pants, as adrenaline raced through her system. Beside her Erin's growl was a low threat that Lakshmi felt as much as heard. The tension in the room was palpable, and Lakshmi felt like her nerves were drawn so tight they might snap. He had the drug. He had a syringe. He would incapacitate her again. She'd be at his mercy.

Despite logic, despite knowing she'd be in even greater danger, her instincts screamed, *Attack!*

He rose, a rippling of muscle and dangerous intent. It was all Lakshmi could do not to take a step back. She was panting in fear, her heart racing too fast. She held his gaze, through an act of will, because if she looked at the syringe, he'd know. He'd know her weakness.

He paused so close to her, the scent of his insanity nearly choked her. She flexed her nostrils in an attempt not to take the smell in. His gaze dropped to her mouth, then farther down to her breasts. She fisted her hands, her every nerve trained on him, waiting for his next move. Her skin crawled with awareness of the syringe he held casually at his side.

"When the time comes," he said, his face close to hers, his voice quiet, "you *will* bear me children, as is your duty. And you will be glad of it."

"Never."

His eyes narrowed. And then he laughed, so abrupt and loudly, she startled and stepped back from him despite herself.

He turned away from her, sauntering toward the door as if there was no tension in the room and nothing had happened. He knocked on the door, but as it opened, he turned to face her again.

"Your estrous is in two days," he said, and he held up the syringe, tilting his head to one side as he studied it. He glanced at her again, moving just his eyes to meet hers. "We'll see."

He swept out of the room, and Lakshmi caught sight of Ryan just beyond the door being held back by two other males. She locked gazes with him. He jerked against the males restraining him, taking a step toward her.

The door closed in his face with an ominous thud.

R yan struggled against the two males gripping his arms as he tried to reach the door, to reach Lakshmi. The door wasn't soundproofed and Gregory had made no effort to keep the discussion quite. Ryan heard every threat. He heard the panic and fear in Lakshmi's voice. Her wide, terror-filled eyes just now had been too much. Ryan couldn't think beyond getting to her, protecting her.

Gregory stopped in front of him, his eyes narrowed. "Problem, doctor?"

He spoke so reasonably it was like he hadn't just threatened the women, invaded their privacy, or implied things that made Ryan's stomach heave. Ryan bit back a growl and jerked his arms again to dislodge the males restraining him. At a glance from Gregory, they released Ryan.

He straightened his shoulders. "They weren't ready for that confrontation," he said, trying to keep his rage in check. It was almost impossible, though. He was choking on disgust and terror. And at least some of that was in his scent because he was too upset to keep it all out. He forced himself to argue from a medical perspective, trying to keep from antagonizing Gregory, but his tiger's rage was too raw, too close to the surface.

"We have no idea what side-effects that drug will have," he said, gesturing at the door. "Look what it's done to Megan. They are *not* fully recovered yet."

Ryan's tiger clawed to be let out. He wanted to rend Gregory limb from limb for threatening Lakshmi, for bringing that drug into the room with her when Ryan knew damned well how terrified all the women were of it.

"Lakshmi was able to fight off Karl's advances," Gregory said, again much too reasonably. "I think she's recovered. Erin appears to have shaken off the results of her head injury. The others will follow. Poor Megan is an anomaly."

"Gregory…" Ryan's tone was deeper than usual, full of warning and threat.

And he knew immediately he'd pushed too far.

Gregory's expression hardened, all hints of reason gone. "You're overstepping again, doctor. Beyond their medical care, the women are no concern of yours."

"Christ man, you brought Isabella Tarasova here. Elizaveta's granddaughter! Of course I'm concerned."

The two males who'd restrained Ryan stepped closer. Gregory shook his head just slightly, and they backed off again.

"You're tired, doctor," Gregory said, his hard tone belying the polite words. "You haven't had a chance to sleep much since arriving. You'll feel better after a rest."

The last thing Ryan wanted in that moment was sleep. But he said, "Fine. I'll sleep here. On the floor. In case they need me."

"We have a room prepared for you. You'll sleep there."

"What if something happens? What if Megan needs me?" Desperation had him on the verge of pleading. He couldn't leave Lakshmi unprotected. What if Gregory went in there again? What if another male decided to go in, despite what had happened to Karl? "I can sleep just fine on the floor. I don't need a room. You brought me here to be their doctor. Let me."

Gregory stared at him for a long moment. Ryan held his breath.

"If one of them needs medical attention," Gregory finally said, "someone will come get you."

"No, that could take too long. Please."

But he could tell, looking into Gregory's dark eyes, he wasn't going to be budged.

He continued to hold Ryan's gaze, his head tilted to one side as if he were examining a strange phenomenon, trying to decide what, if anything, to do about it. After a moment, he blinked and walked away.

But over his shoulder, Gregory said, "Escort Dr. Yin to his room."

One of the males who'd restrained Ryan earlier nudged him in the back. "This way, doc."

Ryan didn't look at the man. He couldn't look away from the locked doors. His tiger refused to move. Lakshmi was in danger and that was all his tiger could think about.

"Doc, you need to move. Now. Or I'll have to force you."

A part of Ryan thought, *Try it, boy. I will squash you like a bug.*

But the logical part of Ryan knew he had to follow Gregory's order. He'd pushed the crazy leader too far this time, he could sense it. If Gregory locked Ryan up, or worse had him killed the way he'd killed Karl, Ryan wouldn't be able to protect Lakshmi, or any of the women. Still, it wasn't until the male actually pushed Ryan that Ryan could summon the will to move.

But it cost him dearly to walk away from that door and leave Lakshmi behind.

CHAPTER ELEVEN

Ryan had the impression of the sun being up for hours when he finally forced himself awake, his eyes gritty and blurry from too little rest over the last week. While he'd made an effort to sleep, despite his churning anxiety, he kept waking up every hour or so, listening to the corridor outside his door, waiting for someone to come get him…dreading the news he might receive.

He was so exhausted he couldn't see straight, but he kept going over the entire conversation between Gregory and Lakshmi in his head. The terror in her eyes just before the guards slammed the door in Ryan's face had haunted him through his restless sleep. He hadn't known the male who'd attacked her had been killed until Gregory told her. The news didn't reassure Ryan even though he had no sympathy for Karl. The fact that Gregory was now issuing death sentences to his own followers pushed the whole situation into new realms of disaster.

And Ryan hadn't thought things could get much worse.

He rolled to a sitting position and ran his hands through his hair, studying the little cell that was his assigned room in the complex. It was a basic rectangle with the same white walls as the rest of the place. A single cot set against one side left just enough space for a grown man to walk into and out of the room. A tan blanket covered the bed, and a comfortable but thin pillow rested at the head. There was no headboard, no bedside table, and no adornments on the wall. It was a single cot in a white room that was barely six feet wide and eight feet deep. The only thing that kept the room from feeling like a tomb was the ten-foot-high ceiling.

He glanced at the door. He needed to check on Lakshmi and the others. His tiger was edgy and restless, anxious to get to Lakshmi now that he was awake. Scrubbing his hands over his face, he pushed to his feet. To his surprise, the door to his cell was no longer locked—he'd been locked in when they'd brought him here. But there was a guard just outside, waiting for him.

"Gregory wants to see you, doc," the male said—another virtual stranger to Ryan.

"I need to check on my patients first."

"After Gregory."

Ryan snarled, but there was no point in arguing. He'd already pushed Gregory as far as he dared. Better to meet with the man and get that over with so he could get to the harem room and make sure Lakshmi was still safe.

"Are the women doing okay?" he asked as he was led through the corridors.

"Gregory says they're fine."

"Has Gregory been in to see them again?" He had to grit his teeth to keep his fears and anger in check.

"No. No one has since Gregory went in last night."

That was something at least. Ryan relaxed his jaw and rolled his head until his neck cracked, trying to force away his tension before he saw Gregory.

The male glanced back at him. "The fights will start soon."

"Fights? The elders' army has found us?"

"No. Fights for the two females coming into estrous. Gregory says we have to fight for them. Winners will get them."

"Shit." Ryan's gut tightened. He was almost out of time. He still had no way out of this complex. And he'd pushed his luck too far with Gregory last night, costing whatever bit of leeway he might have gotten from the bastard.

What the hell was he going to do?

That question dogged him through the corridors until his escort stopped suddenly. Ryan looked around him and came face-to-face with Gregory.

"Good afternoon, doctor," Gregory said, smiling pleasantly. "So glad you could join me."

Not that Ryan had had a choice. "Afternoon. How are the women?"

Gregory blinked slowly, in a way that Ryan could never interpret. He usually watched the other man do that when he was calculating his reaction to someone. But occasionally, Ryan had the impression Gregory simply used the gesture to intimidate those he was talking to.

It worked on Ryan. But he didn't let it show, in either his scent or his expression. Meeting the crazy tiger's dark gaze was harder than usual, but Ryan forced himself not to look away.

"They're sleeping," Gregory finally said, his tone expressionless.

"Has Megan shifted yet?"

"Not yet."

Ryan nodded absently. He'd been hoping for some bit of good news, anything at all would do. Megan shifting would have fit the bill.

"Doctor?"

Ryan snapped back to attention. "Yes. Sorry. I need to check on them. Megan not shifting is a bad sign."

"Later. I need to speak with you first. Privately."

Wariness wrapped a tight claw around Ryan's chest. "Sure. What about?"

Gregory smiled very slightly, that devious and creepy expression that made Ryan's hackles rise.

"This way, doctor."

Gregory sent Ryan's escort away with a sharp head gesture, then led Ryan down more of the indistinguishable corridors to a nondescript door. They passed several other males, but Gregory waved them all away. As he proceeded Ryan into a room Ryan hadn't seen before, Ryan realized Gregory wasn't flanked by any of his guards. Not inside the room, not at the door.

Ryan's heart beat a little harder when Gregory closed the door behind him.

To cover his sudden spike of fear, he took in the new space—a decent sized office with a black lacquer desk at the far wall, facing the door, a swivel desk chair behind it, and the wooden floors covered with a simple blue rug. Bright light flooded the room and it took Ryan several seconds to realize the light was from an actual window. The first window he'd seen in the complex. Ryan had believed the whole place was built without them.

He stared out that large, clear glass at the forest beyond —tall evergreen spruce trees dominated the view, the rocky gray ground beneath covered in spongy brown detritus, dried spruce needles and little cylindrical cones. He wasn't versed in flora enough to identify the species of trees—if he could it might give him a better idea of where they were— but spruce made him think higher altitudes. The sky was blue with a few fluffy white clouds gently floating past. Plenty of sun flooded the room despite the thick trees, and when Ryan moved closer to the window, he could see that the area outside the complex had been cleared back to leave several feet of muddy gray-brown earth between the complex wall and the start of the tree line. Thick puddles in that mud revealed a recent rain.

None of it gave him any clue where they were in the world, though. The only thing he could say for sure was that he didn't know the view. It wasn't the woods around Gregory's primary residence, the cabin in the Green Ridge State Forest outside Baltimore, which didn't surprise Ryan. The Trackers knew where that cabin was located and would have already searched it the minute they realized Gregory was responsible for the kidnappings.

This was someplace new. Someplace Ryan hadn't been with the young males before.

"Beautiful view, isn't it?" Gregory asked from just behind Ryan.

Ryan didn't jump or reveal his surprise at Gregory's nearness in any way. But inside he balked at how close the crazy tiger had gotten to him without him noticing.

"Yeah, it's great," he said in a surprisingly even voice. "Where the hell are we?"

He didn't expect an answer, so he wasn't disappointed when Gregory merely smiled that knowing, creepy smile of his as he moved away from the window.

"Have a seat, doctor." He motioned to a large brown leather couch set against the left wall.

Despite his jumping nerves, Ryan sat as if this sort of private conversation was normal between the two of them. He pulled his arrogant doctor guise around him like a shield and waited for Gregory to make the next move.

Gregory watched him for an unnerving minute before settling into the black swivel chair behind the desk. "We've received word on the ransom demands from the elders," he said bluntly.

"I'm not surprised. They'll pay the money part, obviously. But they can't tell you where the hybrids are, right?"

"Money and the hybrid locations weren't my only demands."

"Of course not," Ryan muttered. "You want the Mate Run dissolved. Was that part of the ransom?"

Gregory hadn't told any of them what demands he'd sent the elders exactly—not that Ryan had been able to uncover. None of the young males he'd spoken to knew anyway. Ryan had assumed money was involved, and Gregory had said he was looking for the hybrids. Ryan knew the women's families would pay any amount. Even if that money had to come from the elders' own funds, Ryan knew a monetary ransom would be paid. He also knew even if Gregory demanded it, *no one* could reveal more hybrids.

But he'd been afraid Gregory's demands would involve more, things within the elders' control that they'd deny. That denial would give Gregory more fodder to stir up the other males. This conversation confirmed Ryan's worst fears.

"Of course," Gregory answered without any expression whatsoever.

"And they said no." Ryan shook his head. "Tell me that's not a surprise to you?"

"It's not. Entirely. Though I'm surprised there wasn't more pressure from the women's families to meet my demands."

"There probably was. The elders aren't going to bow to that pressure, though, or they lose their power over the community."

Gregory dipped his head in a slight nod of acknowledgment. "I expected their response."

"Then why are we talking? I should check on the women."

"You slept well," Gregory asked, ignoring Ryan's question.

"Fine, I guess. I would have slept better if you'd let me stay closer to the women. I kept waking up, thinking I heard someone coming to get me."

"Hazards of your job? What did you do during your residency when you slept at the hospital?"

"Slept badly," Ryan said with feeling. "Can I go now?"

"You must need a run? When was the last time your tiger was out?"

Ryan forced himself not to sigh or roll his eyes. Gregory was stalling and it was maddening, but Ryan was already on dangerous ground with the man. "It's been a while."

"Your own fault for insisting on keeping that job at a human hospital."

Ryan didn't answer. He'd had this discussion with Gregory before—when he'd first joined the young males during a planned hiatus from his job. Gregory asked him why he'd bother going back. Ryan gave Gregory the same answer he gave his own parents when they asked why he insisted on working for humans rather than dedicating his skills to looking after other tigers. He kept his job because he was good at it, and working with humans meant he could distance himself from the tigers. He didn't explain to anyone why he wanted to do that—even his parents.

But he was intent on keeping his current job, working mostly with humans instead of tigers, because he had grown convinced the tiger world was doomed, and he didn't want any part of it. Beyond his immediate family—his parents, his brother and sister, nephews and niece, his brother-in-law—he had removed himself from contact with other tigers. He didn't share his sister's hope that their people could avoid extinction. And he didn't want to watch it happen. The more distance he could keep between himself and the other tigers, the better.

He'd been successful, too. Until the elders had come to him and asked him to be their spy.

"You didn't want to see me to talk about my job," Ryan said. "Why are we here? Why are you telling me about the elders' response to the ransom in private?"

"Would you like that run?" Gregory asked.

"Yes. But I'd like answers to my questions first."

Gregory's mouth lifted in a half-smile. He leaned back in his chair and settled his hands on the armrests, looking at ease and in command of his space. "You're the only one of my tigers who questions me. Did you know that, doctor?"

"I always considered it part of my job."

"Because you're a doctor?"

"Because I'm older than the rest of you. You brought me in *because* I asked questions and don't accept things at face value."

"I have always liked that about you."

Ryan was positive that wasn't true. He often got the impression Gregory would prefer him to be as devoted and unquestioningly loyal as the others. But he couldn't have admitted that without losing face.

"I would like your…advice," Gregory said, "as the only one of my men willing to tell me things I might not want to hear."

Ryan raised his brows at that. Gregory had never taken him into his confidence like this and certainly never sought him out as an advisor. Gregory liked them all to believe he knew exactly what he was doing at all times. Ryan asking Gregory questions was one thing. Ryan being consulted *by* Gregory was something else altogether.

And after last night, Ryan's hackles rose in instinctive concern over Gregory's motivations for this conversation.

"Advice on what, exactly?" Ryan asked cautiously.

Thoughts of Lakshmi, of the way Gregory had threatened her last night, flashed through him, cutting through his façade for just a moment, sending claws of fear and worry into his gut before he controlled the reaction. Gregory's eyes narrowed, as if he'd caught something in Ryan's scent. Ryan made sure his scent revealed only his curiosity and wariness—because Gregory would never believe that Ryan wasn't wary of this request for advice—and held Gregory's gaze until the other man relaxed.

When he did, Ryan allowed himself to blink as a way to release his relief without revealing it. It took a great deal of effort not to show Gregory his fear, but underneath the act he put on for Gregory's sake, Ryan's pulse thumped in hard, nervous bumps.

"The Mate Run must end," Gregory said. "We both know this."

Ryan nodded, a completely honest response to Gregory's statements.

"The elders won't bow to pressure only from the males. We must have the entire community rise up against the Run."

Ryan didn't respond. He actually did agree with Gregory's statement, but since he wasn't sure where the other man was going with this, he didn't want to tip his hand yet.

"I had assumed…" He pursed his lips and looked out the window. "I had assumed the hybrids would break open our community's attachment to the Run."

"It has in some ways."

"Not enough. There are still too many who feel the hybrids will be our downfall."

"The elders really don't know how many hybrids there are, you know?" Ryan said quietly, carefully. "They aren't hiding them from us."

"I know."

Ryan was surprised enough by that, he didn't even think to hide his reaction until after he'd revealed it.

Gregory looked at him again, that slight smile lifting his lips. "I'm much more aware of what the elders know and don't know than you think, doctor."

"How?"

Gregory just smiled and looked back out the window again. "Hybrids are not the answer, though they will help. And because they can't take part in the Runs if they're human hybrids, the rules of reproduction and mating have to change. But too many of the elders are refusing to acknowledge this change."

"How did you expect to change their minds by kidnapping tiger females? That will only make them dig in deeper to the belief that we males are too dangerous without the Run to govern mate choice."

"The hybrids change everything," Gregory insisted. "They refuse to acknowledge it."

"They acknowledge it. They just don't know what to do about it."

That earned Ryan a raised brow and a slight nod. "Though they'll never admit they don't know what to do."

"The arguments in the community are admission enough."

"The arguments will take too long. Our people will move too slowly to settle on an answer. And we males will lose any hope of our own children to their sluggish politics."

"What are you hoping to accomplish with this, Gregory?" Ryan asked again.

Gregory faced him, and this time the arrogant half-smile was gone. When Gregory met Ryan's gaze, his expression was as uncertain as Ryan had ever seen it. That couldn't be a good sign.

"I was assured this move would push the elders to make the changes we want."

"By who?" Ryan frowned.

"Now they're refusing those changes."

"They called your bluff?"

"It was never a bluff. The females are ours now. They won't be released."

Ryan clenched his hands into tight fists to keep from reacting in a way that might get him killed. Instead, he said, very slowly, "You can't keep them, Gregory. The women will fight. You heard Lakshmi last night. You have to know they'll fight to the death rather than accept this."

"I know."

Ryan jerked his hands into the air. "You want them to die? Females? Some of the very few left for our people? Doesn't that defeat the purpose? You *still won't get children*. The elders won't end the Run, and they can't give you any more information about hybrids than they already have. What is the point of all this?"

"Doctor, you assume I'll allow the women to be killed."

"But you just said…"

"I acknowledged that they would fight to the death—if given the opportunity."

Ryan's stomach bottomed out, as it had last night when Gregory went into the harem room with a syringe. Panic almost overwhelmed him again. "You can't use that drug anymore, Gregory. How many times do I have to say that? You can't. It will kill them as surely as any fight."

"They won't fight to the death if they're pregnant. They'll want to preserve those precious lives."

Ryan thought he might be sick. His stomach heaved so hard, he actually leaned forward and put his head between his knees, breathing deeply so he wouldn't throw up. He probably shouldn't have put himself in such a vulnerable position in front of Gregory, but his physical reaction was so strong and fast, he couldn't help it.

"So…" He breathed through his teeth, his head still down. "So you're going to drug them, and rape them until they're pregnant?"

Some part of Ryan must have hoped all Gregory's threats last night were just talk, because in the light of day, with the bright blue sky just beyond the window, Gregory's disgusting plan suddenly seemed so much more real, too likely.

Ryan's tiger roared in denial.

"They'll be happy for the children," Gregory said.

"No, Gregory. They won't. You heard Lakshmi. They will not accept this."

"We're all happy when more tiger children are conceived."

Ryan raised his head. "Not this way. Damn it, Gregory. *Not this way.*"

"The elders have left us no options. They refused our compromise."

"Compromise?"

"End the Run. Tell us where the hybrids that they know of are. We return the females."

"How is that a compromise? And they don't know where the hybrids are. You just admitted you knew that."

Gregory ignored Ryan's outburst. "They have refused to accept the truth. So we will do what we must to have children. Three of our five females are coming into estrous over the next week. The challenge fights will begin tomorrow for the honor of mating with them. They'll be pregnant by the end of this cycle. That will encourage the others to…accept their new position."

"Damn it, Gregory. Isabella isn't even old enough to be in estrous yet! She's a child. She can't reproduce yet. Will you still rape her, just for the hell of it?"

Even the question made Ryan's stomach heave again. He swallowed hard to keep the bile down.

"This is about producing children, doctor. Of course she will be preserved until her first estrous."

"You're talking about eight years from now."

"Not likely, given the changes. Isabella will likely come in early as others in her generation are."

"But you can't be sure of that. Gregory, this is not going to work. Alexis and the Trackers will find this place well before you can accomplish anything. They'll recover the women and kill all of us. You know that. You *have* to know that." Ryan sat forward on the couch and tried, really tried to appeal to whatever logic Gregory might still possess.

There were no witnesses here, like there had been last night, no other young males around to see Gregory change his mind. Gregory could present his change of plan in any way he wanted that maintained his status outside this room, and Ryan would never gainsay Gregory's story. But Ryan had to convince Gregory that this plan would not work.

"Gregory, please. You wanted my advice. Here it is. We can't keep the women. This ploy isn't going to work. You don't get anything from it but a death sentence. No children. No mates—full tiger or hybrid. The only end to this, Gregory, is death for you and the rest of us. The elders will win this round if you don't send the women home. If you stay this course, the *elders will win*."

He watched something move through Gregory's dark eyes, and held his breath as he waited to see how the man would react. Ryan had played his strong card—that the elders would win this game if Gregory didn't change his plans. It was the one thing Gregory detested more than anything else, the idea that the elders would come out on top, that he would lose to them.

Gregory stared hard at Ryan. Ryan stared back.

"Doctor," Gregory said slowly, his voice even and mild, "I asked you here to tell me how much of that drug I can use on the females during their estrous to ensure compliance. That's the advice I want. The only advice I want from you."

"Gregory…" Ryan half rose, determined to put a stop to this madness. But a hard pounding knock on the door stopped him mid-movement.

Gregory jerked and looked at the door, frowning. "Enter."

Sanjay swung inside, his eyes wide and panic filling his scent. "It's the Trackers, Gregory. They've found us."

CHAPTER TWELVE

Ryan raced down the corridors toward the harem room—unfortunately with three other young males in tow, thanks to a barked order from Gregory.

Chaos had erupted around the complex with the announcement of the incoming Tracker army. People were charging past Ryan, heading in various directions, everyone serious, some of the young males too excited to Ryan's way of thinking. Those poor bastards had no idea what was about to happen. He shouldered through a clump of four males arguing over which sector Gregory had ordered them to, and the scent of their anticipation and fear coated his nose and tongue.

He pushed his speed, knowing they only had a brief window of time. He had to get the women out of the compound before the attack. If things turned against Gregory, the crazy tiger would have no compunction about using the women to get out of this mess. Ryan and the three males running with him were supposed to guard the women in their room. Ryan had no intention of following that order, but he needed the other males to find the damned place since he never had figured it out on his own.

Slamming through the doors without knocking, he skidded to a stop halfway inside the harem room. "We have to go. The Trackers are here."

All of the women—two of them in tiger form—were on a single large bed. Lakshmi leapt to her feet, her jump putting her only a yard away from where Ryan had stopped. One of the tigers, Erin from the scent, launched off the mattress to stand next to Lakshmi. They were both between the males and the women remaining on the bed. A brief glance and a quick breath confirmed Violet was the other woman in tiger form.

"What's happening?" Lakshmi said.

"Hey, doc, Gregory didn't say anything about moving the women," one of the males behind Ryan said.

Ryan closed his eyes. He didn't know these three. That didn't make what he was about to do any easier. He opened his eyes and held Lakshmi's gaze for a heartbeat. Then he swung around and pounced.

Not one of the three males was ready for his attack. Ryan slammed one against a wall, knocking him out, flipped another across the room into the tiled pool, and faced off against the third who'd had a split second of time to prepare.

"You don't fight, doc," the male said, panic in his scent and voice. "What the hell are you doing?"

"Saving lives," Ryan said, and launched at the male.

They came together in a swirl of movement, the young man swinging fists and lashing out at Ryan. Ryan was too fast—and too well trained. He broke the males arm, flipped him over his back, slamming him hard onto the floor, then he lifted him by a leg and spun him across the room to crash high against a wall, near the ceiling. The young male slid to the floor unconscious.

The male from the fountain regained his sense and roared, charging Ryan. Ryan swung to face him but before he could return the attack, Erin jumped onto the young male. Ryan winced when her jaws closed over his throat and snapped tight.

Erin eased off the dead male, the white fur around her mouth covered in blood, her tongue hanging out as she panted.

Lakshmi put a hand on Ryan's shoulder. "He was one of the males that took us. He…touched Erin when the other males weren't paying attention. I wasn't sure she even remembered…"

Ryan didn't need to hear anymore. He'd been trying not to kill anyone—despite his tiger's desire to destroy all the males that threatened Lakshmi—but he couldn't blame Erin at all for her actions.

"Come on," he said, motioning to the other women. "We need to leave."

"Where?" Lakshmi asked. "How?"

The other women, Erin included, gathered around Lakshmi, but all their gazes were focused on him.

"There's a window in Gregory's office. We'll have to break out there."

There wasn't much Ryan could be grateful to Gregory for, but bringing him into the office to talk had been a fortuitous bit of luck. Ryan had no idea how else to get the women out. Even with the orders Ryan had overheard Gregory bark at the young males, getting them mobilized for the fight, Gregory hadn't revealed where any of the damned exits were. The window was Ryan and the women's only option.

"Can you find it again?" Lakshmi asked even as they hurried from the harem room.

She kept pace beside him, the other women following as they made their way through the corridors.

"I left a trail." He pointed to a corner where he'd left a visible dent in the wall.

He'd pretended to grip the corners in his hurry to get to the women, squeezing hard enough to mark the path. The other males hadn't questioned or even commented on the dents, thanks to the mayhem surrounding their race to the women.

Ryan paused at the corner, listening down the next corridor, stretching out his tiger senses to feel for other males. Nothing. Most of them were no doubt in position to face the approaching army.

Over his shoulder, he said, "Keep sharp. I'm not sure if anyone has been sent back to check on us."

As they made their way quickly and cautiously to Gregory's office, Ryan's gut tight with anxiety, he considered their options once they got out of the building. They needed to meet the Tracker army. But he didn't want to get the women caught up in the middle of the fighting.

"We should circle around behind the army," Lakshmi said, as if reading his thoughts. "We'll be able to sense where most everyone is."

"And hopefully there'll be a way around," he said, pausing again to scent and sense the area ahead of them.

"How much farther?" she asked.

"Not much. Two more turns and we're in the right corridor."

"Gregory?"

Ryan pulled in a breath. "Last I saw, on his way to face the Trackers. Looking very determined and serious."

"Can they fight the army?"

"They've been training with Gregory. But he's no Tracker. He's a decent fighter but nothing compared to the tigers trained by people like Alexis."

Lakshmi's eyes narrowed and her lips lifted in a fierce, snarling kind of grin. "Like us."

He snorted. "Exactly."

"You're a pretty vicious fighter yourself, doctor."

He glanced at her, the note of admiration in her tone catching him off guard. Her scent, spiced with just a hint of desire, almost made him trip.

"My brother-in-law trained me," he said, looking ahead again so he didn't forget what they were doing. "Payment for a favor."

"Daniel Borowski? Sarah's husband. The Tracker."

"That's the one."

"What favor?"

"Dug a bullet out of his shoulder."

He paused one more time, then motioned them around

the last corner. The corridor ahead was free, but he could sense two males somewhere ahead of them. He waved everyone to silence and they eased toward their goal.

His muscles tensed tighter as they neared the door they needed. The males weren't moving, but they had to sense Ryan and the others. They might just be far enough away that the weird air cleaning aspect of this building would keep the other males from scenting the females, maybe they'd just assume other males…

An instant after Ryan thought that, the males moved, fast. He shook his head and raced forward to meet them.

He charged past one male, spun around, and came up behind him, grabbing the male around the neck with one arm and using his other as a lever to choke the male into unconsciousness. When he dropped his own opponent to the ground, he wasn't even a little surprised to see Lakshmi standing over the second male, holding his arm wrenched up in an awkward angle, her foot on his neck. He thrashed a few times and she pressed harder until he stopped moving.

When he was still, she edged back. Ryan dropped down to check the man's pulse. Unconscious.

"You didn't kill him," he commented as he backtracked to Gregory's office door.

"It was close," she said, a growl in her voice.

At a glance, he noted her eyes were brighter, starting to glow. Her tiger was close to the surface.

"Why didn't you?" He was genuinely curious. He didn't want to kill because it went against everything he did with his life. His tiger's need to kill was an impulse he rejected regularly. But he hadn't been ripped from his home and threatened with rape and murder by a bunch of crazy males.

Well, okay, he had been ripped from his home, and he was pretty sure he'd been close to being killed a few times since arriving here, but really he'd put himself in the position that got him to this point. He and the elders. The women were innocent victims. Erin had killed. He had no doubt Lakshmi would have killed the male who'd tried to rape her if she'd had a chance. He was surprised she held back now.

He tried Gregory's office door, sensing no one inside, and almost crowed when he found it unlocked. Luck, coincidence, forgetfulness on Gregory's part or just the bastard's arrogance. Whatever it was, Ryan was just glad he didn't have to figure out a way through a door designed to keep tigers from breaking it down.

They were inside, and he'd eased the door shut, before Lakshmi answered his question.

"You aren't killing them," she said quietly. "You can but you aren't."

"I don't have the same motivation as you. They brought this on themselves."

"I won't argue with that. But they should be punished by tiger law, made to live with the crimes they've committed. They can't do that if they're already dead."

He couldn't help but wonder if she felt that way about Karl or if she was glad Gregory had executed him.

Quieter, her gaze diverted, she added, "And you weren't killing them. I wanted to…honor that."

She frowned, her brow bunched, little crinkles between her eyebrows. A very light pink color rose to her cheeks.

Ryan had no idea what either her expression, the blush, or her comment meant, but he knew it made his tiger rumble in approval. That slight touch of desire from her scent earlier came back to tease him. He blinked when he realized he was losing control of his own scent.

As quietly as she'd spoken, so only she would hear him, he said, "We'll come back to this conversation once you're safe."

She met his gaze and nodded.

Shaking off the moment, he gestured to the window. "That's our way out."

It only took a quick assessment to discover that while the window didn't open, it was something they could break.

"Why not a tiger-proof window?" Isabella asked.

"Everything else in this place is tiger proof," Megan added. She had her arms wrapped around her waist as she stared out the window to the forest beyond.

Violet and Erin, still in tiger form as neither had had time to change yet, sat near the window, just behind Megan as if protecting her.

"Maybe he couldn't afford to tiger proof everything," Ryan said. "We never discussed it."

In all honesty, Ryan wasn't sure where Gregory had gotten the money to build a place like this. He wasn't rich. He'd taken "tithes" from the other males to afford the cabin, but even with that, there wasn't enough money for a complex like this.

Unless Gregory was getting help from someone a lot richer than any of his young males.

Another problem for later. And for other people. Now, they had to get out of here.

"Why are we running out into the fight?" Megan asked. "Isn't it safer to wait for the Trackers to come get us?"

"If Gregory gets desperate, he might use you to protect himself and escape," Ryan said. "I don't want to take that chance."

Erin made a chuffing noise and stood, nosing at the window, then looking over her shoulder at him.

"I know," he said. "Breaking the glass will be messy and noisy. It's our only way out." He motioned the women aside. "The couch should do it."

He lifted one side while Lakshmi lifted the other. Isabella and Megan moved Gregory's desk and chair back against the wall, giving Ryan and Lakshmi more room to maneuver the couch.

"On three," Ryan said.

He and Lakshmi swung the couch back and launched it through the window, the glass shattering in a crescendo of noise and sharp shards.

"Not even shatter-proof glass," Isabella noted.

"Maybe that's on purpose," Lakshmi said, nodding to the floor just in front of the window.

Most of the broken glass was outside but a few sharp shards remained inside. And Ryan remembered none of the women had shoes. Tiger shifters, even in human form, had very tough soles, but glass could still be a problem.

He stepped up to the window—his shoes adding extra

protection—and looked out to see how far the glass had scattered.

"It's gonna be close," he said, "but I can boost you through and over most of it, I think. If you don't mind being thrown." He opened his senses, gauging the location of the other tigers. "The fighting is farther west of here. But we need to hurry. Someone's bound to have heard the window shattering."

Lakshmi stepped forward. "I'll go through first and help the others."

He took her outstretched hand. The contact sent a shock of sensation over his nerves, a tingling of awareness that made his pulse jump. She held his gaze a moment, emotions in her expression that he didn't have time to decipher.

He braced himself and lifted her so she balanced on one of his legs, then, his hands on her waist and using all his shifter strength, he threw her head first out the window, tossing her as far past the glass as he could manage.

CHAPTER THIRTEEN

Lakshmi flew over the broken couch and shards of window, hitting the dirt in a controlled roll that brought her back up to her feet and swinging around to face Ryan again. She grinned as her stomach danced, the burst of adrenaline coupled with a touch of fear and a lot of excitement similar to how she felt when she rode roller coasters.

Then the realization sunk in that she was outside, the cool, fresh air kissing her skin.

Forest scents overwhelmed and surrounded her instantly—piney spruce and fir trees, the thick loam of detritus covering the rocky ground, the fresh, clean air, the pungent tang of marmots and squirrels, and faintly, the clean, wet, mossy scent of a lake.

She sucked in a big breath, momentarily forgetting everything with that first taste of freedom.

A heartbeat later she remembered she was supposed to

be helping the other women. She motioned to Ryan, counted to two, and Isabella flew from the window, her shifter reflexes coupled with Ryan's strength ensured she reached Lakshmi. Lakshmi caught her, spinning in a circle to offset the momentum of her flight.

"You okay?" Lakshmi asked as she helped Isabella regain her footing.

"That was fun," she said with a little grin. "I never realized I'd like being thrown out a window."

Lakshmi laughed. "I know, right!" She glanced around. "Shift while the others are coming out. You'll be able to get through the forest easier in your tiger form."

"You?"

"I'll stay human. Someone will need to talk to the Trackers when we reach them."

As Isabella pulled her shirt off, Lakshmi turned back to the window in time to see Megan fly through.

Despite her inability to feel her tiger, Megan's reactions were as sharp and graceful as any shifter. She flipped mid-air and landed on her feet, with only a little help from Lakshmi to keep her balance.

Erin and Violet made the jump easily, their tiger forms and shifter strength sending them sailing beyond Lakshmi and the other women. Erin faced the battle happening somewhere off to the west of their position. Isabella, now fully tiger, turned to them, her lips lifted in a tiger grin that anyone but a tiger shifter would see as a threat.

While she waited for Ryan, Lakshmi opened her senses. The fighting was loud enough that she could just hear the shouts, curses and growls—a mix of human and tigers in combat. That surprised her a little as most tigers fought in their tiger forms. It was why Alexis had trained the women to fight a tiger while still in their human forms as well as tiger to tiger. It gave the women an element of surprise. Most males couldn't even fight a tiger while in their human form.

The combatants were far enough away that she doubted they'd heard the window break, but she was still antsy to get moving. She faced the window again, automatically counting in her head as she waited on Ryan. When she reached twenty, she frowned. What was wrong? She took a step toward the window, prepared to ignore the glass if he needed her help.

Before she got closer than that single step, he came sailing out the window in tiger form.

She'd been so focused on the fight, she hadn't realized he was shifting. His tiger was a magnificent Amur, large and thick, with heavy muscles under the russet and black striped fur. His neck ruff was almost entirely white, framing his tiger face like a cloud. And in tiger form, his dark brown eyes were even darker, almost black with a hint of gold glowing in their depths. Her heart thumped a little faster.

"Nice jump," she commented.

He grunted in response around his clothing, which he carried in his mouth. She couldn't read anything from his scent beyond his concentration and anxiety, but she'd swear she saw him preen a little under her compliment.

She was still trying not to think about how his hands had felt on her when he'd thrown her through the window.

They didn't have time for those thoughts. But whatever chemistry had been there before, it was starting to tick upward—no doubt helped along by her impending estrous.

His promise to get back to their earlier conversation returned to her, and she almost smiled. She was looking forward to that talk.

She took his bundle of clothes from him and tucked them under her arm. The shirt and jeans smelled like him. If they weren't in a hurry, she'd probably embarrass herself by putting the material up to her face for a good sniff. Before she could do something so mortifying, though, Erin chuffed loudly, getting all their attention. Lakshmi realized instantly the fight was moving their way.

"Come on," she motioned the others into the trees. "Head north and east, around the fighting." She snatched up Isabella's clothing as well before following the others.

They all set off at a loping run, moving at shifter speeds. The trees blurred. She was so thrilled to be free, to be able to run that as soon as she could, Lakshmi wanted to go tiger. Her muscles, her lungs, her bones needed the release.

She was so caught up in the speed and focus it took to race so fast through an unfamiliar forest, she almost missed when the fighting shifted again, moving toward them. The closer they got to the other tigers, the stronger the scents of musk, anger, and blood. Angry hisses and chuffing sounds traveled on the cool breeze. Everything else in the forest was quiet. From the sounds and smells, most of the local wildlife had scattered, escaping the violence that was a tiger battle.

With her attention turned toward the fighting to the east of them, she nearly missed Erin's sudden stop. Skidding to a halt at Erin's side, Lakshmi faced the forest in front of them.

A huge crash sounded from just ahead, the ground shook, and then a roar echoed so full of anger Lakshmi could feel it as much as hear it. The scream of a wounded animal rent the air.

Isabella's head came up and before anyone could stop her, she took off in the direction of the roar.

"Isabella!" Lakshmi raced after her without thought. The girl had no idea what she might be running into.

In her peripheral vision, she realized Ryan was keeping pace with her, a silent, deadly presence in his tiger form.

They burst into a clearing two steps behind Isabella. The young girl raced toward a whirling blur of tiger fur, three tigers in a deadly battle.

"That's Alexis," Lakshmi said, before charging forward to help.

Not that they needed to. Alexis, in her huge Amur tiger form, roared loud enough to make the leaves tremble and tossed the two attacking tigers around like rag dolls. In fact, one of the males didn't even look to be moving as Alexis picked him up in her huge teeth and threw him into a tree. There were two more tigers, bleeding and unmoving, at the edges of the clearing. And not far from one, what looked to be the body parts of a human.

Lakshmi scanned the area, looking for more wounded, and spotted a man under a fallen spruce. She had to look twice before she realized it was Victor Romanov, Alexis' husband and Isabella's father. She started for the wounded man, but swung back when she realized Isabella was working her way into the middle of her mother's fight.

She grabbed the young woman by the scruff around her neck before she jumped between her mother and one of the fumbling males, then shouted, "Alexis! We have Isabella."

The tiger looked up, her eyes glowing yellow, her mouth covered in blood. She spotted her daughter and in a blink was at her side, bumping her head against the young tigress' shoulder.

"She's not hurt," Lakshmi said, though she was sure Alexis could tell that already. But the former Tracker looked so crazed, Lakshmi wasn't entirely sure she was thinking with any of her human logic at the moment.

The one male still conscious after fighting Alexis tried to slink into the trees. Ryan jumped in front of him and shook his head.

"Don't run," Lakshmi called to the male attempting escape. "You'll only provoke her to kill you."

The male collapsed in a heap of orange and white fur and panted, his tongue hanging out of the side of his mouth.

Alexis nuzzled her daughter, the two making quiet grumbling noises—the equivalent of a tiger purr—and the stench of rage eased from Alexis' scent. But when Alexis looked away from her daughter, she caught sight of Ryan's tiger standing a few feet from Victor. Alexis charged again, so fast Lakshmi almost missed it.

Acting on pure instinct, she raced to stand between a crouched and growling Alexis and Ryan who'd dropped onto his stomach in a passive pose designed to placate the angry mother.

"Don't, Alexis," Lakshmi said. "He helped us. He helped Isabella."

Alexis launched past her, going for Ryan anyway, her mouth open, her sharp teeth dripping blood from the earlier fights.

Lakshmi dove onto Alexis' back, rolling the tiger away from Ryan. They stopped with Alexis crouched over Lakshmi. Alexis snapped her jaw at Lakshmi's face and Lakshmi only barely avoided the strike, holding onto Alexis' neck ruff in an attempt to keep her out of range of a killing lunge.

"Alexis," she shouted. "Enough. Ryan helped us."

A moment later Isabella was there with her mouth on her mother's neck, holding without pressing her teeth in, a warning to get her mother's attention. Alexis grunted and snapped at her daughter but Isabella held on, shaking her head just a little.

Lakshmi held still, not wanting to provoke Alexis any further, though she didn't let go of her neck ruff, just in case.

Finally, Alexis' muscles relaxed under Lakshmi's grip and she eased off Lakshmi. The angry tiger looked around, nudged her daughter, then sat, her eyes narrowed as Lakshmi rolled to her feet.

Meeting the tiger's stare, Lakshmi said, "Dr. Yin isn't a threat. He helped us. I promise. You don't need to attack him."

Isabella grunted and bumped her mother in the shoulder

with her big head. When Alexis lifted her lips in a near-silent growl in Ryan's direction, both Lakshmi and Isabella stepped between her and Ryan. Lakshmi could hear him shifting back to human form. He was incredibly vulnerable at the moment. And Alexis' anger was still palatable. Lakshmi didn't dare let the former Tracker anywhere near him yet.

Alexis grunted at Isabella. Then swung around and hurried to her husband where he lay under a tree. Isabella followed. Lakshmi released a relieved sigh as her shoulders slumped. But she didn't have time to relax. The other women came trotting into the clearing so she hurried to them to explain the situation. When she looked back toward the tree and Victor, she realized Ryan had finished his shift as was examining Victor. Isabella stood between Ryan and her mother, because Alexis was still growling.

A tight knot formed in the pit of Lakshmi's stomach as she hurried to them.

Alexis bumped the tree with her head a few times, but Ryan waved her off without looking at her. A brave move considering Alexis had just attacked him—and would have killed him if Lakshmi and Isabella hadn't interfered.

"Let me make sure that won't kill him," he said, his focus on his patient.

"How can we help?" Lakshmi asked, coming to his side, collecting the clothes she'd dropped keeping Alexis away from him as she went.

She set the bundle on the ground next to him, so her hands would be free to help if he needed her. Ryan ignored the clothing, his full focus on Victor. Seeing a male she'd met, a man she respected half buried under the dense spruce trunk made her head spin. It was covered in spiraling rows of thick branches, any of which could have easily pierced Victor through. Lakshmi's first instinct matched Alexis'—to get that damned tree off him.

Ryan ran his hands over Victor's side, his touch gentle as he assessed Victor's injuries and studied the ground under him.

"No bleeding," he said, almost to himself. "No visible punctures. Broken ribs, those will heal. Can't tell if there's any internal bleeding, though." He glanced at Alexis, cursed, and looked back at Victor just as the man started to struggle. "Don't. Stay still until I finish."

Lakshmi almost gasped as Ryan's scent filled with command and assurance—a complicated mix that reminded her of white hot metal and pine needles. The scent was strong, and while it was always a part of him, it almost seemed like he'd pushed that smell out stronger, a jolt to make sure his orders were followed.

How the hell did he do that?

"Alexis," he said, "we need help. I need to get him somewhere clean and dry, where I can ensure his injuries heal properly."

Alexis shook her head, her ruff rolling with the sharp movement, her lip lifting in a silent snarl. Isabella, still between her mother and Ryan, nudged her mother in the shoulder, a wordless attempt to calm her.

"He's going to be okay," Ryan said, finally meeting Alexis' gaze, his own expression steady and sure.

And his scent filled with that same reassurance he'd had while helping Lakshmi when she was still drugged.

"But," he added, "I need to get him away from the fighting so it doesn't roll over us. And I need to ensure his ribs heal correctly." Victor struggled again, and Ryan turned on him. "Don't you dare. And no shifting until I tell you. Understand."

Victor subsided. Alexis looked between Victor, Ryan and Isabella. Isabella nudged her mother away and that seemed to be the deciding factor. Alexis padded around to give Victor's nose a small lick then her tiger form blurred as she sped toward the fight.

Now that Lakshmi was reminded of it, she realized the fight was much closer than it had been even a few minutes ago. Ryan was right, they'd be overrun soon.

"Can we lift the tree off him yet?" she asked. "If Gregory's tigers get here while he's still vulnerable…"

She swallowed hard, not able to finish the sentence.

Erin and Isabella took up a position facing the coming fight, crouched and ready to jump into the fray.

Violet, who'd shifted back to her human form for the first time since going tiger last night, crowded with Megan behind Lakshmi, looking to Ryan for their next move.

He stared toward the fighting for several minutes, then glanced at the males Alexis had fought. Lakshmi followed his gaze. The one Ryan had stopped from running was lying on his side, panting heavily, but not moving. The second lay absolutely motionless, and Lakshmi couldn't even see his sides moving with his breathing. There was blood in his fur, a lot of blood. The remaining two tigers weren't moving either, though she wasn't close enough to see if they were alive. Given the human body parts next to them, she doubted it. None of the five young males in that clearing were going to cause any problems.

Only in that moment did something sink into Lakshmi's consciousness—Alexis hadn't been wounded. All the blood painting the clearing belonged to the males.

Ryan looked back at her and nodded to the tiger Lakshmi thought might still be breathing but couldn't tell.

"He's not dead," Ryan said. "Yet. But she would have torn them to bloody shreds if Isabella hadn't intervened."

Lakshmi tried to be bothered by that and couldn't find any sympathy in her. "They deserved to be ripped to shreds," she said, her voice quiet.

Megan grunted in agreement.

Ryan didn't comment. He just looked back at Victor and studied the tree and surroundings.

"Okay," he said finally. "I think it's safe enough to lift the tree's pressure. Lakshmi, can you pull him out as the rest of us lift?"

"Got him." She crouched down near Victor's head, positioning herself so she could slide her arm under his shoulder. She set her other just under his head, ready to move it lower when she could get underneath him. He winced, then looked up and smiled a little at her.

Ryan, Violet, and Megan took up positions around the tree trunk, and Ryan counted to three. The huge spruce wasn't much of a strain for three adult shifters, but they lifted carefully, slowly so as to minimize any disturbance to Victor.

As soon as the tree's weight was off him, Lakshmi wrapped him in a more secure hold and, as gently as possible, slid him to clear ground. Once he was free, the others set the tree down, making sure it was stable and wouldn't roll before walking away.

Ryan hurried to Victor, snatching his clothes up off the ground where Lakshmi had left them and pulling on his jeans before he knelt at Victor's side. After tugging his shirt over his head, Ryan set to reexamining Victor's wounds without the tree in the way.

Victor flinched as Ryan pressed a hand to his ribs, but Victor was conscious so Lakshmi hoped that was a good sign.

"I don't suppose anyone here knows sign language?" Ryan asked without looking up from his patient. "I mean anyone still in human form." He glanced at Isabella. "I don't want you to shift back yet, but I might need you to so he can answer my questions."

Victor was mute, he could hear, but he couldn't speak thanks to an incident in his early childhood. Which meant in order to answer Ryan's questions he either had to write out a response or sign it. And given his condition, Lakshmi was positive he couldn't write.

She adjusted her position to face Victor better. Over her shoulder, she said, "Don't change yet, Isabella. I think I know enough for this to work."

Ryan blinked at her. She shrugged.

"I have a bookkeeper at one of my businesses who's deaf," she said. "She's brilliant with numbers. I couldn't run the place without her. So I learned to sign so we could talk." She frowned a little, and faced Victor. "Unfortunately, most of what I know is business centered, so I'm not sure I'll understand everything."

Victor nodded once in understanding, his face pinched from the pain.

"Can you move your hands enough to sign?" she asked.

With one hand, he signed, *"Yes."*

But she could see moving his other arm would hurt him.

"That's the side where his ribs are broken," Ryan said. "And already healing. Damn tiger speed."

"I thought our healing speed was a good thing," she said. She thought of her own broken ankle, the pain of that injury before it had fully healed, and her sympathy for Victor tripled.

"It is," Ryan said. "It'll save his life. If he was a human he'd have been crushed beyond repair. But our healing doesn't always happen in the right order to make sure everything goes back the way it should."

Ryan proceeded to ask a series of questions and Lakshmi did her best to translate Victor's answers. While they went through the exam, Isabella settled on her stomach near her father's head, not quite touching him but close enough that she could lean in and nudge her head against his. He glanced back at her a few times and smiled wanly, signing reassurances.

Violet replaced Isabella next to Erin to guard the group, while Megan hovered a few feet away, her gaze moving between Ryan and the approaching fight.

"They'll be here soon," she said, and there was a growl in her voice.

Lakshmi exchanged a look with Ryan.

"You stay with him," she said. "Protect him if they get near. We'll take care of keeping the fight away from you two."

"You're sure?" he asked, frowning.

She smiled, just a little. The crease between his brows was adorable, and the fact that she was noticing it at such an inappropriate time made her wince inwardly.

"We've got this," she said. "Alexis trained us, remember."

At that he dipped his head in acknowledgement. Victor started to lift up, but Isabella put a gentle paw on his chest even as Ryan shook his head.

"Stay where you are," Ryan said. "I might have to re-break those ribs as it is. You start trying to move and fight, you'll do more damage than good."

Victor snarled silently and looked up at Isabella, signing, *"Stay close. Your mother will lose what's left of her mind if you get hurt. So will I."*

Isabella let out a low rumbling sound, the equivalent of a tiger purr, and scooted closer to her father. Victor ran a hand through her ruff before pulling his arm close again with a wince.

Ryan cursed under his breath.

Lakshmi put a hand on his arm and leaned close. "In case things go crazy." She rolled her eyes. "Crazier. I wanted to say thank you. For everything."

"You're not safe yet."

"You kept us alive, and we'll be safe now. Thank you." She stared at his beautiful brown eyes, the compassion and strength there touching her heart.

Without thought, she leaned closer and kissed him, just a brief brushing of lips. Her reaction to that light contact surprised a gasp from her. Electricity, sizzle, power…rightness.

She pulled back to stare at him again. Had he felt that? Did he realize what had just happened?

He cupped her cheek. "Don't get dead."

She nodded, resisting the urge to kiss him again, and went to join the other three women, now arrayed in a half circle to protect Victor, Isabella and Ryan. She'd barely settled herself when she caught the first combatants coming into view.

CHAPTER FOURTEEN

The minute the young male in his tiger form hit her, Lakshmi regretted being in her human form. But there hadn't been enough time to shift before the moving battle reached them. She could fight this way. It was just so much easier in the heavy, muscular cat body.

She fell backward with the attack, rolling onto her back and bringing her hands up to the large male's shoulders to both keep his mouth from her throat and to give her a hand hold. The momentum helped her lift her feet up under him, the motion almost effortless, giving her the perfect position to brace her feet against her attacker's stomach.

She flipped the male over her head and behind her as she finished the roll and popped back up to her feet, whirling to face the fallen tiger. It all happened so smoothly she was a little surprised. She'd practiced these moves for years, but it was a thrill knowing all that training had prepared her so well for a fight she'd never expected to have.

The male she'd thrown growled as he hopped up to his paws, shaking off her blow and charging her in a blink.

She was ready, spinning aside and kicking him in his shoulder in a single fluid move. The kick sent him in a different direction from his attack and he hit a nearby tree hard. He dropped to the ground under it, still for a moment, and then he was on his feet again, blinking against the breath-stealing impact, but not ready to call off his attack.

Before he could charge again, though, Isabella in tiger form plowed into his side, sending them both tumbling into the center of the clearing just as another tiger lunged toward Lakshmi.

Lakshmi tossed this one over her head, remaining on her feet this time but squatting low to use his momentum against him. And then the clearing was full of roaring, spitting, hissing, cursing bodies. Lakshmi did all she could to keep all those bodies away from Ryan.

In the midst of the chaos, she found herself back to back with Erin, still in tiger form, as they fought three males who had gotten entirely too close to the wounded Victor. She worked well with Erin, as if they'd fought as partners for years.

She was pretty sure she tossed a Tracker or two about as well when they got in the way or too near the people she was protecting, but those males never turned on her or the other females, so she didn't think they took offense.

She spotted Alexis cutting a swath through the fight and

charged in that direction, helping to clear the path for her and three men as they rushed toward Victor.

The fighting shifted directions, pushed she was sure by the Trackers, and Lakshmi let it. Megan and Erin stayed with the fight longer than Lakshmi, overwhelming any male stupid enough to attack them. Despite the fact that Megan couldn't sense her tiger, she fought like a wild animal in pain—vicious and bloody.

Lakshmi continued to guard Ryan and the others, knocking away the occasional pair of fighters, but the bulk of the battle moved away from them. Once most of the fighting was out of sight, Megan and Erin rejoined Lakshmi.

Lakshmi turned to see the three new males—all in human form, though without clothes so obviously they'd been fighting as tigers—hovering around Victor as Ryan gave orders.

"The helicopter will meet us a mile from here," one man said as another, the largest of the three newcomers, bent to gently lift Victor.

Victor winced a little.

"Sorry," the man said.

Victor shook his head, waving off the apology.

Lakshmi noticed the three newcomers bore a familial resemblance. And with that recognition, she realized who they were—the infamous Chernikov brothers. Elizaveta Chernikova's grandsons, practically brothers to Alexis. The Chernikov boys were only infamous because of their mother's suicide and their father's crimes against humans, and their relationship to an elder. As far as Lakshmi knew, the three men had never been accused of any crimes themselves. But most of the tiger community considered them *damaged* because of their parents' sad history.

Lakshmi had only seen them in passing, once or twice at the elders' West Virginia compound. She knew them mostly by reputation. She wasn't even sure which was which, though she had some vague memory that the largest one, the one holding Victor, was the middle son, Dmitry.

They were all handsome males, with varying shades of light brown hair and light colored eyes, their Russian ancestry apparent in their sharp features. Under normal circumstances, they'd have been welcome at any female's Mate Run, and probably would have mated years ago.

But more than one female had warned her off accepting any of the men into her Run. Last she heard, they'd all stopped trying for a tiger mate.

Except some recent rumors reminded her that one of them—the youngest, Mikhail—was involved with the first human hybrid brought before the community. And the oldest, Nikolai, had somehow ended up mated to a tiger female.

Alexis didn't talk about her family much during her self-defense training classes, but Lakshmi couldn't help her curiosity now that she was face-to-face with the infamous brothers. What kind of female would take on that kind of challenge—knowing they would face difficulties within the community because of their choices? Well, the human hybrid probably didn't care. What was her name again? Nila something? But the tiger female…she would understand what being mated to a Chernikov meant.

Lakshmi caught Ryan's gaze, wondering if he knew the brothers at all. She noticed he seemed…uncomfortable, and she couldn't quite put her finger on how she knew that. There was nothing in his scent, nothing in his tone of voice or gestures. But she still got the feeling he wasn't entirely at ease around the Chernikovs.

Something to worry about once they were safe.

Ryan nodded to Alexis, and the huge Amur led the way over the uneven forest floor, the three brothers, carrying Victor, behind her. Ryan stayed close to the Chernikov carrying Victor, talking quietly as they moved. She caught some of it, mostly assurances that he'd be okay, a few detailed explanations of what had to be done once they reached safety. He was in his full doctor mode and she smiled a little as she listened to him. His voice was so reassuring, so full of confidence, it was hard not to feel reassured and confident.

She and the other women took up the rear of the group, guarding their backs as they moved eastward, away from the fight, which from the sounds was starting to wind down. She wasn't sure who was winning, impossible to tell at this stage, but given the fact that they were left to make their way to safety, she had to guess the elders' army was the group on top.

The sound of a helicopter's engines reached her well before they cleared the tree line. The smell of fuel and hot metal mixed oddly with the fresh scents of the forest. Since that helicopter represented freedom and safety, she decided she liked the mix, even if it was a little discordant.

They came out of the thick trees into an open, grassy

meadow, dotted with multi-colored wildflowers. The sun was almost too bright, the sky blue and cloudless. If not for the helicopter—and the now distant sounds of fighting—she would have found the setting idyllic. The kind of place she'd like to let her tiger out to run.

As they made their way to the noisy copter, leaning into the wind its blades created, she hunted for a clue to their location. She still had no idea where they were. And her surroundings didn't help. This could be any forest, any meadow, anywhere in the world for all she could tell. The air tasted clean so likely not a wooded area too near a major metropolis. And the spruce trees made her think of the northern and north western forests in the US, maybe in the Rockies?

As they ducked low coming up to the back of the helicopter, she turned her focus toward their escape vehicle. The helicopter was huge, one of those military transport kinds she'd only seen in movies. It's tannish-green color blended with the forest setting, but the smell of it, the sounds of the whirring blades on the top as well as on the huge tail, and the drone of the motor would never have kept it concealed from a tiger shifter. The thing was so huge, it could have easily accommodated four or five times their numbers.

"How many Trackers did that bring here?" she asked no one in particular.

A rear ramp lowered to allow them inside. They all climbed into the huge cargo bay, and Lakshmi had her first moment of trepidation. She'd never flown in a helicopter before. Airplanes, yes. Helicopters, no. And this beast had a big, echoing bay that felt more like an aircraft hangar than something that should fly.

Alexis led the group to a row of benches lining one wall of the bay. Boxes lined the wall opposite them, presumably with equipment of some kind, though Lakshmi couldn't guess what.

Part of the answer came a moment later. As the rear ramp closed, one of the Chernikov brothers opened a side door in one of the larger boxes and pulled out an orange, padded transportation stretcher. He positioned it near the bench and strapped it down with clip hooks attached to thick straps locking into metal loops on the floor. He pushed at it a few times to ensure it was stable, then the brother carrying Victor knelt and gently placed the injured man in the stretcher. While they strapped him in under Ryan's supervision, Alexis went forward to the cockpit. And then the helicopter lifted off.

Lakshmi's stomach dropped as they rose. She swallowed hard and gripped the edge of the bench. Isabella and Erin laid tummy down on the metal floor of the bay, wedging themselves against the benches. Megan and Violet sat to one side of Lakshmi. Megan seemed blank, neither bothered by the helicopter nor particularly excited by the ride. Violet looked as green as Lakshmi felt. One of the Chernikovs handed Violet a blanket, and another set a pile of clothes at her feet. Violet gave them a woozy half-smile and wrapped the blanket around her bare shoulders.

"Don't worry," the brother who'd handed Violet the blanket said. "We don't have far to go. Just over the boarder to a private hanger where the doctor can help Victor."

"Border to where?" Lakshmi asked, startled. She'd just assumed they were still in the US.

"Canada," the tallest Chernikov said. "Elizaveta got special permission to fly the army in and recover you all. She has friends in the Canadian military." He smiled before returning to Victor's side, settling on the bay floor next to the stretcher.

As the Chernikov brothers settled around Victor, Ryan moved to sit next to Lakshmi. "You doing okay?" he asked quietly.

"Better once we land," she said.

He smiled crookedly, and Lakshmi forgot she was scared. A slight sound caught her attention and she looked toward the cockpit to see Alexis shifting back to her human form.

Lakshmi turned back to Ryan, and for the first time it really sank in that they were safe. She blinked a few times and her shoulders relaxed even as tears stung her eyes.

"So we'll be going home soon," she said, half to herself, half to him.

"You're safe now. You'll be back with your families within twenty-four hours."

"It's…strange."

"Strange?" He frowned.

She waved a hand, not sure how to explain. "It just feels…weird. To have been so stressed and worried and afraid for days and suddenly, it's just…over. We're safe. We're with people who will help us." She shrugged. "If

Victor weren't hurt, I'd want to dance. And maybe pass out." She laughed. "Good thing you're a doctor."

He gripped her hand.

The contact had been meant to reassure her, she was sure. The reassurance and comfort were strong in his scent —like warm blankets fresh from a dryer. But the physical contact did more to her than comfort. A shock of awareness, of that same sort of knowing she'd had when she'd kissed him, washed over her.

Another realization hit her then. Soon, she'd have to say goodbye to Ryan. Maybe forever.

Her tiger objected instantly. Loudly in her head. All Lakshmi could do was stare at him as this new knowing swept through her.

He was her mate. He was *hers*.

When the hell had that happened?

CHAPTER FIFTEEN

The minute the helicopter settled, the back ramp lowered. Bright sunshine flooded the huge bay, and Lakshmi had to blink while her eyes adjusted to the change in lighting. The small porthole windows in the bay had let in some light, but the interior had still been dim…and calming. At the bottom of the ramp she spotted the stretch of gray tarmac that was the landing pad, and the scents of warm concrete, metal, airplane fuel, mountain grasses, and fir and spruce trees blew in on a cool wind.

The Chernikov brothers—now dressed—gently lifted the stretcher and carried Victor off the helicopter. Victor rolled his eyes at them and tugged at the straps holding him in place.

"Stay put," Ryan said, walking alongside the stretcher. "You might feel better, but there's still a real danger if you had any internal bleeding or if your ribs have healed awkwardly."

Victor settled, not looking particularly happy about it.

Alexis smiled at him, though he didn't see it, and Lakshmi smiled at that. Obviously, Alexis wasn't nearly as worried about her husband anymore.

Isabella stayed near her mother and father, though she remained in tiger form. Lakshmi and the other four women followed, making their way slowly down the ramp and out into the open air.

Lakshmi breathed in deeply when her feet touched the tarmac. She was safe. She was free. She could leave. Now if she wanted. Make her way home. Shift and run the whole way if she wanted.

She glanced across the barren tarmac to a huge, tan, metal hangar a few hundred yards away. The building had a rounded roof, a huge set of doors taking up one full edge, and a bay large enough to hold several small private jets and smaller helicopters. From her vantage, she could see the long side of the building had a few people-sized doors, but the main bay doors were wide open, and that was the direction everyone was headed.

She stared at Ryan's back as he disappeared inside with the stretcher, directed by Alexis to an interior door Lakshmi assumed went to a smaller room or office. Her tiger pulled her in the direction of the hangar, toward Ryan. Her mate.

He couldn't be her mate, though. He wouldn't run. And according to tiger law, she couldn't take a mate outside the Run.

If Gregory hadn't kidnapped her, Lakshmi probably would never have met Ryan. And even if she had met him in passing at the elders' compound, since he didn't run, they'd have never had a chance at being mates.

But now… Now, there was no point to her running anymore. He was hers.

Her estrous was only two days away. She might be able to beg off this Run because of what she'd just lived through. But she'd be expected to run at her next estrous. Which meant she had to somehow convince Ryan to join her, convince the elders to let him participate in a Mate Run so far from his own territory.

No mean feat.

Following the other women as they slowly made their way to the hangar, she pulled in another deep breath of fresh air, tainted with chemicals and metal from the small airstrip, and contemplated her future. When she finally stepped into the cool, shaded building interior, Alexis and one of the Chernikov men had set out some chairs for the group against one of the metal walls. Although there were two small jets inside the hangar, the place seemed abandoned.

"Are there any humans here?" Lakshmi asked as she sat next to Alexis. She couldn't smell any, but inside, the scents from the plane engines were strong enough to confuse her senses.

Alexis nodded back outside. "There are two controllers in a tower at the end of the runway, but this is a quiet, private strip. Elizaveta is friends with the owner of one of those planes and got permission to use the site."

"Good thing Elizaveta has so many friends."

Alexis smiled a little at that. This close, Lakshmi saw

the creases around her eyes and the strain in her jaw. She realized, despite her attempt to look otherwise, Alexis *was* still worried about Victor.

Lakshmi took her hand and squeezed. "He'll be fine. Ryan is a good doctor."

Alexis looked at her, her head tilted to one side. "How well do you know Ryan Yin?"

"Just what I know of him from the last few days. I know he's Sarah Chu's brother. I know he's been very gentle with us and helped us all recover from the drug Gregory gave us. I know he tried to protect us when things got…bad. And from the beginning, he was looking for a way to help us escape."

Megan, sitting on the hard concrete floor a few feet away, looked up from contemplating a crack in the blue paint. "He made Gregory stop giving us the drug," she said. "He probably saved my life by doing that."

Alexis frowned at her. "Tell me everything that happened."

Isabella bumped against her mother, on the side opposite Lakshmi, and settled on her haunches while Alexis rested a gentle hand on her shoulder. Erin hadn't bothered to shift back to human form yet either. Megan and Violet both looked to Lakshmi.

With Megan and Violet filling in their personal experiences, Lakshmi told Alexis everything she knew. She skimmed over the details of her attack because Isabella was listening, but she did tell Alexis everything about the confrontation they'd had with Gregory—was that just last night?

Megan explained how the other female she'd been kidnapped with, Anna, had been killed by the drug before they'd even reached Gregory's compound.

"We were the first ones taken," Megan said, "and Gregory didn't know how to use the drug. He gave us both too much."

"You and Anna," Alexis said, her brow creased, "you've been missing for almost a month. There was another tigress taken—she was killed by the human serial killer, the man who gave Gregory the drug."

"Gregory gave one of our females to that monster?" Violet said, her voice faint.

Lakshmi's stomach heaved with disgust. How could a tiger male hand over one of the very few remaining females to a killer? It was just inconceivable. She saw her own disbelief reflected in Violet's expression. Megan didn't look at all surprised.

Alexis' fingers flexed in her daughter's fur. "Don't worry, though. The human murderer is dead. Finally."

Lakshmi leaned back in the metal fold-out chair and blinked at nothing. The serial killer that had killed Su-jin, the creator of the drug that was responsible for their kidnapping, the human male they'd all been avoiding for almost eleven years…was finally dead.

Silence stretched for long minutes. Then Violet said, "At least that's one less thing we have to worry about."

Megan snorted an almost laugh.

Lakshmi let out a long, slow breath. So much had happened. So much. She just wasn't sure she could process it all. Not yet. It was going to take her months to work through her emotions and how she felt about all this.

She shook off the complex confusion when Alexis spoke again.

"There's five of you here," Alexis said. "One we know was killed by Gregory, and one killed by the serial killer. Seven women. Do any of you know what's happened to the eighth?"

"The eighth?" Lakshmi sat forward again, staring at Alexis.

"Eight females have gone missing in total." She looked at them all, including her daughter. "You haven't heard of anyone else?"

"No," Lakshmi said.

"I was in a cage up until yesterday," Megan said, "but the guards talked around me before that. They didn't think I understood." She swallowed visibly. "I was pretty far gone."

Erin scooted closer to Megan, nudging her with her large tiger head. Lakshmi knew she was trying to comfort the other woman, but unless something had changed in the last few hours, Megan still couldn't feel her tiger. Erin's comfort might be a too-painful reminder of what Megan had lost.

"Did they mention more tigresses?" Alexis asked.

"Yes, but never in numbers. I knew there were others. Not how many."

Alexis stared at one of the small airplanes in the hanger, not speaking for long moments. Lakshmi could practically see her mind working through all the possibilities and options.

Finally, Alexis pulled in a deep breath and blinked, refocusing on their group. "We'll question Gregory when he's brought before the elders. We'll find the other female."

To Lakshmi, Alexis sounded more confident than her scent revealed. There was worry and unease, like the faint hint of bitter fruit just under the surface. A worry that made Lakshmi's stomach tight.

She tried not to think too much about it. The elders would fix things, get the other female back, or at least find her. Everything would work out. But…

"Has Gregory been taken captive then?" she asked, realizing she didn't know and wasn't sure even Alexis would know at this stage. "He's so crazy, I thought for sure he'd go down fighting."

"We'll find out soon," Alexis said. She nodded outside the hangar.

The helicopter was winding up, its huge top blade and smaller tail blade thumping faster and faster as the engines rumbled to full life.

"They'll collect whoever is left," Alexis said. "Then come back here to collect us." She looked at the women around her. "Your families are waiting at the elders' compound for you. We'll all head there first. You'll be questioned. Sorry about that, but it'll be necessary. Then you'll be free to return to your lives."

"Is the elders' compound a good idea?" Lakshmi asked. She looked between Isabella and Alexis. "You had reason not to bring Isabella there. And…we were talking… It came up that, if an elder was helping Gregory…" She was almost afraid to say this out loud. Especially to Alexis whose adopted mother *was* an elder. But she knew Alexis and Victor had been worried enough to keep Isabella away from the compound. "Is the compound going to be safe for us?" she finally said.

A long moment passed in silence. Then Alexis met Lakshmi's gaze. "For the moment, the compound will be safe because your families are there, and after the uproar of your kidnapping, you'll be watched closely. I have no evidence that there are still traitors in the compound. We were being overly cautious with Isabella." She cursed under her breath. "And that didn't work out so well."

Isabella rumbled a soft crooning noise, an attempt to comfort her mother.

Alexis smiled slightly. "At any rate, for the moment, the compound is perfectly safe for you because there is too much attention focused on the situation to allow for anything bad to happen." She looked at them all. "But just in case, stick close to your families or friends you trust while there."

Lakshmi glanced at Megan. "We might need some… counseling," she said quietly. "And more medical help."

Megan didn't meet Lakshmi's gaze, but her shoulders stiffened, just a little.

"We'll ensure you have everything you need," Alexis said.

"And after we leave?" Violet asked. "Will we be any safer then?"

"As safe as you've ever been," Alexis said.

Lakshmi wasn't entirely reassured by that, wasn't even sure Alexis had meant it to be reassuring. Lakshmi had assumed she was safe all these years, but she hadn't been, not really. Did that mean she'd have to be on guard for the rest of her life?

Silence descended as they waited for Ryan.

The room behind them was quiet. All three brothers were in there with Victor and Ryan. Lakshmi kept glancing at the door, wondering if Ryan was okay. She hadn't been able to discern from any of their scents how they felt about the doctor, but Ryan had been aligned with Gregory's young males before this. Did they see him as a friend or the enemy?

Worry over Ryan, and how she might convince him he was her mate, kept her from thinking too much about the rest of the situation, so she focused on that. It was enough of a problem that she lost track of time, so when the door to the room behind them opened, she jolted in surprise.

The Chernikov brothers emerged first, followed by Ryan who was wiping his wet hands dry on a clean white towel. Lakshmi could smell the soap he'd used. It added a deliciously clean element to his tangy scent signature.

He immediately looked for her, smiling when their eyes met, and her heartbeat thumped hard in her chest. She felt both silly and happy all at once. She was probably too old for this giddy reaction to a man, but at the same time, it was so lovely to finally feel what her mother must have felt when she'd met Lakshmi's father.

His smile changed but didn't drop away when he

looked at Alexis and Isabella. "He'll be fine," he told them. "Strong bastard."

That he muttered quietly and Alexis barked a laugh in response.

"Fortunately, there was no internal bleeding," Ryan continued. "But three of his ribs had already knitted crooked and were compressing his lungs. I got them reset. He'll be healed up properly soon. I've told him not to shift for another three hours. He needs to follow that instruction or he risks causing more damage." Ryan held Alexis' gaze as he said this.

"I'll make sure he doesn't shift yet," she assured him. "Can I go see him?"

"Sure. He's still a little groggy from the anesthesia, but he's awake."

When Alexis, Isabella and the Chernikovs disappeared back into the room, Lakshmi joined Ryan, who was scowling at the towel in his hands.

He looked up and gave her a rueful half-smile. "I forgot how hard it is to operate on tigers. We heal too damned fast and even local anesthesia wears off too quickly. I can't remember the last time I moved at that speed during surgery."

"If you did that at the hospital, they'd probably notice you weren't human," she pointed out. A ridiculous comment but she had to say something and now that she knew he was her mate, she felt suddenly…awkward.

He smelled really good. Particularly yummy. She wanted to lean into him, to breathe him in. With her estrous approaching, she knew her scent would be affecting him soon, if not already. Did he notice? Did he realize how much things had changed between them?

He held her gaze a brief moment before looking at the other women. "Are you all okay? Any injuries of your own I should look at?"

"We're good," Violet said. She glanced at Megan who couldn't see the look and said, "Mostly good."

Ryan nodded.

Lakshmi knew he wanted to help Megan more. It was in the tensing in his shoulders and the tightness around his beautiful dark eyes. There was just a tiny thread of it in his scent. She loved how caring he was, how focused on healing. But she realized, now that she could consider something beyond her own situation, she didn't know the man very well. And she wanted to know more. A lot more. Everything there was to know about him.

Instead of anything clever or deep, though, the first thing that came out of her mouth was, "Are you hungry? There's a vending machine…"

"Starved actually," he said. "But I'll take care of it." He smiled, that adorable, brightening of his expression.

"You've been operating." She waved him to her chair. "I'll break into the machine and bring over a selection."

She brushed against him as she passed, because somewhere inside she was a teenager and feeling flirty. She grinned when he sucked in an audible breath. Well that was a good sign.

She stood, staring at the vending machine for a long moment, deciding how to break in, since she didn't have any money on her, without actually damaging the machine too much. It was filled with junk—chips and chocolate bars, a few granola bars that pretended at being health food. She sighed, a deep longing for comfort food filling her. A rajma chawal would be delicious. She could practically taste the beans and spices. Or maybe her mother's roasted chicken or her unbeatable fish tacos. Even some mashed potato stuffed bread pakoras sounded perfect, childhood comfort food at its finest. Followed by one of her father's eclectic dessert concoctions that he served at his fusion restaurant. Her stomach actually growled at the thought.

Behind her, she heard Isabella's voice and turned to see the young woman emerging from her father's operating room, fully dressed, her jaw tight and her eyes narrowed.

"Dad, if you even consider shifting against the doctor's orders, I will never forgive you," she said over her shoulder.

She paused to face her father so he could respond. He signed something Lakshmi couldn't see well enough to interpret, and Isabella's scowl turned murderous. Her father grinned, raising his hands palms out, the universal gesture of surrender.

Alexis shook her head. "You shouldn't tease her like that."

Victor smiled at his wife, then pulled his daughter into his arms for a tight hug, kissing her on her temple.

Lakshmi's heart tightened. She missed her own father. And her mother. A lot.

She still saw her family all the time. Most tiger shifters, once grown, moved into their own homes. Tiger shifters tended to prefer extra space and privacy, so you didn't get extended families living under one roof—even in cultures where that was more common. Families lived close sometimes, though, and Lakshmi had stayed in La Jolla near her parents. Two of her four brothers still lived in San Diego as well. Her family got together regularly for huge meals, gossip, watching sports, and lots of fighting and fun.

This was probably the longest she'd gone in her life without visiting her mother and father. She'd even gone to college close to home so she could drop in for regular visits and her mother's cooking.

Her stomach rumbled again and she sighed. Granola bars and chips would have to do for now.

She was about to simply pull the door off the vending machine to get at the food when she heard the distant *whomp whomp whomp* of the helicopter returning.

That was fast. Everyone in the bay looked toward the landing pad, then Alexis pulled in a deep breath and put her hands on her hips, hanging her head.

After a moment, Alexis looked up and said, "Dr. Ryan Yin, you are officially under confinement orders, by command of the Tiger Shifter Elders Council. You will accompany me to West Virginia where you will face tiger law and the justice of the elders."

CHAPTER SIXTEEN

"No." Lakshmi gasped and crossed the room in a blink to stand in front of Ryan. "You can't arrest him. He saved Victor's life. He saved all our lives. Why are you taking him in?"

The other women moved in front of Ryan, too. Even Isabella pulled out of her father's arms to join them. The group formed a half circle of protection between Ryan and Alexis. Because Lakshmi was so aware of him, she caught the surprise in his scent before it vanished.

Alexis stared at them, her brows slightly raised. But she didn't back down.

"He's been an associate of Gregory's for nine months. Every member of Gregory's group of young tigers is officially being brought in, under confinement orders. I can't make an exception for Dr. Yin."

"But you're not a Tracker anymore," Lakshmi said, desperate. "The others aren't here yet." A statement belied by the sound of the huge helicopter nearing. "He could just leave—"

Lakshmi stopped short when she felt a hand on her shoulder. She turned to face Ryan. He looked at her with that soft half-smile she loved.

"It's okay," he said. "I expected this. In fact, I expected worse." He looked past Lakshmi to Alexis. "I'll go willingly."

"Thank you, doctor," Alexis said.

"Thank you for not killing me in the forest," he said.

She snorted. "Thank Lakshmi and my daughter for that. If not for them, I would have."

He nodded in understanding.

Lakshmi didn't turn away from him. "You didn't do anything wrong," she said. "I won't let the elders punish you. You saved us. All of us."

He touched her cheek, gently, with just the tips of his fingers. Then dropped his hand to his side. There was so much more in his expression than in his scent, a confusion of emotion Lakshmi couldn't interpret without the help of his scent. All she got from that was…acceptance and that same calming aura he gave out when he was dealing with patients.

But there was something under it, something sharp and spicy she just couldn't catch. Not being able to latch onto that elusive flavor was maddening because she was sure she'd understand him better, if she could just…scent what he was feeling.

"I'm glad you're all safe now," he said. "And I'm sorry you had to go through what you did."

"I'll talk to the elders."

"We all will," Isabella said.

"Yes," Violet added. "We won't let them punish you."

The corner of his mouth tilted up in the most charming, melancholy smile Lakshmi had ever seen. And it was all she could do not to kiss him.

But the helicopter was landing, the wind from its huge blades blowing dust into the open hangar. Without looking, she knew their time was up. No more delaying. No more excuses.

No privacy to tell Ryan everything she needed to tell him.

She opened her mouth to say something, but nothing came out and then it was too late.

Six Trackers jogged into the hangar and, at a hand gesture from Alexis, surrounded Ryan, gently forcing the women away from him. He went without argument, just like he'd promised, as the Trackers led him to the helicopter.

"I can't promise he won't receive some punishment for his association with Gregory," Alexis said, "but his actions will speak in his favor."

Lakshmi met her gaze, nibbling on her lower lip as she considered the older woman. "I'll speak for him, too," she said.

The other women agreed. Even Erin, in tiger form, let out a soft rumbling growl of affirmation.

Alexis gestured them all out to the helicopter.

They went, without the enthusiasm Lakshmi would

have expected given they'd be reunited with their families soon. Worry for Ryan wrapped tight around her stomach.

It didn't help that Ryan was kept at the opposite side of the helicopter's cargo bay, sitting amidst fourteen other males—none of whom were Gregory—surrounded by more than thirty Trackers. And he refused to look at her even once, despite her best efforts to catch his gaze.

The nagging sense that he wasn't going to be okay hung over her all the way to West Virginia.

* * *

Ryan sat on the twin-sized bed in his holding cell, staring across the small eight foot by eight foot box at the clear, tiger-proof plexi-screen covering the cell's bars. Three of the four walls were solid brick, painted a cool light green, blank except for a sink and toilet to the left. The plexi-screen had holes drilled into its thick surface, helping air circulate and giving him brief hints of scent beyond the cell. Sound carried easily through those holes, easier than scent, but he didn't need sound to know she was here.

He could feel her approaching, her scent a subtle tease in the air ahead of her. He'd know Lakshmi's scent anywhere, anytime.

Which sucked. A lot.

He didn't move as she came into view, just stared at her, trying to decide if he was happy to see her or angry that she'd come. Seeing her brought too many needs and wants. Wants he wouldn't be allowed to pursue. Not now.

And even though it wasn't her fault, a small part of him resented her for the fact that he now wanted something he could never have.

"I talked to the elders," she said into the growing silence between them. "We all did."

"Thank you."

"You don't want to know what they said?"

"I know."

"Someone's already told you?"

"They made their verdict clear to me earlier."

She looked away. "You shouldn't be punished."

He couldn't help his half-smile. Technically, he was being compensated financially for his "punishment." But no one, not even his family, could know that.

"I appreciate your advocating for me," he said. "You didn't have to."

"Of course we did. You saved our lives."

"I could have done more."

"No. You did all you could."

"How's Megan?" He needed a change of subject. At least a slight change. Something that didn't involve what he did or didn't do at Gregory's compound.

"She's better. She still can't shift, but she doesn't look so haunted since being reunited with her family."

"Can she sense her tiger?"

Lakshmi shook her head and met his gaze again. The sadness there echoed in his heart. He couldn't imagine what Megan was going through right now. Their tiger was so much a part of them, a part of their souls and essences. It was inconceivable, the thought of not being able to access that part of himself.

"Gregory got away," Lakshmi said, another change of subject. "You knew?"

"They told me."

"I hoped he was dead."

So had Ryan. His "punishment" might have been lighter if Gregory had been killed. Because the crazy tiger was still on the loose along with a half dozen of his followers, Ryan had to keep up the appearance of a traitor, and his official punishment had to be severe enough to maintain the illusion of his crimes. To protect his family. And, in some ways, the elders themselves. They couldn't afford to let the community know they'd sent a civilian tiger to spy on other tigers. Tracker spies were one thing. That was an expected part of their job. But an ordinary tiger being used that way… That would just pit the community against itself, and they had enough problems already.

"He won't come after you," he told Lakshmi. "Not now while he's being hunted. The Trackers will catch him, and he'll pay for his crimes against you."

"I'm worried about you, not me."

His brows jumped up at that. What did she know? The elders would hardly tell her the truth.

"Why worry about me?" he asked, cautiously, keeping the confusion from his scent. She would have difficulty parsing out the levels of his scent from outside the bars and plexi-screen, but she would pick up on something as strong as his spike of concern if he wasn't careful.

"Gregory could consider you a traitor to his cause and come after you. You aren't being confined for long."

Not really much at all, actually. A week here before being released. His punishment came in another area. Which wouldn't have bothered him much before meeting Lakshmi. Now…

Now it was a real sacrifice.

"I'll be okay," he said. "There's no reason for him to waste his time on me. He'll be too busy hiding."

"He's insane. You can't predict what he'll do."

Ryan shrugged. That was true enough.

"Are you safe in here? If Gregory had help…" She didn't glance over her shoulder at the cameras focused on his cell, but she nodded toward them subtly.

He knew what she meant without her having to say it aloud. He was vulnerable inside this cell, if anyone wanted to get at him here. But since there were cameras on him at all times, guards at the entrance to the holding area, and he was confined to this small cell in isolation, he figured he was safe enough. Especially since his family visited regularly.

"I'll be fine."

They were silent for a moment. Then Lakshmi said, "They told me you were banned from the Mate Run."

She held his gaze as she spoke, but her shoulders were stiff and her hands flexed and unflexed at her sides. In her scent was something he tried very hard to ignore.

He attempted to affect nonchalance about the punishment. "I never intended to run anyway. You know how I feel about it."

"But...now..."

He swallowed hard, because he could scent what she meant. She didn't have to say it. She wasn't hiding her feelings from him. And it was driving him crazy, knowing she wanted him.

"I'm surprised they're letting you talk to me," he said instead of acknowledging the tension between them.

"Special circumstances."

"You skipped this Run." He didn't need to ask. He knew because she was in the second day of her estrous and still here at the compound.

The added spice in her scent was beyond delicious, a flavor any male tiger found hard to resist. With Lakshmi, it was all he could do to stay on the bed. But it was necessary to keep his distance. He couldn't have her, and there was no point pretending otherwise. She'd only get hurt.

The thought that she'd be running at her next cycle, taking another male, fucking him for days in the hopes of getting pregnant, made his vision cloud as blood roared through his head. His tiger wanted to rip the unknown male to pieces. That flash of anger and jealousy was so beyond anything Ryan had ever experienced, it took everything he had to stay still and not show her his reaction.

He had to let her go. She wasn't allowed to choose a male outside the Run, and he was officially banned from the Run. There was no option of a future for them.

He didn't want to compete in a Run for her anyway. He wanted her. There was no denying it. But he only hated the Mate Run more now that he wanted a tiger female. The entire institution sucked, the rules sucked. That wasn't how he wanted to form a relationship with a woman. Even Lakshmi.

Maybe especially Lakshmi. Because what he wanted from her was…

More.

She finally spoke into the silence that had grown between them. "They'll expect me to run at my next cycle, but given what we went through, everyone assumed we'd all be a little…off the idea of mating right now. None of us are running this cycle."

There was a slight tremor in her voice that broke his heart. "Have you talked to someone? A counselor?"

She nodded, her half-smile doing nothing to hide her pain. "Though, I think I'd feel better if I could kick Gregory's ass."

He snorted. "Yeah, I wouldn't mind beating him to a pulp, too."

She grinned, her first smile, and it made his pulse speed up. Unfortunately, it also drew his gaze to her lips, and for a moment, he couldn't think about anything but how full and soft they looked, how utterly kissable.

She pulled in a deep breath, and he knew he'd given himself away. He was pretty sure he'd done that already, though. She had to realize he wanted her, even if he could keep it mostly out of his scent.

Quietly, so quietly he could barely hear her—and he was sure the camera over her shoulder wouldn't pick up the sound—she said, "It's not fair that you can't run."

He didn't know what to say to that.

"It's not fair," she said again, her voice just a little louder.

"Life generally isn't fair."

"You want me," she said.

So blunt and so true he could only stare at her. There was no point in denying it, but to admit it would be to cross a line he shouldn't cross.

"I want you," she said.

He shuddered at hearing her speak the words aloud. He closed his eyes briefly, as his tiger soaked in the shear perfection of knowing she wanted him as much as he wanted her.

"You saved my life."

"I didn't." He opened his eyes to look at her. "Is that the only reason you want me? It happens a lot between doctors and patients."

Her expression turned stormy and her scent filled with anger, like a forest fire.

"I have *not* fixated on you because you functioned as my doctor."

"It was…a difficult situation. Don't discount the reaction."

"Stop it," she growled.

He heard her tiger in her voice and almost smiled.

"You're trying to piss me off. It won't work."

"It has worked. You're pissed."

She scowled. "Fine. You pissed me off. But it's not going to send me away."

"Lakshmi…"

"Don't. You're mine."

His entire body tightened at the declaration, then exploded with heat. His breathing sped and his pulse hammered in his veins.

"I don't know how to make things work yet. But I'm not letting you go because of some stupid ruling by the elders."

"Don't let them hear you say that," he warned, his voice low as he nodded to the camera behind her.

"I don't care if they hear. You're mine."

"Please stop saying that."

"No. It's true. And you know it. I know you know it."

He didn't answer, but he didn't look away from her either.

"You and I are meant to be together."

"I don't believe in fated mates. Not among our kind anyway."

"I don't care if you believe or not. My tiger has claimed you. I claim you. You are mine."

Damn her, he was. She was his and he was hers. And there was no way he could consider another woman now. He wasn't even sure how it had happened. Or when. But his tiger agreed wholeheartedly with everything she said.

Despite that, he had to try convincing her to move on. "You have to run at your next cycle. You'll have to choose another male." He clenched his jaw to keep from snarling at the idea.

"No."

Said simply. With no embellishments. She straightened her shoulders, put her hands on her hips, and tilted her chin slightly up.

She was magnificent. Powerful and primal and so awesomely female she took his breath away.

It wouldn't work. They both knew it *couldn't* work. But in that moment, with her looking so fierce and beautiful, he wanted to believe she could conquer anything, overcome even the elders.

He wanted to believe they could be together.

Looking at her made his chest ache painfully. He turned to stare at the floor.

"You should probably go," he said without facing her. "They'll separate us soon anyway."

"I'm only going because I need to talk to some people," she said, her voice steely. "But just so you know, Ryan Yin, this is not over."

He looked up in time to see her whirl away and stalk out of the holding cells area, all beautiful curves and fierce determination. He stared at the place she'd been for a long time after she left, letting the remains of her scent fill his head, wishing for the impossible.

Lakshmi waited until she was well out of the holding area before letting her angry tears fall. Wet drops plopped onto her cheeks and she swiped them away with a snarl. It wasn't fair. Ryan was hers and she would have him. Not even the elders could stop her.

She hunted through the compound until she found Alexis in one of the dining rooms, quietly sharing a meal with Isabella. When Lakshmi joined them, Isabella popped out of her chair to give Lakshmi a hug.

"How are you doing? Is Ryan okay?" Isabella asked as she sat across the large oak table from her mother.

Lakshmi settled into the chair next to her. "He seems okay. Resigned to his fate. I'm furious. How are you?"

"A little better now." She motioned to the full plate in front of her and the empty one next to it. "Apparently, I handle stress by eating." She grinned, and her mother barked a short laugh.

"My mother has already fed me at least three of my favorite comfort meals and my father has taken over a section of the kitchen for making me my favorite sweet treats." Lakshmi smiled, glad the lighter conversation mitigated her anger a little. She knew talking to Alexis was a risk, but of all the women Lakshmi knew, Alexis would understand Lakshmi's position.

She faced Isabella's mother, studying the older woman. "I need some advice."

Alexis sat back in the cushioned, wooden chair and studied Lakshmi, her blue eyes unreadable, her scent blank —the kind of blank that the elders and their assistants used to keep their thoughts to themselves. Different from whatever it was Ryan could do, but still frustrating.

"You want to know," Alexis said, "how to get around the elders' ruling that bans Dr. Yin from the Mate Run."

"He's my mate," Lakshmi said, tilting her chin up.

"I can't change their minds, if that's what you're asking." Alexis glanced at Isabella. "I tried. Because my daughter asked it of me."

A small sliver of jealousy poked Lakshmi as she faced Isabella.

Isabella blushed. "I knew you two were meant for each other the first time I saw you together. If he can't run, you can't be together. You deserve each other."

"Isabella…" Lakshmi squeezed her forearm, not sure how to respond to that. Lakshmi hadn't realized the other women knew she had feelings for Ryan. It was both humbling and a relief.

She faced Alexis. "There has to be a way. He's mine. Victor was banned, and you two still ended up together."

"And only just stopped paying off the fine the elders imposed a few years ago," she said. "The punishment would have been worse, too, except that the elders themselves forced our hands."

"They're forcing my hand now. I have money. I can pay a fine. And if I don't have enough now, I'll make more money and pay them off when I can."

Alexis smiled. "I figured you'd say that, so I talked, quietly, to Elizaveta."

"And?"

"She says since my day, the elders have gotten more 'pig-headed,' her word, about compliance with the Mate Run rules. With the introduction of the hybrids, who don't have to—or can't—run, and the realization that the world is changing but our extinction problem hasn't, there's a lot of…debate."

Lakshmi groaned and rolled her eyes. "Not elder debates! I'll be as old as an elder myself before they solve anything."

Isabella snorted a laugh.

"Chances are good," Alexis continued, "that if you're caught breaking the Run rules now, Ryan would be placed in long-term confinement and you'd be…"

"What? What?"

"You'd have a mate selected for you."

"What?" Lakshmi screeched. "After what I've just been through, you're telling me the elders themselves would force me to mate with someone?"

"Not physically. Artificial insemination."

"No!"

"I agree with you," Alexis said, surprising Lakshmi into silence. "The Mate Run has…for lack of a better word, run its course. Many of the elders realize this. The hybrid option has only emphasized it. Gregory's young males— though they went about things in exactly the *wrong* way— were speaking what a lot of tigers already think."

Alexis leaned forward, setting her arms on the table as she held Lakshmi's gaze. "With only eight elders, the vote is split and all the arguing in the world hasn't been able to break the stalemate. But the truth is, the Mate Run isn't working anymore. It was developed to prevent violence against our females, and that part worked for the last two centuries—mostly." She blinked a few times, then shook her head. "But now, with Gregory and—" She cut herself off and waved a hand. "Anyway, the violence is starting up again. The extinction problem is still a problem. And we need a new answer. At least some of the elders realize this."

"But…?" Lakshmi asked, hearing it in Alexis' voice.

"But the change won't come soon enough for you and Dr. Yin."

"There *has* to be a way. I won't run anymore if I can't have him. I don't want another male. There's no point. And I will break the rules to have him."

Isabella gripped Lakshmi's knee under cover of the table and squeezed, her eyes narrow and her scent filled with a warning like burnt toast.

Lakshmi fell silent, heeding the warning, but keeping the facts to herself made them no less true. She'd run away with Ryan if she had to. She'd do whatever it took to keep him. The elders, the rest of the community be damned.

If Ryan would break the rules for her…

That thought stopped her mid-tirade. He was resigned to his fate. He'd made no sign that he'd fight the elders to be with her. He wanted her, she knew he did. He hadn't denied that part. But he hadn't fought the elders on their ruling…

She glanced away from Alexis and Isabella as her eyes burned with tears she didn't want to shed. Damn her emotions right now. She'd managed to get through the entire situation at Gregory's complex without crying. Now she couldn't seem to stop.

Alexis reached across the table and squeezed her hand. "I truly understand your position. I was in the same place myself, in love with a man who was banned from the Run. I wish I could wave my hand and say everything will be okay. But I can't. The unrest and upheaval moving through the community has made the elders even more stubborn than usual. They're digging into their beliefs, and arguing like never before."

"I find that hard to believe," Lakshmi said.

Alexis half-laughed, but the humor didn't reach her eyes. "You're in a terrible position." Very quietly, her gaze intent on Lakshmi's she said, "The only way you can avoid a forced pregnancy is to get pregnant before they can insist. Elizaveta implied that once pregnant, there wouldn't be much the elders could do."

"Even to the…male involved?" Lakshmi asked, frowning.

"A male proven capable of successful reproduction? While we face extinction? It would be very shortsighted to eliminate him from the breeding pool. Even more so if the pregnancy happened to produce a girl…"

"There's no guarantee of that, though," Lakshmi said, her eyes narrowed as she considered what Alexis was saying.

"Never is. No. But the researchers at the Chernikov Institute have uncovered some interesting correlations over the last twenty or so years between…love matches and the probability of female offspring." In a seeming change of subject, Alexis said, "You're not running now. I'm sure the elders will let you off from your next run if you plead the trauma of your kidnapping."

Lakshmi tried to follow Alexis' unspoken implications, hope sparking in her heart even as she forced that reaction from her expression. "I'm sure I'll still be feeling the… effects of my kidnapping by my next cycle," she said slowly.

"Then you should take that time off. All the time you need to recover. Maybe see a doctor for additional… support." Alexis stood, circled the table and dropped a kiss on her daughter's head. "I have to check on Victor. He launched back into work as soon as we got here. Stubborn man. I want to make sure he's eating. You two enjoy your afternoon."

Alexis waved over her shoulder as she sauntered out of the dining hall.

When Lakshmi faced Isabella, the girl was grinning, her eyes sparkling with mischief.

"I'll talk to the other women," Isabella said, quiet but the excitement in her tone obvious. "What can we do to help?"

CHAPTER SEVENTEEN

Ryan pushed into his small Victorian house with a groan, his body sore from too much time in confinement and the residuals of his *adventures*. The place smelled good, at least, like lemon polish and an apple-spice air freshener. After visiting him in confinement, his mother had insisted on coming to his home and cleaning it so it would be ready for his return. She'd been more than a little angry at his punishment and had apparently taken it out on his house's dust bunny population.

His father had shown up at the elders' compound with a backpack of clean clothing for Ryan and a stoic expression that hid his own anger from anyone who didn't know him. To Ryan's surprise, his parents were angrier at the elders for sentencing him to confinement than they were angry with him for being part of Gregory's group.

Ryan had never been able to lie to his mother. Even disguising his scent, she always managed to ferret out his and his siblings' secrets. So Ryan had purposefully avoided talking about Gregory with his mother. He'd been sure his parents would, at the very least, express disappointment in him for aligning with the young males.

Instead, they'd hugged him and praised his efforts to help the women, and his mother had loudly and insistently decried his punishment to anyone who would listen.

Ryan smiled at that memory. His mother was a fireball when she wanted to be.

He dropped his backpack onto the hardwood floor just inside the front door, then shuffled down the narrow hall to the kitchen for some of the food his mother promised was waiting for him.

Familiar surroundings went a long way toward soothing his tired brain. The cream-colored walls and dark wood accents of his house, the overstuffed red couch in his living room, the Persian rugs on polished floors, the dark wine-colored runner lining the wooden stairs to the second floor. All the warmth and bright colors, the distinct and prevalent scents of home, were a sharp contrast to Gregory's white compound.

Ryan scrubbed his hands through his hair as he entered his well-lit kitchen and headed straight for the fridge. As promised there were containers of pre-made meals waiting in the freezer and fresh fruits and vegetables in the fridge. He pulled out a container of his mother's pork dumplings, his stomach growling as he put the plastic container into the microwave.

He leaned against the light gray granite countertop as he waited, soaking up the smells of his mother's excellent food and the comfort of his surroundings. It was really nice to be home.

If only home could take his mind off his worries…

From confinement, he'd been permitted to call the hospital and ensure he still had a job to return to, but he got the impression the hospital administrator wasn't too happy with him at the moment. Earlier in the year—to allow time to get in with Gregory's group—he'd taken a sanctioned sabbatical. Two weeks of unplanned "holidays" after that weren't viewed kindly. Especially when he'd had patients, scheduled surgeries that had to be delayed or assigned to another surgeon.

He pushed away from the counter to get out a bowl, thoughts of the hospital bringing back the last conversation he'd had with his parents, and his father's dangling carrot of a new job in a new city.

Ryan loved his job. He loved Boston. He loved his home and the life he had here. But the new position in Toronto would put more distance between Ryan and the young males who had survived the raid on Gregory's compound.

Because of the bear and wolf shifter populations, not a lot of tigers had settled in Canada. There were some, particularly in the cold northern regions where few humans lived. But most of the Canadian territories were occupied by other shifter groups. Tigers were so insular they didn't tend to set up territories that risked a lot of interaction with other shifter species.

There were only a handful of tigers in and around the Toronto area, and all of them were males. There were three females living on the eastern coast of Canada, a mother and her six-year-old daughter and one female old enough to Run. All three lived closer to Montreal, and the one female who'd been running had just mated a few months ago. So there were no Mate Runs currently in the area.

All of that made the move very tempting for Ryan. He'd primarily be surrounded by humans and wouldn't have to have much dealings with other tiger shifters. Now more than ever he preferred the company of humans to his own kind.

Especially because his own kind would only know the public story of what had happened at Gregory's compound.

Ryan had been a little disgusted to hear he was being hailed as a hero by some—not for saving the women, but because he'd been part of Gregory's group. More males than even Ryan had suspected were secretly supporting Gregory's efforts to end the Mate Run. They didn't necessarily agree with his solution to start challenge fights for females again. And almost everyone who spoke publicly claimed that Gregory had gone too far in kidnapping the women. But Ryan was shocked to discover just how many tigers wanted to see the Run end.

The news reached him quietly through "helpful" supporters hoping the elders didn't find out how they really felt.

His sister Sarah and her Tracker husband Daniel had visited him in confinement, too. Ryan hadn't expected to see Daniel, and he'd been sure his brother-in-law would take him to task for siding with the young males. Daniel hadn't said a word about it, though. He hadn't looked particularly happy, but then neither had Sarah. Yet they didn't abandon him. And when Ryan finally left confinement, Daniel had been the one to tell him they still hadn't found the one remaining missing female and that Gregory was still on the loose.

The microwave beeped cheerfully, pulling Ryan from his thoughts. He poured the hot, succulent dumplings into his bowl, grabbed a fork, and headed to the living room and the comfort of his overstuffed couch. He savored the pork and spice filling as he stared at the blank, big screen TV on the wall and debated his future.

A future that seemed less…satisfying without Lakshmi.

She hadn't come to see him again while he'd been in confinement, and he'd learned through Sarah that Lakshmi had left for home the day before he got out. Each of the other women from the compound had stopped by to check on him. Megan had even stayed with him, talking quietly for several hours one day. Isabella checked on him once a day, always ensuring he had enough to eat. The fact that the seventeen-year-old girl fussed over him like his own mother amused him.

But Lakshmi had stayed away.

He tried to tell himself it was for the best. He had made it clear they didn't have a chance together. No doubt she'd come to that realization herself and had decided not to make matters worse.

He shoveled in another dumpling, scowling because no one was there to see his expression, letting his irritation and hurt fill his scent because no one was there to smell it.

Maybe he should go to Toronto. Massachusetts was the

entire length of the US away from Lakshmi's territory in southern California. But Toronto would put an international border between them. Maybe then he could convince his tiger to stop pushing him to head to the West Coast.

He was halfway through his dumplings, still brooding, when his doorbell rang.

Groaning, he set the bowl on his oak coffee table and went to answer the insistent noise. He could sense the tiger outside and assumed it was a member of his family come to check on him…until he hit the entryway.

He had his scent under control before he opened the door, but his heartbeat hammered hard in his chest, making breathing more difficult than it should have been.

The sight of Lakshmi on his front stoop, smiling at him, her dark eyes bright, her scent filled with more emotion than he wanted to face, took his breath away completely for a moment. All he could do was stare at her. And his tiger grumbled a low purr of approval.

"What are you doing here?" he asked, then scowled at his rough tone.

She raised her brows. "I told you this wasn't over between us." When he didn't move out of the doorway, she put her hands on her hips and scowled. "Are you inviting me in or not?"

"I haven't decided yet."

"We can't talk like this."

"We've talked already."

"Ryan Yin, you're being rude."

Her pout only made it harder for him to concentrate. She had the most delicious mouth.

When he still didn't budge from the doorway, she narrowed her eyes. "Do I have to strip on your doorstep and give your neighbors a show?"

For a full thirty seconds he couldn't think beyond the idea of Lakshmi naked. He dropped his gaze to her body, dressed in fitted jeans, a simple white t-shirt, and a short jacket. Nothing overtly seductive. But her high-heeled boots made her legs look particularly long. And the idea of her stripping out of that casual outfit, revealing all her deliciously soft skin inch by inch, made his entire body pulse with heat. He swallowed and tried to drag his gaze up to her face. Her seductive, heavy-lidded expression didn't help restart his brain cells even a little.

He fisted his hands to keep from reaching for her, some instinct keeping him just inside the door instead of pulling her into his arms. She wouldn't actually take her clothes off in the middle of the day on a public street. Tiger shifters might not think about nudity much—under non-sexual circumstances—but humans would notice. They might call the cops on her.

Then he realized if she went through with her threat, his neighbors—other men—would *see* her beautifully naked and that made his tiger growl.

She reached up to remove her jacket, flashing a sultry smile.

"Get in here." He gestured sharply toward the entryway, stepping aside so she could pass. Her scent wrapped around him, warm and spicy, with all the undertones of deliciously erotic desire. The flavor of her scent on his tongue was beyond anything he'd known before, rivaling any food he'd ever tasted. Though he'd never admit that to his mother.

The thought of his mother was just enough of a slap of cold water to keep him from touching Lakshmi.

"Why are you here?" he asked, closing the door very carefully.

"You know why I'm here. You can't come to my Run, so I'm coming to you."

"You know very well this isn't allowed. Someone will find out. There will be consequences."

"No one will turn us in."

He narrowed his eyes. She hadn't said *no one will find out*. "Who knows about this?"

She grinned and turned her back on him, ambling into his living room. "Those dumplings smell amazing. I don't suppose you have more?"

"Who knows you're here, Lakshmi?"

She faced him, still smiling but there was a touch of hesitance in her eyes.

"Erin and the others," she said.

He blinked a few times. "Maybe you should explain."

"Can I get some dumplings if I do?"

"Lakshmi."

"Fine. We hatched a plan so no one would miss us, everyone would think they knew where we were, *and* they'd give us privacy. We said Megan was still so upset about her tiger, we all wanted to take her to her territory so she wouldn't be under the gaze of the rest of the community."

"Megan was okay with you using her condition for your own ends?"

"It was her idea." Lakshmi raised her chin defensively. "She knew the others wouldn't question the excuse. We all claimed we would stay with her, try to help her release her tiger, because we'd been through this together and were the only ones who could really understand."

"And then?"

"We just said it might take a few weeks, maybe a month or more of privacy. None of us were going to go to our next Runs, but the community would know where we were and that we were safe. We'd be sure to check in regularly with our families so no one worried. But we insisted on the privacy."

"Did Isabella go along with this?"

"Her mother helped her pack for the trip."

"Alexis is helping you with this scheme?"

"Not…officially." She shrugged. "She did mention we should all take the time we needed to recover. Thought I should maybe see a doctor." She grinned now and took a step closer. "I thought that was a very good idea."

Almost without meaning to, he took a step toward her, his hands reaching for her before he knew what he was doing. He scowled at the reaction and stepped away again.

"This is dangerous. To you. You need to leave."

"No. You want me. I want you. I'm not letting you go just because of some elder ruling."

"There's no future in it, Lakshmi. Or do you just want a few nights together?"

"You know better than that."

The trembling along her jaw when she spoke made him regret his words almost immediately. But he didn't let up. "Even if that's the case…no matter what happens today, we aren't allowed a future together. Not outside the Run."

"If I'm pregnant, they can't argue."

He opened his mouth. Closed it. Stared at her for a long moment. Swallowing hard, he said, "You aren't in estrous right now."

"Do you want kids, Ryan?" she asked quietly, her hands clasped in front of her. "I know you said you hadn't intended to have them, but you never really said if you wanted them or not. If it was an option, would you want them?"

"Yes." He frowned. He'd answered without even thinking, going purely on instinct. He hadn't even known the answer was yes until that moment.

Everything had changed because of Lakshmi—including that deeply buried desire. He loved his sister's children, adored them. And somewhere deep inside, a part of him wanted what his sister had—a family, kids, a mate. But he'd never allowed himself to see that desire, to acknowledge it existed in him somewhere.

"It doesn't matter," he said, trying to believe that. "Only a pregnancy during the Run counts. Outside of the Run, it's still against the law, still something you'll be punished for. You've been through enough already. I can't do that to you."

"This is my decision. My choice. You're my choice."

He opened his mouth to deny her words, but she raised a hand, silencing him.

"Just, please, listen," she said. "When we talked, you agreed meeting and dating and getting to know someone before jumping into bed with them would be a good way to form a relationship. Like the way humans do things. Dating."

He nodded. The conversation was etched in his mind, that quiet moment, the door separating them, her scent filled with things he never wanted to forget.

"Well, that's what we're going to do."

"What?"

"The others have bought us some time. To date. To get to know one another outside of the…tense situation we met in. If we still want each other, if we can see a future together after that, something you can't write off as my attachment to you as a doctor…"

She scowled at him and he winced, knowing she wouldn't let him forget that comment any time soon.

"We're going to date, Dr. Yin," she finished. "And fall in love the way you wanted to. Not forced by the Run to be together, but together because we want to be."

"And then what? It's still against the law."

"*If* we decide we want to be together, and *if* I can get pregnant in the next cycle or two, we can make an argument to stay together. And *if* I happen to have a girl…"

"You know as well as I do that's unlikely."

"My mother did. Your sister did. Your mother did. Genetically speaking, we stand a good chance. And… Alexis said there's some evidence that within the last twenty years, the chances of a female baby are increased if the couple is…in love."

Her gaze danced away from his when she said "love." That didn't stop him from catching the insecurity and hope in her scent. It didn't stop his heart hammering with hope and possibilities he'd never thought to have.

"Do you see that between us?" he asked, his voice strained. "Do you think we might have that kind of…relationship?"

"I do."

She faced him again, her chin raised in that stubborn defiance he was growing to adore.

"I think I could love you, Ryan. I think I might already."

So fucking brave. She was so amazingly brave. If he hadn't been in love with her already, he was pretty sure her declaration tipped him over the top.

It didn't change anything. It didn't repeal the law or change his public ban from the Run or make any of those challenges go away.

It just made them seem less impossible.

"So how do we go about this…dating plan of yours?" he asked.

Her smile bloomed so full and bright he thought he could die right then and be happy.

"Well, I do need to stay relatively hidden from other tigers," she said. "But since there's only a few in Massachusetts, I think we're safe enough if we steer clear of their usual haunts. I assume you know where the others live and all that?"

He nodded. Tiger shifters always knew where the other tigers near their territory lived and worked and moved.

She glanced around. "I haven't arranged a place to stay yet, because I didn't want to call attention to myself by getting a hotel room. I can do that, using cash so I can't be traced. But if you have a spare room here, that might help keep my presence in Boston secret longer."

Help? If she stayed in his home, he wasn't sure they'd stay out of bed long enough to actually go on a date. Or even leave the house.

And yet, he still opened his mouth and said, "I have a spare room."

His voice sounded thicker than normal, deeper and huskier, even to him. His tiger rumbled happily, pleased with this turn of events.

"Thank you," Lakshmi said. She glanced down at the bowl of dumplings still sitting on his coffee table. "Did you make those?"

"My mother left them for me. For when I got out."

"My mother cleaned my apartment for me, so it will be ready when I get home."

He smiled. "My mother did that, too."

"I met her and your father," she said, almost hesitantly. "At the elders' compound. I told them you didn't deserve to be in confinement."

"They didn't tell me you spoke to them."

He wondered about that. Despite his insistence that he'd never run, his parents hadn't given up on him finding a tiger mate. They'd hardly condone breaking the law. At least, he didn't think they would condone what he and Lakshmi were doing. But he was pretty sure his parents would approve of her as a prospective mate for him. It wouldn't surprise him if his mother already knew Lakshmi was more to him than just a patient.

"I like them." Lakshmi glanced away, a beautiful blush climbing her cheeks. "I'd like them as parents-in-law."

She spoke quietly, but still loud enough that he easily heard her. His chest tightened at her admission. It spoke of a future, marriage, family. Things he hadn't allowed himself to want.

Until now.

"Did you...drive here? Do you have luggage?" he asked, because he needed something to talk about that didn't make him want to propose to her right there on the spot.

"I have a car parked around the corner, on the street. I didn't want to park out front. In case someone noticed." She shrugged.

"Do you want to go get your luggage?"

"Actually, if you have any extras, I really would like some of these dumplings. I haven't eaten in a while."

"Oh. Sorry. Of course. Have a seat. I'll be right back."

He stalked off to the kitchen, certain he'd gone insane for even considering her "dating plan." And letting her stay in his house was masochistic in a way he couldn't even fathom.

He was in way too deep, probably making the biggest mistake of his life.

And he just couldn't seem to care.

CHAPTER EIGHTEEN

Lakshmi waited for Ryan by his bookshelf, idly running a finger over the medical texts lining the shelf at eye level. They'd shared a wonderful meal—her father and Ryan's mother would have a lot of food things to talk about one day—with conversation that had flowed pretty easily after a few minutes of awkward small talk. Discussing their families had broken the ice, which made her happy because he was as close to his family as she was with hers and somehow that proved to her that he was the right mate for her.

After dinner, he went to get her suitcase from her rental car, leaving her to tap her foot and anticipate the night ahead.

Her plan, vague as it was, had been to put off seducing him for at least a few days, to really give this traditional dating idea a fair chance. It was how they both wanted to develop a relationship, so she'd ensure it happened that way.

But she was starting to waver in her conviction to delay sex. Most of the meal had felt like a kind of foreplay, sexy and easy at the same time. She was surrounded by his scent here in his home, and the delicious tang of it on her tongue was hard to ignore. She wanted to taste his skin and see how it blended with the flavor of his scent. She wanted to wallow in his touch and taste and everything about him. Now that she was so certain he was hers, resisting him was a lot more difficult than she'd assumed it would be.

She was doing this for him, though, for her and for their future. She needed him to accept her as his mate, to let go of his concern over the laws they were breaking, and to give their future a real chance. To do that, they needed this —dating, getting to know each other, then jumping into bed, not to reproduce at first but just for fun.

She pulled a random book off the shelf and flipped through it, and Ryan's scent rose up to envelope her, strong and tempting. She wavered again. She wanted him so much she could almost feel his hands on her. A shiver raced between her shoulder blades as heat tightened her belly and made her exceptionally aware of her clothing. And how much she wanted to take them off…

No. She had to wait. They weren't in a hurry. She could wait and give him the start he wanted. The start she'd always wanted.

The errant thought that she had to get pregnant to keep him rose up to poke a hole in her determination. She pushed it ruthlessly away. She had weeks before her next cycle. And that was the whole point. They could date for a few weeks, have sex as it evolved naturally, and not have to adhere to the way tiger shifters had been forming bonds for the last two centuries. Sex now would just be for fun, nothing to do with reproduction. Being with Ryan that way was, in and of itself, worth every risk she was taking.

Yet she couldn't quiet the nagging, worried voice that kept reminding her—being able to keep him meant they had to get pregnant.

For the first time since she started running, she'd found a man whose baby she actually wanted to carry. She loved the idea of having a baby with Ryan. She ached with so much feeling at the image, it was breath-stealing.

She just hoped they'd get the chance for all of that.

She blinked when she heard the front door lock turn and the door open. She'd been so deep in thought, she hadn't felt his return. Now, her heart pounded hard, almost as hard as when she'd stood at his front door, brazenly threatening to strip naked to get him to let her in. She'd put on a confident air, but inside she'd been terrified he'd still turn her away. That same excitement, anticipation, lust, and terror raced through her now, and it was all she could do to keep from rushing to the front door to meet him.

Instead, she stayed where she was, flicking through the medical book with pictures of human bodies in various states of dissection, and tried to focus on her plan.

When he entered the living room, it took her a few minutes to find her voice. He was so handsome… She smiled in greeting and thrilled when his scent spiked with desire.

"You didn't have trouble finding the car?" she asked.

He tapped his nose. "Nope. What are you reading?"

"Human anatomy text." She held up the thick book. "I still don't know how you do it."

He shrugged. "I'm good at it. Come on, I'll show you the spare room."

He led the way back through the living room's large double doors into the entry and up the wooden steps to the second floor. Pictures of his family and a few nature photographs in frames lined the cream-colored walls up the stairway, and Lakshmi kept stopping to look closer. Especially at the pictures of his family, all smiling and strong. She recognized Sarah as a younger woman, and a few with a much younger Ryan.

Seeing him as a boy made Lakshmi grin, and her chest tightened with another overwhelming wash of emotion.

Ryan glanced back over his shoulder and caught her studying a photo of him and his sister making faces at each other.

"You were both very cute," she said.

"My mom and Sarah looked almost identical at that age." He nodded to the picture. "We have a yellowing one of Mom throwing snowballs at her oldest brother and she's even making the same silly face as Sarah is in that shot."

"How funny." And sweet.

At the second floor landing, he turned back toward the front of the house and led her to an open door.

He set her small suitcase down just inside, but didn't go in. "Here you go. If I know my mom, the sheets are clean and fresh. You can hang anything you need to in the closet. The bathroom is two doors back down the hall."

"Your room?"

He blinked, but his scent stayed frustratingly neutral so she couldn't read his reaction to her question.

After a hesitant beat, he said, "Back of the house, just at the top of the stairs. That's my door. Let me know if you need anything."

"What are you doing now?"

"I'm pretty beat. And I have to start back at the hospital tomorrow. I need to get some sleep."

"Okay." She pressed her lips together, not really wanting to say goodnight, but she knew she needed to let him rest. "Can I ask something first?"

He nodded.

"Would you consider dinner and conversation a typical date?"

He frowned. "I suppose. Is that what you'd like to do for our first date?"

"Well, technically, that's what we did tonight. Which means, technically, we could count this as our first date." She eased a little bit closer to him.

He swallowed visibly, and a very satisfying edge of desire darkened his eyes and wove through his scent. Lakshmi didn't smile, but her tiger growled quietly in triumph.

"I suppose. Technically," he said, his voice rougher than just a moment before.

"And don't dates typically end with a goodnight kiss?"

"If the date went well."

His voice was deep enough now to make her shiver. He leaned in to her, though she suspected he didn't realize he was doing it, and his gaze dropped to her lips—a brief glance that she felt like a touch. Her pulse pounded.

"I think this date has gone very well. Don't you?" she murmured.

His answer was barely a grunt.

She rose up on her toes, just a little, enough to put her lips close to his, to feel his breath on her skin. His scent wasn't neutral now, it was spiced with the rich, thick flavor of need and lust. And his scent mixed with her own as they hovered in that position, a combination of textures and flavors blending to make something uniquely perfect.

She brushed her lips against his, lightly, only just touching, and whispered, "I think you should kiss me goodnight."

He captured her mouth, hard and fast, his arms coming around her waist in an embrace that flattened her against the hard planes of his chest. Heat flashed through her belly and down between her legs as she wrapped her arms around his neck and kissed him with all the pent-up needs and frustrations of the last week. He tasted as good as he smelled and she couldn't get enough.

Savoring the sweep of his tongue against hers, she ran her fingers up his neck and into the thick, short strands of hair she'd wanted to touch for what felt like eternity. His grip tightened further and she rubbed against him, her hips instinctively finding his. She'd intended for this to be just a kiss, the kind of kiss an ordinary, non-tiger shifter couple might exchange before saying goodnight.

This kiss was oh so much more. It was lust and need and desire. But it was also more than just lust, more than just basic desire. She'd never experienced anything quite like it, not on any Run, certainly not with any other man. She couldn't get enough of Ryan, like she was drunk on his flavor. Even in her most estrous-driven lusts, she couldn't remember ever wanting anyone this much.

Not just in her bed, though she was desperate to strip him and explore every hard inch of him. Now. But she wanted him…period. For life. Forever. *Hers.*

She might have given in to her need if not for thoughts of forever intruding. Forever meant following her plan. Forever meant doing things differently, not the way tiger shifters did. And while she wasn't in estrous, and this wasn't a Mate Run, she was pretty sure jumping into bed after only one *technical* date didn't qualify as "dating and getting to know each other before jumping into bed."

Easing away from his kiss was incredibly hard to do— she wasn't used to denying herself anything she really wanted. And she really, *really* wanted Ryan.

But she wanted him for forever. That meant taking a little more time.

She broke the kiss with a huffing pout and set her forehead against his for one moment before settling back onto her feet. She cupped his cheek, not at all unhappy when he didn't loosen his grip right away. The feel of his strong, solid arms around her was like heaven.

"Dating first," she reminded him, softly, her voice a little shaky. "I intend to give you what you want."

"What I want is you."

She almost kissed him again. She almost gave in.

But she didn't. "I want you, too," she said. "Which is why I want this to work. Goodnight, Ryan. Sleep well."

His grip tightened for just a moment as she started to ease away. The reaction thrilled her to her core. He let go reluctantly and took a step away from her.

"Sleep well," he said.

She didn't break eye contact with him until she'd closed the bedroom door fully. Then she rested her forehead against the cool wood, savoring his scent on her skin, her stomach giddy with anticipation.

Grinning, she realized that anticipation would make giving in to the chemistry between them even more explosive. She couldn't wait for the moment. Especially because she knew it would be the start of their forever.

So long as nothing went wrong.

* * *

Thanks to work—and having to make up to the hospital administrator for his long absence—Ryan didn't see much of Lakshmi the next day. Her scent permeated his house so that as he'd gotten ready for work that morning, he'd been on edge, turning toward her bedroom more than once.

He hadn't slept well either. Which meant he was a little more irritable at work than usual. The good thing about being a surgeon, though, was most people expected him to have irritable moments, and the nurses, interns, and luckier residents avoided him as much as was possible.

By the time he got home, he was antsy, restless, and in need of a run in his tiger form more than he'd ever been before. Something he wasn't likely to get tonight since it was well after midnight and he had an early start in the morning—a patient whose condition had worsened in his absence so that surgery was now the only option. He felt enough guilt about that to further dampen his mood.

The only bright spot was anticipating seeing Lakshmi, even if only for a short time before he had to go to bed.

But as he stepped inside, he realized he couldn't sense her.

Where was she?

Panic made his pulse jump. He wasn't sure what triggered that panic, but it rushed through him so fast, he was up the stairs before stopping to think. He pushed into her bedroom—a place he'd always think of as hers now. Her suitcase sat open on the floor, empty. The double bed was neatly made. Her clothes were hanging in the closet. Three different pairs of shoes lined the closet's wooden floor.

The room was thick with her scent but nothing in it indicated distress. Just her usual cinnamon and allspice essence. He stalked to the bathroom. Her toiletry bag was neatly placed on a shelf next to the sink, and she'd dropped her toothbrush into the holder by the sink, next to his own. For a split second, seeing her toothbrush next to his filled him with a strange sense of intimacy and rightness. Such a little thing, and yet it felt like a sign that they were meant to be together.

He blinked the image of domestic bliss away and continued his search of the house.

In the kitchen, he found her dinner dishes soaking in the sink—and a note.

"Ryan, needed a run. Be back soon. I have my cellphone if you need to reach me. Missed you today. Love, Lakshmi."

He read the note four times, lingering over the "Love, Lakshmi" part, before he realized her scent was quite strong on the paper. She hadn't been gone for long.

Not bothering to consider why he was doing it, he programmed her number into his own cellphone, then he called her.

Her voice, when she answered, was breathy and happy and possibly the best sound he'd ever heard.

"Where are you?" he said, flinching at his sharp tone.

She laughed. "You weren't worried, were you?" she asked.

"Of course I was worried. Gregory is still on the loose."

"He'd hardly look for me here. I'm not supposed to be in Boston, am I?"

She sounded like she was moving, the faint whoosh of cars covering her voice. Which meant she'd moved beyond his quiet neighborhood to a busier road.

"Where are you?"

"Near the baseball stadium."

"You ran all that way?" It wasn't that huge a distance for a tiger shifter, but she'd have to move at human speeds or risk discovery. And he hadn't thought she'd been gone long enough.

"I ran at human speed," she said with a note of wry amusement.

He scowled at the phone, wondering how the hell she knew what he'd been thinking. "When did you leave?"

"Couple hours ago. I wasn't tired enough for bed yet."

"You should still get home. Just in case."

He couldn't begin to explain why he was so worried about her. She was a grown woman, a tiger shifter who had trained in fighting techniques with one of their people's best combat instructors, more than capable of handling herself with any human that came along. Especially now that the one human serial killer who'd been a threat to them was dead.

But there was still a crazy tiger on the loose, along with some of his followers, all of whom might consider Ryan a traitor at this point. It was also possible Gregory hadn't discovered how Ryan had helped the women at the complex. He could still see Ryan as one of his followers and come to Boston looking for Ryan's help.

Having Gregory out there somewhere put Lakshmi in danger, and, for reasons Ryan couldn't entirely explain to himself, he was driven by an instinct to keep her safe. If Gregory discovered her here in Boston, whatever reason might bring him to Ryan's territory, Gregory wouldn't hesitate to go after her.

"Did you realize you just told me to come 'home'?" she asked quietly.

The question pulled him from his worry, and he froze as her words sank in. He hadn't actually realized what he'd said—or the implication.

Damn, but he was in deep. Already. Well and truly lost to her even without this dating plan of hers. For the first time in years, he actually preferred the idea of doing things the tiger way—a Run where he got to spend three days with Lakshmi, alone and making love as often as possible.

He couldn't deny his tiger had claimed her as surely as she'd claimed him. He couldn't deny they were meant for each other. And all his previous ideas of falling in love over time seemed ridiculous in the face of the absolute surety that he was well and truly in love with her already.

"I didn't realize I'd said that," he answered. "But I meant it. Please come home."

"Be there soon."

She disconnected, and he smiled at the pleasure in her voice.

He wasn't sure whether to be pleased or irritated when she pushed into the house a half hour later.

"It takes longer to get here from the ball park if you're running at human speeds," he said.

She grinned. "I took a taxi." Then she stepped into his arms and kissed him.

So easy. So natural.

He wrapped her close and dove into her kiss, taking and savoring, a man desperate for just a sip of her perfection.

How the hell had this happened? When had he stopped resisting her and started thinking of her as his? Last night? Last week?

Time seemed to have changed somehow, distorted, lengthening and shortening and making itself all twisted until he couldn't quite remember life before her. Yet, in reality, they'd known each other practically no time at all and half of that had been while she was a captive.

How had this happened?

He filled himself with her scent, absorbed the soft heat of her skin, let his need and desperation fill his own scent without hesitation.

She eased back and smiled at him, her dark eyes sparkling and bright. "I could get used to that kind of welcome home."

"Me, too."

"Have you eaten dinner?" she asked.

He thought of his early morning, his busy day tomorrow, and said, "I'm starved. You hungry after your run?"

"I could eat." She laughed. "Okay, I can always eat."

He took her hand and led her to the kitchen. "This counts as a second date." It wasn't a question.

"I think it has to. A good sign right?"

"Good sign?"

"A sign of a good first date is wanting to go on a second."

"Absolutely," he said with feeling.

This time they ate at the little two-person table in his kitchen, near a window. She dug up candles while he warmed up some more of his mother's frozen food—this time a pan of lasagna, a recipe she'd learned from an Italian neighbor and gone on to make her own. There were three large trays of it in the freezer, which would make him and Lakshmi three good meals. While he whipped up some garlic bread—mostly to impress Lakshmi that he could manage some cooking—she opened a bottle of wine.

The meal was romantic and relaxed. And fun. She asked about his day at work, letting him moan about the troubles he had with the administrator and a few of the senior surgeons. He asked about her businesses and marveled at her savvy, entrepreneurial mind. Her face lit up as she discussed her newest business venture—the retail clothing store she'd told him about at Gregory's complex.

"That was what my mother and I were discussing over dinner that night before…" She trailed off and waved her fork, some of her light dimming.

He cursed Gregory silently. Again.

"Anyway." She forced a smile. "She was trying to hire my manager away from me." Her smile turned genuine again and her eyes narrowed slyly. "I have *the* best manager for this store. She's a genius with layout and pricing. And she handles employees exactly the way I would."

As she told him how she'd hired the woman away from some other store, she glowed. He couldn't look away and was surprised when he'd finished his half of the lasagna without noticing.

They both laughed a lot. He needed that after his days at the hospital, especially the harder days like today. She made him forget to worry about the future, his entire being focused on the present. A present moment he could live in forever.

She glanced at the small silver watch on her right wrist and her eyes widened. "It's after three. What time do you have to be up?"

He waved it away. "I'll be fine. Used to very little sleep, remember?"

"Still." She rose and took his hands. "Leave the dishes to me. You need to sleep."

He couldn't have resisted her even if he'd wanted to. Which he didn't. He followed her up the stairs, his gaze traveling over her lush body, smiling when she increased the swing of her hips because he wasn't hiding the desire lacing his scent. She walked him to his door tonight and melted against him when he pulled her into his arms for a kiss.

A kiss that lit all his nerves and made his head spin. He ran his hands up into her hair, crushing the silk thickness as he angled his head to deepen their contact. It wasn't enough. He wanted more. Naked skin and heat and sweat. He wanted her moaning beneath him. He wanted the taste of her on his tongue. He wanted to spend hours exploring every beautiful, delectable inch of her.

He could do without sleep to be with Lakshmi.

But she stuck to the plan, despite him dragging her back twice before she finally succeeded in pulling out of his arms.

"Goodnight, Ryan," she said, her tone stern. But she was grinning. And breathing hard.

And she was a little unsteady on her feet as she went back down the stairs.

He considered that progress in the right direction.

CHAPTER NINETEEN

Because of his schedule and the fact that he had to do some ass-kissing to the people who'd covered for him during his unexpected "vacation," it took another three days before Ryan could take Lakshmi out for a proper date. But when his schedule lined up with an early enough evening off and a late start the following morning, he insisted they go out. Movie and a meal, like a typical dating couple. It was a late show, and an even later dinner, but he didn't care because he was with Lakshmi.

He kept his senses open while they were in public, unconsciously checking their surroundings for signs of other tigers. Any tiger discovering them together would be bad. But he admitted, if only to himself, that he was most worried about Gregory. Two weeks had passed since the raid on Gregory's complex in Canada, and the Trackers still hadn't caught the males who'd escaped. Until they did, Ryan would be on edge.

Lakshmi didn't seem nearly as jumpy as he felt, but he did catch her occasional nervous glance when someone with a similar build or hair color to Gregory's walked by. Those instances made Ryan's tiger raise his head and growl. His rational side knew she'd have moments of fear, bad memories, post-traumatic stress for months, maybe years. She'd been through something awful and wouldn't recover from it overnight. In fact, it frankly amazed him how well she was doing. But his tiger didn't understand that her jumpiness was a residual reaction to her kidnapping. His tiger wanted her to be happy and content.

His tiger wanted him to kill the man who'd given her even a moment's discomfort.

He didn't let those feelings into his scent or reveal them in his conversation. If she realized he was holding something back, she didn't show any sign of it either. She recovered quickly, if she did have a nervous moment. And outside of those brief flashes, the night was...perfect. Exactly the kind of easy, flirty, slow build he'd always wanted.

From a woman he couldn't keep his hands off of.

He held her hand when they walked, put his arm around her shoulders in the movie, made excuses to touch her during dinner. Anticipation hummed in his blood like alcohol.

After dinner, they took a walk around the downtown area, near Boston Commons, an excuse to hold hands and talk more. The night air was cool and pleasant, which meant even at this late hour, Bostonians and tourists alike were on the streets, the area buzzing with life and energy.

"I can't remember the last time I had a night like this," Ryan said, squeezing her hand as he let his gaze roam their surroundings, the trees lining cobbled sidewalks next to the Commons, the soft street lights, the modern, glass-covered skyscrapers butting up against brick and stone buildings from centuries past. He wasn't sure he'd ever experienced the city quite like this before, and he was sure the change had everything to do with Lakshmi.

"I don't know how you deal with your job," she said, squeezing his hand. "Having to adhere to someone else's schedule…" She shook her head. "I couldn't do it."

If they worked with humans, tiger shifters typically took freelance jobs or owned their own businesses so they could be flexible in their schedules—to accommodate the Mate Run or even just to have the freedom to let their tigers out when they needed to. Most tiger shifter doctors ended up working in small, private practices or entirely with other tiger shifters. As far as Ryan knew, no current working tiger restricted himself to a human hospital the way he did.

He shrugged. "I like working at the hospital. I help people. I do a lot of good."

"I know. I just don't know how you do it without getting antsy and restless for some open air and freedom."

"How does your father do it? He owns a restaurant. That takes a lot of time and attention."

"He's hired an excellent executive chef and has family to take up the slack." She grinned. "But he says as an old married tiger, he doesn't need to get out as much as we young cubs do." Her expression softened as she spoke of her father. "He'd like the work you do," she said, glancing at him with a little smile.

He tugged her closer and draped his arm around her shoulders. "You're very easy to talk to," he said.

"I'm glad. Because if I get my way, you'll be talking with me for the rest of our lives."

His heart thudded hard at the casual way she spoke of their future, so assured and confident he wanted to believe everything she told him.

He paused to face her. "I want that, too, Lakshmi. I really do."

"Then all this dating has worked?"

He laughed. "I've wanted you for a lot longer than our 'dating.' Thank you for being willing to…risk this."

She cupped his cheek. "It would have been more of a risk not to."

"You know we might be ostracized from our people if we make this work? At the very least, we'll be in debt to the elders for the rest of our lives. And that's if they don't throw me into confinement."

"They won't. Not again. I won't let them." She pulled in a big breath, glancing away. "I don't care what our people say. You're mine."

"Will your family be upset?" She was so close to her family, just like he was. But he had a feeling his mother already approved this breach in the law by her youngest son —otherwise she wouldn't have made up the spare bedroom. He needed to be sure Lakshmi's family would forgive her for breaking the rules, though. It would hurt her too much to lose them.

"They'll understand. My mother is… Well, she met my father during her Run, so she knows it can work. But my unsuccessful Runs have led her to believe we should explore alternatives."

Ryan frowned. "Does she know you're here? I thought your family believed you were with the other women."

"They do. Or at least that's the story I told them, over the phone so they couldn't scent the lie. But my mother is…astute. I'm pretty sure she knows."

He laughed and they started walking again, holding hands. "I'm pretty sure my mother suspected something, too. She left a lot more food than she normally would have. And made up the spare room. They spoke with you at the compound?"

She nodded.

"Then she must approve of you."

"That's a relief," she said with real feeling. "Have you spoken to them since coming home?"

"Not yet. I was afraid I'd give away the fact that you're here. My mother is impossible to hide anything from. She might as well be a walking lie detector. I never could keep a secret from her for long. The only way to avoid giving myself away is to say nothing at all."

"How did she feel about your…association with the young males?" Lakshmi asked.

"She didn't approve. But mostly because Gregory is crazy. She knows my feelings on the Mate Run."

"And doesn't object? Didn't she want you to find a mate, have children?"

"Both my parents want me to be happy, and yes, settled

with children. But I'm a male so they'd never been counting on it."

It was Lakshmi's turn to squeeze his hand.

"Can I change the subject a little and ask you a question?" she said.

"Of course." He frowned at her sudden unease.

"Your scent is…very difficult to read," she said quietly.

Shit. He should have expected this. He knew she'd suspected something at the complex. He released a slow breath. So few people knew the truth, and he wanted it kept that way. Other tigers wouldn't trust him, ever, if they knew he could manipulate his scent.

But he wanted to marry Lakshmi. He wanted to father her children and live a long life with her by his side. That kind of future required honesty between them. At least about the things he was allowed to admit.

"That wasn't a question," he said, stalling despite his intention to tell her the truth. He wasn't sure why except that the long-time habit of keeping his secret was so ingrained it was hard to break.

"You don't just…control your scent the way the elders and their assistants do, the way some of the very old tigers can. You…change it depending on what you want others to think you're feeling."

"Damn, but you're smart."

"So it's true, you really can alter your scent, on purpose?"

He shrugged. "It's true." As a demonstration, he shifted his scent to hide his desire and discomfort and instead infused it with the disinterest he usually used to cover anger.

They had walked a few yards before she stopped to face him, her eyes wide. "You just did it. You just changed your scent. I can't detect any of the things you were feeling a moment ago."

She dropped his hand and Ryan had to fight down the panic that tightened in his gut, a panic that made him want to reach out for her.

"How do you do that?" she demanded, her hands on her hips.

"I just do. I've always been able to do it, from as early as I can remember. According to my sister, it's a very rare genetic trait, but it does happen from time to time."

"Why didn't you tell me?"

"I don't tell anyone."

"Who else knows?"

"My family, obviously. My brother-in-law figured it out a few years ago."

"Only then?" She lowered her hands to her sides, her eyes wide. "But he's a Tracker. How'd he miss it?"

"I don't do it all the time. Just when I need to."

"Like at the complex. So we'd trust you."

"So you wouldn't be afraid of me. I use it a lot with patients."

"Humans? It works with humans?"

"They don't know why, but they trust me to take care of them because I infuse that into my scent. It works on an unconscious level for them."

She blinked, glancing at the cars passing behind him on

the street. "I knew…we all suspected there was something about your scent."

"I thought you might. I had to hide my real feelings a lot more there than I normally do."

She fell silent, and Ryan had to work hard not to rush the conversation. If she couldn't trust him now, best they got that out in the open, before things went any farther. His heart would shatter if she left, but better now than after they were discovered. She could still have a life, find a mate, so long as no one learned of their dating.

He fisted his hands as the silence drew his nerves tight.

Finally, finally, she faced him, her dark eyes serious as she studied him. "I want to ask how I can trust you if I can't read your scent."

"But?"

"But…I do trust you. I have even when we knew you were part of Gregory's group. I don't know why I do." She scowled. "I haven't the faintest idea why I trusted you then. I just knew you were a good man and I could rely on you to help us."

The tight muscles along his back and shoulders eased. "I haven't hidden anything from you since you got here. If that helps."

"Maybe a little. Mostly, I'm just going on instinct, though. Something beyond your scent…" She paused. "Wait, if you can manipulate your scent, how does your mother uncover your secrets?"

"She's never needed scent to sniff out lies. She saw mine despite my best efforts for most of my life. I don't know how."

"I need to ask her about that."

Another kind of panic bubbled up, but with it came amusement. And a lot of relief. He finally reached for Lakshmi's hand again, and she didn't resist.

She pulled him a step closer, looked him right in the eye, and said, "Promise me something."

"What?"

"No lying to me. Not to *me*."

He hesitated. He had one secret he couldn't tell her—that he'd been working for the elders infiltrating Gregory's group. That was as much the elders' secret as his own and he was sworn never to reveal the truth. It was a lie of omission rather than an outright lie. He had a feeling it still counted.

But Lakshmi deserved as much truth from him as he could give her.

"I might have to change my scent while you're around," he said, working to be absolutely honest, "to reassure others, to hide something from someone else. But I'll let my scent reveal my feelings whenever we're alone. I won't hold anything back." Even if he couldn't admit the whole truth. "Will that do?"

She pursed her lips and lifted her chin. "For now."

To prove she could trust him, he released the control he'd had on his scent, allowing it to flow with every worry, fear, desire, hope, and anxiety he was feeling in that moment. So much, he was pretty sure she still wouldn't be able to dissect out all the various emotions. But she *would* know he wasn't hiding anything.

Her half-grin sent a race of raw need through him.

"That's better," she said. "Now. Let's get home." She glanced at him from under her lashes. "This was our sixth date."

"What's the significance of the sixth date?"

She didn't answer, just smiled to herself as they strolled back to his car.

That look heated his blood, making his body pulse with wanting her. And he couldn't wait to get home and find out what that look meant.

* * *

Lakshmi could barely walk up the steps to Ryan's front door, her knees were wobbling with so much need and lust. The waiting had built her desire into something so fierce she barely recognized herself. His scent—open and uncontrolled—drove her wild because she could *taste* his desire, like richly spiced honey sweets melting on her tongue. She stumbled through the door, waited impatiently for him to close and lock it, then wrapped herself around him, desperate for his heat and the strength of his hard body against hers.

And oh he was hard. She rubbed herself against him, savoring every solid inch of him, swallowing his groan with a kind of triumph she'd never felt. Before him, sex had been fun, exciting, often satisfying. With Ryan, though, this moment felt as vital as her next breath, as fundamental as food. She dug her fingers through his thick hair, tilted her head just a little and deepened the kiss.

"Upstairs?" he muttered between kisses.

"Yes, yes, yes." But she was too caught up in his mouth to remember which direction the stairs were.

His lips moved from hers to her neck, licking and nipping, scraping over sensitive skin until she trembled. He cupped her breast in one hand, his fingers sliding gently over her peaked nipple through her silk blouse, the contrast between his soft touch and his aggressive mouth driving her so close to an orgasm she wanted to scream. She wasn't even sure how it was possible, but the things he was doing to her body—while they were both still fully dressed!—robbed her of any control she might have had over her lust.

Lost in sensation, she gasped when he leaned over and picked her up, one arm under her knees, the other around her back. Every feminine bone in her body purred at the show of strength. She trailed her lips over his jaw, down his throat, his skin smooth and hot, tasting his salty flavor as he carried her up the stairs. She nuzzled against his neck to absorb his scent, all that warm, musky, earthiness that made her stomach dance, then flicked her tongue out in a quick taste, smiling when he gasped.

"Just a warning," he said, his voice tight and husky, "if you do that again before we reach the landing, I might not make it all the way up these stairs."

She chuckled, letting her breath brush over the wet mark she'd left on his throat, and he shivered.

Somehow they did reach the landing, and even made it all the way to his bedroom door before he released her legs to press her back against a wall, kissing her hard. The feel of his cock against her stomach, thick and hard, made her body jerk to get closer. It wasn't enough. She braced her hands on his shoulders and wrapped her legs around his waist, enveloping him, trying to feel all of him at once.

But they had too much damned clothing on.

She wasn't used to getting this far with a tiger and still being dressed. No one wore clothing during the Mate Run—between shifting from tiger to human and back again, and all the sex, clothing just got in the way. She'd had a few encounters with human men before her Runs started, and those had involved stripping off clothes in order to have sex, but she'd never been as desperate with any of them as she was now. The hassle of removing the barrier between her skin and Ryan's was so irritating, she actually growled.

He pulled back from their kiss, cupping her cheek. "You're so beautiful it sometimes hurts to look at you."

"You're beautiful, too. Now get me naked before I scream."

"I'm really glad this wasn't just an intense goodnight kiss."

She laughed as he slammed open his bedroom door and carried her to his bed.

Getting her naked involved some ripped clothing, a few curses, and some giggling, but eventually she managed to wiggle out of her pants and blouse, her heals tossed into a corner in a careless way she'd never normally treat good shoes. She stripped Ryan's shirt over his head, then reached for her bra clasp. But he stopped her with a touch.

She narrowed her eyes in warning because she wanted them both naked five minutes ago. He just grinned and gently pinned her wrists to the mattress as he bent over her, trailing a hot fire kiss across her throat. He straddled her hips as he moved down, licking the hollow at the base of her throat, nipping the tender skin over her collar bone. He tasted her with quick, random flicks of his tongue, the unpredictability of it driving her a little mad.

Then he reached her breasts, nuzzling at her silk bra, pushing the edge over just a little with his teeth before kissing the plump inner edge. She arched under him, wiggling, trying to get his mouth to her nipple, but he resisted. She jerked her arms against his hold and he released her wrists, moving his hands to her ribs, just underneath her breast. Still not touching her where she wanted him to touch her.

She tried moving him, tugging at his wrists to get his hands to her breasts, pulling none too gently at his hair to move his mouth, but he didn't give in. And she lost track of what she was trying to make him do because what he was doing was sending so many ripples of pleasure through her that she couldn't think. She almost sobbed when he nudged her bra aside enough to get at her nipple, sucking the peaked bud into his mouth in a hot, wet kiss. He suckled hard, and the sensation tugged a tight line between her breast and her core.

Delirious with need, she didn't even notice he'd pushed aside the silk covering her other breast until she felt his warm fingers on her skin, pinching her other nipple. He altered the pressure he used on each breast—his fingers hard and demanding as his mouth moved over her gently, his mouth sharp and rough as his fingers eased to a barely-there pressure. The combination, the way she couldn't predict what kind of sensation she'd get from where, left her on a knife's edge of pleasure so intense it was almost pain. By the time he left her breasts to move across her stomach, down to the lacy scrap of underwear she'd donned especially for tonight, she was practically begging him to let her come.

He still didn't rush. He licked a wet line across her inner thigh, then blew a hot breath over her skin, the contrast making her shiver. He flicked his tongue against her mound, through her underwear and her hips bucked. When he closed his mouth over her heat, her underwear still separating his tongue from her clit, she thought he actually might kill her. She covered her eyes with one hand and dug the fingers of her other hand into his hair, gripping hard enough that she was sure it hurt but not caring because he had driven her beyond being able to think about anything but the throbbing, building pressure between her legs.

With her eyes closed, their scents got stronger, the mixture coming together in a complex harmony of tastes and textures, weaving so thoroughly into a single scent she couldn't even tell where he started and she left off. That realization momentarily caught her attention, because she'd never had that happen before, and she breathed in deeply to absorb the perfection of their scents coming together.

Then he nuzzled aside her underwear and his tongue touched her clit without any material in the way, and she was so ready, so tightly wound, that he barely sucked her into his mouth before she was coming, her body jerking, her insides bursting apart in such raw release she screamed.

She went limp as the powerful orgasm eased, though residual shivers and ripples raced over her skin. She removed her hand from her eyes so she could look down at Ryan. His expression was a little smug, but she didn't have the energy to do anything about it. She figured he'd earned that smugness for giving her the best orgasm of her life.

He eased up her body, settling over her, and kissed her lightly.

She realized then he still had his pants on and frowned. "We lost track of getting naked."

"I didn't. I had a plan."

"It was a very good plan. But now I have a plan. Which involves you having no clothes on." She pushed at the waistband of his dark slacks. "If these don't come off now, I'm going to rip them off."

His chuckle sent a wave of lust through her.

He didn't make her wait this time, though. He pushed out of his pants while she stripped off her bra and underwear, then she crawled over him, forcing him onto his back so she could play. And play she did, returning at least a little of the torture he'd inflicted on her. She wasn't nearly as patient, but she was just as determined to drive him crazy. Exploring his beautiful male physique was so distracting, she even forgot this was supposed to be torture.

She savored and licked and kissed each dip and rise, all hard male muscle and solid strength. When she discovered his waist was quite sensitive to her kisses, she remembered the torture part of her plan and proceeded to drive him as mad as he'd driven her, until his growled demands were almost unintelligible. She, of course, ignored his demands, because it turned out she enjoyed repaying him for his earlier erotic torment.

By the time she reached the straining length of his cock, he was panting, sweat beaded his brow, and she was pretty sure he'd shredded the sheet in his tight grip.

She trailed her lips over him lightly, tasting him with little flicks of her tongue, before taking him into her mouth, sucking hard. Every muscle in his body tensed and strained, his jaw tight. She gentled the suctioning pressure of her mouth, and he growled down at her, looking so fierce and demanding she laughed. He gasped and dropped back against the mattress again, his eyes clenched closed.

"Lakshmi," he muttered tightly, his voice gravel rough. "I… Up. Now." He reached for her shoulders, dragging her away from his cock.

She gave him one last, teasing lick, then let him roll her onto her back. She was so ready, so primed to take him, he slid into her like a homecoming, stretching her, the friction of his entrance sending her spiraling high.

They rocked together in a rhythm as ancient as time, finding their pace and timing easily, as if they'd always been lovers, as if they knew exactly what the other would do. Lakshmi clung to him, watching his face, kissing him when she could pull in enough breath, panting and groaning as they strained toward the edge, urging him on with quiet murmurs and when she could no longer speak, with her hands and body. He sent her surging into another climax that stole her breath and blanked out all thought. The only thing she knew was the sound of him following her, groaning her name when he came, the sweetest sound she'd ever heard.

Lakshmi rolled close to Ryan's side when he flopped onto his back, and he wrapped his arms around her almost without thought, hugging her close even though his muscles felt like jelly. He kept his eyes closed, trying to regain his balance, his body twitching with the aftershocks of a pleasure he was pretty sure he was addicted to now. He pulled in a deep breath, held it, and then released the air on a low, satisfied sigh.

"I think the way we smell together might just be my new favorite thing," he said.

"It's wonderful, isn't it?" she murmured. "Perfect. I've never had that happen before, my scent mixing with a lovers so thoroughly it's like one scent."

He growled softly. "Good. Because I'm not just any lover."

"No," she agreed, levering up to brush his cheek with a soft kiss. "You're my mate."

"Damn straight." He finally opened his eyes to look at her. For a heartbeat, all he could do was stare. She was glowing and he'd never seen anything quite so stunning. He tugged her close for another kiss, a gentle brush of lips, before settling back against the pillows piled up at the head of his bed.

"Now," he said, with feigned seriousness, "what was all that earlier about this being our sixth date? What did that have to do with anything?"

She grinned. "The younger women who work at my sundries store tell me there's a rule that the sixth date equals sex."

"It does?"

"Among humans apparently. But then, the manager at my coffee shop says a woman should make a man wait for at least three months. And an article Erin found me online said some human women make men wait up to a year." She shivered and wrinkled her nose in distaste. "I could never wait that long."

"Thank. God."

He spoke with such feeling, she laughed and hugged him.

"And I will be eternally grateful to the women who told you six dates was the charm."

She snuggled closer to his side, gliding her fingers gently over his chest, the feel of her caress sending a slow burn through his blood again. She folded a leg over his thighs, and he was only a little surprised when his cock twitched in reaction, starting to harden again despite the mind-blowing orgasm he'd just had. The one really great thing about being a tiger male—with the right female, recovery time was quick. He rolled to his side, pulled her close, and kissed her deeply, letting the liquid slide of lust pull him under again.

He had a feeling he'd need a lifetime of orgasms with Lakshmi to quiet some of his lust. Though even a lifetime might not be enough.

CHAPTER TWENTY

The next three days were like bliss for Lakshmi. She couldn't remember ever being so happy in her entire life. Even when she opened a new business.

During the day, sometimes into the night, Ryan worked at the hospital while she worked from his house, keeping tabs on her two businesses and the new one opening via email and the occasional conference calls with her managers. She called her parents twice so they wouldn't worry, but otherwise she avoided contact with other tigers —just in case.

When Ryan came home, they'd either stay in for a romantic dinner or he'd take her out to one of his favorite local restaurants. She couldn't miss how edgy he was when they were out, though, so she didn't push public dates. In fact, she preferred when they stayed home because she got him up to bed a lot quicker.

By the fourth day, Lakshmi couldn't imagine her life

without Ryan in it. And she wasn't sure how she'd sleep without him beside her.

But worry for her friends dimmed her happiness somewhat.

So after Ryan had left for the hospital and she'd finished the most important work tasks for the day, she called them—Megan's retreat was so wonderfully isolated, she had a satellite phone because cellphones didn't get service.

Lakshmi didn't get an answer the first time she tried, so she went back to work for another half hour and tried again. This time, Erin answered.

"Have you seduced him?" she asked before Lakshmi could say more than *Hi*.

Lakshmi laughed. "Yes. And everything is going really well. So long as no one discovers us before we're ready."

"That's the best news we've had in two days."

"What's wrong? Is it Megan?" Lakshmi frowned at Erin's tone. She sounded worried and tense.

"Megan is doing okay. Still can't shift but she's with us more than she's away if you know what I mean."

"That's something. The others?"

"Oh, we're all okay here. The privacy has been great, actually. Isabella went home for two days and came racing back to get away from the rest of the community. Said there was too much cloying attention. I'm afraid we'll all have to deal with that for a while."

"I'm not surprised." Lakshmi sighed. "Our kidnappings really shook things up."

"The attention wasn't the worst of the news Isabella

brought back, though."

"What's happened?" She'd been so purposefully avoiding other tigers, Lakshmi hadn't a clue there could be *worse* news.

"Couple of things. Gregory is still on the loose."

Lakshmi had figured that—her parents or Ryan's would have been in touch if he'd been caught. "Are the Trackers closing in?"

"Isabella said he keeps giving them the slip somehow."

"Somehow?"

"Like he's being…warned when they get close."

"What? He's getting help? From who?"

"They don't know. But…it might have something to do with the other bad news."

Lakshmi closed her eyes. "Tell me."

"That complex where we were kept, it's been around a long time. Longer than Gregory's been alive."

"So…he didn't build it for us. Okay, that makes some sense. Ryan said he didn't have that kind of money. Gregory probably bought it and updated it to hold us."

"That's the weird part. It was already reinforced against shifter strength. Those reinforcements were built into the foundations of the building, part of the original design, not added later."

"But that doesn't make since. Is it something the elders own? Or another shifter group? Why would anyone design a building in the middle of nowhere that was able to confine shifters…?" She sat back in her seat at the kitchen table as a thought struck panic in her gut. "It wasn't built by humans was it?"

"That's the problem. According to Isabella, we don't know who built it or why. The land and building are owned by a corporation that's just a front. No one has been able to trace the corporation back to its owner—they just keep coming up with more dummy corporations."

"Someone went to a lot of trouble to hide that place. That's more than a little scary."

"Tell me about it."

"So how did Gregory find it? Was he just squatting? Or does he know the owner?"

"They'll know when they capture him. *If* they capture him."

Lakshmi stared at the kitchen wall without seeing it. "He's getting help to escape the Trackers. He was able to use an established shifter-proof compound from…someone…" She trailed off as half-formed connections tried to come together. "Didn't the hybrid-hater, the one who tried to kill that first hybrid-human woman Nila—Petrov… Petrov Dubrovsky, that was his name. Didn't he get help escaping the Trackers—from other Trackers?"

"I'd forgotten that, but yes. They caught a lot of those Trackers, but not all."

"And wasn't there some rumors that an elder was behind all that?"

"Yes, but everyone assumed it was the elder who killed himself after kidnapping the hybrid child—Petrov's son's child." Erin paused. "That's really twisted. Anyway, Elder Lei was as fanatical as Petrov, and one of the Dubrovsky sons admitted Lei was the elder helping his father."

"But according to rumors, Lei claimed he was being framed before he killed himself."

"Well, he'd been caught attacking a child. Of course he'd tried to blame others."

"Yes, but what if someone was framing him?"

"He was a fanatic, Lakshmi. He'd have said anything. Besides, Gregory *isn't* an anti-hybrid tiger. Why would the same people who helped Petrov have any interest in helping Gregory?"

Lakshmi shook her head. "You're right. I'm sure. It's just… I don't know. I get the feeling there's more happening here."

"You think another elder might be…involved?"

"I don't know. I mean, we were worried about that, but when the Trackers came for us, and Alexis said we'd be safe at the compound, I guess I stopped worrying about it so much." Lakshmi pressed a hand to her temple. "I don't even know what I'm saying. It just seems so…odd. Maybe I'm complicating things too much. That complex could have been for anything, and Gregory would only need help from one tiger close to the chase to keep him ahead of the Trackers. Neither of those two things could have anything to do with the other. I'm just looking for conspiracies. Paranoid now, I guess."

"Well, don't feel bad. You're not the only one. Isabella didn't come running back just because of the attention but because her parents still don't want her around other tigers." Erin lowered her voice even though the only people that would be able to hear their conversation were the other women. "Alexis and Victor are worried. They're not the only ones. My father told me to stay at Megan's retreat until they catch Gregory—and maybe stay longer. When I asked why, he said there were very quiet rumors circulating about the complex."

"What rumors?"

"That maybe one of our people built it."

"But why, if it's been around for so long?"

"That's the question. And the worry." Erin growled softly. "I hate rumors without fact. I hate the way fear and innuendo can spread through our community without any real information. I like information, and I hate when I don't have good information to work from."

Lakshmi sympathized. She preferred facts to assumptions, too. "Now I know why you sounded so tense."

"I called my father this morning after Isabella got back. He was so worried it's left me edgy. But I don't know why he was worried, because he couldn't *say* why he was worried."

"After our kidnapping, he's probably seeing danger everywhere. The same paranoia that's making me look for conspiracies," Lakshmi said. But she wasn't sure she believed what she was saying even if it was logical.

"Maybe. But it feels like our community is imploding. Doesn't it to you?"

"I hadn't thought so a few months ago. Now..." She ran a hand over her hair and settled back in her seat. "Have they found Mia yet?" The eighth missing female, Mia Li-Orlova, had still been missing when Lakshmi left the elders' compound.

"Not yet. No sign of her. Her father is frantic."

"Her mother?"

"Her mother is…well, I guess frantic would be the right word. Just a strange, selfish sort of frantic, like the daughter being missing is a blight on her. She's always been a strange one."

Lakshmi tried to remember what she knew of Mia's mother… Mostly that Ning Li had been very fecund and produced something like thirteen or fourteen children over the years, from ten, maybe eleven different males, and three of her children were actually females. It was almost unprecedented to have one tigress produce so many female children, and it had made the woman something of a celebrity among the tigers who supported a female taking new mates for each child.

Since Lakshmi had always wanted a long-term partner in her mate—a relationship like her parents had—she hadn't paid a lot of attention to Ning. Now that Lakshmi had the kind of relationship she'd always wanted, she couldn't imagine taking a new mate for each child.

"I'm sure she's worried in her own way," Lakshmi said. "I'm still hopeful that when they find Gregory, we'll get answers about Mia."

"Hopefully. She must be terrified."

Lakshmi heard the tremor in Erin's voice, felt her own shudder of fear and worry. They were silent for a long moment after that.

Later, after Lakshmi got off the phone with Erin, she paced through Ryan's house, trying to pinpoint exactly why the conversation had disturbed her so much. And wishing

Ryan would get home soon so she could discuss it with him.

* * *

Ryan walked through the door that evening to find Lakshmi pacing the ground floor. She smiled when she saw him and launched into his arms. Immediate worry mixed with the satisfaction of coming home and having her close.

"What's wrong?" he asked into her hair.

Slowly, she eased back from the hug, kissed him lightly —which wasn't nearly enough for him, but she was too worried for him to push the kiss into something deeper— and took his hand.

"Let's eat while we talk," she said. "I forgot about lunch."

The idea of her being hungry bothered him on a deep level, and his tiger grumbled at knowing his mate was upset.

After they'd heated up the rest of his mother's frozen food—a hodgepodge of left-over lasagna, the few remaining pork dumplings, some rich chicken and rice soup, and the remains of a rump roast and vegetables meal —they settled at the kitchen table and Lakshmi told him about her conversation with Erin.

"I don't know why I'm so antsy about the news. I mean, I know why I'm bothered that Gregory is still on the loose."

Ryan had to suppress a growl when her shoulders shook

with a slight tremor and her scent flashed with just a touch of fear and anger.

"But it's the weird coincidence of someone high up having helped Petrov and someone high up helping Gregory." She rolled her eyes. "I'm seeing things where there's nothing, aren't I? Gregory is crazy. Petrov was a fanatic. But they both had completely different views. Didn't they even fight over the hybrid woman at one point? So there's no reason the same person would help them both."

"Especially when the elder who helped Petrov is dead," Ryan added, keeping his tone neutral, but allowing his scent to show his unease at the mention of Nila De Luca.

Lakshmi didn't miss the change. "Why are you uneasy?"

He smiled. "It's easier if I can hide that kind of things. This being open with my scent takes more of an effort than hiding my emotions."

"Ryan…"

He sighed. "I was with Gregory when the young males took in Nila and Mitch Chernikov. I was there when Petrov's tigers attacked, trying to get her back. We fought them off. Gregory and Petrov were most definitely on opposite side of the hybrid issue."

"Is that why you were uncomfortable around the Chernikov brothers? Because of what happened with Nila and Mitch?"

He nodded.

"You regret being there?"

"No. I regret I couldn't get them out before Mitch had to fight for her. He could have been killed."

At the time, Ryan had only been with the young males for about a month and his position was tenuous at best. He couldn't afford to have blown his cover. That didn't stop the twinge of guilt for being any part of that particular incident. Oh, he'd reported a lot of information to the elders afterward. But in the moment, his hands had been tied by the job he was supposed to be doing.

Unfortunately, that situation reminded him too sharply of Lakshmi's kidnapping, and how helpless he'd felt to do anything for the women.

Lakshmi reached across the small table and squeezed his hand. "You helped us, Ryan. Stop beating yourself up over what Gregory did."

He squeezed back and forced a half-smile he didn't feel. "Anyway, my guilt aside. You've run through the logic of why it can't be the same person helping Petrov and Gregory. But you're still worried about…what exactly?"

She jerked her hands up into the air. "I don't know. That's the trouble. I don't know what my instincts are telling me. I just have this feeling that there's a connection of some kind. But every logical part of me tells me there isn't."

"It is pretty coincidental that both Gregory and Petrov received help escaping the Trackers. But it probably is *just* a coincidence."

"I hate coincidences."

"Me, too. Doesn't mean they don't exist."

"The complex Gregory used… It also worries me."

"I'm with you on that. If it was designed to hold shifters but predated Gregory by years, there's something we don't know. Maybe the elders do know and just aren't telling because Gregory found the place. You know how they are with their machinations."

"That doesn't make me feel any better," she said, her tone dry.

He snorted in agreement.

"I guess I'll have to let it go. Until they capture Gregory and he talks, we have no way of knowing."

"I know it's irritating. But hopefully, it doesn't have anything to do with us."

"Alexis and Victor sent Isabella back to the retreat because they were so worried," she said quietly.

That had Ryan's gut tightening. Something was very wrong in their community. "At least Megan is doing better," he said, trying to get on to a more positive topic.

"They all seemed to be happier in Megan's territory. Maybe that's what we should do. Run away to my territory during my estrous."

He smiled. "I'd lose my job for sure then. But it'd be worth it."

She grinned and ducked her head but not before he saw the beautiful pink coloring her cheeks. The spices in her scent mixed with that lovely sweet flavor of desire and pleasure, like honey and cinnamon. He could probably live on that scent alone.

"How was work?" she said, changing the subject completely. And he let her because he hated to see her worried.

Later, when he had a free moment with no one around to listen in, he'd called Elizaveta—or at least her assistant

—and find out if there was any basis to Lakshmi's worries. He'd have to somehow explain how he came by the information without giving Lakshmi away, but he'd figure that out. Anything to ease Lakshmi's mind. She'd been through enough.

* * *

Lakshmi's earsplitting screech wrenched Ryan from a deep sleep. He was reaching for her, ready to fight whatever had scared her, before he was even fully awake. She fell against him, panting, sweating, her heartbeat hammering so hard he felt it where she pressed into him.

"Shh. I've got you." He smoothed his hand down her spine, up again in soothing strokes. "What's wrong? What's happened?" He'd already scanned their surroundings and confirmed there wasn't another shifter around. No scent of a human intruder either.

"Bad dream. Nightmare." She rubbed her face against his neck as she held onto him, her grip tight. "Damn it, I thought I was doing okay."

"The kidnapping." Ryan didn't have to ask. And he should have expected this. "That kind of trauma leaves damage. It's going to take time."

She nodded, her breathing slowly returning to normal, her hold around his waist loosening a little. He didn't let go because she didn't.

"Do you want to talk about it? Or talk about something else so you can forget it?" he asked.

"Which will help more?" There was just a thread of

annoyance in her tone. "I hate nightmares. I never have them. If I meet up with Gregory again, I might just kill him for this alone."

Ryan snorted an almost laugh. "I'll help. That scream of yours gave me a heart attack."

"Sorry."

"Don't be. I'm glad I was here." He stroked her hair, letting his fingers tangle in the thick softness.

"You didn't answer my question," she said, shifting positions so she could snuggle against him better.

He leaned back on his pillow, pulling her with him, keeping her tight against his chest. "About which will help more, talking about it or ignoring the dream? It depends on you. Eventually, you need to deal with it all. And keep seeing a counselor for as long as necessary. But if you don't want to live in the nightmare again for tonight, I'm sure we can find other things to talk about."

She leaned up a little to look at him and he got his first clear view of her. There were very faint circles under her eyes, a touch of tension in her mouth, and her scent was laced with the musk of terror that had come out of her dream with her. He cupped her face with one hand, rubbing his thumb over her high cheekbone.

"I couldn't move," she said. "I was screaming in my head, trying to force my body to obey, my tiger was roaring in my head, but I couldn't move. Gregory stood over me laughing. There were shadows in the dark, circling me. I could sense them, so many of them. But I couldn't fight. I couldn't do anything." She swallowed visibly and looked away. "That was always the worst part for me. The effects of that drug…" She looked him in the eye. "I'd rather fight and lose than not be able to fight."

"I know. I think I fell in love with you the first time you told me that."

She blinked, sitting up a little. "You…you love me?"

"Of course. What do you think I'm doing here?"

"Living in your own home that I invaded."

He chuckled. "If I didn't want you, the future you've offered me…if I wasn't in love with you, I wouldn't be risking this much to have you."

"I love you, too."

He kissed her, very softly because words wouldn't suffice.

"This is better than thinking about the nightmare," she murmured against his mouth. "Much better."

"Good." And he kissed her deeper, savoring her sweet, spicy flavor. Her scent signature had shifted, the fear musk gone, replaced by something infinitely more delicate and yet full of strength, like honeysuckle but more…more than he had words for. He pulled in that smell, wrapped it around his soul to sooth his own worries, allowing all he was feeling to flood his own scent.

With Lakshmi, he held nothing back. It felt so damned right, he knew he'd never be able to hide from her again, not even if he tried. He *had* to let her know him on this level, let her know all his emotions, his love, his fear, his anger for what Gregory had done to her, and his need. So much need swamping him as she shifted to straddle his hips, pressing her lush body close.

He gripped her hips, making an effort to be gentle even

as desire roared through his blood. Her turn to lead the way, to set the pace and decide where they went. She needed control after her dream, and he wanted to give that to her. She was so damned strong, so magnificently fierce, he needed her to know he saw her that way. Saw who she was, not what Gregory had done to her.

She set a slow pace, which was both delicious and torturous.

Her hands were magic as they stroked across his shoulders, down his chest, setting his skin on fire everywhere she touched. He touched in turn, letting her moans and approving murmurs dictate the places he lingered, the sensitive spots he knew drove her crazy. The inside of her elbows, the back of her knee, the sides of her neck, her waist and across her hips. She shivered when he caressed her ass, his touch as gentle as his need would allow him.

"Harder," she demanded.

He complied, but only a little harder, just enough to continue the torture. She growled and nipped at his lower lip.

"Harder," she said.

He gave up any pretense of gentleness then, letting all his lust roar through him as he gripped her ass and lifted her, settling her over his cock, easing her down, pausing just long enough to watch her eyes close. Then he slammed up into her, as hard as she wanted him to, and their groans echoed together in the darkness.

She was so hot and perfect, so right. He couldn't imagine anything more right than having Lakshmi wrapped around him. She rocked against him, again taking the lead, setting a rhythm that was steady but not too slow. He watched where their bodies joined, the sight more erotic than anything he'd ever seen. She leaned back, her hands gripping his thighs and the change in position tightened her inner muscles around him.

The slap of her skin against his filled the room, matching their pants and moans. Her scent layered through his, mixing together to form that blend that was uniquely theirs, the perfect combining of two souls into one essence. A bead of sweat slipped down her neck and over her chest, between her breasts. He followed it with a finger, before turning his attention to her breasts, pinching one of her nipples just hard enough to make her cry out and arch into his touch.

She came with a shuddering scream, the kind of primal sound his tiger adored, and he followed her, unable to resist anything she demanded of him. He held her hips tight as her body pulled his into an orgasm that ripped him apart, and he happily went to that hot, sharp place of pure sensation where only Lakshmi existed.

As the storm eased, she dropped slowly forward, wrapping around him in a full body hug that settled him in a way nothing else ever had. He stroked her back, cradling her close as she drifted back to sleep. He didn't loosen his hold for a long time, wanting her to know, even in sleep, that he'd be there for her—to protect her, to stand with her, to comfort her. To be her mate, no matter what their laws demanded.

And somehow, some way, he'd make sure Gregory and his kind never threatened her again.

CHAPTER TWENTY-ONE

Lakshmi was still shaken by her nightmare the next day, but she refused to let Ryan stay home from work to keep her company. Mostly because it made her feel weak. She hated feeling weak, and he seemed to understand that because he left even though his scent was full of his reluctance.

She loved him even more for it.

After wishing him well, she fired up her laptop, then called her parents so they knew she was okay.

Her father delivered the news that Gregory had almost been caught but had managed to get away. "He's injured now," he said quietly. "Your mother wants to join the hunt. She's more afraid of him now that he's wounded."

Lakshmi hummed under her breath. "Don't let her go after him."

"I won't." He half-laughed. "But mostly because it protects innocent bystanders from her maternal anger."

Lakshmi smiled. "Thanks, papa."

"You're safe?" His voice got even quieter. "We know you're…not with the others."

She opened her mouth to explain, but her father didn't give her a chance.

"Don't say anything. I don't need to know what you're doing or where you are. Only that you're happy. And safe."

"I'm safe. And very, very happy."

"Ah, my child. It makes my heart rejoice to hear that. I expect…a full accounting when you're able."

"There might be difficulties ahead, papa."

"There always are with love matches. It won't matter in the end."

She frowned a little at the kitchen wall. "Are you sure? I want to believe that, but…"

"If it makes you feel better, your mother and I will support any decision you make. No matter what. As we always have."

Her shoulders relaxed from a tension she hadn't realized she'd held. "I love you."

"I love you, too. Stay safe. Keep your senses open for Gregory."

"I will. You too. Just in case."

"He wouldn't dare come here, even as crazy and unpredictable as he is. Your mother would tear him into unrecognizable pieces."

"That didn't stop him from kidnapping Alexis' daughter."

"And look what that got him. He'll be lucky if a neutral Tracker brings him in before Alexis' tigers find him."

Lakshmi snorted at the truth in that statement.

She spent the rest of the day handling the invoices and ordering for the new store, several calls with the new manager as well as a conference call with her bookkeeper and accountant over the finances at her coffee shop, then she did some research into a new clothing brand she was considering stocking.

The light was already starting to dim when she looked up from her laptop and realized she'd missed lunch and had rolled right into dinner time.

She'd never been much of a cook—despite her father's innate talent and her mother's many lessons over the years, Lakshmi had never developed the love of preparing meals. So after a search of Ryan's fridge revealed they'd eaten all the food his mother had left, she decided some take-out was in order.

She glanced at the clock on the microwave. Ryan wouldn't be home for another couple of hours. But she was too hungry to wait. And she was sure she'd be able to eat again after he got home. A quick internet search turned up a New York style pizza restaurant in the neighborhood. So she grabbed her keys, texted Ryan so he wouldn't worry if he came home early—and knowing he would made her smile—and headed out into the Boston twilight. She raised her head after locking the house, pulling in the local scents, testing the taste of the air. A slight shiver of awareness moved over her skin.

She narrowed her eyes, opening her senses. She couldn't feel another tiger nearby. But after what she'd been through, she didn't want to take anything for granted

—even the fact that she might be imagining things because of her nightmare.

Forcing a casual gate, she ambled to the pizza joint, a long enough walk to work off some of her antsiness. She kept her senses open to her surroundings, stretched as far as they would go. But she couldn't pinpoint anything suspicious.

The restaurant was a long, narrow place surrounded by other mom-and-pop owned shops and restaurants on a busy commercial street. The smell of garlic, tomato, and cheese made her stomach growl when she stepped inside, the bell over the glass front door ringing a happy jingle. She ordered a large, loaded pie, and then moved to the side of the tall wooden counter to wait, hovering near the parmesan and pepper flake shakers lined up on little metal trays.

Her senses were still jumping with the sensation of being watched, even though she couldn't find a source for her unease. She let her gaze travel over the patrons sitting at checkered cloth-covered tables in the back of the restaurant, all humans completely unaware of anything beyond their food and the people they were sitting with.

She was used to humans ignoring their own instincts. All tiger shifters learned to keep an unassuming aura that wouldn't alarm the humans around them. Her people's extinction issues meant they had to stay under human radar, and many of the tiger laws were designed to accomplish just that. But it never ceased to amaze Lakshmi how easy it was for humans to miss a predator standing right next to them.

And it bothered her that she'd somehow fallen into that

human habit and missed the predators who'd kidnapped her.

Not a mistake she'd ever make again.

She was still scanning her surroundings when her cellphone rang. She smiled at Ryan's number. "Did you get my text?" she asked by way of a hello.

"I did. Are you okay?"

"Yes. As usual. Why do you sound worried?"

"I just got a call from my brother-in-law. Gregory has been spotted on this coast."

"My father said they almost had him in Michigan just yesterday. And that he was wounded and may be even more dangerous now."

"All true, according to Daniel. He's afraid Gregory is making his way to Boston."

"Because of you?"

"Where are you now? Still at the restaurant?"

She glanced at the clock on her phone. "Pizza should be ready in another ten minutes."

"Stay there. In public. I'll meet you there in half an hour."

She looked back at all the happy, unaware humans sitting around the cheap tables, eating their delicious smelling meals. "Not sure that's a good idea. Innocent bystanders and all." She'd lowered her voice but the cell made it impossible to talk in the almost inaudible tones they could use in person.

Ryan was silent a moment. "I understand. But stay there anyway. Crazy as he is, he's never shown any signs he'd reveal the shifters to humans."

Lakshmi's conscience argued with her pragmatic side but pragmatism won out. "I'll order a second pizza for you before you get here. And if anything goes…wrong I'll text you. Keep your phone available."

"I'll be there as soon as traffic allows."

"Be safe. If he's here it's because of you."

She disconnected, staring at the blank screen with its screen saver of a lush green forest, and patted the phone as she might Ryan's hand. Her instincts were jumping as frantically as her nerves. And all her worry now was for Ryan.

Ryan climbed out of his Jeep and closed the door gently, ignoring his instincts to race across the street and slam into the little pizza restaurant. It still took all his self-control to move at human speed through the parking lot of the office supply store and across the street to the row of shops and restaurants. He sent Daniel a pre-programmed text, then turned on his cellphone's GPS all at an even, unhurried pace. He crossed at a traffic light, waiting for the lights to change without any outward sign of impatience.

Finally, he pushed into the delicious smelling restaurant like an ordinary human man and strolled past the counter to the back room. Where he sensed Lakshmi waiting…

With Gregory.

Lakshmi stared at the insane tiger sitting across from her, her expression impossible to read, her body language casual. She sat with her hands in plain sight on the edge of the table, a slice of pizza in front of her, a plastic cup of water next to that. She was leaning back in her wooden chair, giving all onlookers the appearance of a woman at ease. But her feet were planted firmly on the ground, as if she were ready to move at the slightest provocation. Even with all the oregano, garlic and olive oil scents filling the air, Ryan could smell the violence of her anger. And under that, just the faintest hint of her fear.

Gregory looked equally casual, one arm resting on the table, the other hand holding a slice of half-eaten pizza. But Gregory's gaze was on Ryan as he crossed to their table. And Gregory's smile was that sinister lifting of lips that raised Ryan's hackles.

"Doctor! So glad you could join us," Gregory said, indicating a free seat.

Ryan looked him over first, noting the way Gregory kept one foot more firmly on the ground than the other. Daniel said Gregory's leg bones had been broken when he escaped the Trackers in Michigan. Without a doctor, those bones likely healed badly, which would leave Gregory in some pain, and not nearly as dexterous as usual.

Ryan didn't underestimate the strength the pain probably lent the bastard, though.

"You okay?" he said to Lakshmi, keeping his gaze on Gregory the way she was.

"Fine." Clipped and simple, no elaboration, her voice tight and just a little deeper than usual.

"Join us," Gregory said again, gesturing with his half-eaten slice to a chair.

Tension tightened the lines around Gregory's eyes,

despite his pleasant tone, and his scent was full of so much crazy and pain now, Ryan couldn't detect anything around it. Not even a hint if his intentions.

Taking his seat, which he scooted close enough to Lakshmi that they could both keep Gregory in sight without getting in each other's way, he said, "Pizza good here?"

Gregory smiled. "Delicious. Almost as good as real New York pizza."

"I've always preferred Chicago style," Ryan said, just to be contrary. "Why are you here?"

Gregory made a grand gesture with the hand not holding food. "This is my first trip to Boston. You'll have to give me a tour." He glanced between them, then focused on Lakshmi and tisked. In a tone too low for the people around them to hear, he said, "Spending time with the good doctor outside the Mate Run? Lakshmi, what a bad little tigress you are." His gaze dipped to her breast before he met her gaze again. "Wish I'd known that."

Ryan swallowed his growl because if he let it out, he wasn't sure he'd be able to keep his tiger controlled. He let his disgust and anger into his scent, though, knowing Gregory would expect it.

He risked a glance at Lakshmi, keeping Gregory in his peripheral vision. She was smiling, a brittle-looking baring of teeth.

"Would you like to go a round with me?" she asked, as quietly as he'd spoken. "I could show you exactly how *bad* I am."

Gregory laughed, the sound loud and abrupt, startling several people around them. He ignored the stares and the way the humans shifted their chairs a little farther away from him.

"Are you in a hurry to get caught?" Ryan asked.

"They won't interfere." Gregory flicked his fingers in a dismissive gesture at the other customers.

"Don't count on it," Ryan said. "You really want to tangle with the human police?"

"Doctor. I'm under a death sentence. What do I care about paltry human law?"

"The elders might not put you to death."

"Even though you deserve it," Lakshmi added.

"But if you cooperate," Ryan continued, not even trying to contradict her statement, "they might spare your life."

"Did they tell you to tell me that?" Gregory asked. "Seeing as how you work for them, I assume you know."

Ryan held perfectly still, not revealing his reaction to Gregory's statement in his body language or scent. But inside, his brain exploded with shock. "What are you talking about?" he asked, keeping his tone light.

"Breaking the laws by being with a tigress, and you a spy for the elders. Shame, doctor."

Beside him, Ryan felt Lakshmi stiffen, and a thread of shock moved into her scent. She turned to face him. He kept his gaze on Gregory. The surprise, like drops of acid, increased in her scent.

He shut his own scent down, letting only irritation show, and hoped like hell Lakshmi recognized what he was doing.

"You're paranoid," Ryan said. "You always have been. You know how I feel about the Mate Run."

"True. True. And wasn't that a nice little bonus. That you actually *did* hate the Run as much as the rest of us. Is that why they chose you to spy on me? Because you can lie so well by telling some truths?"

Ryan forced down his knee-jerk snarl, and the equally instinctive reaction to deny everything Gregory was saying. He kept his scent carefully controlled, revealing only irritation and a very slight edge of offense. But he didn't jump to defending himself against the accusation.

Instead, he asked, "What makes you think I've been spying on you, Gregory? Because I got away from the mess you created with only a week in confinement?" He shook his head, as if the answer to that was obvious. "I told you from the start that taking the women was a mistake. I got them out to save lives. And I've been banned forever from the Mate Run for my efforts. Where in all that do you get the idea I'm a spy?"

Gregory stared at him, his expression thoughtful. "You are such a good liar, Ryan. How do you do that?"

Ryan startled at Gregory's use of his first name. He'd almost always called him "doctor" before this. The use of his name couldn't be good.

"I still don't know what you think I'm lying about. I *did* get banned from the Run forever. I *did* spend a week in confinement, even though I got the women out and had nothing to do with your stupid-ass plan to kidnap them. What the hell am I lying about?"

"I know about confinement and the ban. That was very carefully disseminated among our people so that I couldn't help but know." Gregory leaned forward, putting his face in Ryan's.

Ryan didn't flinch, but he wanted to as Gregory's stench washed over him.

"I'm not as crazy as everyone thinks," Gregory said.

"Yes, you are," Ryan said.

Gregory smiled and leaned back. "That's why I let you stay, doctor. I've always liked you, despite the fact that you came to our group to betray it. I had hoped we could win you over. I'm not the only one."

He murmured the last very quietly.

Before Ryan could respond, a large, heavy human man came to the table, wiping his hands on a dish cloth. He stopped next to Lakshmi, drawing all their attention.

"Everything here okay?" The human man looked at Lakshmi as he asked, his raised brows and intent stare easy to read even if his concern wasn't obvious to all of them in his scent.

"We're fine." She smiled at him, a reassuring look that didn't reveal any hints of her tension.

Ryan filled his scent with the calm, confident reassurance he used on patients, hoping the man picked it up and relaxed. The last thing they needed was some well-meaning human getting involved and getting hurt.

"May we get the check?" Lakshmi asked. "And a box for the rest of the pizza. It's the best I've had in a long time. Can't wait for the cold slice for breakfast tomorrow morning."

The man's smiled flashed before he frowned again and

glanced at Gregory. "If you're sure I can't do anything else for you…"

"Thank you," Lakshmi said.

The man nodded and walked back to the front counter, glancing at them as he got their check ready.

"We need to leave," she said, facing Ryan and Gregory again. "This isn't business to discuss in front of humans."

"Someplace…private then?" Gregory asked. "You surprise me."

"The Trackers are on their way," Ryan said. "You'd do well to run again, Gregory. They'll be here any minute."

Gregory's gaze swiveled to Ryan, something dark moving through the depths of his eyes even though he kept his pleasant expression firmly in place.

"You called the Trackers?" Gregory asked.

"I sent a message to my brother-in-law." Ryan saw no reason to deny it if it meant Gregory would leave without any of the humans or Lakshmi being hurt. "They already knew you were coming this way."

"Because I know you're a spy, and they thought I'd come to kill you?" Gregory asked.

The human man returned with the check and a take-away box. Lakshmi took the check from him before he could hand it to Ryan. She paid, leaving a substantial tip Ryan noted, and the man reluctantly left them again. Ryan put the rest of the pizza into the box, maintaining the illusion that the humans didn't need to worry about them.

Lakshmi stood. "I need some fresh air." And she started for the door without waiting for either Ryan or Gregory.

Gregory met Ryan's gaze as he rose slowly to his feet,

tossing the half-eaten slice of pizza in his hand back on the table.

"You lied to her about working for the elders? She seems a little annoyed." Gregory smirked. "Oops."

"You're not nearly as funny as you think you are," Ryan said, taking the box and heading out ahead of him.

It took a great deal of willpower for Ryan to turn his back on the insane bastard, and the fine hairs on the back of his neck stood on end as he pushed through the restaurant's front door, giving the proprietor a friendly wave on the way out.

Lakshmi was waiting on the sidewalk, her gaze moving over the busy street.

"We need to talk later," she murmured to Ryan just before Gregory walked out.

Then Gregory was next to them and Ryan had to focus on what to do next. Gregory wouldn't stay here and just wait for the Trackers to arrive. And like the restaurant, anywhere public would put humans in danger.

Gregory pulled in a deep breath. "Boston smells delicious. But it's time for us to be away."

Ryan reacted to Gregory's tone more than his words, moving faster than he should have in front of humans, out of instinct more than a conscious realization of what Gregory was about to do.

And Ryan still wasn't fast enough to avoid the needle prick.

CHAPTER TWENTY-TWO

Ryan started fighting the effects of the drug immediately, but it didn't stop the loss of control, the way his limbs froze, like they didn't belong to him anymore. He could feel Gregory pulling him up from behind, the sting of Gregory's knife against his waist, carefully hidden from the passing pedestrians. Ryan could see the fear in Lakshmi's eyes, and despite his difficulty breathing, he could still clearly scent her terror. For him.

But most of that was peripheral to his battle against the drug's effects. He knew as a male he could break out of the drug quicker than the females could, but it would still take time, precious time. Vaguely, he heard Gregory order Lakshmi into a car parked on the street not far from the restaurant, threatening Ryan's life if she didn't cooperate. Ryan wanted to shout at her to run, get away from the bastard now, but like the rest of his body, his voice was locked up by the drug.

He'd known in a clinical, empathic sense how horrible this must have been for the women, but having his own body out of his control, not being able to move or fight though he could still feel and was aware of everything… It was like a nightmare. The vulnerability of it was appalling, and having his mate in danger without being able to defend her was a kind of torture.

So he fought the drug with every ounce of rage and fear he had, letting out emotions he'd spent most of his life controlling with so much force, the air inside Gregory's car stank with it. Ryan let his tiger take the lead, that vital primitive part of him fighting ferociously to move.

He had no idea how long they were in the car, or where they went. Lakshmi had been forced into the front seat while Ryan was laid out on the backseat, a blanket carelessly tossed over him to keep any passing observers from being suspicious. The only part of him not fighting the drug was the part monitoring her scent, keeping track of her emotions. The tone of her conversation with Gregory penetrated into Ryan's awareness a little, but mostly he paid attention to the unspoken conversation, in a way he'd have trouble explaining to a human.

Time blurred, and Ryan only realized it was pitch dark after the car stopped and Gregory threw open the door. The tiger's tone was cocky and laced with hate, but Ryan could no longer decipher words. He was moving too far into his tiger, relying on his animal to break out.

Lakshmi touched his arm briefly before Ryan was jerked away under Gregory's hold. The quick contact was a comfort that also sent his tiger into roaring, mindless rage.

His mate was in danger. He had to move… He. Had. To. Move…

Lakshmi followed Gregory down a long, narrow, wooden pier to a floating dock, covered by an open-sided wooden shelter. There were houses behind them, along a hillside and farther down the dark road, but the pier and dock were blocked from view by thick trees. Before the pier moved out over the water, she spotted a small stretch of sand beneath them, with some rough shrubbery and rocks leading back up a slight hill to the road. She could see lights in the distance, across the water on some spit of land, but couldn't tell if it was an island or part of the mainland. The area was quiet except for the slosh of rolling water and gentle waves, and the scent of fish, salt and seaweed was thick in the cool night air. Very distantly, she heard the faint sound of a fog horn, but she couldn't see a lighthouse.

They were some distance outside Boston, but she had no idea where exactly since she didn't know the area well. Likely they were at an inlet rather than right on the Atlantic because the waves were too gentle. Other than that, she couldn't be sure. Even the names on the road signs hadn't meant much to her. She really should have taken the time to get to know her surroundings better.

The fact that Gregory had a place to take them, even though he'd just arrived in Boston that day worried her. Had he been planning this the entire time he was running from the Trackers? And if so…how?

Gregory was rambling nonsense conspiracy stuff about the elders, about the Mate Run, about death matches being the only true way forward. She mostly ignored him because her attention was so fully focused on Ryan. She could scent everything he was feeling, and knew he was fighting. She knew exactly how he felt in that moment, and it hurt her heart that he'd been subjected to the drug that had caused her so much trauma.

Her own fear at seeing the syringe in Gregory's hand, watching him inject Ryan before she could react…the terror and helplessness were a living thing in her gut— matched only by an anger she could barely keep in check. Her tiger wanted out, to rip and tear and protect her mate. But Gregory had his knife at Ryan's throat now. Tiger shifters healed fast, but a deep enough slice through the neck could kill Ryan. Worse, Gregory might not even bother with the knife. He could easily tear Ryan's head right off while he was so vulnerable—a sure way to kill him.

Lakshmi couldn't shift fast enough to prevent Ryan from getting hurt, not while Gregory kept him like a shield in front of him, so she followed and watched for an opening, keeping her senses open to Ryan's fight against the drug.

The smell of salt water, wet plant life, and molding wood surrounded her as Gregory stepped onto the floating dock and moved underneath the wooden roof. The dock was cut in a blocky U-shape, allowing a single boat to moor up inside it and be covered by the protective roof. Wooden posts held the roof over the dock, and little silver line hooks dotted the inner edge of the platform. The wooden planking around the open center was a little warped, the water beneath them black as ink. There wasn't a boat there at the moment, so the central area was like a pit waiting to swallow them.

She had a horrifying thought that Gregory would just toss Ryan into that pit. Without the ability to control his limbs, Ryan would drown. And because he could feel everything, he'd feel that slow, suffocating death.

She shivered.

"Cold, bitch?" Gregory said. "Good."

"What are we doing here?" She almost hated to ask, but she wanted Gregory talking. If he kept talking, he'd give Ryan more time to break out from under the drug.

She balanced on her toes, ready to move in an instant, and kept her gaze on Gregory as he moved down one side of the floating dock. When she tried to follow, he shook his head and grinned, pointing to the opposite side of the U, across the open area from him.

"I know it's an easy jump," he commented casually. "For our kind. But I like keeping you in sight."

"What are we doing here?" she asked again. From her peripheral vision, she saw Ryan's hand twitch. She hid her reaction as best she could, but she'd never wished for Ryan's ability to change his scent so much as she did right then.

"Boat's on its way," Gregory said, his tone now distant and distracted as he looked out to the lapping waves of water in the channel. "A ship is moored off the coast, waiting for us."

She ignored the punch of fear that comment sent through her. "And then what? Why are you doing this?" She kept her own tone even because Ryan's fingers were flexing and she didn't want Gregory to notice.

"We escape. There's an island. You'll bear me the children I deserve, as you were meant to. And he'll be our doctor. Chained of course. Can't trust him. Never trust the doctor. That's what he told me. Made sure I knew. Did you know that, my little bitch? He's been helping me all along. He'll give me the kingdom I deserve. The one I've earned."

Lakshmi swallowed hard. "Who's he, Gregory?"

She forced down the image of the future Gregory was proposing. She had no intention of letting things get that far. In the distance, she did hear a boat approaching, a single outboard motor chugging closer. Their time to act was running out. She had to do something.

It took her brain a moment to recognize the change in Ryan's scent. Or rather the fact that it hadn't actually changed.

The emotions in it *were* subtly different now. Still anger, fear, frustration, desperation. But all a lot stronger than they were just moments ago, even though he was breaking free of the drug. Another few moments passed before she caught up to what he was doing. When she did, she almost smiled.

He was letting Gregory smell what he wanted him to, ensuring Gregory didn't realize Ryan was almost free. There was no triumph in Ryan's scent, no satisfaction when he made a fist and relaxed it. He continued to hang heavy against the arm Gregory had around his chest, his head flopped to one side, which left his neck vulnerable to the knife.

But he was almost out of the drug now, hiding it well, which meant she had to keep Gregory distracted just a little longer.

"Who is 'he', Gregory?" she said again, making the tiger look at her.

She had a hard time meeting his glittering gaze. There was almost no recognizable logic left in it, none of the part of him she might consider human. Yet she wasn't looking at the beautiful danger of a tiger's gaze either. Something much worse moved in the clouded, sparkling depths of brown, something not at all natural.

"He?" Gregory asked, blinking slowly. "He is my servant. He pretends to lead our people all while ensuring I gain my throne."

"What the hell happened to you?" she muttered.

She'd never seen a tiger go so far crazy like this before, not and survive it. Her people were harsh and merciless when it came to perceived mental flaws. They didn't want those genes endangering their already precarious survival. How had Gregory been allowed to get this insane without being locked up? Or killed?

"I was born superior," Gregory said, misinterpreting her question. "He knew it. He came to me."

"He?"

"My servant. He came to me, told me the truth."

"What truth?"

"That I was born to be king of our people. A ruler. That

I should have as many mates and children as I deemed worthy of me."

Someone had purposefully fed him that story? Did they know what they were doing, playing into his delusion?

"When did he come to you?" she asked.

"When he told me not to trust the doctor." Gregory glanced at the side of Ryan's face. "I knew all along," he murmured to Ryan. "I knew you were the elders' spy. He told me. You were useful, though. I was happy to make you one of my servants. He said I should send you away, but I didn't want to. How do you do that with your scent?" His voice had gone even lower, almost sing-songy as he stared, unblinking, at Ryan.

The mention of how Ryan could control his scent started Lakshmi's heartbeat thumping painfully in her chest. He knew. If he knew, he'd realize soon that Ryan's scent right now was a lie. She hadn't seen Gregory take out another syringe of the drug, but that didn't mean he didn't have more. Or worse, he'd simply kill Ryan before Ryan could protect himself.

She started to inch around the edge of the dock. The sound of the outboard motor was getting closer, even if she couldn't see any running lights yet. Time was almost up.

Gregory's gaze flashed back to hers. "Aren't you angry? That he lied to you? I know you are. I saw it in the restaurant. He's been the elders' spy, and you didn't know." Gregory grinned. "Don't worry, my little bitch, I'll make sure he's punished for his impudence."

Gregory blinked, his expression turning thoughtful and almost reasonable if you weren't looking into his eyes. "I think you will be my queen, my first wife, above all my wives. If you serve me well, that will be your reward. I thought it would be Irina. But she's been the slut of that other male for too long. She's ruined. I'll just kill her. And then you can be my queen."

"Irina?" If he was talking about the tigress Irina Gorbin, she'd given birth last winter to a female tiger and was mated to Max Rudikov. Lakshmi had a vague memory of some connection between Gregory, Max and Irina, but she couldn't recall the rumors just then.

"Irina was always supposed to be mine," Gregory said, quietly, sadly. "She just wouldn't face the truth. Now she's been replaced. You will be my queen."

"Why me?" Not that she really cared, but Ryan was staring out to the open water now, toward the sound of the approaching boat. He'd make his move soon. She just had to keep Gregory distracted a few minutes longer.

"At the complex, when I came to you in the harem room, you didn't back down from me. You're strong. You'll breed many healthy tiger children for me. You're beautiful. Not Irina, but still beautiful."

"Gee, thanks," she mumbled, barely resisting the impulse to roll her eyes.

"And the doctor loves you," Gregory finished. "It will be a fitting punishment for his betrayal that the tigress he loves becomes my queen."

"That's almost logical, Gregory," she said, keeping her gaze on him even though the boat was getting closer. "I wouldn't have thought you capable of logic at this point."

He barked a laugh. "See! You'll make a superior queen.

All the tigers will bow down to you. You'll thank me for placing you above the others."

"Who's coming to get us?" She inched another few steps to the back of the dock. From here, she could leap across to Gregory and take his knife hand without getting in Ryan's way.

"His emissary," Gregory said. "He too will be one of my devoted followers. The others are already waiting for us on the ship."

Others? She assumed those were the young males that had escaped with Gregory. At least, she hoped so. Worry for more female captives, for the still-missing tigress clenched in her gut. To keep from letting that fear out, she said, "You still haven't mentioned who 'he' is?"

"I told you. He's my servant."

"Who pretends to lead our people? An elder then?"

"What is an elder? An old man with no sense and too much money. Worthless and out of date. Past all usefulness."

"So your…servant isn't an elder? Or is he?"

"He's certainly old," Gregory said. Then laughed like he'd made a joke.

The boat came into view then, angling across the open water toward the dock. It was a speedboat, but it was chugging slowly toward them, the sounds of the motor quieter as it approached the coastline. The window shield on the front of the boat was salted and dark, and the boat still didn't have any running lights on, so Lakshmi couldn't see the driver. He wasn't close enough yet for her to sense whether he was a tiger or not.

She was still staring at the boat when movement from Gregory's side of the dock had her swinging around, ready to face an attack…

In time to see Ryan flip Gregory over his head and into the black water.

CHAPTER TWENTY-THREE

L akshmi watched Gregory sink, the impenetrable cold darkness swallowing him in one gulp. She moved to leap across to Ryan, afraid if he wasn't fully recovered he'd lose his balance and follow Gregory into the lapping waves. Ryan gestured her still, his gaze intent on the water.

She froze, ready to leap, and the stillness saved her.

Gregory exploded back out of the blackness, strands of muck and weeds clinging to him as he reached for Ryan. Ryan leapt back, bounced against one of the wooden posts holding up the roof, and stumbled toward the front of the dock as the planks he'd been standing on shattered under Gregory's lunge.

Lakshmi raced around the edge of the dock toward Ryan as Gregory sank under the water again. Awareness of the open water beneath her sent a tingling wave of anxiety through her nerves, expecting to feel the wood beneath her give way at any moment.

She reached Ryan just as the place she'd been standing erupted, the wood exploding out in a shower of sharp shards. She raised an arm to protect her face from flying splinters, positioning herself in front of Ryan even as she felt his arms come around her to pull her away from the source of the chaos.

Gregory landed on what remained of the dock at the end closest to the open water, a small section of still-floating plank barely connected now to the main structure of the platform. The speedboat hovered within sight but had stopped in the lapping waves, not approaching. Lakshmi still couldn't see who was driving the thing.

"You two are dead," Gregory growled. "I will have your heads when I'm done."

Without any indication of what he intended, Ryan launched across the length of the dock, wrapping his arms around Gregory's chest, a rugby tackle that sent them careening into the water.

"Ryan!" Lakshmi dove in after them, and the sharp cold water stole her breath.

She surfaced and swam toward the two men, ignoring the freezing chill racking her. The sounds of splashing and cursing directed her as she cut through the low waves. Her night vision was excellent but the rolling rise and fall of the water, gentle though it was, the cold, and the darkness still disoriented her. It took her painfully long moments to reach the fighting men.

The boat motor started again. She looked up in time to see it approaching, circling them.

She swallowed a splash of water, choking as she

reached the fight, and had to take another long moment to differentiate between the two men. Then she dove beneath the surface, using her tiger sense to feel Gregory because the water was too murky to see. She grabbed one thrashing leg, lost her grip, then grabbed him again. And jerked down hard.

The move sent her bobbing to the surface. She broke for a single gulp of air before strong hands grabbed her calves and jerked her beneath the water again. She kicked and thrashed, reaching down to grab hair she couldn't see, pulling up with all her strength. Thick nails ripped through her jeans and scraped over her skin as her assailant was lurched away. She broke the surface again for another breath. And the boat motored past nearly close enough to clip her head.

She back-paddled, fighting the water's resistance, to put space between her and the boat. As it swung around toward her again, she took a huge gulp of air and dove under water. She swam through the murk toward Ryan and Gregory still fighting beneath the surface. She gripped Gregory's hair hard and yanking his head back, the motion not nearly as effective as it would have been on land. She felt Gregory convulse and then she had to launch toward the surface again to breathe. Kicking hard, she didn't release her hold on Gregory, but when she broke into the open air, he twisted away from her, breaking her grip. He sucked in a breath before diving under again.

The waves were larger now, caused by the circling boat, and Lakshmi choked on more water spray.

Ryan surfaced a few feet away and swam to her, his

gaze scanning their surroundings. "Feel him. Can't see him."

She treaded water, spinning in a circle, Ryan at her back as they searched for Gregory. She couldn't hear well above the sounds of the boat, her sense of smell was useless over the strong, thick punch of seawater and fish, and while she could sense Gregory out there, she couldn't pinpoint him.

"Damn it, where is he?" she shouted, her throat tight, her stomach in knots as anxiety crawled over her skin. She was starting to shiver—even a shifter's high metabolism was no match for long against icy, spring ocean water.

The boat was closing in, coming directly at them, picking up speed as it got closer. She swung around to face Ryan just as a sharp pain sliced into her thigh. She screamed, her body jerking against the shocking wound. Warm blood leaked into the water around her even as a chill raced through the rest of her limbs.

Ryan grabbed her by the shoulders, keeping her head above the waterline. He kicked out hard and pushed them both through the water, away from the boat as it surged past, the hull barely missing Ryan's foot.

"What's happened?" he asked when they were out of the boat's immediate path.

She reached beneath the surface, touched the jagged edge of her ripped jeans. "Knife, I think. I'm bleeding."

She glanced toward the boat, trying to gauge its direction and her vision blurred for a minute. Shock. Shit, she couldn't afford to go into shock. She blinked against the rising nausea.

"Gregory still has the knife," she said through chattering teeth.

"Can you stay up?" he asked, looking around, one arm wrapped around her for support, the other swishing across the water's surface.

"Find him," she said. "I'll be okay." She eased back, using her arms to tread water so she wouldn't have to move her injured leg.

Ryan dove under again, disappearing into the spray.

She swung around, hissing as salt water made the pain in her leg infinitely worse. She was so disoriented she had no idea which direction the shore was now. Or how far away she was from it. She did know the water was going to leech blood from her fast, even though the wound was already closing. And she was a little afraid of what that blood might attract.

The roar of the boat motor closing in again pulled her attention. It chugged slower this time, getting close without trying to ram her. She swam back from it, keeping it in sight as it maneuvered to a bumping stop near her.

The male tiger driving wasn't someone she knew personally, not one of the young males she'd seen at Gregory's compound, though she was sure she hadn't seen all of them. But he was smiling at her in a way that made her almost forget the shooting pain in her thigh.

He stopped the motor and reached over the edge toward her. "You don't want to drown, you'll get aboard," he shouted.

"I'd rather drown, thanks," she said and paddled back a little farther.

His eyes narrowed, but before he could say more the boat lurched sharply, rolling sideways so far the male was almost tossed into the water. He gripped the railing as the boat rocked back so far the other way it nearly capsized again.

The waves knocked Lakshmi farther from the boat, and she took advantage of the momentum to put space between her and the strange male. When the boat flopped back onto its hull, Gregory was standing in the middle of it, blood covering his chest and neck. He stared at her, not even trying to cover the deep slice on his throat to stem the blood. She could see it wasn't a killing blow, it would heal, but his blood was still spilling out. He wobbled in the rocking boat, snarling at her when he had to sit.

"Go," Gregory ordered the male.

"The woman?"

"Leave her."

With a shrug the male started the motor again, and the boat swung around, heading back into the open water.

Lakshmi treaded water, frantically looking for Ryan, pulling herself in a circle with long swings of her arms and an occasional leg kick to keep her at the surface. Her nerves were raw and pain was still pulsing through her limbs, making it hard to concentrate enough to sense him.

"Ryan!" She swam a few feet in one direction. Spun again, hunting the rolling water for signs of him. "Ryan!"

Panic clenched around her chest, her throat and stomach tight, terror making it hard to think. Where was he? He couldn't hold his breath this long. Even a shifter had to breathe. She dragged a hand down her face to clear away the water spray and called to him again. The sound of her voice faded into the quiet.

And then he exploded into the air like a rocket, coming halfway out of the water before dropping back. She swam to him as fast as she could manage, her arms and legs slicing through the cold wetness, all thoughts of her own pain vanished in the face of her relief. When she reached him, she grabbed him around the shoulders to keep him above the waterline, just as he'd done for her.

"Ryan. Are you okay? Are you hurt?" She patted his face, wiping water off his cheek and pushing his wet hair out of his eyes. She kept her legs moving underwater, keeping them both at the surface as she searched him for wounds.

He hugged her close, his hand coming to her face. "Fine. A few slices that are healing." He looked toward the retreating boat. "But he got away."

"Why did you take so long to surface?"

"After I stabbed him through his neck, he kicked me in the head and I got turned around. Took a minute to figure out which way was up."

"Sonofabitch," she breathed and hugged him closer. The realization that Ryan could have drown, that she wouldn't have been able to stop it… Her sob was as wretched as the pain in her thigh, maybe even more painful because just the thought of losing him devastated her.

"Your leg," he murmured into her ear, one hand cradling the back of her head, his fingers tangled in her hair.

"I'm okay. We need to get to shore, though." She eased

back enough that she could see the faint shadow of the distant boat. "What are we going to do about him?"

"We'll figure it out after we get back to land."

They'd just turned toward the faint lights that showed the way to the nearest shore, kicking gently in that direction, when an explosion roared into the night, lighting up the sky in a fiery red inferno. Lakshmi gasped as they watched the remains of Gregory's boat fall in chunks into the water, glowing on the surface in a chaotic scatter.

"Jesus," Ryan breathed.

"What the hell?" Lakshmi whispered. "Do you suppose they were both on the boat when that happened?"

"Good question. Come on. We need to get out of here."

They swam in easy strokes, making it to land a few hundred yards from the shattered dock. Stumbling onto the mucky ground, Lakshmi felt like she weighed a hundred pounds more than she had just moments before. She lurched up a small hill to a grassy patch and collapsed, blinking away tiredness and a faint dizziness from the earlier blood loss. Ryan half-walked, half-crawled up next to her and immediately started examining her leg wound.

She laughed faintly. "Always the doctor."

"Looks like it's sealed completely. The scar is already clearing up."

She nodded toward the still-glowing remains of Gregory's escape boat. "That's going to draw attention. We'd better get back to the car…" A thought stopped her and she groaned. "I don't suppose you got the keys from Gregory during the fight?"

"'Fraid not. Looks like we're walking. At least until we can hitch a ride." He rubbed her arms.

The night air was chilly though not freezing, but being wet already meant she was shuddering with cold.

He stood and held out a hand to help her to her feet. "We could shift. But given that"—he gestured toward the explosion— "we might want to stay in human form."

"We're still going to attract attention," she said, indicating their wet, torn clothing. "If the human authorities see us, they're going to want to question us."

"We'll deal with that when and if it happens. My first priority is getting you warm."

She pulled him into her arms, kissing him soundly. "You scared the hell out of me out there," she muttered, then dove in for another kiss.

"Same," he managed when he released her long enough to run his lips over her jaw, along her neck, then back up to her mouth.

His kiss was as deep and desperate as she felt, all her terror and love pouring out of her in ways she could never put into words. She tunneled her fingers into his hair to keep him close, pressing tight to his body, reassuring herself they were both whole and safe. His hands caressed over her back, down her arms, then he cupped the back of her head in one palm and wrapped his other arm around her waist.

When they finally eased away from the kiss, Lakshmi was breathless and significantly warmer than she'd been a few moments earlier.

He held her gaze, cupping her face in a gentle hold. Then he took her hand. "Let's go home."

They clambered up a low rise and headed back in the direction of the Gregory's car.

They were only a half mile down the road, walking toward the brighter lights of a main street, when a dark, four-door car rolled to a stop next to them.

Ryan shook his head as his brother-in-law leaned out the open car window.

"Are you guys okay?" Daniel said, looking them over.

"About time you showed up," Ryan said. "What the hell took you so long?"

"Your GPS signal died before I could get close enough to pinpoint you. I've been trolling the area for the last twenty minutes trying to find you."

Ryan groaned and patted his pockets. "Phone must have fallen out in the water."

"Where's Gregory?"

Ryan exchanged a look with Lakshmi. "That'll take some explaining."

"Get in. There are emergency vehicles heading this way."

"That would be part of the long story," Ryan said.

He held open the back door for Lakshmi to climb in, then he slid in beside her, holding her close as Daniel turned up the car's heater.

"Thanks," she said, snuggling against Ryan.

"Where are the other Trackers?" Ryan asked.

"Swarming the area. Most on foot."

"There was an explosion out in the inlet," Ryan said. "Gregory was on the boat last we saw him."

"Is he dead?"

Daniel didn't sound even a little bothered by the possibility, and Lakshmi found she couldn't care much either.

"Hopefully," Ryan said. "If he and the tiger with him were still in the boat, they died."

"Okay, you'd better tell me everything. It'll take us a little time to get to safety."

"Where are we going?" Lakshmi asked.

"First, a hotel farther south. We'll get you into warm clothes and you can rest. Then the elders will be expecting an accounting."

Lakshmi exchanged another long look with Ryan. Their ruse was up. The elders would know they'd broken the law and been together.

Even as worry wormed under her relief at being safe, she remembered Gregory's comment that Ryan had been working for the elders all along. She leaned in and whispered in his ear so Daniel wouldn't hear, "We have something to discuss when we're alone—the fact that you've been working with the elders…"

He went very still for a beat and then let out a long breath that made his shoulders slump. He nodded.

On the drive, Ryan told Daniel everything that had happened with Gregory that evening. Ryan never released his hold on Lakshmi. And despite the troubles still ahead, she relaxed into him, content for the moment just to be in her mate's arms.

CHAPTER TWENTY-FOUR

Lakshmi exchanged a look with Ryan as the elders continued to argue. Neither she nor Ryan had had a chance to speak yet. The elders were nothing if not verbose.

They'd spent a relatively hectic night in a small hotel room. Daniel had been on the phone into the early hours, keeping track of what was happening around the boat explosion and body recovery. If the human authorities recovered either the mysterious tiger shifter or Gregory, the Trackers would have to go in and make those bodies disappear. They didn't dare allow humans to get documented, scientific proof that tiger shifters existed, so one of the Trackers' many jobs was to ensure anything related to the tigers that fell into the hands of the humans quietly disappeared before the humans could examine things too closely.

The next morning, after a few hours of sleep and a lot more phone calls, Daniel drove Lakshmi and Ryan straight to West Virginia, to the elders' compound. Though they'd been treated respectfully when they arrived, and shown to separate rooms in the guest wing, they hadn't been given any time to recover from their ordeal before being called to the Meeting Hall to face the elders and "explain" what had happened.

And for the last hour, Lakshmi and Ryan had sat silently in two mildly uncomfortable straight-back chairs, surrounded by the impressive opulence of the Meeting Hall, listening to the elders argue.

She dropped her head against the chair back and rolled her head to face Ryan. He looked like he might fall asleep, though she suspected that was a façade to hide his worry. Because of Daniel's presence, they hadn't really had a chance to talk about anything—what had happened with Gregory, their future, the fact that Ryan had been supposedly working with the elders all this time, how they would get around the fact that they'd broken all kinds of tiger laws by being together for the last few weeks. She'd hoped they'd have some time here at the compound, at least to discuss how Ryan had ended up working as a spy for the elders, but the old bastards hadn't seen fit to give her and Ryan any real rest.

Ryan's scent was unreadable at the moment—not the way the elders' were, with all emotion carefully disguised so that none of their true feelings were revealed, but that unique way of Ryan's where his scent conveyed what he wanted it to. And it seemed what he wanted the elders to think was that he was tired and a little bit bored.

She might have smiled if their future wasn't at stake. Honestly, she *was* a little bored, or might be if she wasn't also very worried. She wanted to say something into the arguing drone of voices washing over her, but doing so risked putting her and Ryan on the elders' bad sides. At the moment, they were walking a very fine line and she really didn't want to start off wrong when they finally allowed her to speak.

The noise got louder, the arguments impossible to follow. A lot of shouting over Gregory being crazy, being dead, maybe not dead, how had this happened, who was to blame, how would they handle the humans…and on and on.

Lakshmi reached for Ryan's hand without looking at him. He took hers and squeezed, just a hint of reassurance coming through his scent. She did smile now, glad she and her mate were facing this together.

Elder Pavel, at one end of the long wooden table where the elders presided over the Meeting Hall, narrowed his eyes and scowled at Lakshmi and Ryan's linked hands.

"You will remove your touch from her, Dr. Yin," Pavel said. "You are in enough trouble as it is."

Lakshmi growled and came half out of her seat. "Why the hell would he be in trouble?"

She almost bit her tongue the minute the words came out. Of course they were both in trouble for being together outside the Mate Run. But the bigger issue was the fact that a crazy tiger had come after her twice and almost killed her. And it was that reminder that had her speaking again, her anger rising fast and hard.

"That sonofabitch Gregory killed females. Endangered more female lives. If Ryan and I had been forced onto that boat, we might be dead now. Yet another female dead. And you have the nerve to reprimand the man who helped not once, but twice." She stood fully now, her justified anger growing. "A good man who doesn't deserve your scorn. Especially since he was only associated with Gregory because *you* sent him in as a spy."

She caught just a hint of something in Ryan's scent when she made the bold statement, but it was gone before she could analyze it.

The entire council had fallen quiet at her accusation. Then, one by one, they looked at Ryan.

Elizaveta, the only female on the council, sitting at the opposite end of the long table from Pavel, said, "Did you tell her this, Dr. Yin?"

"No," he said, his voice strong and steady. "Gregory did. He claimed he knew all along and had gotten the information from an elder."

There was no accusation or anger or even irritation in Ryan's voice. He had risen to stand beside her, but showed no signs of preparing for a fight, and his tone was perfectly neutral, as if he was giving a report.

Another elder in the center of the long table, Elder Qiang said to Lakshmi, "You believed the word of a crazy tiger?"

"Your reactions confirm Gregory's accusations," she said.

"No one was supposed to know," Elizaveta said softly, her expression serious but unreadable, her Russian accent stronger than usual. "Ever. Not even Dr. Yin's family." She looked down the length of the table at the other elders, her eyes just a little narrower. "For his safety and the safety of his family," she added as if speaking to the other elders and not Lakshmi.

"Well, Gregory knew," Lakshmi said. She looked at Ryan. "You should know I'm not mad at you for lying. I understand why you did. I was annoyed to find out from Gregory. But knowing you weren't ever really one of his is a huge relief, and I'm glad I found out."

His shoulders relaxed a fraction, and only then did Lakshmi realize he'd been tense at all. His smile was crooked and charming.

"Thanks for that," he said. "I was worried."

She took his hand again, her turn to reassure. She ignored the warning growls from three different elders and kept Ryan's hand in hers as she faced them again.

"So here's the deal," she said in her business voice, the one that was no-nonsense and full of confident command. "The laws didn't protect me as they were supposed to. The Trackers have been compromised—at least enough of them to allow the escape of yet another criminal, a criminal who endangered my life. For a second time. Said criminal—crazy as he was—implied there was a tiger of significant power and clout helping him."

"Did he say he was helped by an elder?" Pavel demanded.

"He implied," she said. "He insinuated. He made it quite clear without saying the words."

"Then it means nothing," Qiang said. "He was insane and not capable of telling a truth."

"But he was receiving help from someone high ranking

enough to convince him he would be king of the tigers," she said, keeping her calm even though she wanted to roar at them for trying to deny their responsibility in all this.

"And he *did* know I was with his young males as a spy," Ryan said. "As Elizaveta said, no one other than the elders was ever supposed to know that. Not just for my safety and the safety of my family either." His voice got much quieter on the last sentence, not quite a warning, but a close cousin to one.

Lakshmi wondered at that for a moment before realizing what he was implying. If it got out that the elders had recruited an ordinary tiger—not a Tracker, not one of their assistants or personal staff—to spy on other tigers…chaos might erupt. Tigers would no longer be able to trust anyone. And that kind of suspicion would make the tigers' already precarious situation worse.

She latched on to that fact like her tiger would a wounded deer. "Esteemed elders, after the incident with Elder Lei, do you really think you could maintain some semblance of order among our kind if the community learned about any of this? If they knew you'd recruited an ordinary tiger to spy on other tigers? If they learned it was likely that yet *another* elder has betrayed us all—and through that betrayal was responsible for the death of two, possibly three *precious* females."

She hoped her emphasize on the word "precious" didn't ring too sarcastic. She didn't feel as if they viewed her as "precious" right now, but the entire community pushed that term onto all females. A rebellious part of her soul—that part that had gone after her true mate even though it meant breaking tiger law—resented the term because despite all the coddling and monitoring and supposed value placed on the females, the elders still hadn't protected her from a demented male and his followers. How fucking *precious* could they really consider the females if they had allowed Gregory to remain free for so long?

With as even a voice as she could muster, she said, "News of what has happened in the last few weeks could throw us all into chaos once more. And send us toward extinction as surely as our lack of female numbers. Tiger against tiger. Civil war." She pursed her lips. "Very bad. Very bad."

From the corner of her eye, she saw Elizaveta's mouth tick up at the corner, just a little. It was impossible to judge the elder's expression, but Lakshmi got the impression of a smile, gone before most would have noticed.

"Are you...blackmailing us?" Elder Kamal asked, his dark eyes narrowed, but a very slight smile lifted his lips.

Kamal was the only other elder on the council who was as vocally pro-hybrid as Elizaveta. And until that moment, Lakshmi considered him and Elizaveta her best hope of getting out of this mess without losing Ryan. She wasn't sure whether Kamal's half-smile was threat or amusement, though. The elders to the left and right of him didn't look pleased. Pavel looked downright enraged.

"You would *dare*," Pavel hissed.

"I would dare," she told him without allowing any hint of nerves to show. "You didn't protect me the way you promised in exchange for my participation in the Mate Run.

One of you may be actively working against the community. And I could have been killed in that boat explosion."

"What are you saying?" Qiang asked tonelessly.

"I want restitution."

She was playing a very deadly game with the elders. If they wanted to, they could execute both her and Ryan under some trumped-up charge and no one would be able to argue the verdict because no one would know the truth. Even Daniel didn't know everything, and Lakshmi knew now that no one outside this room had a clue what Ryan had really been doing with Gregory's group. Well, except Gregory, thanks to whichever elder had been helping him.

Beside her, Ryan tensed almost imperceptibly. His hand tightened on hers. But his scent didn't reveal his reaction. In fact, something soothing and relaxing was starting to weave through his scent signature.

She let her words hang in the air, not rushing to speak her demands, letting the elders digest what she was telling them, making them ask her what she wanted.

As Ryan's scent grew subtly stronger, she realized it was the same soothing scent he used with patients, the scent that got them to relax and trust him despite being in pain or scared. Given the elders' expressions, ranging from unreadable to outraged, Lakshmi hoped Ryan's scent helped.

The silence stretched, and Lakshmi's heartbeat thumped a little harder. She controlled her breathing, careful not to show her nerves outwardly. She couldn't change her scent like Ryan, or even control it the way the elders did, but she could ensure her body language spoke of strength and self-assurance. Despite that, though, her palm was starting to sweat where she still gripped Ryan's hand tightly.

Finally, Elizaveta said, "What do you want, little one?" Her gaze flicked to her fellow elders. "In exchange for your discretion."

"I want Ryan."

Pavel launched out of his seat, his body vibrating with his anger. "No! We cannot destroy the laws, not for you, not for anyone. It would be our undoing."

"Someone important is already undermining our laws," Ryan said into the ringing sound of Pavel's denial. "Someone in power. That someone is ultimately responsible for the deaths of two, possibly three females."

"Almost four," Lakshmi added, meeting their gazes, one at a time.

"We're already on the verge of change," Ryan continued. "Gregory was crazy, but he amassed a large number of loyal followers despite that. Because the Mate Run, and our mating laws, are no longer viable. The hybrids are forcing a change in our laws, the extinction issue hasn't been resolved by the Run, and our females are in danger once again. Something has to give."

"Not this," Pavel said. "Not now."

"What's wrong with now?" Lakshmi asked.

"No," Pavel said again without answering her. He did take his seat again, but he scowled at them as if they were the criminals.

And given the fact that they'd broken the mating laws, she supposed she and Ryan were criminals. But she wasn't giving up just because Pavel growled at her.

"If you refuse to compensate me, with my requested demand, then I'll have no choice but to run away with Ryan. And reveal what's happened to the rest of the community."

Ryan's soothing scent got stronger, more obvious. Kamal glanced at him. Pavel's shoulders relaxed a little. Then he scowled and sat up straighter as if annoyed.

Elizaveta said, "Dr. Yin, I thank you for your considered calming influence, but I think we would all prefer not to be manipulated in this moment."

Lakshmi wasn't sure whether to be relieved by the amusement in Elizaveta's voice or not.

"My apologies," Ryan said, without sounding the least bit sorry. "It seemed a good time for…calm."

Elizaveta gave a nod of agreement. "How do you feel about Lakshmi's request?" she asked. "You have risked a lot to be with her."

"And I'd risk more," Ryan said. "Everything. I love her."

Lakshmi's heart thudded hard then, for the first time that afternoon from something other than nerves. She smiled at Ryan and brushed a very soft kiss across his lips, ignoring the growls of irritation from the table.

"Well, that's that then," Elizaveta said.

Lakshmi swung to look at her, not sure she'd heard her right. Not entirely sure what the elder was saying. She eased closer to Ryan, seeking reassurance in his heat and strength.

"If…*if* we allow this," Qiang said, "you will sign a

contract and swear an oath of silence that none of the facts discussed here will ever be revealed."

"We can promise *we* won't reveal anything," Ryan said. "Neither of us can promise the things discussed here won't get out eventually, via another source. But we won't speak."

"Good enough?" Elder Rajesh said, the first time he'd spoken since Lakshmi and Ryan had begun to talk.

Rajesh looked left and right along the table, his dark brows raised over sharp features that didn't show a hint of his age. He sat closest to Elizaveta and was generally considered the calmest, most circumspect member of the council, though Lakshmi couldn't have sworn to that in the midst of the earlier arguments.

"No," Pavel said. "I cannot approve this."

"What would be our excuse for allowing it?" Qiang asked.

"We could come up with something," Kamal said. "After all, Lakshmi *has* suffered. And Ryan did protect her —as well as other females. The community already knows this. We can say it was our way of…rewarding them both for their part in bringing down Gregory—someone all tigers would agree was a severe threat to our people."

"After we have already punished Dr. Yin," Pavel said, "before the entire community and banned him from the Mate Run because he was associated with the young males? No one will believe that."

"But no one can prove it's anything other than the truth," Rajesh pointed out quietly.

"Unless we reveal everything," Elizaveta added.

"The other males will rebel," Pavel insisted. "They will not tolerate this after everything that's happened."

"The males are already starting to rebel," Ryan said. "That's what Gregory's group was about. They weren't the only ones. What happens with Lakshmi and me won't make that any worse."

"And it might actually stall the inevitable," Elizaveta said, quietly. "Because for a little while longer, we can maintain the status quo. Until we have a better plan."

"Elizaveta is right," Kamal said. "We have no other good option to offer the community yet—even with the hybrids—and until we do, we must try to maintain the laws as they are."

"Which we would not be doing if we let Lakshmi and Ryan mate outside the Run," Pavel said.

"An exception to preserve the laws," Lakshmi said.

"We have already had too many of those," Pavel said, turning his glare on Elizaveta.

She stared back without reacting to whatever barb he'd just thrown at her.

Qiang leaned forward in his seat, drawing everyone's attention. "A vote. Lakshmi and Ryan are allowed to mate in exchange for their silence. Or they are forced apart and the cracks in our situation get larger when everything discussed here is revealed."

Pavel rolled his eyes at the wording. The other elders ignored him.

"A vote," Elizaveta concurred. "Lakshmi and Ryan are allowed to become permanent mates without the necessity of a Mate Run pregnancy, in compensation for Lakshmi's pain and suffering and Ryan's loyal service to this council. All in favor?"

Elizaveta raised her hand without hesitation. Elder Chen, who'd been arguing against relaxing their Mate Run laws earlier, surprised Lakshmi by raising his hand at the same moment as Elizaveta. Kamal put his hand up a moment later, and Rajesh followed after that.

Half the council. Just one more would be a majority vote.

But with eight elders, the vote could be tied. And Lakshmi could lose her gamble to keep her love.

CHAPTER TWENTY-FIVE

Ryan tried not to hold his breath and failed. He stared at the four elders who hadn't yet raised their hands, keeping his jaw tight so he wouldn't shout or demand or in any other way disturb the situation.

If the vote went against him and Lakshmi, he'd run away with her. It wasn't the best option. Running would mean they'd have to cut off all contact with their families and neither of them wanted that. But he'd do it for Lakshmi. He was pretty sure his family, at least, would understand.

Her hand in his was trembling, though none of that showed in her expression. She looked fierce and confident. As if she fully expected the elders to vote in her favor.

He hadn't thought it possible, but he loved her all the more in that moment.

The silence stretched. Pavel crossed his arms, staring at the other elders as if daring them to approve this step. The tension drew out so long that Ryan was sure Elizaveta would call the vote and declare a tie.

Then slowly, his expression thoughtful, Qiang raised his hand.

"A majority vote," Rajesh said. "Lakshmi and Ryan may mate permanently, and Lakshmi is no longer required to participate in the Mate Run—unless and until such time as she wishes to resume running."

Pavel stood and stalked out of the Hall.

The other elders ignored him.

Ryan kept his expression neutral, but his body vibrated with so much excitement he wasn't sure how he could contain it.

"And now," Elizaveta said, "we will have the contract drawn up. But you will give us your oath of silence now."

"I give my oath," Lakshmi said.

"My solemn oath," Ryan said.

"Then it is done," Kamal said.

Without another word, the elders rose and filed out of the Meeting Hall through the two side doors at the back of the room that led into the elders' private offices. The Hall's huge main doors opened in the next instant, startling Lakshmi into a little jump. She laughed at her reaction, a lovely blush coloring her cheeks.

"Shall we," Ryan said, motioning toward the now open door with his free hand, still holding tight to her with his other hand.

They returned to the guest wing without speaking, but before they reached the elevators that would take them upstairs to their rooms, Ryan stopped Lakshmi, pulling her to face him.

She looked so beautiful it stole his breath for a moment and he had to blink a few times to remember what he wanted to say.

"I love you," he finally said. "I'll be a good mate to you, for as long as you'll have me."

"That will be forever so I hope you're prepared." She grinned, her dark eyes sparkling.

"Would you like to go for a run?"

"A run?" She half-laughed but her eyes narrowed in question.

"My tiger needs out. And I'd like to run with my future wife."

Her mouth opened in a little *O* of surprise at his use of "wife." Then she said, "I'd love to go for a run with my future husband."

Grinning like a fool, he tugged her into a trot, leading her to a door that would take them out of the building into the surrounding woods.

At the door, he paused to strip so he could leave his clothes in the cubbyholes lining the wall next to the door— a way to store clothes in an easy-to-find spot when a shifter wanted to go tiger.

Lakshmi let her gaze travel over his chest when he had his shirt off and her smile sent his blood boiling. She met his gaze and pushed open the door, still dressed.

"Find me when you've changed," she said, her eyes sparkling wickedly.

And she was gone.

Ryan was pretty sure he'd never stripped as fast as he did in that moment. His shift took another two minutes, his muscles stretching and pulling, bones cracking as tawny fur rippled along his body. He'd shifted so rarely in recent weeks, the change felt amazing, like stretching out muscles that had been in one position too long. It reminded him of the way he felt after hours in the operating room, finally looking up and stepping away from a successful procedure.

When he'd finished the shift, he dropped onto all four paws and shook hard, blinking a few times to reorient in his new form. The one problem with working so much in the human world had always been finding enough time to let his tiger run free.

He caught the lingering tendrils of Lakshmi's scent then and growled, his eyes narrowing. He rose on his hind legs, pressed the bar release to open the steel door, and pushed out of the building. The door closed slowly behind him with a quiet click.

Cool spring air washed over his face, bringing with it the scents of the surrounding forest, maple, white oak and beech trees, warm, rich earth, the local deer herd and a few smaller mammals willing to venture into the open forest surrounding the compound—tiger territory.

A deep breath pulled in Lakshmi's trail. He followed it, chuffing when he spotted her clothes scattered across the forest floor, leaving him another kind of trail. His tail twitched, his whiskers bristled as he stalked through the spare undergrowth, too quietly to be heard by most creatures. She wouldn't need to hear him, she'd be able to feel him. But the wind worked in his favor, along with his silence, making the stalking fun.

She wasn't passive prey, though, and never had been. When he found the last of her clothes, he sniffed the ground beside the discarded bra and panties, and he realized she'd moved deeper into the forest before shifting. Gaze narrowed, he hunted the trees, sensing her to the west and south, farther than he'd anticipated. And running.

He bolted after her, his tiger no more able to resist her than he could resist taking his next breath. Her roar echoed through the trees, sending a shiver of predatory delight through him, and he ran harder, chasing her across the uneven ground, letting his instincts take him around and over obstacles as he focused on following her.

She led him on a wild run, unpredictable and fast. He had to work hard to outsmart her, and twice she fooled him, getting him to run one way before she took off in the opposite direction.

He loved every minute of it.

He loved it more when he finally leapt from a low oak branch into her path, bringing her to a skidding stop. She crouched low, backing up a little, giving him an excellent view of her in her tiger form—all sinewy muscle and sleek russet coat. Her stripes created a flowing pattern that would have been a good distraction if he weren't so focused on catching her. The white fur lining her stomach was soft and bright in the afternoon sunshine.

She growled at him, and he replied in kind, his voice low and reverberating. She straightened, sitting on her haunches and tucking her long tail around her legs. Then she licked her lips.

He huffed a tiger chuckle and joined her, rubbing his head against hers, letting her scent cling to his fur, tangling with his.

She nipped his ear lightly, then stepped back and started to shift. He watched quietly, staying in tiger form for the moment so he could admire her human form when she finally stood at her human height.

"Was that a good enough run?" she asked, stretching her arms over her head.

The position raised her breasts and made his blood pound. He grunted an affirmative, letting his lust fill his scent.

She grinned at that. "Good. Change. I want you. And I'm close enough to estrous that I won't be denied."

His shift back to human went even faster than his shift to tiger. The additional stretch made him feel strong, his lungs and muscles pumped, his blood rushing through his veins.

She chuckled when he pulled her into his arms, the sound cut off when he kissed her.

Almost immediately their scents tangled, creating that perfect combination that was theirs alone, a scent he would forever consider his favorite smell in the world. He drank her in, his hands moving over her lush body, savoring the fact that she was officially his.

His.

No one could dispute it anymore, no one could tell them they had to separate. There would be no waiting weeks between her estrous cycles to see her until they got pregnant, no other males chasing her, hoping she'd pick them. No Mate Run to endure just so he could marry her.

And she'd said yes. The magnificent woman in his arms had given him more than he ever thought possible in his life. His arms clenched tighter, his hands grew a little rougher, as thoughts of what might have been taunted him. But she was here, hot and soft, and he intended to make her happy for the rest of her life.

He eased her against an oak trunk, nibbling the sensitive skin along her throat, caressing her breast with one hand, her ass with his other. She moaned into his mouth, moving against him until he burned with wanting her. He didn't even have to urge her into position, just grunted something nonsensical and she was lifting up, wrapping her legs around his waist, settling over his erection, hot and wet and ready.

Sliding into her was as easy as breathing, as perfect as a sunrise over the ocean, as hot as a desert breeze. He rocked into her, all his focus, all thought on her, on the feel of her clenched tight around him, the rasp of her panting breaths against his cheek, the rise of their mingled scents—full of spice and heat, musk and blood, with the earthy loam of the forest under it all.

When she tightened, when she came, he watched her beautiful face, the flush across her skin, the release in her expression, until he couldn't keep his own eyes open. Then he followed her, letting go of any last fear and worry in a blinding burst of pure pleasure.

Breathing hard, he hugged her close, not ready to

release her even though his body trembled. Now that they were able, he thought he might just keep her naked in this forest for the rest of the afternoon.

"I love you," she murmured against his temple.

He tightened his hold, too overwhelmed for that moment to even answer. But he let his love, his joy flow through his scent like the clean wash of fresh spring water.

Finally, when he thought he might be able to form words, he leaned back to smile at her. "So will your mother expect a big wedding?"

"Huge," she confirmed with an answering grin. "In fact, if we have any hope of enjoying the build-up to the wedding, we should just let her take over and organize it all."

"My mother will want her say, too. I'm not sure she ever expected to marry me off. She'll have…ideas."

Lakshmi dropped her head back and laughed. "This should be fun to watch. I hope they don't fight. Too much."

"They love us. They'll figure it out."

"My father will want to make the desserts and the wedding cake."

"Perfect. My mom will want a say in the menu."

"So long as my mother gets some of her favorites in there, we should be okay." She frowned a little. "This is going to be crazy."

"Probably. I don't care what sort of madness they create. Just so long as I get to call you my wife at the end of the day."

"Or week. We might end up with a week of parties."

"That'll be okay, too."

Her eyes widened. "Where are we going to live?"

"Wherever you want. If you want to stay in Boston, you could always open up East Coast versions of the businesses you already have."

She pressed her lips together, but it didn't hide her grin. "I could be bicoastal." She raised her brows, then brought them together in a slight frown. "Your work is in Boston. We should stay there." Her tone and scent were hesitant, though.

"Only if you want to. I can move. I'm sure someone in San Diego needs a general surgeon on staff. I understand if you don't want to live too far from your family."

"But then you'd be far from yours."

"That's what airplanes are for." He kissed the tip of her nose. "My parents will understand. They'll just be thrilled I've finally found a wonderful woman to love."

Her expression softened, her eyes glistening, a wobbly smile lifting her lips, and her scent filled with the rich, sweet flavors of her love. She hugged him tight, then kissed him hard, and Ryan decided he could do and take anything…so long as Lakshmi was in his arms.

Without the Run, he'd finally caught his mate.

Elder Kamal Ghosh sat in a large, softly-padded chair in his private office in the elders' compound, staring at the pale blue walls, his hands steepled in front of him, his fingers pointing toward the ceiling.

Ivan Sokolov had been Kamal's assistant for nearly thirty years now. He was good at judging the elder's moods, had kept his secrets and supported his efforts to save their species—even when those efforts weren't something Ivan approved of. Frankly, some of what Kamal had done over the years, Ivan had found appalling. Not because of any ethical or moral objection but because the years of failure hadn't dissuaded the elder into giving up his experiments. If it had been Ivan, he'd have let this madness go a decade earlier.

Now, however, it looked like Kamal might have been right. At least, they were closer now than they'd ever been to making things work the way Kamal envisioned.

The elder's gaze lifted to Ivan where he stood off to the side of Kamal's desk. Ivan didn't blink or change his relaxed stance, simply met the older tiger's dark eyes and waited. It was part of his job to wait on Kamal. A job he took very, very seriously.

"Ensure the complex in Alberta is leveled, all evidence hidden," Kamal said quietly. He frowned a little and shook his head. "Probably shouldn't have let Gregory use it, but…" He shrugged. "Hindsight, right, Ivan."

"Right, sir. All links between you and the complex have been erased, so the rest should be easy enough."

"No deaths please. That would cause even more suspicion."

"It will look like an accident."

"The rest of the drug?"

"The few remaining vials in Gregory's possession have been recovered and returned to our processing lab."

"Kind of Gregory to provide us with the updated sample Williams gave him so we could reproduce it," Kamal said thoughtfully. "It will be useful in our research, but I could never have asked Elizaveta for some of the original sample."

"Of course. This version is much improved anyway."

"Good point, Ivan. Gregory's remaining young males?"

"Have all been taken care of. With the help of an anonymous tip, the ship will be found by the Trackers in a few weeks, the bodies aboard too far damaged and decomposed to give up much information."

Kamal nodded, then fell silent again. Ivan continued to wait.

"Gregory's remains?" Kamal asked after a few minutes.

"The pieces have disappeared from the human morgue."

"When left to it, the Trackers really are good at their jobs, aren't they?"

"Yes, sir."

Kamal sighed. "It would have been better had Dr. Yin died with Gregory in that explosion," he said quietly. "Lakshmi's loss would have been regrettable, but the doctor… He might have discovered more from Gregory than he's admitted."

"You should have let me arrange for Dr. Yin's death while he was in confinement."

"I told you, no more of that in the compound, Ivan. We can't afford it. It was enough taking out a fellow elder here without drawing attention to us. If something had happened to Dr. Yin inside the compound, it would confirm Victor's suspicions."

Ivan acknowledged the truth of that. Victor Romanov was entirely too good at his job, and extremely tenacious. Getting around him again to produce another security breach would not only be difficult, it would be almost impossible to erase the trail before Victor tracked it to Kamal's door.

"Dr. Yin doesn't know you were involved with Gregory," Ivan said. "And now that he has a mate to worry over, I doubt he'll think about it much more. He got what he wanted with the information he had."

"But the question has been raised. Gregory went against my orders and got Alexis and Victor…and by extension

Elizaveta involved. I need Elizaveta's support for a little longer. My work isn't ready to be revealed yet."

"The last experiment…"

"Another failure. We're close, though, Ivan. I can feel it. The hybrids were the key, along with the research Elizaveta's company has been doing. The next one, maybe the one after that… We'll get the process perfected. Then I can reveal everything. And save our people from extinction."

"Yes, sir." Ivan didn't show any signs of his disgust at the idea. While he didn't object morally to Kamal's… research, the idea of *them* becoming a part of the tiger population was still unsavory.

"We need the time to ensure acceptance anyway," Kamal continued. "Gregory was a good distraction until he became a liability. The late Elder Lei and the other fanatic anti-hybrid tigers are still causing issues. The split among the Trackers, yet another screen of smoke to complicate matters." Kamal met Ivan's gaze again. "Stir that pot, Ivan. Make sure the Tracker split and the anti-hybrid movement continue to make things difficult for the elder council."

"It will be done. What of the new elder…?" With only eight, the council was vulnerable. A ninth elder had to be vetted and approved—by the community as well as the other elders—soon. There were a few candidates but none of them appealed to Kamal and his vision. They'd gotten rid of Zhang Lei on purpose. And not just because his treason created a lot of mess and confusion.

Kamal waved his hand at the question of a ninth elder. "It won't matter who is chosen in the end. Let the others argue and debate. I can take care of that end of things. You just ensure our people continue to have doubts and fears and worries about the future. Gregory, his young males, and Ryan Yin aren't the only males resistant to the Mate Run. And with the kidnappings, you'll see the females start to rebel more. The breakdown of that convention will add even more upheaval. That works for us, too."

Kamal's dark eyes glowed just a little yellow, his tiger close to the surface, old and crafty and deadly. "When the dust settles, Ivan, I'll be triumphant. And the tigers will thank me for it."

"Yes, sir," Ivan said quietly, keeping his body purposefully relaxed, his emotions well hidden and out of his scent.

"We're nearly there," Kamal said with a very small smile. "We're nearly ready."

Thank you for reading To Catch a Tiger. I hope you're enjoying the Tiger Shifters series. For an excerpt from book 8, What a Tiger Wants, keep reading!

CHAPTER ONE

Dmitry Chernikov parked his truck outside his older brother's cozy house in Eirene, Colorado, opened the driver's side door and pulled in a deep breath. Pine and snow, rich earth, squirrels, the faint scent of Nick's diner a short walk away on Main Street, and the definite scents of his brother, his sister-in-law, and—Dom smiled—their five-month-old baby girl.

He climbed out of the truck, stretching sore muscles and savoring the crisp, sharp bite of Colorado in December. The late afternoon sun hung low in the sky. He'd driven for several days to get here, stopping a few times to sleep but otherwise continuing straight through from West Virginia. He'd been spending so damned much time at the elders' US compound lately, helping his friend Victor Romanov with the compound's security, he'd barely seen the inside of his own home in Vermont. Not that it had much lure. It was just the building where he stored his stuff.

He looked in the direction of Nick's diner. Dom's heart had been in Eirene for a long time…

The door to Nick's house opened. Dom glanced back to see his older brother framed against a riot of bright, colorful Christmas decorations.

"Tiana says to come inside," Nick called, "before the ladies get a look at you and invade the house."

Dom rolled his eyes and snorted softly as he climbed the two wooden steps up to Nick's front porch. "That would be Mitch causing all the female rioting. How's Chrissy?"

"Sleeping so keep your voice down. I, on the other hand, haven't slept in months."

"You want a nap now?"

"Nah." Nick grinned. "Just need a little more quiet before the excitement starts again."

Dom had never seen his brother look so light and happy. Not since they were kids. In fact, Nick hadn't looked this easy and content since before they'd found their mother's body when they were both so young.

"What smells like peppermint?" he asked when the faint scent wafted out to him from somewhere close to his brother.

"Nothing," Nick said. "I don't know. Maybe Tiana's hot chocolate. Get inside before we freeze."

Dom raised his brows at Nick's weird tone but shrugged it off, figuring the sleep deprivation was getting to him. Dom stomped his boots off on the mat outside the front door—a new addition he attributed to Nick's wife—and walked into the house, shrugging out of the light jacket he used more as camouflage than for actual warmth.

"Who's cooking at the diner today?" he asked, then looked into the living room and spotted his sister-in-law. "Tiana. You look beautiful."

He spoke quietly because she was cradling a sleeping baby across her lap, one hand supporting the now quite large five-month-old and the other holding a tablet. The coffee table had been scooted close to the couch and held a cup of what smelled like mint-flavored hot chocolate.

Dom nodded to the cup. "Guess that is the mint smell."

Tiana looked past him to Nick with an amused expression Dom couldn't interpret. When he glanced at Nick, Nick was scowling.

"Hey, Dom," Tiana greeted, facing him again and smiling. "Come on in and get comfortable. Chrissy should be waking up soon. We weren't expecting you for a couple more days. I'm surprised Victor let you leave ahead of him."

The whole extended Chernikov clan was gathering in Eirene for the winter holidays and to celebrate little Chrissy's five-month birthday. Christina Loban-Chernikov was the first female born into the Chernikov family in more than a century—since Dom's grandmother, as far as he knew. Which meant Chrissy was going to be extremely spoiled and doted on. The five-month birthday celebration was actually his grandmother, the elder Elizaveta Chernikova's idea because she wanted another excuse to come visit her great-granddaughter.

"Last I saw," Dom said, "Alexis was dragging Victor away from his ongoing campaign to keep the security at the compound from ever being compromised again. They'll fly into Denver at the end of the week."

"You drove?" Nick asked, motioning Dom into the living room. "Did they have a room for you at the motel or do you need to stay here?"

Dom took a free chair across from the couch so Tiana wouldn't have to turn too much to talk to him. The chair was large and soft, the light from a huge front window at his back giving the room a warm glow. There was a small fire in the fireplace, but a window somewhere in the back was open to keep the house from getting too warm for their higher tiger shifter metabolisms.

"I checked into the motel before coming here," Dom said. "And yeah, I drove from West Virginia. I needed the quiet."

Since he'd started helping Victor with the security at the compound—neglecting his own security business to do it—he'd been surrounded by other tigers almost constantly for months now. He never spent that much time with his own kind. Even his brothers, though they were close and talked a lot. He was, in a lot of ways, a stereotypical tiger— much happier on his own than surrounding by others.

Except, for some reason, here in Eirene he felt comfortable. Not crowded. Never hemmed in. Not even with the place full of other tigers—like it had been for Nick and Tiana's wedding back in May. Something about the place…

Or maybe it was because *she* lived here.

He shook off the thought, but it did remind him. "You

didn't answer my question earlier. Who's watching the diner?"

"That new cook who came into town a few months back. She's working out really well. Been doing a fine job giving me a little extra time to spend with Tiana and Chrissy."

"Which means you'll be buying her her own restaurant soon, then?" Dom asked, not entirely joking. His stoic, grumpy, occasionally broody big brother was a secret philanthropist who kept giving his best cooks money to open their own restaurants in other towns. One, a place in Vail, was starting to get international notice now. All because Nick fronted the owner enough money to open her restaurant.

Nick scowled. Tiana laughed softly. Chrissy snuffled a little in her sleep and rolled closer to Tiana, snuggling against her arm. Tiana smiled down at the baby's soft, fuzzy head.

"Anyway," Nick said, "Lulu has the grill, and Jane is minding the front."

Dom had perfected not reacting to the mention of Nick's head waitress over the last six years. He kept everything he was feeling neatly tucked under a casual screen of curiosity.

"How's Jane doing? Ben started college this fall, didn't he?"

"He did," Tiana answered. "Jane survived. But barely." She grinned. "She's better now, but I think that's because Ben is home for the winter break."

"Is he? I'll have to stop in and say hi."

"Bet he'd love that," Tiana said.

"I'm sure Jane will be glad to see you, too," Nick added without any hint of innuendo.

That didn't keep Dom from a knee-jerk suspicion that Nick already knew his secret.

Not that it mattered. Jane had made the situation clear when they'd first met, not long after Nick had moved to Eirene and Dom had come for a visit. She wasn't interested in dating or relationships. She was well and truly done with men. And the woman was just stubborn enough to mean it.

Dom decided thinking about Jane would get him into trouble, so he switched to other topics. "How are things with the wolf pack?" he asked Nick. "They're okay with another invasion of tigers at the edge of their territory?"

"Since the tigers are coming into my territory, it's none of their business," Nick said, his voice just a little deeper than it had been a moment earlier. "Their businesses in town are doing good—especially Siobhan Walsh's boutique."

"But?"

"But there's infighting." Nick shrugged. "You know how it is when a new alpha takes over. There can be years of settling out."

Dom nodded. He knew very little about wolf politics, and cared even less. But the Colorado pack's territory butted up against Nick's, close enough to be trouble. Anyone or anything that might cause trouble for either of his brothers was Dom's business.

"You hungry?" Nick asked. "I'm sure I can whip something up."

"You're tired." Dom waved him away. "For good reason. I'll go across to the diner, see how good this new cook of yours really is. Before you lose her." Dom stood and grinned unrepentantly at his brother's frown.

He crossed to Tiana and kissed her lightly on the head, letting his gaze linger on his new niece. A baby girl in the family. He was still a little stunned by the reality of it. None of the Chernikov brothers thought they'd have kids. He let his hand hover above Chrissy's soft, sweet-smelling head, afraid if he touched her he'd wake her up, then smiled at Tiana and headed back to the front door.

"You guys rest," he said, slipping into his coat. "While you can. I'll be back in a few hour."

"Say hi to Jane for us," Tiana said, casually.

"Will do." He turned toward the door but didn't miss the look Tiana exchanged with her husband. He just chose to ignore it.

Nick's diner was a classic, homey place, with tables lined in paper that children could draw on, wooden accents, and a Formica counter with bar stools facing the kitchen, visible through a large order window. It always smelled of delicious food and good, fresh coffee.

The entire town congregated at Nick's diner to eat and visit. This time of the afternoon, between the dinner and lunch rushes, the place was relatively quiet. Old Charlie Sanchez—an Eirene fixture—sat at the counter regaling a tourist with town "history," which if Charlie was telling it would be embellished past the point of recognizable fact. Dom caught a few sentences and had to hide his smile—

Charlie was telling a story about an ancient mythical beast that had stalked the area at night when Charlie was a kid, the beast preying on the unsuspecting.

If only Charlie knew the diner he sat in was owned by a "mythical beast."

A handful of other people sat at the tables and booths filling the dining area. Dom recognized a few locals, but the rest were tourists.

He sat at the counter, a few stools down from Charlie and his unwitting victim, and let the feel of the place settle into his bones. More than most anywhere Dom had ever been, the diner felt like home.

Though he tried not to make it obvious, Dom watched for Jane, carefully pulling in the various scents of the place, looking for hers… And there it was, under the perpetual coffee and grease smell, under the more pervasive, territorial scent of Nick and Tiana, the very faint touch of Jane's human, earthy, pine and fresh grass scent.

As if taking in her essence called her, Jane came out of the kitchen carrying a tray with two plates of sandwiches and fries. She was dressed in her work uniform—a pair of snug-fitting, low-rise jeans that always did amazing things to her ass, a light blue polyester shirt that should not have been sexy but somehow was because it hugged her glorious curves, and a short apron where she stored her pen and order book. Her thick, dark brown hair was pulled up into a bun, but tendrils of springy curls had escaped to frame her face, highlighting her high cheekbones. Her dark eyes were framed by thick lashes. Her full lips, as always, looked lush and kissable.

His heartbeat thudded hard and he flexed his hands against the counter, working to control the instant hit of lust.

She spotted him and nodded, smiling faintly as she carried the tray to a couple obviously in Colorado for the skiing.

"Be right with you, Dom," she said in passing.

He returned her nod of greeting and remained casually seated at the counter, not following her with his gaze, not straining to hear her speaking to the customers…and impressed he managed that much. He hadn't seen her since Nick and Tiana's big wedding bash in May, which wasn't unusual. He made an effort to go as long as he could without seeing her. Somehow he was always drawn back to Eirene, to Jane, and to the certain and hopeless knowledge that she refused to admit to the attraction between them.

He smiled in greeting when she rounded the counter, keeping the barrier between them, and stopped to pour him a coffee.

"How did you know?" he asked.

"Everyone needs coffee or tea at this time of the afternoon."

She looked up from the cup to grin, the expression crinkling the corners of her eyes in that way he adored. He wrapped his hands around the mug to keep from reaching for her.

"When did you arrive?" she asked.

"Half hour ago. Chrissy is napping so I thought I'd get some food. And try out this new cook Nick's hired."

"You're gonna be impressed. She's almost as good as Nick. What'll you have?"

You. Aloud, he said, "What's best?"

She narrowed her eyes at him, her mouth pursed as she considered. The expression drew his attention to her mouth and he almost groaned aloud. He loved her mouth. She had such perfect heart-shaped lips, and all he could think about in that moment was pulling her into his arms and kissing her hard.

"Think you'll love the fajita sandwich," she finally said.

He blinked and focused on her eyes. Which didn't actually help the erotic fantasies his imagination was torturing him with.

"It's one of Lulu's specialties," she added. "Be right back." She paused on her way into the kitchen, looking over her shoulder at him. "It's good seeing you again, Dom. Always nice to have you back in town."

He didn't let the pain show in his expression, but he was grateful Nick wasn't around because Dom's scent filled with a longing he knew was pointless. He should have stayed away, despite his grandmother's insistence that everyone be here. He really needed to keep as far from Jane as he could get. For his own mental well-being. She didn't want him, or any man for that matter—a small mercy—and she'd made it clear years ago that she wasn't ever going to change her mind.

The worst of it was, she was attracted to him. He caught delicious, tempting hints of it in her scent, and tormented himself by memorizing those elusive flavors of spice and want. If she hadn't revealed that much to him, if his *tiger* could just be convinced there was no hope, Dom was pretty sure he'd have been over this obsession by now.

His heart thumped harder when she came back out of the kitchen and he sighed quietly. Well, maybe not exactly over the obsession. But at least there wouldn't be even a hint of hope in his soul. There wouldn't be this nagging sense that maybe, just maybe she'd change her mind.

Jane forced a casual smile. She stopped at the counter again to exchange small talk with Nick's younger brother, and all the while she had a running monologue rolling through her mind, the irritating voice of her wiser self, telling her to get over this attraction to Dmitry Chernikov.

Stop acting like a silly girl. You're too old for this. You're too old for a crush on a man this young. He's not really interested in you so stop acting like a fool—even if only in your head.

She'd nearly dropped a hot pot of coffee the first time Dom had walked into the diner. Jane had stood like a love-struck fool for what felt like an eternity, just staring at him. To this day, she wasn't sure what it was about him, exactly. He was sexy as all hell, and his eyes could turn most women to mush. But her boss was gorgeous enough to be a male model, and she'd never reacted to Nick that way. She'd been done with men for more than two years when she'd first met Dom, and she'd been completely unprepared for the impact he had on her, the way he'd turned her inside out.

A little taller than Nick by an inch or two, Dom was thickly muscled even though he was a computer geek—his words—which made her way too curious about what he did to earn those muscles. His hair was a little more brown than blond, and his hazel eyes sometimes looked green and other times more gold. His features were sharp and strong, his voice deep and husky. And his smile… His smile made her knees wobble.

When Nick had arrived in town, he'd turned the female population of Eirene on its head, but Jane had always seen him as…well her boss and a friend. She was protective of him, the way she was protective of the town. And she was amused by what other women had done to get his attention, but she'd never been attracted to Nick.

Dom, on the other hand… She'd felt like she'd been hit with a two-by-four when he'd smiled at her and had barely managed an intelligible hello when he'd taken her hand in greeting as Nick introduced them.

The last time Jane had reacted to a man that way had been…a long time ago and led to yet another very bad situation. Before Dom, she'd been certain she'd finally gotten over all the romantic longings nonsense she'd harbored in her youth. Dom proved just how wrong she'd been.

And she'd run from that attraction as fast as a woman could go. Not physically. Eirene was her home, and she'd be damned if she'd be chased away just because she got all hot and bothered by her boss' brother. The man didn't live here. She didn't have to see him all the time. But she'd rolled up all those girly feelings of desire and stomped them down deep, under her cynical, battered and scarred soul.

"How's the coffee?" she asked when she realized she'd been staring at him without speaking.

"Perfect. As always."

She needed casual things to discuss, stuff you'd talk to your boss' brother about. Nothing too personal. Nothing to hint that she was restlessly trying not to notice how good he smelled, or how fantastic he looked. His hair was a little shaggier than usual, a bit longer than the last time she'd seen him, and it was all she could do not to reach across the counter and brush a few stray strands off his forehead.

No! Act like the grown woman you are. Stop panting after the younger man. He'd probably be embarrassed for you if he knew what you were thinking.

"You staying with Nick?" she asked.

"No, I'm at the motel by the highway for the next few days. I didn't want to crowd them, with the baby and all."

"You'll get more sleep at the motel," she said.

Dom chuckled, and her thighs clenched. Jesus wept, the man had a sexy laugh.

"Elizaveta rented that cabin she loves," he said. "I'll move up there once the rest of the clan descends later in the week."

A beat of silence and she almost got lost in his eyes. Damn it. She blinked. "So how's your work going?"

"Good. Busy. Working with Alexis' husband at the moment."

At the mention of Nick's aunt, Jane smiled. She liked Alexis. A lot. Woman was down to earth and didn't suffer fools lightly. Just the kind of person Jane could relate to.

"She and Victor coming to the big family reunion Tiana's been gushing about for a month?"

His crooked grin sent an obscene amount of lust through Jane. She ignored it. Forcefully.

"They're coming," he said. "Bringing Isabella and Scott. James will be arriving a little late. He's got some college exams to finish or something."

"Good to hear. Good to hear." She bit the inside of her cheek to keep from saying anything else inane and shifted gears. "Ben's home for the winter break, too."

"Nick told me. How's he doing?"

"Seems to be doing well. What he tells his old mom, anyway."

"You must be proud of him."

"Too much for words," she said, with complete honesty.

"Think he'd like a visit?"

"He'd love it."

Her son adored Dom, and had since they'd first met and fell easily into talking about computers. Ben's conversation could be a little hard to follow sometimes—even now. At twelve, Ben had almost been able to hold a conversation like a neuro-typical kid, but he'd still stumbled over words and the order to put them in when he got excited about a topic. Dom hadn't even blinked, just followed Ben's rambling and disjointed discussion without missing a beat.

Jane had been attracted to Dom from the start, but she was pretty sure she'd fallen in love with him in that moment.

Which had set off so many alarm bells in her head, she'd gotten a headache from them.

"How's Ben adjusting to college life so far from home?" Dom asked.

She blinked away the memories. "Better than my worst fears. The college has a group for kids like Ben, to help them adapt to the social stuff. He says he's enjoying it. It can be hard to tell with him, you know."

"How are you doing?" he asked with a knowing nod as he sipped his coffee.

She snorted. "As well as can be expected. Empty nesting and fussing like a mother hen whenever he calls. The usual. I'd have preferred him going to school somewhere closer to home, but the local places didn't have strong support systems for autistic kids. And at least Washington isn't a long flight from here."

Dom grinned. Her heart thumped faster. She ignored the reaction.

"He's at the house now," she said, "if you want to stop by after you eat."

She almost hated to invite Dom into her home—his scent lingered and tortured her—but she did every time he was in town. Ben was crazy about him, and Jane never had been able to refuse her son much when it came to socializing. That was her excuse anyway. An excuse she acknowledged as bullshit only in the middle of the night when she couldn't avoid her own guilt.

"I will," Dom said. "Thanks."

A ding from the bell on the order counter drew her back to her job, a blessing of a distraction. She retrieved Dom's sandwich, then excused herself to fill coffee cups and check on the other customers, making an effort to chat and act normal. To her everlasting irritation and supreme embarrassment, old Charlie Sanchez flashed a gummy and lecherous grin at her when she filled his cup, waggling his eyebrows in Dom's direction.

Nosey old coot, she thought, scowling at him despite the heat crawling over her cheeks. Charlie just chortled wickedly and raised his mug to her in a silent toast. She glared a warning at him and stalked away, swearing she'd put him in his place as soon as Dom was out of earshot.

Then she'd put herself in her place, too. Because her lust-fueled obsession was too obvious if Charlie was teasing her about it. Her only hope was that Dom would continue to be a gentleman and ignore her inappropriate feelings. Someone had to be the grown-up.

Even if it was the younger man.

Look for What A Tiger Wants
Book 8 in the Tiger Shifters series
Out now!

BOOKS BY KAT SIMONS

TIGER SHIFTERS SERIES

1 - Once Upon a Tiger

2 - Along Came a Tiger

3 - Here There Be Tigers

4 - Her Tiger To Take

5 - To Tempt a Tiger

6 - Down Will Come Tiger

7 - To Catch a Tiger

8 - What a Tiger Wants

9 - Taming Her Tiger

Tiger Shifters Series Vol 1 (Books 1 - 3)

Tiger Shifters Series Vol 2 (Books 4 - 6)

ABOUT THE AUTHOR

Kat Simons earned her Ph.D in animal behavior, working with animals as diverse as dolphins and deer. She brought her experience and knowledge of biology to her paranormal romance fiction, where she delights in taking nature and turning it on its ear. After traveling the world, she now lives in New York City with her family. Kat is a stay-at-home mom and a full time writer.

For more on Kat and her future books:

Website: http://www.katsimons.com
Newsletter: http://eepurl.com/OxQQL

www.ingramcontent.com/pod-product-compliance
Lightning Source LLC
Chambersburg PA
CBHW032202180726

48284CB00001B/153